"I'll do my best either of you."

That small smile crept onto her lips and he wanted to shout his victory. Her smooth skin beneath his thumb sent electricity down his spine. His body tensed at the sudden flood of desire pumping through his veins.

"I know you won't." She placed her hand over his on her cheek.

Trust. Had he ever known anyone quite like Maggie Brown? From a starry-eyed girl to a sultry teenager to this glorious woman standing before him, Maggie would never cease to amaze him.

He kissed her. He'd only meant to kiss her briefly. He wasn't even sure why. He wanted to, so he did. He could taste the vanilla ice cream. Her lips were incredibly soft beneath his. His only thought was he didn't want to stop kissing her.

FATHER
BY CHOICE

BY
AMANDA BERRY

First published in Great Britain 2013
by Mills & Boon, an imprint of Harlequin (UK) Limited,
Eton House, 18-24 Paradise Road, Richmond, Surrey TW9 1SR

© Amanda Berry 2013

ISBN: 978 0 263 90636 3
ebook ISBN: 978 1 472 01203 6

23-0613

Harlequin (UK) policy is to use papers that are natural, renewable and recyclable products and made from wood grown in sustainable forests. The logging and manufacturing processes conform to the legal environmental regulations of the country of origin.

Printed and bound in Spain
by Blackprint CPI, Barcelona

To my critique partners,
Jeannie Lin, Shawntelle Madison, Kristi Lea
and Dawn Blankenship, who helped me develop
my idea and create a cohesive story and kept me sane.
I'd be lost without them. To Stephanie Draven,
who helped me make my synopsis the best it could be.
To Missouri Romance Writers, who inspire me and
provide a safe space for those of us with stories to tell.
To my family for putting up with the craziness of a
writer. To my husband for allowing me to live
my dream.

Prologue

Eight years earlier

Brady Ward didn't stir as the bed dipped and rose. Maggie's bare feet slapped lightly against the wood floor. The sound of her gathering her scattered clothes from around his childhood room broke the otherwise silent morning. Even the old rooster hadn't woken to greet the day.

The last few stragglers from Luke's graduation party had left minutes before. The sound of engines starting had awakened him from the light sleep. Apparently, it had woken Maggie, as well. His side cooled where her body had been moments before.

Brady remained still so she could slip out of his life as easily as she had slipped into his bed last night. He could almost taste the potential in the air. That this could be more if they wanted it to be. If things were different, they could be more than just one night.

The metal rattle of his doorknob stopped suddenly and he

swore he could feel her gaze on his bare back. As if giving him that final moment to reach out and welcome her back into his bed, give her the promise of something more. But he couldn't give anyone that.

The light floral scent of Maggie drifted over him like a Siren beckoning. Her soft voice lingered in his mind—*I don't normally do this.* Her rich, blond hair had felt like silk in his hands while her hazel eyes had made him feel like the only man in the world.

The door whispered open with a sigh, and she was gone.

Brady rolled and stared up at the ceiling. The graying plaster had cracked, and a daddy longlegs had taken up residence in the corner of his room. He rubbed the dull, familiar ache in his chest.

Last summer had been hard enough. He'd come home from college to help Sam with the farm and tried to keep Luke from getting into too much trouble. Burying the fact that without their mother and father, the three brothers weren't as close a family as they once were.

No use pretending sleep would come. Brady rolled out of bed and pulled on some jeans before plodding down to the only bathroom in the house for a quick, cold shower.

As if he hadn't been away at college for a full year, he fell into the rhythm of chores like he'd always done, because it was expected. Summer break didn't mean he got to laze around the house all day.

By the time the cows were fed and milked, the sheep moved into a new pasture and the pigs slopped, Brady's muscles ached. Being home felt like slipping on a suit that didn't fit right. It had never fit.

Kicking off his muddy boots on the porch, he walked into the kitchen in his socked feet.

"Morning." Sam stood at the stove with a spatula, pushing around brown chunks of what might have been sausage at one point in Mom's cast-iron skillet.

"Morning." Brady started the coffee and hoped there was some cereal or something that didn't need to be cooked—or in Sam's case, burned—for breakfast.

"Glad you could make it out of bed this morning."

Noting the sarcasm, Brady said, "I'm not here to argue with you."

Sam grunted but kept pushing around the darkened meat. "The back forty needs to be plowed. I promised John at least two loads of hay. The barn needs repair and a fresh coat of paint."

"Where's Luke?" Brady tried to divert the conversation from the long litany of chores.

The back of Sam's neck tinged red like it did when Mom had caught him out late. "He went out this morning."

"What did you do?" Reaching into the old white metal cupboards, Brady pulled out their father's favorite coffee mug with #1 Dad emblazoned on the side in red.

"Nothing." Sam cranked the stove off and slammed down the spatula. "Breakfast is ready."

"That *nothing* is definitely something," Brady mumbled as he found a box of Cheerios toward the back of the cupboard. Even stale, it would be more edible.

"Leave it, Brady." Sam's tone left no room for additional conversation. Typical Sam. Which meant that something had happened but Sam was unwilling to confront it. Instead, it would stew inside until he lashed out. Confrontation had never been the Ward family way.

Luke had only been fourteen when Dad died and sixteen when Mom died. If that weren't enough, dealing with Sam for the past two years as his guardian couldn't have been easy. The kid had promised Brady he would straighten out for his senior year. And he had. Luke had graduated with honors and a full-ride scholarship to University of Illinois. He'd managed to escape Tawnee Valley High without a permanent record, an unplanned fatherhood and with all his limbs intact.

With a bowl of cereal and a slightly bent spoon, Brady joined Sam at the table. Sam scarfed down the burned food on his plate. Probably so he wouldn't have to taste it. When he finished, he leaned back in the chair with his cup of coffee and studied Brady.

Undaunted by the appraisal, Brady ate his cereal at his own pace. He might have slowed down slightly to irk his brother. Each bite felt like a lump into his stomach. He should have written a note and left. But he needed to act like the man he wanted to be.

"Maggie Brown is a good kid," Sam said.

Brady knew it had been coming. Ever since Mom got sick, Sam stuck his nose into everyone's business.

"She's not a kid." Even though Brady had seen Maggie around for years, he'd never gotten to know her. Two years behind him in school, she'd just graduated with Luke.

"I suppose not." Sam folded his hands over his stomach. "She seems to have her head on straight. I'm not sure why she slept with you."

The spoon clattered against the bowl. Heat flooded Brady's system, rising until even the tips of his ears were warm. "What of it?"

"She isn't a one-night kind of girl." Sam's fatherly tone had Brady biting his tongue.

Not that it was any of Sam's business, but neither of them had made any promises last night except one night was as far as their relationship would go. There wouldn't be any holding hands in Parson's Park or heading over to Owen, the next town over, to watch a movie and get some dinner. Even if he wanted to, they were at different points in their lives. His plans were taking him far from this place.

"She's the kind of girl you settle down with," Sam added.

Brady shoved away from the table and rose slowly to glare down at Sam's dark hair. "Are you going to arrange a shot-gun wedding?"

Sam didn't budge. "I'm thinking you should give the girl a chance. You've only got two more years of school before you come home. She'd make you a good wife and would probably be a better cook than I am."

"If you want a woman's touch around the house, why don't *you* get married?" Brady tried not to think of what Sam was proposing.

"I'm not exactly the catch of the county." Sam's smirk was Brady's undoing. The same damn smirk Sam used to give him when they were kids and Brady had made better grades than Sam had.

"Neither am I." Brady ran his hand through his hair and stared up at the yellowed ceiling tiles. "Don't you see how the people in town treat us? Don't you see the pity? The poor Ward brothers who lost their parents. Hell, in their eyes, you are probably a saint for raising Luke, while I'm the coward that ran away."

"You didn't run away."

"Didn't I?" Brady stared into the blue eyes of his brother that were duplicates of his father's and his. "You don't think I wanted to escape when Mom died? That I needed to escape?"

"And you did. And I didn't stop you." Sam's voice had a slight edge to it. "You went to college, and I stayed here with Luke. I kept the farm going and when you get done with col-lege, you can come home and help out."

"Home?" The word was so foreign to Brady that it tasted bad in his mouth.

"Like Dad always wanted. Like Mom wanted. The three of us together."

The backs of Brady's ears burned. "This isn't home."

Sam's lips tightened. The humor and patience drained from his face. He stood, but the extra inch of height Sam had on Brady wouldn't intimidate him today.

"God, Sam, have you deluded yourself that much?" Brady wouldn't back down. "This can't be home, because home is Mom and Dad. Home was an illusion we had as kids. A safety net to keep us protected. Now? Home is shattered all around us."

"Stop it." The threat behind Sam's words only made Brady push harder. This had been building for too long.

"Luke is a mess. You are a mess. I'm a freaking mess. We don't belong anywhere. You can't keep trying to bind us to this place. We don't belong together."

"Stop." The word was an angry whisper.

"I'm not staying here anymore, Sam." Brady took in a deep breath and the weight released off his shoulders. "I have an internship and scholarship waiting for me. In London."

"England?" Sam staggered backward as if Brady had hit him.

"It's the opportunity of a lifetime. It's what *I* always wanted." Brady changed tactics as some of the anger drained from him. "They don't offer this to just any student, Sam. I'd be a fool not to jump on it. Most people who go end up getting a job overseas. My flight leaves in two days."

"And that's what you want?" Sam straightened to his full height. "To be as far away from here as possible?"

"It's not like after school I'd return to Tawnee Valley, settle down with someone like Maggie Brown and raise a passel of children. The farm is your dream. Not mine."

"What about Luke?"

"Luke?" Brady looked out the window toward the old barn across the drive.

"Who's going to protect Luke? Who's going to watch his back as he tries to become a man?" Sam's voice was tight.

"You were—"

Sam shoved Brady. Caught off guard, Brady almost fell over a chair. The sibling rivalry that had been playing out for years rose to the surface, bringing with it the pent-up rage. But Brady held himself in check, even though he wanted to plant his fist in Sam's face.

"That's right. Me. I'm the one who left college to come home when Mom got sick and Dad died. I'm the one who is stuck on this farm, destined to watch everyone leave our dying hometown. I'm the one who had to step in when Luke made bad decisions. I'm the one who will have to clean up the messes you two leave behind."

"I never asked—"

"Mom did." Sam didn't raise his voice, but he'd struck for Brady's heart.

"But you didn't have to." Brady knew his reply was weak as it left his mouth. The venom from Sam's words seeped through Brady's veins and sapped away his anger.

Their mother meant the world to them. Their parents had tried for years to have children before finally getting pregnant with Sam. Their father had a heart attack when he was fifty-three. That same year their mother found out she had widespread cancer. If the boys could have, they would have taken her place. But none of them could and it was time to get on with their lives.

"I can't keep coming back." Brady took in a deep breath. "Mom's in every square inch of this house. I keep expecting her to come around the corner, to shout from the bedroom for help, to be here. Every time that door squeaks and slams shut I keep hoping to see Dad coming in from work. You have to stay. But I don't have to."

Sam turned and braced his hands against the sink as he stared out the window.

"Please don't ask me to." Brady tried to sound confident, but the words were a shaky whisper.

Sam stared out the window for so long Brady lost track of time. Sam's shoulders sagged from the weight he carried and Brady had helped put it there. Away from Tawnee Valley, Brady could pretend that everything was fine, but here... it hurt to breathe.

Sam finally pushed away from the counter and turned to face him. Brady braced himself to defend his decision. Sam wouldn't understand how hard this was on him. The opportunity was too good to pass up.

"I won't ask you to stay." Sam lifted his gaze to meet Brady's. He didn't raise his voice, but Brady knew he meant every word. "I won't ask you to come home. Not now or ever."

"I wouldn't expect you to." Brady knew this was goodbye. He'd hoped to be leaving on better terms, but knowing Sam, how else could he leave?

"I'll tell Luke." Sam picked up the dishes and took them to the sink.

The conversation was over and so was their relationship. "I'll send what money I can."

The dishes crashed into the sink. Brady winced as the cup he'd given his father cracked.

Sam's words were stilted as he bit out, "I don't need your money."

Brady nodded, but he would send some, anyway. "Bye, Sam."

Chapter One

Eight years later

"Amber! You need to get out to the bus stop now!" Maggie Brown flipped over another paper on the desk. More bills. They just kept piling up.

"I'm going." Amber bounced into the dining room with her backpack strapped tightly to her shoulders, her dark hair swinging from side to side. Her blue eyes were serious, even as she paused next to Maggie's chair for a quick hug.

"You don't have to wait with me." Amber skipped her way out the front door, calling over her shoulder, "I'll be fine by myself."

Maggie rose and followed her. "I like to wait with you."

Amber swung around in a circle, so carefree and full of life. Maggie could barely breathe with the weight on her chest. It had been only a few months since her mother succumbed to cancer. Amber had been their blessing during the hard times.

She'd given Maggie and her mother the chance to focus on life instead of death.

"You all right, Mommy?" Amber had stopped her twirling and walked over to take Maggie's hand. Through the bad times, they had each other.

"Yeah, baby. I'm good."

The squeal of the bus's brakes announced its arrival.

"Time to go." Maggie squeezed Amber's hand and dropped it.

"Love you." Amber flung her arms around Maggie's waist. Before Maggie could return the hug, Amber took off for the school bus.

"Love you," Maggie shouted as the doors folded shut. She wrapped her arms around her waist against the chill of the early autumn breeze that swept the first fallen leaves across the sidewalk. The leaves continued past her neighbor's house. The air felt light and free, but Maggie's insides kept tying themselves into knots.

As the bus pulled away, Maggie noticed a truck across the street in front of the Andersons' house. Not unusual given the teenage kids. It seemed as if a different vehicle was parked there every day. Shrugging off a nagging feeling, she turned to go inside.

Her mom's house needed work. The old Victorian had seen better days, and the wraparound porch needed a fresh coat of paint. But painting would have to wait. Other bills needed to be paid this month.

"Maggie!"

She froze. She'd recognize that voice anywhere.

Spinning around, she saw Sam Ward jogging over from the old white truck. His familiar black hair, blue eyes and strong build marked him as one the Ward brothers. Brady had always seemed more approachable than his stern older brother, though.

Sam stopped in front of her with a grim look on his face. "I'm glad I caught you."

"I was just leaving," she said coldly.

"I saw you at the store with Amber the other day. She's growing up fast." His smile had an edge of worry to it.

Even though everyone in town speculated which Ward brother had done the deed, Maggie had never told anyone except her mom and her best friend.

Luke was always the first guess. They were the same age. It lined up perfectly with their graduation. A few thought it was Sam. Sam didn't talk to her or Amber unless to say a brusque hi if they passed in a store. Not one person in town laid the blame on Brady. He was their golden child, football hero, the most likely to succeed; and he had. He'd gone off to England without a backward glance. She hadn't expected any long goodbyes. And when she'd sent Brady a letter with the fact she was pregnant, Sam had started dropping off money to help. Sam had never said anything, just handed her the envelope or left it with her mother. Brady hadn't even written a note.

As embarrassed as Maggie had been, she'd been grateful for the financial help. But the fact that the Wards, who had lost so much family, didn't want Amber to be a part of their lives left a sour taste in Maggie's mouth.

As far as she knew, Sam hadn't spent any time with Amber. He never stuck around long enough for conversation. Maybe Brady shared the pictures that she sent once a year by mail to the Ward farm like everything else she had to share with Brady. Never any response, but the money always came. Never a note or any request to see his child. Just money, as though that was all Amber needed from her father.

"We go to the same store every week, Sam." She emphasized his name as if he had a few screws loose. "What's this all about? I have to get ready for work."

"I heard about your mom." Sam rubbed the back of his neck. His nervousness was starting to make her worry. What if something had happened to Brady? "I'm real sorry to hear she passed."

"It was the end of a long battle," Maggie said automatically. Even though it had been a different cancer that had taken Mrs. Ward, Maggie knew that in this respect Sam and she had something in common. Her gut clenched momentarily.

They stood there awkwardly for a moment. He looked around as if he wanted to be anywhere but here. The feeling was mutual. "I really need to…" She gestured to the screen door.

He hesitantly stepped on the first step. Apparently, he wasn't going to leave until he'd had his say. "Would you mind if I came in? I need to talk to you."

She stared him down, trying to determine whether she was willing to listen to anything a Ward had to say. But he seemed open and sincere.

She shrugged and opened the screen door. "Is everyone okay?"

"Yeah. Fine as far as I know." Sam followed her into the small living room. Out of habit, she gestured to one of the worn recliners. Her furniture may be worn but it was clean and paid for.

"Would you like something to drink?" Manners won out over the burn of anger. Why now? After eight years of silence, why was Sam here? Was he coming to tell her that Brady was through sending money? She'd have to put in more hours as secretary at the furniture store if that were the case.

"No, thanks." He sat on the edge of the chair, leaned his elbows on his knees and clasped his hands. Then he sat upright and half stood. He gestured to the chair opposite. "This would be easier if you sat."

Her stomach knotted. She moved toward the chair but didn't sit. What would be easier?

"I've done some stupid things in the past, Maggie." Sam seemed to think she was in the mood for confessions.

"I'm sure you have, but I have work to do—"

"Sit down, Maggie Brown." His stern expression had her lowering to the edge of the seat. Obviously remembering where he was, he added, "Please."

"You have a lot of nerve—"

"Yes, I do." Sam ran a shaking hand through his shaggy hair. "You have no idea how much nerve I have."

She crossed her arms over her chest and waited.

"I've done some really stupid things—"

"You said that part already."

He looked up to the ceiling before returning his gaze to her. His eyes softened. "I know Amber is Brady's."

She flushed and started to rise.

"But Brady doesn't."

She fell into the chair as if he'd punched her in the stomach. The air sucked out of the room and she gasped to draw it back in. Blood thundered in her ears. Her thoughts scattered into a million shards. "What are you talking about? I...I told him. He sends money."

His eyes remained sad but determined as Sam reached into his pocket and pulled out some opened envelopes. "I'm sorry, Maggie. I thought I was doing right by my brother. Protecting him. I didn't mean to hurt you or Amber."

She took the envelopes. Each one was a letter she wrote to Brady, including the first one. One for every birthday.

"Brady doesn't know about Amber?" Maggie felt as if the room had turned upside down. With her mother needing constant care after chemotherapy, Maggie had been so startled and scared when she found out she was pregnant that she hadn't known what to do. Brady had vanished overseas somewhere. Taking the cowardly approach, she'd written a letter and sent it to the farm. When Sam dropped off the money, she'd been crushed that Brady didn't want anything to do with Amber, but maybe a little relieved, too.

"I messed up." Sam leaned forward again, his hands clasped before him and his head hung. "I want to make this right."

"Right?" She felt like a mockingbird, but her chest felt hollow and her mind couldn't put her world right side up. All these years, she'd been angry with Brady and he hadn't even known.

All those missed birthdays. The long nights awake with Amber when she'd been sick. Brady had missed everything from Amber's birth to kissing her scrapes and bruises better to holding her when she cried at her grandma's funeral.

A rush of heat went to her cheeks. She could have tried harder to reach out. Even searched for Brady on the internet. But she'd been too afraid of further rejection to reach out through any means but the letters.

"I got you a plane ticket for this weekend and talked with Penny about watching Amber. I didn't open your last letter. You should give it to him in person." He held out the sealed envelope.

She looked at him as if he was the Mad Hatter. "What are you talking about? You walk into my house to tell me you've lied to me and Brady for eight years. Do you know how hard it is to raise a child alone? How hard it is to care for your mother and your daughter when both are sick?"

Maggie jumped up and paced away. This was Sam's fault, not hers. Her mind raced to keep up with her emotions. "You had no right."

"You're right." Sam didn't move from his spot. His face was grim.

"Why?" Her shoulders shook with the anger bubbling

within, but tears pressed against her eyes. A million what-ifs weighed heavy on her soul. Would she have had to do it on her own? Would Brady have held her when her world fell apart? Would he have been the strong one when she felt small and overwhelmed? Would he have grown to resent her for keeping him from his dreams? Or would he have rejected her like his brother had made her think? "Why would you do something like that? How could you treat your brother that way? What did *I* ever do to *you?*"

Sam rose and set the letter and another envelope on the table. He took a heavy breath and blew it out. "I didn't think about you. I had my reasons. It's time to fix this. Go to New York and let Brady know."

"New York?"

"Luke told me Brady transferred to the New York office of Matin Enterprises a month ago. I figured if Brady was this close again, it was time he knew."

"Why don't you tell him?" She shoved the envelopes toward him.

His lips drew into a thin line. For a moment, it seemed as if he wouldn't say anything. But something inside him broke. She recognized defeat because she'd felt it far too frequently herself. She refused to feel any sympathy for Sam, though.

"Because Brady won't talk to me." His words came out stilted and harsh. "He hasn't spoken to me in eight years. The only reason I know anything about his life is through Luke, and he barely speaks to me, either. This is the only way to clean up this mess."

She stared at the plane tickets that had fallen out of the envelope. "I can't go to New York and leave Amber at the drop of a hat. I have a job. I need to work." Her gaze fell on the stack of bills. "I have obligations."

"I'll take care of it." Sam stopped by the front door.

"What? Like you took care of this?" She held the old letters crumpled in her tight grip. Her stomach clenched. Heat flushed through her. This couldn't be happening. Brady had to know. How could he not?

"Damn you, Sam Ward." She made sure all the anger and frustration she felt were directed solely at him.

"I can't change the past, Maggie."

She refused to see the pain in his eyes.

"All I can do is try to fix the future. Brady needs to know about Amber."

Chapter Two

"This project will bring in twenty percent more revenue," Brady said as a trickle of sweat ran along his spine. Senior management filled the boardroom, and he had their undivided attention.

"The project appears to be sound," Kyle Bradford, the CEO of Matin Enterprises, said. In his mid-fifties, Kyle seemed more a friend than Brady's boss. The past month he'd treated Brady to a few football games and a couple of dinners out to discuss where Kyle felt the company needed to go in the future.

Jules cleared her throat and stood, showing off her dark red suit as it hugged her killer curves, though they were nothing compared to the sharpness of her mind. "We put together this project to show exactly what Matin Enterprises can be in the future."

Brady and Jules had put in long hours and weeks of planning to get this project ready for this presentation. Before he'd made the move to New York, Brady had started with the concept and played with the numbers. Now was his chance, and he had known Jules was the right person to help with the project.

"I agree, Kyle." Dave Peterson stood at the far end of the conference table. "However, as a higher-level manager, I would like to help oversee it. That is, unless Brady—" he paused and winked at Jules "—or Jules objects."

Jules had told Brady that Peterson had been asking her out since she started at Matin. Even though she always turned him down, it didn't seem to make a difference. His condescending attitude toward her made Brady want to punch the smug man. The fact that no one else in the boardroom seemed aware of the issue made him more frustrated.

Peterson raised his eyebrow, daring him to make a scene in front of the corporate heads.

"Of course Peterson would be a great asset to have on our team." That way, Brady could keep an eye out for the dagger Peterson would stick in his back.

"Wonderful. Keep us updated as the project moves forward." Kyle stood. The rest of the men and women took it as their cue that the meeting was over.

Brady collected his papers and disconnected his laptop from the projector. Three months of planning had hinged on a one-minute decision.

"Nicely done, Brady." Jules gathered the remainder of their presentation materials. She kept busy as Peterson approached.

Brady shut his laptop and met Peterson's brown eyes. Peterson was only a few years older than Brady, but the man had let himself go over the years. His shirt buttons strained over his stomach, and his receding hairline was a mixture of black and gray.

"Great presentation, you two." Peterson's eyes strayed over Jules's figure. "I couldn't have done better myself."

"Thank you." Brady stopped from adding *because you*

couldn't have. It was well-known among the staff and lower management that Peterson made his way up the ladder on other people's backs, taking credit for their work.

"I expect to be added to all correspondence from now on." Peterson shifted his body closer to Jules. "And included in any meetings you two might have, Jules."

Brady fought the urge to jerk the guy away from her. "Sure, Peterson."

Jules lifted frosty green eyes to Peterson. "We'll make sure you are included in all meetings, but the decisions come from us."

"As long as you're there, I'll be there." Peterson grinned and left the room.

Brady and Jules were both out for the same thing— recognition for the work they did. Their initial attraction had ended with a fizzle after a week. Both of them were driven to succeed and compatible in a lot of ways, but love wasn't in his five-year plan. Jules agreed with him that love was something you sought when your career was firmly in place. Right now, it would get in the way.

"I'll do my best to intervene with Peterson," Brady said, knowing he could do nothing unless Jules wanted to file a harassment report.

She lifted her gaze to his and smiled. "I can hold my own with guys like Peterson. I've been doing it my whole career."

Brady nodded and held the door open for her as she swept by. If he let down his guard for a moment, Peterson would take over his project and get the boost in his career that was meant to be Brady's and Jules's.

An email notification pinged on his phone. He clicked over to it. His blood pressure started to rise as he read the email Peterson had sent out to all the employees working on the project. He'd worded the email perfectly. It implied the project was his baby and that he was *letting* Brady and Jules work it.

Brady would need to keep close tabs on this project if he wanted to keep Peterson from taking over.

"This is ridiculous." Maggie pulled the jeans out of the suitcase and folded them before returning them to the dresser drawer. It had taken every ounce of will Maggie had not to drive out to Sam's farm and cram the tickets down his throat.

"What's ridiculous is how long it is taking to pack a simple suitcase." Penny rested against the headboard with her coppery hair pulled in a knot. Her brown eyes sparkled as she held up a lacy nightgown. "You should take this."

Maggie snatched the nightgown from her best friend's hands and stuffed it into the bottom of her nightgown drawer. She sank on the edge of the bed and put her hands over her face.

"What am I doing?"

"I've been wondering that for the past half hour. Are you packing to go to New York or just testing out your suitcase? I'm fairly certain it can hold more than the blouse you left in it." Penny leaned forward to consider the insides of the suitcase.

"How can I walk up to Brady Ward and tell him, 'Hey, you have a seven-year-old you know nothing about. By the way, it totally wasn't my fault.'" The lump in the pit of her stomach said otherwise, though.

"It *wasn't* your fault." Penny patted her back. "Now pack up and enjoy life a little."

"I should have tried harder."

"To pack. I agree. This is no way to pack to confront the one-night stand you had a baby with." Penny shifted off the bed and started opening drawers. "Not to mention the biggest crush you ever had."

"That's it, Penny. It isn't about me. It's the fact that we weren't anything more than bed buddies for a night."

Penny stopped with a red sweater dangling in her hand and quirked an eyebrow at Maggie. "Bed buddies?"

"Whatever." Maggie took a deep breath. "Shouldn't I call him or email him? Like I should have done in the first place?"

With an armful of clothes, Penny made her way over to the suitcase. "Bygones."

"What if he's too busy to see me? Shouldn't I at least call and schedule an appointment?" Maggie pulled the lacy nightgown out of the suitcase again and tightened her grip when Penny reached for it.

"Okay. I get it." Penny sat next to her on the bed and took Maggie's hand in hers. All playfulness put aside for a moment. "What are you really worried about?"

Maggie's eyes filled with unshed tears. "What if he doesn't want her?"

Eight years ago, her mother had held her tight while she cried over the fact that Brady didn't want anything to do with their baby. Part of Maggie had dreamed that he'd show up on her porch and sweep her off her feet. They'd shared something special that night and relationships had been started under worse circumstances than an unplanned pregnancy.

"Why wouldn't he want her?" Penny squeezed Maggie's hand.

Maggie took a deep breath in. "If he's a self-involved nut job."

Penny smiled. "Then we wouldn't want him around our girl, anyway. Now about this nightgown…"

"No way. Grab my sweats."

"You afraid you'll be tempted to show him your pretty nightgown?" Penny laughed, but Maggie had no idea what to expect when she saw Brady. Would she feel anything? Would her old crush rear its head? Or would she resent him for not being there?

"There won't be anything to worry about. I'll be in a hotel.

By myself." Maggie stood and took charge of the packing. "I should call first, though."

"What could you possibly say on the phone?" Penny tried to mimic Maggie's voice. "I'm planning on being in New York this weekend and ran into Sam. Even though you apparently haven't spoken to him in years, he told me your phone and address so that we could hook up. You don't have time because you are a busy man? That's fine. I'll tell you some other time that you have a daughter."

"I get it." Maggie held up her hands in defeat. She hadn't been able to figure out a better plan for the past few days. "I guess this is the way it will have to be."

Penny grinned and held up a different lacy nightie.

"I'm not going for me. I'm going for Amber." Maggie pointed to the drawer until Penny returned the nightie to its proper place.

"Yes, ma'am." Penny saluted with two fingers. "I guess I don't need to run to the drugstore and get some condoms?"

"No!" Maggie blushed as a little remembered heat flushed her body. "I don't need a man. I've done fine on my own for years now."

Penny muttered, "It isn't about need."

"Where are you going, Mommy?" Amber hugged her brown bear close to her small body. Her hair spread on the pillow, making her look like a dark-haired angel.

Maggie drew the covers to Amber's chin. "I'm going to New York for a few days. Penny is staying with you."

"I like Penny. She orders pizza for dinner." Amber smiled. Her front tooth had come out a few days ago, prompting a visit from the tooth fairy. Another thing Brady had missed out on. If he even wanted to be part of their lives. She tried not to dwell on it, but she had to be prepared for him to reject her like she thought he'd already done. What would he want with a small-town family when he had New York?

"Are you going to see the Statue of Liberty?" Amber asked with awe in her voice.

Maggie smiled. "Maybe."

"Will you bring me something?"

"Definitely." She tickled Amber until she laughed. Maggie had her own ideas of what she wanted to bring home for her, but she wouldn't dare to get Amber's hopes up. It was bad enough that Maggie was thinking hopefully. She'd been kicked enough to only have doubt left, but apparently, a little spark of hope had survived.

"Go to sleep. Penny promised she'd get doughnuts." Maggie dropped a kiss on her daughter's cheek.

Amber linked her small arms around Maggie's neck and pulled her down to the bed. "I'll miss you."

"I'll miss you more, baby." Maggie hugged her as best she could with all the bedding and stuffed animals in the way. She stood and walked over to the light switch. "Good night."

"Night." Amber squeezed her eyes shut like she always did at bedtime with her hands clasped together. What she prayed for, she never said aloud. Maybe Maggie, maybe her father.

Amber knew her daddy lived far away. But Maggie couldn't bear to break Amber's heart by telling her that her father didn't want to be part of their family. Now she was glad she hadn't.

A whole week hadn't been long enough to figure out what to do or say. She'd never imagined Brady didn't know. Over the years, she'd come to terms with the fact that he didn't want her or Amber. Okay, maybe she was upset with him not wanting to be a father, but Maggie didn't need him to want her.

That knot twisted a little tighter in her stomach.

How was she going to tell Brady about their child?

Chapter Three

"This is stupid," Maggie muttered as she stood in front of Brady's apartment building. She should have called. Sam had said she could catch Brady in the morning when he left for work.

The cold day seeped through her jeans and she hugged her blue sweater closer. Her ponytail whipped around into her face again. Just a few more moments then she'd go in and ask for him. Just a few...

Brady lived in a luxury apartment building off Central Park. Housing wasn't cheap in New York, but his building seemed to be the cream of the crop. On the taxi ride over, Central Park had emerged among the buildings. The trees gave an illusion of open spaces, but the massive buildings dwarfed the park, holding it captive. Metal-and-glass structures on concrete. She'd never felt more lost or frightened.

Too many people shoved into one space. Even now, people walked or jogged past her. There didn't seem to be a spare area anywhere in the city to step aside and take a deep breath.

Her heart raced and she could barely breathe with the hustle and bustle.

She didn't understand how Brady could live here when he'd grown up with the open spaces in Tawnee Valley. Where you didn't have to clutch your purse to your side and fear the stranger walking toward you.

She moved closer to the door. Maybe she should return to the hotel and call him. A jogger in hot-pink short shorts weaving between the business people in their gray-and-black suits caught her attention. She followed the woman with her gaze, wondering if she could ever feel that comfortable here, surrounded by strangers.

"Maggie?" Brady's baritone voice rushed over her like a warm waterfall.

Her breath caught in her throat as she turned to find Brady staring at her from a few feet away by the apartment building door. The sun chose that moment to come out from under the clouds, lighting his handsome face as he came toward her. His dark hair was cut more conservatively now, and crinkles formed in the corners of his blue eyes. He was even more handsome than she remembered.

Maggie returned his smile but couldn't form any words. Up close, she could see the similarities between him and Amber. And those eyes, they caused her heart to stutter as he focused solely on her.

Brady had a huge grin on his face. "Maggie Brown! What are you doing here?"

"I came to see you," she pushed out through her numb lips. "I mean, I'm visiting New York and..."

What else could she say? And how was she supposed to think when he looked at her like that? As if he knew her inside and out. It had been a long time since she'd been in his arms, but her body tingled with memories. Should she hug him?

"God, it's good to see you." His genuine smile didn't

change, but his voice sounded different from high school, more sophisticated, colder. "Are you living nearby?"

"No, I'm still in Tawnee Valley." She didn't want to blurt it out, but how was she supposed to ease him into knowing he had a seven-year-old daughter? Even though she'd known Brady since they were kids, they hadn't been close friends, and right now he felt like a stranger. "I need to talk to you about something."

Brady's eyebrows drew together in concern, and he reached out his hand to grip her elbow. "Is everything all right? Is Sam…?"

Shocked at the intense surge of giddiness flowing through her at his touch, Maggie shook her head. No stranger had ever made her feel like that. "Everything's fine."

She wanted to drop her eyes, but his eyes held her entranced. It was on the tip of her tongue to tell him about Amber, but she couldn't make her mouth form the right words.

With his pressed suit, he could have stepped off the cover of *GQ*. The Brady she knew had been headed for big things, but she didn't know this man in front of her. To be honest, she hadn't known Brady even back then. Not truly, just the facade he put on for the town. A facade he let drop during their night together.

"I wish I had more time right now, but I have to get to work. There's an early morning meeting." He pulled out his BlackBerry and checked the screen for a moment.

The cold wind swept through her when he backed away slightly. A reminder that they had shared only one night together. It had been a great night, but it wasn't as if they'd had a meaningful relationship.

Now wasn't the time to tell him about Amber. A little of the weight lifted off her stomach. She couldn't tell him when there were people surging down the sidewalk like salmon around them. When he glanced at her, she shivered and nodded. "Maybe later?"

"How long are you in town?" He gave her the same expression Amber got when she wanted to reassure Maggie. It was unnerving. How could Amber have his expressions when she'd never met him? "I'm not trying to brush you off. Honestly."

He tapped on his phone again.

"I didn't think you were blowing me off." What if this was her only chance? *You have a daughter. I got pregnant. Surprise, you're a daddy!* Maggie swallowed hard.

"Good." He barely looked at her. "How about one? For lunch? Unless you have other plans."

"Sounds great." She forced a smile. *By the way, you have a daughter.*

His return smile stole her breath and emptied her mind. "Where are you staying? I'll pick you up."

She rattled off the address of the hotel. She should tell him now. Get it over with. That way it wouldn't sit in the knot that was her stomach until later. But how? His attention was apparently already at his meeting. She tightened her smile as he glanced at his watch. Who had Brady Ward become?

"I have to run. I'll see you at one." He backed away from her. "I'm glad you came."

By the time they were sitting in the restaurant, Maggie was drawn tighter than a bow. Brady couldn't imagine what had her uptight. The Maggie he'd known had been spontaneous and friendly.

Of course, high school had been years before. But he remembered the adoring look in her hazel eyes when she'd been a sophomore and he'd been a senior. He hadn't taken advantage of her crush then, but two years later at Luke's graduation party, that night he couldn't resist. She'd been stunning and forward and one hell of a kisser.

Eight years hadn't faded her beauty at all. Her honey-blond hair framed her face in a no-nonsense style. She had developed some curves since high school. Her soft blue sweater didn't reveal much, but her jeans clung low to her hips and she filled them out nicely. She didn't try to flaunt her assets the way Jules did. She was just Maggie. She put off a natural vibe that was unlike any woman he knew, and it did something to his senses that he couldn't begin to describe.

"What brings you to New York?" Brady set his BlackBerry on the table, trying to ignore the constant barrage of emails. Now that financing had begun, he had to put everything into motion, which was always the hardest phase and required a lot of finesse. It didn't help that Peterson circled every conversation like a shark waiting for blood.

Maggie lifted her gaze to his. He lost track of what he'd asked as he sank into her rich hazel eyes. Warmth. That's what she offered, with no expectation of anything in return. The type of women he usually went for were like Jules. Sophisticated, driven, focused...temporary.

Her gaze dropped to the tablecloth, then to her hands folded neatly in her lap. "Do you remember Luke's party?"

His phone buzzed insistently against the white tablecloth. He smiled apologetically and fought the urge to curse. The number was the contractor for the new facility. Another fire to put out.

"If you need to..." Maggie said.

"I'm sorry. I need to take this." He stood and stepped outside the restaurant to talk to the contractor about the change orders that had been processed that morning. After a hurried five minutes, they'd agreed on the main changes. When Brady hung up, he quickly scrolled through his in-box to try to avoid more interruptions before heading inside.

She was already picking at her salad when he sat across from her. She looked at him expectantly. He wished for a moment that he could put the rest of the world on hold to catch up with Maggie, but he had obligations. He hoped she'd understand that.

"It was important. I swear it won't happen again." He drew the napkin across his lap. "I'm sorry. What were we talking about?"

"Luke's party?" Her cheeks flushed.

His gut tightened as he recalled that night—her sweet smile and soft kisses. He waited until she looked at him before saying, "I remember."

Her lips parted slightly before she shook herself. She inhaled before taking a bite. Whatever she was working herself up to must be major. The Maggie he remembered had been bold that night. Unrelenting, untamed, unashamed.

"It was the last time I was in Tawnee Valley before I left for London," he said, trying to ease her into whatever she needed to say.

She set down her fork. "I don't know how to even begin to explain—"

His phone buzzed. Brady didn't want to answer it. Something had Maggie tied up in knots. He glanced at the screen. An email notification from Peterson, and Jules was calling. "Dammit. I'm truly sorry. I have to get this one."

He didn't know if she looked relieved or upset as he picked up the call and walked outside. When he returned ten minutes later, their lunch was on the table, but the work situation had been resolved...for now.

"Perfect timing." He tried to lighten the mood.

"You're a busy man." Maggie's statement was soft and nonaccusatory, but it was also a little sad.

"I'm in the beginning stages of a major project. New office. New position. New phone." He held up the phone and then dropped it into his suit's inner pocket. "No more interruptions. How have you been?"

She froze with a bite halfway to her mouth. A little war raged in her eyes until she sighed and put the fork down. "I've been better."

"Is every—"

"Things haven't been all sunshine and daisies the past eight years, but we've gotten through."

His mind stuck on the word *we*. He didn't even know if Maggie was married. His gut tightened. She wasn't wearing a ring, but that didn't mean anything. A memory of Maggie being the kind of girl you married hovered in the back of his mind. Not that it would bother him if she were. He choked a little on the word. "We?"

With her gaze firmly on his, she said, "After Luke's graduation, I found out I was pregnant."

The blood flowed heavy in Brady's ears and the air left the room. "Pregnant? But we—"

"Used protection. Yeah, that was my first thought, too, as I was holding five positive pregnancy tests."

"Why didn't you tell me?" Brady asked quietly, too numb to be angry. A child? How could he have not known? He'd lost track of a lot of people, but someone could have reached out. It'd been eight years. Why keep the child a secret?

She bit her lip. "I wrote you a letter. It was childish. I should have called, but I was scared. We weren't anything more than one night to each other."

"I would have wanted to know that you were pregnant. I don't shirk my responsibilities." He automatically defended himself, but then her words sunk in. Brady's fork hit the plate. "I never got the letter."

"I know."

His brows drew together. "Then why didn't you try to reach me?"

Maggie's cheeks brightened and her eyes flashed. "I didn't know then. Shortly after I sent the letter, I started receiving money. I figured you wanted nothing more to do with me or Amber."

A headache started behind his eyes. "Money? I never sent—"

"A week ago, Sam stopped by. He'd been the one receiving my letters and sending me the money."

"Sam?" Brady felt as if his world was crumbling in on itself. Eight years of lies. He'd been across an ocean, but never out of reach. Brady had sent Sam money for the farm and always included his address and a way to reach him in an emergency. His older brother had always been controlling but this went beyond that. His thoughts stumbled. "Wait. Amber?"

"Our daughter." Maggie pulled a photo out of her purse.

Brady was afraid to take it, afraid to touch it, afraid of making this real. She set the photo in front of him.

"Amber is seven. She's in second grade with Mrs. Mason. She plays softball and takes gymnastics. She's a good kid."

Brady glanced at the photo, meaning to take a peek. But his gaze settled on a face so familiar, it broke his heart.

"She looks like my mom." Brady's hand trembled as he lifted the photo. Tears choked in his throat. It had been ten years since Mom died. When she became sick, it had changed their household. After she died, it had been the three of them. Angry, confused teenagers hell-bent on going their own way. Now his mother had a grandchild she'd never be able to spoil. Finally, a girl.

Maggie gave him a wary half smile. "She looks like you. Every time I see her, I see a little of you."

He had a daughter. His phone clattered in his pocket, insistent for his attention.

He ignored it, trying to grab on to one of the emotions flying around in his head. Anger at not being told, frustration that he couldn't ignore work for even an hour to discuss this with Maggie, confusion over the still-vibrant connection he felt for Maggie and uncertainty on how to process all this.

He had a daughter.

Maggie sat across from him with her usually emotion-filled face as serene as the pond in the back field of the Ward farm. He had a daughter with this woman that he barely knew. A daughter who didn't know her father.

The bubble of a grin threatening to expand on his face burst as his phone once again vibrated violently. Taking it from his pocket, he glanced at the screen.

"Damn." Setting down his daughter's picture, he scrolled through the three new emails. One from Peterson and two from the production leads in response to Peterson's email. "Give me a minute."

He didn't look up as Maggie shifted slightly in her chair. Her outgoing breath was a little harsher than normal. He read Peterson's email and held back the vulgar word that came to mind. Peterson was taking over his project and trying to write his name in Brady's blood all over it.

He couldn't regain his focus as Sam and Amber floated through his mind, each vying for his attention. One with anger and the other with curiosity. And then there was Maggie. He connected with her hazel eyes, and he stopped to take a breath. His chest tightened. "I'm a complete ass. Here I am trying to multitask while you've been doing that for the past eight years. Seven years old?"

Maggie nodded. Seven birthdays. What would his parents think about him not knowing about his child growing up in Tawnee Valley without him? How could he not know? Anything he said or did would feel inadequate for the time he'd missed.

He put down the phone without finishing his response and reached out and took her hand in his. "I wish I'd known. I wish I could have been there for you and Amber. To have to do that all on your own…"

Maggie flushed and dropped her gaze. "My mom was there for us when she had good days."

"Good days?" Brady couldn't remember much about Mrs. Grace Brown, but she'd always been nice to all the kids at the town picnics.

Maggie looked back at Brady. "Mom had breast cancer. She underwent treatment while I was pregnant and we had a few good years before…"

With the revived memories of his own mother still battering his heart, Brady lifted a napkin to the tear that trailed down her cheek. "I'm sorry to hear about your mother."

They both froze at his action. Maggie shifted back and he pulled away quickly, looking at his hand as if it were the hand's fault. He'd stepped over a line. They hadn't ever been emotionally involved.

"She fought it to the end." Maggie's smile was distant, as if she caught a glimpse of some memory that strengthened her. Ten years ago he'd been devastated by his parents' absence from his life. He couldn't even stand to be in the community he'd grown up in.

He had no idea how he would have reacted at twenty to Maggie's pregnancy. He glanced at the posed, smiling face with a few scattered freckles across her nose. Amber. It felt as if a fist squeezed his heart. Had his daughter ever needed him? He winced at the thought of not being there for her.

"I want to see her." The words burst out of Brady before he could stop himself.

Maggie's mouth dropped open.

"I want to be part of her life." A sense of rightness went through him. It's what his parents would have wanted. It's what he wanted. "If you'll let me."

Chapter Four

Maggie's heart raced, but she drew in a deep breath to steady herself. Just because Brady wanted to get to know Amber didn't mean he wanted anything more to do with Maggie. Nothing had to change.

"I'd like that." She tried to smile, but it faltered on her face. "I mean, Amber would love that. It's been hard telling her about you when I thought you didn't want any part of our lives."

Brady's blue eyes narrowed. "I'll never forgive Sam for doing that to you."

"No," Maggie rushed out. Her cheeks warmed. How much of it had been her fault for not trying harder? "I'm not saying what he did was right—"

"It was damn conceited." Brady leaned back in his chair. "He always thinks he knows what's best."

Maggie didn't argue. Brady had been twenty when Sam had made the decision for him. Eight years had added a roughness to Brady's boyish face. If anything, he was more handsome now than when she'd mooned over him in high school. His dark suit and blue tie lying against the soft-gray pressed shirt made him feel less approachable than when he'd been on top of the high school food chain dressed in denim and a worn T-shirt.

His face softened. "I'd do anything to take back those years and give Amber the father she deserved and you the support you needed."

His words irritated her. "We got by fine on our own."

He smiled. "Always the fierce one, Maggie."

The intimacy of the statement hit her below the belt and reminded her why she'd slept with him in the first place. If she hadn't thought he was patronizing her, she might have even liked him saying that. She cleared her throat and lifted her fork to toy with her rapidly cooling food.

He reached for his BlackBerry again and started pressing buttons. "I might be able to get away for a day or two..."

His lips tightened as he glared at the small screen. Whatever was on the screen wasn't making him happy.

"The project I'm working on is a multimillion-dollar deal. But I should be able to get away in a month, maybe a Sunday."

"A month?" The food sank like a lump in her stomach.

"If everything goes according to plan. I should be able to make it out and back in a day."

"It might take longer?" Maggie crossed her arms over her chest. "Amber has waited seven years for a father I didn't think wanted her. What am I supposed to tell her? Your father is a busy man and when he finds time, he fully intends to come meet you for the first time? Am I supposed to string her along with promises of her father indefinitely?"

"Amber should come first. You're right—" Brady met her gaze "—but my career is hanging on this project. Can I fly her and you out here?"

"She has school. No one can cover for you for a few days? You don't have vacation time?"

"Of course I have vacation time. I have a few months' worth of vacation time saved, but—"

"But you aren't willing to take them." She stood and clasped her shaking hands together. "I don't have vacation time, but I came here on my weekend off to tell you as soon as I found out you didn't know."

Brady glanced around them. Some of the nearby diners had stopped talking and stared at them with unabashed interest.

"Will you please sit?" Brady asked softly.

She wanted to leave and forget she had ever come to New York, but she had a duty to Amber. For the past seven years, she'd been the one that Amber turned to, the one she relied on. But every now and then, Amber asked about her father. Maggie wasn't willing to disappoint her daughter because her father was turning out to be an ass. She dropped in the seat and crossed her arms.

"I can't tell Amber that her father *might* be able to make it to Tawnee Valley to see her sometime this year. She's seven. She's never met her dad and doesn't know her uncles. Her grandmother died a few months ago. I'm all she has left."

Brady laid his hand on the table. The surrounding diners went back to their food, but they seemed to lean a little closer in the direction of Maggie and Brady's table.

"I'm not trying to blow you off, Maggie." He ran a hand through his hair and looked up to the ceiling before returning to face her. She had a feeling he said that to every woman in his life. "I want to see Amber. The project I've taken on is important—"

"And we're not." Maggie didn't like the hurt in her voice, but she'd worked hard to be everything to Amber. Now someone else had a chance to be part of Amber's life. This man that Maggie had always found fascinating. He'd been her hero in high school, and it was hard not to be disappointed in the man he'd become. She took in a deep breath and closed her eyes briefly, trying to think rationally. "I know that this is a lot. I know I just told you that you have a child. I know your work is important, but is it the only thing that's important?"

"I'm not saying that." Brady closed his eyes and sighed. "What do you want from me, Maggie?"

Everything. The thought startled her into silence. She bit the inside of her cheek and tightened her lips. Romantic dreams were for other people. She had to be rational. "I'd rather not tell her about you at all if we can't work out something definitively."

"I found out I have a daughter ten minutes ago. I'm dealing with the information as best I can." He looked at the photo of Amber and his eyes softened. "I want to do what's right, but I'm eight years too late. Tell me, what should I do?"

Maggie uncrossed her arms and laid her hand on top of his. His heat gave her comfort. She knew what Amber needed, what Amber deserved. What Maggie wished she'd had from the father she barely remembered. She took a deep breath before meeting his eyes.

"Two weeks. Give us two weeks of your time. Let Amber get to know you and adjust to having you in her life. If you decide you only want to be around occasionally after that—" Maggie swallowed the lump forming in her throat "—we can work something out."

His lips tightened into a thin line and she wondered if he would try to bargain more with her. He let out his breath in a puff. "I'll have to work while I'm there..."

Joy welled within Maggie, but it was tainted with concern. What if he didn't love Amber the way she deserved to be loved? What if he decided he didn't want to be a daddy to their daughter? What if Maggie accidentally drove him away and Amber hated her for the rest of her life?

She shook the doubts from her head. "We'll make it work." Realizing she held his hand, she released him and tucked a stray hair behind her ear.

"I'll need a few days to straighten things out, but then we can head back," Brady said.

Maggie's smile slipped as she focused on what Brady was saying. "We?"

"You don't think I'm going to let you go without me?" His half smile reminded her of the high school Brady she'd known. It was the same smile he'd given her when he'd caught her staring at him during gym class. The clanking of plates pulled her out of the small bubble she'd been in, bringing her back to the diner. Back to reality.

The reality was she needed to go home. "My plane ticket is for tomorrow. I have work and I need to take care of Amber—"

"All important details, but Sam obviously owes us. My assistant can take care of the ticket."

"I can't afford to stay at the hotel another night—"

"Stay with me." He cleared his throat. "I meant stay at my apartment."

The background noise faded again as she met his eyes. If only she were eighteen and willing to throw caution to the wind, to have one more night in Brady's arms. If only she'd let Penny pack her pretty nightgown. With her mother's illness and taking care of Amber, Maggie hadn't had time for anything else. She opened her mouth to say no, but the words stuck in her throat.

The girl she'd been would have been happy to let him take control of the situation, but now... "My flight is already booked. Penny is expecting me. Amber is expecting me. I should go home."

"I have a guest room," Brady said. "It will be easier if we head back together. That way you can make sure I get out of here. And you can get to know me better. You can fill me in on the last eight years."

"What do you mean?" Maggie asked, suddenly filled with nervous energy. Time alone with Brady Ward? Her inner teenager squealed with delight. She had to get ahold of herself.

"It's been years, Maggie." Brady sat back and looked for all intents and purposes to be a big-shot CEO as he stared down his fine nose at her. "We don't know each other that well. I've missed so much already. Birthdays, Christmases, her favorite color. All these things a father should know. I don't even know her birth date."

That twinge of guilt for her part in his missing Amber growing up picked at her conscience.

As if reading that she was wavering, Brady added, "You might decide I'm not the type of guy you want to bring home."

Given that he'd insisted that he wanted to meet Amber, Maggie suspected this was his way to make her feel comfortable with his plan by making it appear that it was in *her* best interest.

She wasn't eighteen anymore. Guilt or not. "And if I decide in the next few days that I don't want you to come meet Amber? You'd be fine with that?"

His eyes narrowed, but that cocksure smile of his told her that he had every intention of making sure that didn't happen. He leaned in conspiratorially and suddenly the air surrounding her was sucked away. "Of course. I'd respect your wishes. But you have to promise me something."

She returned his smile, wary but willing to play the game. "We don't make promises. Remember?"

His smile only faltered for a second. "That was years ago. Surely we can make a few promises now."

"Okay." She leaned away, ready to negotiate. "A promise for a promise."

He stroked his chin as he contemplated her. "You drive a hard bargain. Ladies first."

"You won't make any promises you can't keep to Amber. No promises of gifts or time unless you fully intend to live up to that promise."

Brady nodded. "Fair enough."

"And that extends to parenting," Maggie added.

"How so?"

"I've been with her these past seven years. You can come to visit, but she is *my* daughter. What I say goes."

"All right. No promises I can't keep and no going over your head on parenting." Brady's eyes twinkled mischievously though the serious look on his face never changed. "That sounds like two promises."

"Take it or leave it." Maggie shrugged. He'd either accept her decision or he could stay out of their lives. She expected him to ask for two promises, but instead he looked at her with something like...respect. Warmth blasted through her.

"Accepted." Brady moved in close and the diner faded into a distant rumble. "Now for your promise to me."

She squirmed in her chair. Whatever he was about to say she could walk away from if she needed to. She held that thought close to her heart as she gave him a nod to continue.

"You promise you'll give me a chance."

Her eyebrows wrinkled in confusion. "Would I be here if I wasn't ready to do that?"

"I don't know." Brady stroked his fingers along his jaw. "I don't know you any more than you know me."

"We grew up together," Maggie protested.

"We grew up *around* each other and except for one night, we never talked that much. We've both changed over the past eight years, Maggie."

He didn't have to remind her of that. Everything about him had changed. Clothes, hair, even his attitude. Eight years ago he'd had a haunted look about him. Even with his confidence, he hadn't been able to hide that look from her. For a brief moment, she'd met a kindred spirit and she'd let her impulsiveness get the best of her.

She definitely wasn't that girl anymore. Her first one-night stand had given her a daughter and a taste of responsibility she'd only toyed with before that. She was as firmly planted as the oak in her backyard.

"Give me a chance to get to know Amber and give her a chance to get to know me. Trust me to accept responsibility for this child I never knew I had. Trust me to try my best to not hurt Amber's feelings. Allow me to make a few mistakes without cutting me out of her life."

Could she trust him? What choice did she have? He was Amber's biological father. Maybe part of her had actually hoped he'd leave them alone and want nothing to do with them.

Maybe that's why it had been such a shock when Sam had delivered the money. Sure, Brady had been in London, but he probably would have wanted to be involved, somehow. Or maybe he would have been like Maggie's father and tossed her away.

"Maggie?"

She pulled herself from her past pain. This was a new future.

"Can you give me a chance?" Brady asked.

"I'll try." She gave him a halfhearted smile.

"And you'll stay with me until I can get away?"

How could she say no? She needed to get to know this man before she introduced him to her daughter. And she owed him the chance to learn about Amber.

"I don't know if this is a good idea." Insane was what it was; she was actually considering spending the next few days in Brady's apartment. Alone. With him. Certifiable. But if it meant Amber got to meet her daddy...

"It's a large apartment and I barely use it. I bought it as an investment." He glanced at his watch. "There's time to get your things and set you up in my apartment before my next meeting."

"You won't take no for an answer, will you?"

He winked. "Definitely not."

Chapter Five

One meeting rolled into the next, keeping Brady from focusing on the fact that he had a seven-year-old. Amber was never far from his mind as he went over the numbers with the team in London. Neither was Maggie.

When he finally managed to find time to sit at his desk, it was already quarter to five. On his return from lunch, he'd asked his assistant to order some groceries and have them sent to his apartment. As far as he knew, the refrigerator and cabinets were empty. The clock seemed to be marking every second he had left to get things straightened out. If he wanted to talk to Kyle before he left for the game tonight, Brady needed to get over to his office.

"Brady, I have those numbers you asked for yesterday." Jules appeared in his doorway. She looked up from the reports and frowned. "Are you going somewhere?"

Brady walked toward Jules. "Can you talk me through it on the way to Kyle's office?"

"Is there a meeting?"

"No." He waved off her concern. Though he knew in the past things had been done behind her back, that wasn't the way Brady worked. "I need to talk to Kyle about a personal matter before he leaves."

She nodded, though she still had a crease between her eyebrows. They started down the hall, and she handed him a page from the top of her papers. "I've been going through the preliminary budgets we set up. It looks like Peterson has made some changes without giving us notification."

Brady stopped abruptly and gave the sheet his full attention. Funds allocated to construction had been moved to another account. "Dammit."

"I can change it back, but—" She bit her lip and glanced at her watch.

This could take hours to resolve with Peterson and that's probably why he'd done it. If Jules went into his office now, she'd be in there for hours arguing about why it was correct in the first place. All the while, Peterson would be suggestive without being overt enough for her to press sexual harassment charges against him.

Brady took the papers from her. "I'll take care of it."

"Thanks." The tension drained out of Jules's face and shoulders. "I owe you."

"Don't think I won't hold you to that." Brady left Jules and knocked on Kyle's office door.

"Come in."

Kyle stood behind his desk, putting his laptop in his bag. His cell phone was cradled between his cheek and shoulder. He gestured for Brady to come forward.

"No..." Kyle said to the person on the other end of the line. "Thursday won't work. Yes, see you then."

He tucked the phone into its holder and gestured for Brady to take a seat. "If you'd been two minutes later, I would have been out the door."

"Glad I caught you, then." Brady took the offered seat and waited for Kyle to sit.

"What can I do for you today, Brady?"

Brady swallowed. "I know this is the worst timing, but I have a family emergency and need to take some time off."

Kyle leaned his elbows on the desk. "Is everything okay?"

"I honestly don't know." Brady chuckled, suddenly aware how absurd the situation sounded. "I recently found out I have a seven-year-old daughter who knows nothing about me. Her mother thought I knew, but I didn't."

"Congratulations." Kyle leaned back in his chair and it rocked with him. "So what were you thinking? A day? Two?"

Brady released the breath he'd been holding. "I have vacation built up, but I'm planning to continue working on the project while I'm in Illinois."

"How long?" Apparently, Kyle had noticed that Brady had dodged that question.

"Two weeks."

"Starting…"

"Tomorrow or the next day?"

Kyle templed his fingers to his lips as he contemplated Brady. The clock in the corner ticked mercilessly. Kyle's expression didn't change. Brady felt as if he were being silently quizzed on a subject he didn't know a single answer for.

Kyle stopped rocking. "You've just made a transition to this team. We usually like to build vacations into the schedule ahead of time." Kyle smiled. "But this qualifies as a family emergency."

"Great. I'll keep the Detrex project going via email and phone." Brady started to get up.

"No, the Detrex project is a huge account. Since Dave Peterson and Jules Morrison are both on the project, they should handle things while you are gone."

Brady sank back into the seat. If he let Peterson take over

the project, it would sink faster than the *Titanic*. Jules would have to deal with that scumbag every day. "With all due respect, Kyle, Peterson is a decent manager, but the contacts deal with me directly. We have so many balls in the air right now, one could drop and someone might not notice."

"Then you had better get them up to speed before you leave." Kyle rose from his chair, obviously dismissing him.

Brady stood. "Detrex is my project. I'd rather stay here than risk it failing because I left at the wrong time."

"The project won't fail without you." Again, Kyle dismissed his importance.

But Brady knew how this game was played. He'd studied it from every angle. He wasn't going to lose this project and the boost to his career. But if he let Maggie down this time, she might never let him see Amber.

"Let Jules lead it." Brady knew this was a risky move, but he had to play it. "If she has any questions, she can contact me or go to Peterson. It's only two weeks."

He hoped that Kyle would accept this. He could work the project with Jules while he was gone. Peterson wouldn't care if the project failed because it was Brady's and Jules's necks on the line. Until it's time to take credit.

"It's probably time Jules took on some additional responsibility." Kyle walked with Brady to the door and turned out the lights in his office. "But this project is too big to let fail. If I see any indication that she can't handle it, I will pass it off to Peterson."

Brady nodded. "Enjoy the game, Kyle."

Turning on his heels, Brady headed to Peterson's office. It was time to take his project back.

Within thirty minutes after Brady left, Maggie had finished putting away her things. What was she doing here?

She grabbed her phone off the nightstand and dialed Penny's number. It was early afternoon so she should be able to get her before Amber got home. "Did you tell him?" Penny asked immediately.

Maggie fell onto the bed. "Yes. I'm in his apartment right now. How is Amber doing?"

"She's fine. I'm fine. What are you doing on the phone with me?" Penny laughed. "I know it's been a while, but get out there."

"He went to work." Maggie rolled onto her side and stared out the window overlooking Central Park. "I told him."

"Okay." Penny stretched out the word as if trying to pick up the underlying meaning. "What happened?"

Maggie relayed the morning meeting followed by the nerve-racking lunch. And ended with her being dumped off in an apartment that looked like a pristine hotel room.

"It's like no one lives here." Maggie walked to the empty fridge. Her stomach rumbled, reminding her that she'd only eaten a few bites of lunch.

"Did you go in his room yet?" Penny sounded as if she was on the edge of her seat, waiting.

"I'm not going to snoop." Maggie turned to look at the closed bedroom door. She leaned against the refrigerator and wondered what he would have in his bedroom.

"I bet he has kinky sex toys."

"Penny!"

"Or naughty magazines."

"Seriously?"

Penny changed tactics. "Would you want someone like that around Amber? After all, it's important to have a good male role model and not all men can pass muster."

Maggie tapped her finger against her bottom lip. "He did say that he wanted me to find out about him before taking him to meet Amber."

"See?" Penny's triumph was obvious even hundreds of

miles away. "He *wants* you to snoop. Why else leave you in his apartment alone?"

"Because he had to go to work."

"Wrong!" Penny said, sounding like a buzzer. "Excuses, excuses. Get in there. I'll be right beside you. Make sure to use descriptive words like *black leather love swing*."

"Okay, but don't get your hopes up." Maggie crossed the room and turned the doorknob. Just in case, she checked over her shoulder to make sure no one was in the apartment.

"A girl can dream."

Maggie shoved open the door and stepped into a room similar to her own. The hardwood floors from the living room continued into the room, providing the only warmth to the otherwise white, sterile room.

"Dying of suspense over here," Penny said.

"It's bigger than my room. King-size bed." No art. No photos. No spark of personality. Lifeless. Loveless. "Light tan bedspread with matching curtains. Black dresser. Two doors."

"One of them has to lead to the sex chamber." Penny's voice quivered.

"Do you think that if he had a sex chamber I would tell you?" Maggie rolled her eyes as she opened the first door to a bathroom.

"You'll tell me or I promise to read Amber Stephen King tonight."

"You wouldn't. Besides, I would be so shocked to find a sex chamber that I probably would tell you, so you could tell me what all the things were for."

"You know it," Penny said smugly.

"Door number one is a bathroom. Nice. Clean." Lifeless.

"I'll take what's behind door number two."

She opened the door to a walk-in closet the size of her bathroom at home. "Big closet."

The rich scent of sandalwood drifted over her as she entered the closet.

"Dirty mags?" Penny whispered, as if they were on the hunt together, instead of just Maggie waiting to get caught going through Brady's stuff.

The closet was neatly organized with nothing out of place. Suits lined up, next to neatly pressed pants, a few pairs of shoes. "It's as if he doesn't live here."

"That's it! Maybe he's a vampire." Penny snickered.

Maggie backed out of the closet and looked around for some evidence of anyone living there. "Worse, he's a workaholic. No one's house is this clean unless they don't live here."

"Or he stays at his girlfriend's." Penny's tone didn't help matters.

Maggie sank down on the edge of his bed. "I hadn't even thought about that. I didn't even ask. Why didn't I ask?"

"Because you were telling the dude he has a seven-year-old? I think you had more pressing things than 'are you dating?'"

"What if he is?" Maggie's heart clattered to a stop. She stood. "What if I'm getting in the way of his life here?"

"Whoa. Cart. Horse. Slow down, Maggie. It's only one possibility. As you said, this isn't about you hooking up with Brady. This is about Brady getting to know his daughter."

This wasn't about her. It was about Amber, and she shouldn't be in Brady's room at all. She rushed out and closed the door. "You were the one who wanted me to bring sexy nightgowns and bikinis."

Penny sighed. "Only because I want my friend back. The one before all the crap piled on her and made her into the glorious woman she is today. I love you, but you seriously need to get laid."

Checking to make sure she was alone, Maggie said, "I do

not need to get laid. I need to support my daughter and make sure her father is a decent man who won't let her down."

"You can do both, you know." Penny had been trying to get her to go out for the past several years. Saying it wasn't healthy for a woman in her twenties to be cooped up all the time. Between Amber and her mother, there hadn't been time to do the wild and crazy things that Penny did.

Maggie would never regret her daughter or the time she spent helping her mother. Given the choice, she would do it all over again.

"I can't do anything with Brady, Penny." The realization of what that would mean washed over her like a cold shower.

"Why not? He's there. You're there. You had a good time last time." Penny's voice was soft and coaxing.

Maggie let her gaze drift around the white-and-black room with its unused furniture. She squeezed her eyes shut and thought of her well-loved furniture that had been her mother's. She caught a hint of Brady's cologne, a warm rich scent in contrast to his surroundings. She opened her eyes. Regrets were a bitch.

"Because—" Maggie sighed "—if I ruin this for Amber, I'll never forgive myself."

Chapter Six

Brady scrubbed the weariness from his face as he rode the elevator to his apartment. Maggie would be waiting for him. It was such a foreign concept.

He hadn't had any kind of long-term relationship since he'd left Tawnee Valley. Only himself to worry about.

As he opened the door, he heard the sound of the television on low. He set his keys and BlackBerry on the side table. The curtains were all shut, blocking out the night skyline. By the flicker of the television screen he could see the table set for two and Maggie curled up on his couch.

She must've fallen asleep trying to wait for him. He should have told her not to bother. It hadn't crossed his mind to call. He always worked late. Checking the kitchen, he found the groceries he'd ordered, and in the fridge were two wrapped plates of food.

It stirred something in him that hadn't been touched in a while. Something he'd forgotten he wanted, but he couldn't quite name it. Warmth settled in his chest, pushing away the coldness of the New York fall evening. Some guys could work all the time and have a home life. Brady had never considered it. Too many ties, not enough mobility.

He strode over to the couch and squatted in front of Maggie. His future was tied to hers through Amber. Her hands were tucked under her cheek. In sleep, the tension around her was gone.

She was beautiful. Every time they touched, sensation rushed through his body. Could it just be an echo of attraction based on their shared past?

"Maggie," he whispered, almost afraid to wake her.

Her nose crinkled in response, and she tried to snuggle deeper into the couch.

He glanced at the table. He'd been a fool to think he'd have any time for getting to know about Amber or that Maggie would get a chance to know him. Work had always come first.

Peterson had been adamant the figures were incorrect. They'd argued over the numbers for five hours. Once they'd come to an agreement, Brady had written a detailed email to both Jules and the team that explained the changes. He would need all day tomorrow to catch Jules up on the state of the project and what needed to be done.

Complications, all of them. And yet, even knowing that Maggie waited, he hadn't been willing to let any of them drop. What kind of father would he be if he did that to his daughter? Was he even suited to being someone's father?

"Maggie?" he tried again. Still no response.

He went to his room and searched the upper shelf of his closet for the quilt he'd kept. The cotton was worn in spots, but it always felt warm in his hands. The patterned fabric seemed out of place in his apartment in London and even now, it was a misfit for his lifestyle.

When he returned to Maggie's side, he shook it out and gently laid it over her. Children had never been part of his plan. Maybe a wife who would have her own career to deal with, but never a child who would suffer from his lack of attention.

After getting a beer, he settled into the armchair and flipped the channel on the television. He should be in bed exhausted, but it felt good having someone else here. Maggie being here felt good. Most women would have waited up to ream him a good one for staying out late. Maybe he still had that to look forward to when Maggie woke.

Maggie stretched beneath the quilt and rolled onto her back. Her eyes blinked open and tried to focus on him.

"Hi." She sat up, rubbing her eyes. "What time is it?"

"Midnight." Brady held the bottle between his hands as he leaned his elbows on his knees. "I should have called."

Her sleepy smile made him forget to breathe. "I didn't expect you to."

Would she have expected him to if they were more than strangers? But they *were* more than strangers. He cleared the lump from his throat. "Did you want to eat?"

She nodded and started to rise, but froze when she saw the quilt. "This is gorgeous. Hand quilted. Where was this hiding? I didn't see it before."

Her smile dropped, and color rose in her cheeks.

"I mean…" She cut herself off with a groan and sank into the couch. "I shouldn't have, but Penny…"

"It's okay, Maggie." Brady stood and offered her his hand. "It's not like I have corporate secrets lying around my apartment."

He helped her up but didn't let go. Her body's warmth reached for him like a lover's embrace.

"What you see is what you get." Brady wasn't sure if he was trying to warn her off or make it clear that he didn't have anything to hide.

She cleared her throat. "I should have asked before snooping around."

Her gaze lifted to his and it felt like that night again. Energy pulsing between the two of them. Before there had been cattle lulling and the distant howls of coyotes as the backdrop, not the theme from *Law & Order*. He wanted to pull her in those last few inches and kiss her. To see if the spark between them could be coaxed into a fire. But he didn't. He'd never been one to shy away from attraction, but Maggie was different.

She blinked and stepped back. Busying herself with folding the quilt, she said, "I made dinner, but wrapped it up so when you got home, it would be ready."

He didn't know what to say. How could he think of sex when she was vulnerable in his apartment. With nowhere else to go in the middle of the night. She wasn't some random woman or coworker. This was Maggie Brown, resident of Tawnee Valley, his brother's classmate and the mother of his child. The type of girl you settled down with, and his commitment was to his work and his new life in New York.

She draped the quilt over the couch back and went to the kitchen.

His fingers itched to put the quilt away. To hide that piece of Tawnee Valley he'd kept. A memento of better times. He picked up the end, intending to pull it from the couch back.

"Penny was okay with staying an extra day or two. Amber only insisted I bring home something spectacular," Maggie said from the kitchen.

Brady forgot about the quilt. "Hopefully, I don't disappoint her."

"I think she meant a souvenir like a snow globe." Maggie reappeared with the two plates of food and set them on the table. "I'm not sure what to tell her about you."

Brady held out a chair for her, and she took the offered seat.

"What have you told her?" The aroma of fried chicken stirred his taste buds. Potatoes and vegetables rounded out the meal. His stomach rumbled. "It's been forever since I had fried chicken."

"I hope you like dessert because I made cookies, too. Idle hands and all that." She shrugged her shoulders as if embarrassed.

"I should have told you I would be late." Brady bit into a piece of chicken. He couldn't contain his moan of pleasure. He never would have guessed he missed good country cooking. "Heaven."

Maggie flushed with pleasure. "Thank you. Amber hasn't asked about her father too much."

"But when she does?"

"I don't know. I tell her that her father lives far away."

"Which is true." Damn Sam for his interference. Not that it would have changed much. His work had been in England and hadn't left room for a family. Even now he had no idea how he could work a child into his life, but he had to try.

Maggie met his gaze with sincerity. "I wasn't bitter about it. It was what it was. You weren't in the picture, but I wasn't going to bad-mouth you to someone who loves you whether she's met you or not."

"She loves me?" Brady couldn't keep the wonder from his voice. His family had always been a unit. Mother, father, two brothers. He'd never had the opportunity to question whether his parents would be there for him or if he wouldn't love them if they weren't. "Does she say that?"

"She doesn't have to." Maggie folded her hands together and he could see an inner battle being fought.

"Why is that?" He wasn't sure she'd answer, but it seemed to be what she was struggling with. Maybe searching for the words.

Finally, she raised her head to face him. "Because no matter what, a little girl has faith that her father, wherever he is, wants her and that whatever is keeping him from her must be important."

The carefully chosen words made Brady want to question Maggie's relationship with her father. Mrs. Brown had been on her own, but since his mother hadn't been one for gossip and preferred to keep to the farm, he didn't know as much about everyone in their small town as some people. This overwhelming urge to protect Maggie rose within him. Had her father hurt her?

He opened his mouth, ready to grill her for the details so that he could right her wrongs, but Maggie hadn't come to him. She wasn't offering *herself* to him.

"I hope I earn that trust." Brady broke the eye contact and returned to eating.

"I'm sure you'll do fine." Maggie took her plate into the kitchen. He could hear the faucet running. "Do you want cookies now or later?"

What could he say or do to make things right? He stood and headed for the kitchen. Unfortunately, Maggie was heading out at the same time. He caught her shoulders as they ran into each other.

"I—" she started, but stopped herself. Her warm, hazel eyes gazed at him. He could almost smell the fresh-cut grass, the fragrant flowers growing wild, surrounding them. Eight years ago, she'd kissed him, offering him a taste, tantalizing him with the promise of nothing more than a night.

He wanted to kiss her and it had a little to do with the nostalgia that she evoked in him and everything to do with the sexy woman she'd become. She didn't seem aware of her own sexuality. Maybe he was overworked, maybe he had put too little priority on his sex life, because right now, he longed for Maggie to give him an offer like that one night. But what good would that do? No strings attached was what had left

Maggie alone for eight years. But right now, he wanted another stolen moment with her.

Her hands came up on his chest. His heartbeat quickened. Could she feel it below her fingertips? Her lips parted and he couldn't resist the temptation any longer.

He lowered his head slowly, giving her ample time to smack him, run screaming to her room or ask him what in the world he was thinking. Instead, she rose up on her toes and met him halfway.

Her lips were soft under his and her arms clutched around his neck, drawing her body in close to his. Soft curves melted into him as lust hit him hard below the belt. It was all he could do to keep his hands planted on her shoulders.

When she made a little noise of need in the back of her throat, his brain went into meltdown. His hands flowed down her sides until they reached the bottom of her sweater.

Her breath hitched as he touched the skin at her waist. He pulled away from the kiss and met her gaze. His fingers lightly brushed along her sides under the sweater. Giving her every opportunity to stop him and hoping she wouldn't.

Maggie didn't look away, could hardly breathe. Her heart pounded in her chest and her insides had turned molten. *This shouldn't be happening.* Somewhere, little warning bells were going off in her head, but with his gaze on her, she felt as mesmerized as a deer caught in headlights.

His every touch left trails of nerves quaking in its wake. It had been so long since she'd been with a man. With a child and her mother to take care of, she hadn't had time. And pregnancy had scared her out of one-night stands.

But she'd always had a soft spot when it came to Brady Ward. He was definitely the exception and not the rule. Her breath caught when he finally cupped her breasts. She pulled his head down so she could recapture his lips with hers.

His hands lowered to her hips and without breaking lip contact, he started maneuvering her toward his bedroom. All the while his fingers played with the waist of her jeans as her fingers threaded through his hair.

Thinking was not allowed. With the flush of heat building within her, it was a wonder she didn't combust on the spot. He stopped at his bedroom door.

He nipped at her lip as he lifted his head. "This is insane."

"Completely." She pressed her body into his.

"We don't know anything about each other." He pushed open his door and stepped her across the threshold.

"Didn't stop us before." Maggie laughed. It felt good. He felt good. Life was a million miles away. Consequences were things best handled in the morning.

"One would think we had better judgment now," he muttered against her lips. He lifted her sweater off and tossed it on a chair.

His gaze traveled over her and a moment of anxiety surged through her. She wasn't a perky eighteen-year-old anymore. Fighting the urge to cover herself, she let him look at her.

"More beautiful than I remember." He lowered his head and kissed the top of each of her breasts.

Warmth pooled in her chest at his praise and his kisses. "More suave than I remember."

"I've had a little more practice." His fingers began to work on her jeans.

She tried to unbutton his shirt. Frustration bit into her as the buttons refused to come undone. "I'm sadly out of practice."

His lips claimed hers and she completely forgot what she was trying to do. Within moments, she felt him shrug out of his shirt and her skin was touching his. Desire flooded her.

"This wasn't exactly what I meant by getting to know me better." Brady kissed the side of her throat.

She wanted to purr with contentment, to let him take the lead and show her how hot passion could burn. "This is a good way to judge someone's character."

Her hands skimmed over his back. Every muscle twitched under her fingers as they passed. Some sane part of her brain kept intruding. Was she going to have sex with Brady Ward? Why shouldn't she enjoy herself like Penny always insisted? Why shouldn't she let herself go for one night before returning to reality? *It's not real. It's New York.*

Tawnee Valley seemed forever away. Brady's mouth was magical as it pressed against her skin. She wanted to sink into this and forget everything. Escape.

His mouth found hers and she released her thoughts like balloons. Her knees hit the side of his bed. A flash of reasoning rushed through the fog gathered in her brain and the thought balloons crashed all around her.

She put her hands against his chest and pushed a little. He backed off immediately, but his hands held her hips against his.

"Too fast?" The concern in his eyes made her want to yell no, but instead, she nodded. He rested his forehead against hers and drew in a deep breath. "I kind of got carried away."

"Me, too," she admitted, even as her fingertips tingled with the touch of his hard chest beneath them.

He lifted his head and tipped her chin. His eyes searched hers. "It's been a long time since we've been here."

"We don't know each other at all." She sighed. His blue eyes had always been devastating to her. "We shouldn't be doing this."

"I understand." He pulled her into his arms and hugged her tight. Her cheek rested against his heart. There was nothing sensual about the hug, but she could feel his desire pressed against her. Her insides pulsed, but she ignored the craving.

"I should probably go to my room now," she said weakly. *Tell me to stay,* a little part of her whispered.

He released her and stepped away. "I suppose that's for the best."

Trying to play it cool, she retrieved her sweater. She pretended not to hear the little rumble from his chest as she pulled it on. It felt good to be desired, even if she should forget about it entirely.

"Tomorrow is Saturday..." She waited for him to acknowledge her, but didn't dare look his way as she walked toward the doorway.

"Unfortunately, I have to work all day."

She glanced back and he caught her gaze. For a moment, she wanted to toss her cares to the wind. They'd had sex before. The only difference now was they had a connection in their daughter. *Their* daughter. She couldn't afford to start anything with the father of her child, as ridiculous as that sounded.

"We should be free to leave on Sunday." He stuffed his hands in his pockets, drawing her attention away from his eyes and over his chest, down his flat abs to the unbuttoned fly of his pants.

She raised her eyes before venturing lower. "I should go to bed. It's been a long day."

"Maggie?"

She paused and he walked to her, stopping just out of arm's reach.

"You could stay in here. We could just talk. We don't have to..."

A sigh worked its way through her. "I don't think that's a good idea."

His grin had a sheepish quality about it. "You're probably right. Good night, Maggie, and thank you."

"For what?"

"For raising our daughter on your own. For flying here to tell me. For staying. For dinner. For being you."

"Good night, Brady." She gently closed the bedroom door behind her before she changed her mind.

Chapter Seven

Sunday morning, Brady sat at the table with his coffee. Maggie either wasn't awake yet or was still in her bedroom. During work yesterday, Brady had made progress and had packed the necessities from his desk: laptop, cell phone, wireless router. This might not be the best move for the project, but meeting his daughter was essential. When he'd walked into his apartment last night, he'd almost turned around to check the number to make sure he was in the right place.

The quilt remained on the back of the couch. A couple of framed photos sat on the table he threw his keys on. He recognized the frames as a Christmas gift from a work party.

He sat at his table scrolling through emails on his Black-Berry, trying to ignore the centerpiece of flowers in a vase he was fairly certain was new. The changes had made the room feel a little more like home and less like a hotel. Instead of making him feel good, it made him feel like a guest in his own space.

Except in his bedroom. A red silk scarf had been draped

over the foot of the bed, adding a bright spot of color to his drab existence. He had wanted that color to be Maggie draped in red silk across his bed. It even had a hint of her light floral scent to it. Positive she was already asleep last night, he'd made himself pass her door without knocking. But his imagination had kept him awake into the early morning.

"Good morning." Her voice startled him out of his thoughts. The real Maggie was better than his imagination. Her blond hair was damp. The green "I heart N.Y." T-shirt lovingly hugged her curves. His fingers itched from the memory of touching those curves. The scent of her strawberry shampoo floated around him. Far from the seductive scents of the tailor-suited women he was used to. Maggie had him uncomfortably aroused even in her cheap shirt with clean, unstyled hair.

"Morning," he mumbled. This was going to be a long two weeks. Being with her and unable to kiss her was going to be torture. She'd only said it was too fast. Not that she didn't want him. Was she leaving an open window?

"I only packed enough clothes for the weekend." Maggie held out the bottom of the T-shirt and looked at it. "It's not like I could run around naked. I bought this and two more for only ten dollars."

His mind stumbled and held on to the word *naked*. Damn lack of sleep. He shook his head to clear the image as she passed the table on her way to the kitchen and coffeemaker.

"I hope you don't mind the pictures. I found the frames in the guest bedroom closet and had the pictures of Amber with me. They were some I'd sent you over the years."

He could hear her moving around in his kitchen. So domestic. "They are fine."

"I couldn't help it." She leaned against the door frame with a cup of coffee cradled in her hands. Her gaze took in the room. "I know you don't have time, but my mom always said a little color makes life better. Of course, sometimes she got a little carried away with color. I haven't worn that red scarf she got me. Penny must have snuck it in my bag when I wasn't looking."

"We should be able to fly out today." Brady made himself focus on logistics and not the bit of skin peeking out from below her shirt. "My assistant was able to book two tickets on a flight leaving late this afternoon. After we pack, we can grab lunch before heading out."

She sat next to him at the table. Her focus stayed on the coffee cup. "We haven't discussed what's going to happen when we get to Tawnee Valley."

"We can discuss that now."

"We have an extra bedroom, but I'm not sure if I'm ready for you to stay with us." She met his gaze.

"I understand." Brady hadn't thought it through. The only time the two of them had been alone, he hadn't been able to keep his hands off her. He had slept like crap with her a door away for two nights. But he was sure she was thinking of Amber and not the attraction between them.

"I know there aren't any hotels nearby, unless you want to stay in Owen…"

"No, that would take too long." Owen was ten miles away and though the commute wasn't horrible, occasionally a tractor would slow traffic to a crawl, turning the ten minutes to twenty minutes or longer.

Maggie flushed. "I suppose if it's the only option…"

"I can stay with Sam." Brady's chest tightened. "He owes me at least that much for keeping this from me."

The lines of worry faded from Maggie's face and her pretty smile returned, making the bands around his chest ease. "That would be great."

"I'm sure Sam and I have a lot to discuss." Brady stood and took his cup to the sink. "I need to pack and answer a few emails. I'll send a quick email to Sam to expect me. Maybe we can go out and wander a little before our flight."

Because if they stayed here any longer with her smiling like that at him, he wouldn't be responsible for his actions. This attraction was temptation in the flesh. Briefly he thought if they got it out of their systems maybe the tension would go away. Or make it worse.

The ride to Tawnee Valley was a lot more comfortable than Maggie's trip to New York. Brady had booked them in first class. When she'd complained about the cost, he'd said they were the only tickets left.

Now she was sitting in a BMW heading down the highway that led to her small-town life. Maggie couldn't contain her excitement. New York had been intimidating, but she'd managed. It was time to return to Amber and their home.

They'd spent the remainder of their morning in New York wandering through Central Park. With Brady by her side, she hadn't worried like she had the day before. She even relaxed and enjoyed herself. They had chitchatted about this and that. He had asked question after question about Amber. Maggie had answered as best she could. It had been almost easy to ignore the little jolts she got when he put his hand at the small of her back to guide her.

Lunch had been simple and delicious and she could see the appeal of having lots of restaurants within walking distance. But she wouldn't give up the closeness of their community for the anonymity of the city for anything.

The plane ride had brought back the tension. Sitting close to him for two hours had been excruciating. Her body had hummed from the brush of his arm. Maintaining the conversation without wanting to kiss him when he was so close… She was lucky the seat hadn't combusted.

"Not much has changed around here." His voice drew her to the present.

"No, not much," she agreed.

They'd been avoiding eye contact for most of the day. If she looked at him, he looked away. If he looked at her, she looked away. It was crazy, childish. They were the parents of an amazing little girl, but trying to define their relationship with each other seemed impossible.

They'd passed through Owen a few minutes ago and were a few miles from Tawnee Valley. The plan was for Brady to drop her off, but should she introduce him to Amber or wait until they could set up a time so Maggie had time to prepare Amber for her father? Maggie's heart went full throttle and the snack from the plane sat like a lump in her stomach.

Before she knew it, they were stopping in front of her house. What did he think of their town now that he'd lived in England and New York?

"Where do we go from here?" He caught her gaze. His eyes were so blue.

She'd told Penny she wouldn't want Brady, but boy, had she been wrong. It had been too long. The other night hadn't helped. It had stirred all those physical needs she'd ignored while she took care of a growing child and her mother.

"Maggie?"

What she wouldn't give for another kiss. But the cost was too high. For her and for Amber. Amber needed her father. Maggie took in a deep breath and raised her eyes to his. "Why don't you come in? The sooner we get this over the better, I think."

A wrinkle appeared on his forehead as if trying to figure out what was in her mind. Good thing he wasn't a mind reader, because her thoughts were less than pure.

"If you think that's what's best," Brady said.

"Definitely." She pushed out of the car and waited by the

trunk until he opened it for her. She reached for her suitcase, but he beat her to it.

"I've got it."

She nodded and turned stiffly to walk toward the house. What on earth was she going to say to Amber?

Brady didn't have any trouble ignoring the sexual tension between Maggie and him as they approached the house. Nervousness filled him. This wasn't a baby he was meeting for the first time. This was a child. His child. Who had had seven years to build up in her mind what her daddy was like.

Now that he was here, he wasn't sure he could do this. Maybe he should tell Maggie that they'd do it tomorrow. That way he could worry about it through the night and formulate a plan. He reached out to grab Maggie's arm.

A screen door slammed and small footsteps raced down the wooden porch. A streak of purple and black slammed into Maggie. Maggie grabbed her daughter and swung around in a circle.

"I missed you, Mommy." Her voice was beautiful like the whisper of wind on a warm day.

"I missed you, too, baby." Maggie tucked her face into Amber's shoulder.

Brady felt as if he was intruding on a moment, as if he shouldn't be there, but he would never forget how beautiful the two of them looked together. Amber had his dark, almost-black hair but her smile was her grandmother's.

Maggie set Amber on the ground and knelt before her. Amber peeked around her and gazed at Brady with familiar blue eyes. A lump formed in his throat and his chest tightened. Warmth surged behind his eyes. He tried to smile, but he wasn't sure it came through.

"Amber, I have someone I want you to meet."

Amber glanced at her mother and back at Brady. She edged

in closer to Maggie and took her hand. The lump descended into Brady's gut like a lead cannonball. His own daughter didn't know him.

Maggie stood and turned. She took a deep breath, which reminded him he needed to breathe. "Amber, this is—"

"Brady." He stopped her from saying *your father*. "I'm Brady Ward. A friend of your mom's."

Maggie cocked an eyebrow at him. He shrugged. He wasn't ready to deal with being her dad and this way, Amber could decide if she liked him without worrying about him being the father who had never been there for her.

"You have a funny name, Mr. Ward." She peered at him with those gorgeous wide eyes and he couldn't believe that this was his daughter.

"You can call me Brady." He held out his hand.

She took his hand and jerked it up and down before releasing it. "It's nice to meet you."

She turned her back on him and looked up at her mother. Her whole face lit and her body trembled with excitement. "Did you bring me something?"

"Let's go inside. Maybe we can order a pizza, and you can get to know Brady better." Maggie glanced at him for confirmation.

"That sounds great." Brady nodded and followed them up the steps.

Maggie kept throwing confused looks over her shoulder at him. He wished he could explain, but for the first time in years, he felt completely out of control. He had no idea what Amber would say when she realized he was her daddy. Would she instantly like him or instantly hate him? He'd never been there for her. Birthdays, Christmas, the days that mattered and the ones when nothing happened. He hadn't been there. How could he look her in the eyes and say he was here now? What if she didn't believe him? Or what if work pulled him away before he was ready to leave? It was a risk he wasn't ready to take.

The porch steps creaked under his feet, and flecks of paint littered his path. He followed them into the small Victorian and was engulfed in warmth. All around was evidence of a house well loved by the occupants. Pictures of generations of family members were strewn all through the entryway and living room. A rainbow of colors collided anywhere he looked, but the mismatched furniture all seemed to blend together.

"Where would you like me to put the suitcase?" Brady asked.

"Brady Ward." A feminine voice brought his attention away from Maggie and Amber's reunion.

He would need to get used to these voices from his past if he was going to spend the next two weeks in Tawnee Valley. A copper-haired woman came down the narrow staircase. Her outfit hugged every curve, and her style hadn't changed much since high school. "Penny Montgomery?"

"Figures it would take Maggie to go and get you to come for a visit." Penny grabbed him into a hug and whispered in his ear, "You hurt either of them and I will personally lop off any dangly bits you have."

She pulled away. Her smile convinced him she'd be willing to do just that and she'd enjoy doing it. He pulled a tight smile. He hadn't even considered all the people he would run into while in Tawnee Valley. Maggie was the next victim of Penny's embrace.

"You know Brady, too?" Amber asked from behind Maggie.

"Yeah, we all went to school together." Penny knelt next to Amber and whispered something in her ear.

Amber giggled behind her hand and the sound softened the knot of resentment that had begun to form in Brady's chest.

If he hurt them like Penny said, it wouldn't be intentional. He was confident that if he stepped out of line, Maggie would make sure he knew it.

"No more secrets, you two." Maggie took her suitcase and opened it on the table. "Penny, can you order us all a pizza?"

Penny left the room but not before throwing Brady a serious look that said, "I'm watching you."

Just what he needed— another set of eyes watching him. Tawnee Valley was a small enough town. Being back and hanging around Maggie and Amber meant gossip was going to fly. He wouldn't have long before some well-meaning person spilled the beans accidentally to Amber. The speculation he could deal with, but Amber being hurt by it was a whole other story.

"Tell me about New York," Amber said to Maggie as she knelt in one of the chairs near her mother. Her purple gem earrings sparkled in the overhead light. She peered into the bag, looking to find what Maggie had brought her.

Brady should have gotten her something. Would that have been odd? For a friend of her mother's, maybe. Not odd for a father. Dammit, why didn't he let Maggie tell her? Did he think it would be better this way? Was he already screwing things up?

"Brady lives there and before that he lived in London, England." Maggie glanced at him and he saw all the encouragement he needed in her eyes. Maggie seemed to have a spark of faith in him even if Penny didn't.

"You lived in England?" Amber's full attention was on Brady.

"Yes, I did. For eight years."

"I'm almost eight. Did you meet the queen or the prince?" Before he could answer, Amber's attention was drawn away when Maggie held out a plastic bag.

"For you."

Amber quickly unwrapped the snow globe of the Statue of Liberty and the New York skyline. "Thank you, Mommy!"

She shook it and watched the snow fall and swirl. After a couple more times, she shyly lifted her gaze to Brady and he felt his heart sing. "Would you tell me about England?"

"Of course," Brady said.

While they waited for pizza, Brady told Amber all about England, answering the silly questions and the serious ones with complete openness. Maggie watched them with an expression he couldn't read. His daughter was curious, intelligent and everything he could have ever hoped for. If he had hoped for a child.

His career was his life. Work was what he'd return to when these weeks were finished. Work was what would keep him from coming around for every little event in Amber's life.

Work kept him sane, and he was making a difference. Part of him wished he could be that father that grilled on Sundays and played catch and wiped away tears, but that wasn't who he was. As he looked into the innocent eyes of his daughter, he knew he'd better not forget that and start to wish for more. This was all he was capable of.

Chapter Eight

Maggie washed the pizza dishes while Brady told Amber an English story with princes and princesses. He had looked anxiously at Maggie—for approval or strength, she wasn't sure— but she'd smiled softly and nodded. He must have found what he needed as he started a tale of jousting.

This was everything she'd always hoped for in a reunion with her father, but she knew it wouldn't have been the same. Her father had left her. He'd known about her from the beginning and one day got sick of being someone's daddy. Maybe Brady would get sick of it, too, and she'd be left with a broken-hearted daughter. Maybe it was better to not tell Amber who he was. Let her think he was some stranger from Maggie's past who happened into their lives.

"Are you doing okay?" Penny asked from the doorway.

"Yeah." Maggie swiped at a strand of hair. "It's weird, right? Brady being here? With her?"

Maggie couldn't help the anxiety cascading through her

system. She didn't know whether to be happy or sad or worried that Amber had finally met her father.

"You didn't tell me what happened in New York." Penny grabbed a towel and began to dry the dishes.

"There isn't anything to tell. He worked. I waited." *Except that one night when we almost wound up in his bed.* Her knees went a little loose thinking about his lips on her neck.

"I don't believe you, but I'll let it go." Penny took the next dish. "Is he staying here?"

"No, he's staying with Sam." Maggie glanced over her shoulder toward the living room where she could hear Amber laughing. "This is good."

"I sure hope so. Do you want me to stick around?" Penny made comically shifty eyes toward the door. She'd been at Maggie's house for a few days and probably had plans.

"No, we'll be fine. It's almost Amber's bedtime. Brady has to get out to the farm."

"Good, because I have a hot date." Penny grinned and slipped on her jacket.

"I don't think that your DVR counts as a date."

"You haven't seen *Supernatural*. Call me later." Penny kissed Maggie on the cheek. "If he does anything wrong, you tell me and I'll take care of him."

"I'm sure you will." Maggie dried her hands. She could handle Brady in Tawnee Valley.

After Penny left, Maggie finished cleaning before walking toward the voices in her living room. She leaned against the doorjamb, suddenly exhausted.

"Dragons roamed the streets, but Lady Jane was more than a match for them." Brady's voice had taken on a slight accent as he told the English story.

They sat facing each other, lost in their own little world. The same dark hair, the same blue eyes, the same slope of their noses. It would take a fool to realize they weren't father and daughter. Amber leaned forward, straining to listen to every word that came out of Brady's mouth.

Maggie remembered that feeling all too well. Even though he barely knew her in high school, she'd had the biggest crush on him. She'd spent hours doodling her name with his on her folders. It had been a silly, girlish crush.

When he'd left for college, she'd finally let herself believe it wasn't going to happen. He wasn't going to one day see her as anything more than a classmate of his brother's. She'd moved on to Josh. They were together until the end of high school, but it became clear they were going in separate directions and were better friends than lovers. And graduation...a hot summer night spent tangled in Brady's sheets, sheltered by his arms. No expectations. No regrets.

"There are no dragons in England nowadays. But the roads aren't much better." Brady looked up and caught her watching them. His eyes sparkled with happiness. Her heart stuttered. What she wouldn't have given back then to have him look at her like this.

She held her breath. Surely he could hear the rapid beat of her heart from over there.

"Mommy, Brady says that the English call rain boots wellies. Isn't that funny?" Amber's blue eyes were filled with wonder and joy.

Watching the two of them together, Maggie didn't regret bringing Brady into her home. Whether or not she'd regret it in two weeks, she had no way of knowing. After all, Brady hadn't come clean about being Amber's father. She needed to ask him about that. "It's about time for bed. Why don't you thank Brady for the stories and go shower?"

"Thank you," Amber said dutifully. "Are you coming back?"

"Of course. I'll be here for a couple of weeks." Brady kept his attention focused on Amber.

Maggie exhaled. She'd known he was going to stay, but maybe he didn't want to be with them every day. She couldn't expect him to, especially with work, but it had been part of their bargain that she give him a chance. Well, that couldn't happen if he wasn't around.

"You should stay with us. You could use Nana's room. Mommy cleaned it real nice and changed it into a guest bedroom. My nana went to heaven. She won't mind." Amber's expressions changed rapidly during her speech. She hadn't learned how to hide her emotions. With everything she'd been through, Maggie was grateful Amber hadn't grown up too fast.

Brady's mouth dropped open as if he wasn't sure what to say. "I'm going to stay with my brother for now."

"Okay." Amber raced over and hugged him around the waist. His hands went out to the side and he gave Maggie a look that said, "What do I do?" Before he could do anything, it was over.

Maggie smiled and got her own tackle hug before Amber raced upstairs, yelling over her shoulder, "I'll see you tomorrow, Brady."

Brady sank into the chair and rubbed his face.

"How are you holding up?" Maggie stayed where she was in the doorway. Afraid that if she got too much closer she'd want to touch him, and touching him might lead to things best not explored. Her fingers tingled. She knew exactly how tight his muscles were. As well-defined as his younger self.

"Tired." Brady laced his fingers together and hung his head. "This is going to be exhausting."

"She's usually not this wound up." Maggie stepped toward him, wanting to reassure him without scaring him off.

"It's not Amber." He lifted his gaze to hers.

For a moment she thought he was going to say it was her. That she was making him exhausted.

"It's this town."

She let out a sigh of relief.

He pushed himself to his feet and stalked over to the window. "I'd forgotten how soul crushing it is. It wasn't just my parents' deaths that made me want to run, but people like Penny. Everyone thought they were involved in everyone else's business."

Maggie bristled. "It's a community. We care for each other. Penny is protective of Amber and there isn't anything wrong with that. She was there for us."

"It's good to have someone look out for you, but this place is like a virus. Everything spreads quickly and not a thing can stop it." Brady turned back to her, and she could see the anger in his eyes.

"It's a good thing you don't have to live here." Maggie crossed her arms as her spine stiffened. "What time are you coming over tomorrow?"

"I don't mean you or Amber." His tone softened. "I just…"

"You don't want to be in Tawnee Valley. Completely understandable after you've spent the past eight years alone over in England." Damn him for making her care about him even an inch.

"I kept busy and kept my nose out of other people's business." Brady walked over to her until they were close enough to touch. "I don't need to be watched like a hawk or told when I'm out of line by anyone but you, Maggie. Amber is your responsibility and I won't begrudge that, but she's not this town's child and they have no say in what we do."

Her anger softened a little with his words. With him this close, it was like standing next to a live wire. She wanted to grab his shirt and kiss him. Finish what they'd started a few days ago. She breathed deeply and ended up filling her lungs with the scent of him—sandalwood and that underlying scent that was uniquely Brady.

He stepped closer, almost hesitantly, as if to give her the chance to push him away. The angry words faded into the background, just noise that hadn't mattered. Eight years dropped away in an instant and she felt eighteen again, at a crossroads that didn't have a good ending, no matter which way she looked. Her mother's diagnosis had meant staying home and helping her. There had been no other family to turn to, and they couldn't have afforded a nurse with the level of treatment her mother had needed.

For one night, she had wanted to feel free, uncaged. She'd wanted Brady. They had gone upstairs to his room with no backward glances. Every touch had been torture and pleasure, both of them knowing that when the morning came, it would be time to return to their lives as if nothing had happened between them.

"Maggie?" Her name tumbled from his lips and he leaned toward her, daring her to close the last bit of distance like she had in New York.

Her body swayed toward him as if it couldn't resist his pull.

"Mommy, I forgot a towel," Amber yelled over the noise of the shower.

Maggie tried to find something more in Brady's eyes, but the shutters fell and he stepped back.

"I'll be right up." Maggie didn't move. They weren't kids anymore. Both had responsibilities elsewhere, and their paths were only joined by one thing—Amber. That's all they had between them.

Brady cleared his throat. "What time does school let out?"

"Three." Maggie was glad the word came out without being breathless.

"Tell Amber good-night for me." He brushed past her and headed to the front door.

She sighed and let out a little shiver before turning to go upstairs.

"Good night, Maggie," he said softly as the door shut.

Brady stood on the front porch of his childhood home. A whole host of memories had swarmed in to greet him. From toddler to teenager, he'd spent many days on this porch, dreaming of a future far away. He'd loved his parents and wanted to make them proud, but farming had never been his passion.

He'd made sure to be the best at anything he tried. To be better at school and sports than his two brothers. It hadn't mattered. Sam was his father's favorite and Luke had been their mother's favorite. Not that Brady had been neglected. He'd been loved. He'd just been different. Never quite fit in.

As he was getting ready to knock, the door swung open.

"Brady." Sam moved out of the way to let him through.

So many emotions played through Brady's mind. Guilt, hurt, past resentment. Nothing compared to the anger for keeping Brady's daughter a secret.

"Sam." Brady rolled his suitcase into the dining room and shrugged off his laptop bag. Nothing had changed in the house. Sam had kept it exactly as Mom had left it. Everything had aged, though. What was once a cream-colored paint had yellowed. From here he could see that the kitchen vinyl was worn from years of boots treading across its surface. The place was clean but far from spotless.

"I made up your bed." Sam moved farther into the house, going through the doorway that led to the kitchen.

Brady closed his eyes and took a deep breath. It was as if he had only been gone for the school year and not eight years. He should have decked Sam when he answered the door, but nothing would come from a confrontation. Sam wasn't going to change.

From the kitchen came the sounds of a chair rubbing against the floor and a newspaper rustling. If Brady weren't emotionally drained from meeting Amber and dealing with Maggie, he might have gone in there and started in on Sam for his lies. Instead, Brady lifted his suitcase and climbed the stairs to his old room. The doorknob was still loose in the casing and made a metallic rattle when he opened it.

Exactly as he left it with the exception of the quilt. Brady had taken the quilt his mother had made for him when he left. Even though he'd felt compelled to leave everything behind and start a new life, he couldn't let go of such a simple thing as a blanket.

The double bed barely fit in the small room and left little room for the dresser. When he was fourteen, Mom had found the old bed frame at an auction.

As always, if Mom had wanted something done, the three of them would move heaven and earth for her. They'd managed to get the bed up the narrow stairs with a few bruises and a lot of cussing. Brady ran his hand over the smooth wood footboard. Now he barely spoke to his brothers. Luke kept in touch when he could. He had always been the mediator between Brady and Sam. But their lives were all so different and without Mom and Dad to draw them together...

Pushing the thoughts from his head, he quickly unpacked his suitcase and tucked it away under the bed. He hadn't worked at all today but since it was Sunday, it probably didn't matter.

He would have to find somewhere else to work. Sam had to have a computer hidden somewhere in this house, which meant there might be a decent desk and chair for him to work on.

Shouldering his laptop bag, Brady made his way down-

stairs. Anywhere he went in town, he would run into people
from his past and his parents' past. Interruptions would eat
into his work time.

He walked through the farmhouse, trying to ignore the
memories floating on the edge of his mind and to concentrate
on finding somewhere to work. The main difference in the
living room was the fancy flat-screen TV and stereo com-
ponents. Gone was the old tube TV console and rabbit ears.
Their father had always complained that if you had time to sit,
you had time to work. There were always chores to be done.

Obviously, Sam didn't feel the same way.

The little room had a meager office with an old dial-up
modem hooked to the modern computer. Brady wondered
if he could even get a signal for his wireless router this far
down in the valley.

The metal folding chair and particle-board desk wouldn't
be ideal for working long hours. Back in the dining room,
Brady set his laptop on the table and stretched out his shoulders. He could hear the rustle of a newspaper from the kitchen.

If he told Sam off for keeping Amber from him, what good
would it do? Sam had never listened to anyone but their father. In his mind, Sam had probably justified it with some
bullshit he'd decided on when Brady had left.

No. Sam was one demon Brady wasn't ready to face yet.
And given the silence from the kitchen, Sam wasn't ready,
either. Maybe they never would be. Two weeks and Brady
would be gone again. Nothing was going to change that. And
nothing would change between them.

Chapter Nine

Maggie sat at her desk working on some bills for the furniture store while Amber did her homework at the kitchen table. Brady had brought in his laptop and sat next to Amber. Two minutes later, he'd answered a call on his cell phone and wandered out to the front porch.

"Alex Conrad puked in the hallway today. It was so gross." Amber tipped back in her chair to look around the door frame at Maggie.

"That sounds unpleasant. All four on the floor." Referring to the chair legs. Maggie looked at her watch again. Brady had been outside for the past thirty minutes. She'd begun to like the guy yesterday. He'd been attentive and helpful in the airport and the car ride to Tawnee Valley. He'd focused on Amber, answering her nonstop questions like a pro. Just when she thought he was going to give it a real go and leave the workaholic in New York, the New York Brady had shown up at her door jonesing for an internet connection.

She'd wanted to ask how it went with Sam, but he hadn't spared her more than a couple of sentences since he'd arrived.

"There were chunks—"

"That's enough, Amber Marie. Get back to your homework." Maggie finished the last check and started putting things away. "Maybe after homework and dinner, we can go get some ice cream."

"Yay!" Amber bent her head over the page of math problems.

Maggie carried the stamped envelopes out the front door. Brady stood on the far end of the porch, gesturing while he spoke intensely on the phone.

She walked to the mailbox and dropped the bills in. At least he was passionate about his work. What would it be like if he were that passionate about Amber? Would he even give a second thought to the phone when it rang? Would it have been better if Maggie had left it alone? If he'd never found out about Amber? It's not as if he would visit Sam and accidentally run into Amber and her. Besides, half the town thought Amber was Sam's. The other half thought she was Luke's.

"Don't let Peterson take over, Jules." Brady turned, and Maggie could feel his frustration like a heat wave. "We've worked too hard to let him step in and take the credit."

Maggie perched on the porch railing and crossed her arms, waiting for him to be finished with his conversation. She had a thing or two to talk to him about.

"Tell him no." Brady lifted his gaze.

Her body buzzed with energy as he met her eyes. Irritating attraction. It kept popping up when all she wanted to be was mad. He held up one finger to indicate one minute. She resisted the urge to hold up a different finger with a very different meaning.

"Fine. Tell him we're dating and that's the reason you guys can't go out."

Maggie's heart sank like a lead balloon crashing into her gut. Dating? It made sense. The Brady she'd known had rarely been without a girlfriend in school. He was smart, sexy and a good guy. She never would have guessed the Brady she'd known would be a cheater, but New York Brady was some-one entirely different. If she hadn't stopped them, they would have had sex in New York. Thank goodness she'd come to her senses. He'd changed, and she had to remember that.

A different rant was forming in her head, but he wasn't here for Maggie. He was here for Amber. And right now, he was sucking at it.

"It'll be okay. Run the preliminary numbers again and cross-reference the new numbers. Email me the spreadsheet and I'll see what I can do."

Maggie shored up her defensive wall as she prepared to launch her attack. The bubble of heat welling within had nothing to do with the fact that he was a two-timing— She stopped her thoughts and drew in a breath. For Amber.

Brady hit a button on his phone and walked toward her.

When he stopped within touching distance, he looked wor-ried. "Is something wrong?"

"Yes." She swallowed the hurt of finding out he was dat-ing someone as hoity-toity as he was, and the fact her crush on him wasn't affected by that fact. Mother first. "Amber is expecting you to pay attention to her. I'm expecting you to put away the phone for the few hours you get to spend with her."

The worry fell off Brady's face. A little anger crept into its place. "This isn't exactly a cakewalk for me. I didn't ask for any of this and it isn't the best time to be away from the office. I have people relying on me."

Like Jules? The words pressed on her tongue to get out, but she clamped her lips shut.

"I promised I would get to know Amber, and I will." The muscle in his jaw ticked.

"Fine, but no more phone calls. You have all day to take them—you don't need to take them here." She kept her head up and ignored the heat his body stirred in her.

"I can't control when other people need to consult with me." He took a step forward. "That was part of the deal, too. I need to work while I'm here."

"While in Tawnee Valley, yes, but while at my house with my daughter, no." Maggie's heart stuttered against her chest. She hadn't spent the past eight years being brave to crumple under pressure now. She pulled her shoulders back and met his gaze with an uncompromising one.

Eight years ago she would have backed down. So in love with the idea of Brady Ward that she would have done anything he asked of her. But that girl had grown up and could face down anything and anybody. Having a baby out of wedlock wasn't as big a deal now, but with a small town, it hadn't been a *cakewalk,* as Brady put it.

She could almost feel the battle that waged between them. Will against will. She had the advantage. She had the power to stop him from seeing their daughter. His jaw was tight and he looked as if he was about to say something they might both regret.

She tipped her chin up another notch. "Promises or not. She is my daughter."

"She is *our* daughter." He straightened more, towering over her and inside she crumpled a little, but on the outside she remained a rock. "If I have to get a court-ordered DNA sample, I will. But since you don't deny that she is mine, it shouldn't come to that. As long as you don't make unreasonable demands of me, I won't make unreasonable demands of you."

She bristled. "I didn't *have* to tell you about her."

"But you did."

They stood close enough to touch, but neither of them

moved an inch. Neither willing to retreat. She wouldn't give on this one. "If you want to work, stay at the farm."

"Fine." The soft-spoken word caught her off guard.

"What?" Was Brady Ward giving in to her demands? Her confusion made her anger dissipate.

"I'm not going to fight you on this." Brady reached out and took her hand. His whole demeanor changed. The hard businessman shut down and the country boy reemerged. The charmer she'd been half in love with. "I'm here for a short time. If I can't be here one hundred percent for Amber, I'll stay out at the farm. Just don't lose faith in me yet."

Her pulse raced as he lightly held her hand in his. She hadn't won the war, but she'd won this battle. Giddiness filled her. The warmth of his touch caused her breathing to become uneven. The steel look had left his blue eyes until they became warm and she felt herself softening. Swaying ever so much closer.

He has a girlfriend! Her mind had to shout to remind her. Reluctantly, she took her hand back, resisting the urge to rub the tingles away. Just another reason to keep her distance. It would help her remember that Brady was here only for Amber.

She nodded, not trusting her voice. Fortunately, Amber came rushing out the door at that moment, keeping both of them from making a fool out of her.

As they stood in line at the ice cream shop after dinner, Brady couldn't understand why Maggie was still angry. Amber had kept up the conversation during dinner, but Maggie had been visibly upset. When Amber had asked Maggie if she was okay, Maggie had claimed to have a headache. But she'd given him a glance that made him believe he was the headache.

He had business to do. It wasn't as if he could take off

two weeks and not do his work, regardless of what his boss thought. And with the limitations of the internet out at the farm, he could only do so much there. But she didn't seem to understand that.

Besides, Amber had been busy with homework. It wasn't as though she needed his constant attention. Did Maggie expect him to help Amber with her homework? Because from what he'd seen so far, she didn't need it.

"I want the mint chocolate chip in a waffle cone with chocolate sprinkles and chocolate sauce." Amber bubbled over with excitement as she pointed her fingers against the cold glass.

"Keep your hands off the glass, please." Maggie avoided looking at Brady.

If that's the way she wanted it, fine with him. He would figure out how to bridge this gap between them eventually. Her eyes had softened after he'd given in and her lips had parted slightly. Temptation in the flesh. And then she'd gone cold and rigid. Obviously, even if she desired him, she didn't want to. Maybe he was reading her wrong. But he hadn't read her wrong in New York. She'd been as into him as he'd been into her. He mentally shook his head as he pulled out a twenty and handed it to the cashier before Maggie had a chance to dig in her purse.

That got a glare out of her, but he just smiled.

Right now he had to focus on getting to know Amber in the time he had left. As much as he desired Maggie, she needed someone who would be there for her. He wasn't ready for a full-time family.

An elderly man in ripped khakis and a plaid shirt sidled up next to Brady. "You know it's rude to not say hello to your elders."

Brady looked over and recognized Paul Morgan, a friend of his dad's. "When I see an elder, I'll be sure to say hi."

Paul took Brady's offered hand in a hearty handshake. Paul chuckled and gestured toward Amber and Maggie getting the ice cream they'd chosen.

"Good family you got there."

Brady hesitated. He almost said *they're not mine,* but that wasn't exactly true. Amber was his daughter, but Maggie wasn't his wife or his in any way. And at the rate they were going, they wouldn't even be friends by the end of the week.

Brady nodded, not knowing what else to do.

"You been over to see Sam?" Paul asked.

Brady looked at his feet before returning Paul's gaze. How much did he know about the blowup between the brothers? "I'm staying out at the old farm."

"Good that you two let bygones go. Sam's done a great job tending the farm. His livestock is the best in the county. And the way he took over raising you and Luke, that shows real courage. Shame your parents aren't around to see how well you boys grew up."

Even as the familiar burn of jealousy engulfed him from all the praise for Sam, Brady couldn't help but think of how disappointed his parents would be that he and his brothers weren't close like when they were young. His mother had always mended the fences between him and Sam when they fought, but she wasn't here now. Brady wasn't sure their relationship could be mended after what Sam did to Maggie.

"Looks like I should get back to…" Brady gestured to Maggie and Amber, not knowing what to call them. "It was good seeing you."

"You should stop for a visit while you're in town," Paul said.

Brady shook Paul's hand before heading over to the table Maggie and Amber had found.

Paul had a neighboring farm to the Wards'. Brady hadn't even asked how Paul's wife was doing. Or his farm or crops.

Mom would have scolded him for not showing common courtesy.

"Don't you want ice cream?" Amber's nose was coated with a skim layer of green ice cream. She looked at him with those adoring eyes and he melted inside. He did have one thing Sam didn't.

He patted his stomach as he sat. "I'm stuffed from that dinner your mom prepared. She must be the best cook in the tri-county area."

He glanced over at Maggie, but she didn't seem amused by his declaration.

He missed her smiles. And their absence made him try even harder to get one. Apparently, it was going to take more than complimenting her cooking.

"How was school today?" Brady asked.

"Alex puked all over the hallway. It was disgusting." Amber drew out the last word and made the requisite face to go along with it.

"That's what you remember from school?" Brady shook his head and tried to keep a straight face. He'd been expecting something about the math homework she'd had or the spelling test she'd mentioned earlier. Not some kid puking in the hall.

She took a bite of her cone. "It was the most exciting thing that happened all day. It almost splattered all over Jessica and Maddy. Everyone jumped out of the way while the janitor went and got kitty litter."

Brady smiled. "I suppose that would be exciting."

Amber continued to eat her green ice cream as if they'd been discussing art rather than vomit. From what Brady remembered of grade school, it probably would have been the highlight of his day, too.

He turned to Maggie to see how she was reacting. "How was your day today?"

Maybe she would answer a direct question.

"Fine." Maggie kept her gaze out the window past him.

"Anyone puke?" Brady winked at Amber, who giggled.

"Nope."

Nothing. He sighed internally. As he scanned the ice cream shop, people had a familiar look about them. But he'd been away for so long, he couldn't tell who they were.

He'd almost forgotten what it was like to be in a small town. To be recognized by who your parents were, where you'd gone to school and even whose pigtail you'd pulled when you were seven, and not by what you'd accomplished since then.

The other people in the ice cream store pretended not to be looking at them, but Brady wasn't fooled. They knew he was Brady Ward and he was with Maggie Brown and her daughter. If people hadn't put two and two together before, their being together would leave little doubt.

It bothered him that people would see that Maggie wasn't talking to him.

But it bothered him more that Maggie wouldn't meet his eyes. He didn't like that she wouldn't talk to him, except for in clipped words. And he didn't like the pressed thinness of her lush lips.

"Maggie?" he said.

She faced him with a questioning look in her eyes. None of the spunk that had drawn him to her years ago reflected in them.

What could he say to make her happy? To bring back that little smile she'd give him when he said just the right thing.

"I might be late tomorrow." Dumb, dumb man. That wasn't what he'd meant to say, but darn it all, he wasn't used to being around women in a nonwork environment. He wasn't used to someone counting on him outside of work projects.

Her eyes grew frostier, and she nodded briskly. He flinched internally.

"Amber, you need to go wash." She went back to ignoring him as Amber raced off to the bathroom.

Maybe over the years, he'd let his work consume him until work was all he had. There wasn't a separation between the relaxed him and the work him. It was how he protected himself. He couldn't let that go for a couple of weeks to "hang out." He *needed* to work, it had kept away the pain that he'd felt when his mother had passed so soon after his father. The anger and rage that had engulfed him; that had forced his hand and made him flee not a hundred miles away, but across an ocean.

In London, no one had asked him about his parents. No one had offered sympathy for his loss, because they hadn't known. Here, it was in their eyes and words, even if they never said it out loud.

As they walked home in the ebbing twilight, Amber rambled on about this and that. Brady couldn't get out of his head. It didn't help that Maggie continued her silent treatment. The street was lined with trees and though he hadn't walked this particular street much as a kid, it was familiar. Like every other street in Tawnee Valley. The past seemed to press in on him and force his hand in the present. He had nothing to give to anyone. What made him think Amber even wanted *him* for a father?

He had run away from the responsibility of being part of a family. He had run out on Sam and Luke—his own brothers. Even though Sam had been controlling, he could have used some guidance.

As they reached the porch steps, Amber spun around. "Do you want to see the scrapbook Nana and I put together?"

"Sure." Brady didn't know if Maggie wanted him to hang around any later, but he didn't want to leave. He wanted to be part of this family, part of whatever they were creating here. Tonight he didn't want to run.

Amber bounded into the house. The screen door slammed behind her. Maggie climbed a couple of steps before stopping. Brady barely kept himself from running into her.

"I need to know if you are in this." Maggie didn't turn to meet his gaze. The light from inside the house lit her profile, but he couldn't make out her expression.

"I wouldn't have come all this way if I weren't." He wasn't sure what she was referring to, but he could only assume this was a continuation of their earlier argument about work.

"Either you tell Amber you are her father or you don't, but I need to know what you are going to do. I can't keep lying to her." Finally, she turned to face him. On the steps she was the same height as him. In her eyes was the fierce protectiveness of a mother trying to keep her child from harm.

"I've done a lot of things since I left Tawnee Valley." Brady cleared his throat. "I've made a lot of deals and created thousands of jobs."

She crossed her arms over her chest and looked down her nose at him. Not impressed with his resume.

"But…" What could he say to convince her? Years of negotiating multimillion-dollar deals failed him.

"But what, Brady?"

He searched her eyes, trying to figure out what technique would work. Trying to assess the risks versus the rewards of each scenario, but this wasn't work. This was a little girl. His little girl.

"I'm good at what I do, but—" he shrugged and gave up trying to hide "—I suck at the emotional stuff."

Her face softened slightly, but her body remained tense.

He took a deep breath as if he were about to jump into a pool. "I don't know how to be a daddy."

She dropped her arms. "She needs to know you care about her. No one's asking you to be her daddy."

"But I want to be."

"You do?" Skepticism lingered in her expression.

He closed the distance between them. "I've missed so much already. I don't want to miss any more. Amber is an amazing kid." He paused. "Our kid."

"I haven't made my mind up about you yet."

He could tell that he was winning here. Even as he felt more exposed than he had ever felt. "What if she doesn't like me? What if her fantasy of her dad is built up so high in her mind that only Superman could fulfill her dreams?"

Maggie's eyes glistened with unshed tears. "All a little girl wants from her father is for him to be there for her."

"Was your father there for you?" he asked, pushing gently for more information. There was something there. He'd sensed it before.

She shook her head, and a tear escaped down her cheek.

He smoothed it away with his thumb. "I'll do my best to not disappoint either of you."

That small smile crept onto her lips and he wanted to shout his victory. Her smooth skin beneath his thumb sent electricity down his spine. His body tensed at the sudden flood of desire pumping through his veins.

"I know you won't." She placed her hand over his on her cheek.

Trust. Had he ever known anyone quite like Maggie Brown? From a starry-eyed girl to a sultry teenager to this glorious woman standing before him, Maggie would never cease to amaze him.

He kissed her. He'd only meant to kiss her briefly. He wasn't even sure why. He wanted to, so he did. He could taste the vanilla ice cream. Her lips were incredibly soft beneath his. His only thought was he didn't want to stop kissing her.

Chapter Ten

Brady's lips were pressed against hers, firm and questing. Maggie couldn't help but part hers on a sigh, surrendering to the pent-up passion.

Until her mind butted in with the reminder that this was some other woman's man. In New York, she hadn't known, but now...

She pushed her hands on Brady's chest, breaking the connection. His eyes were hazy and confused.

"What about..." She searched for the name she'd heard today. "Jules?"

His eyebrows drew together. "What about Jules?"

"Wow." Her hands were on his chest and she could feel the muscle beneath her fingertips. Heat flushed her cheeks, remembering how his naked skin felt pressed against hers. She pulled her hands away from the fire that he ignited in her. Crossing her arms to keep them from checking out other muscles, she looked down her nose at him as she tried to rally her indignation. "Your girlfriend?"

Brady had the audacity to appear genuinely confused. "Jules?"

"I'm not stupid." Though she was starting to wonder about him. "I heard you on the phone today. You said you were dating."

Clarity transformed his face into a grin. "Aah."

"Do you typically kiss other women when you date someone these days? Because I can tell you, I'm not okay with that." Maggie wished she'd felt that way the minute his lips touched hers, but they hummed with pleasure and longed to jump right back into kissing.

"I'm not dating Jules." He closed the distance between them.

She backed up a step on the porch stairs. "I'm not a fool. Just because I'm here doesn't mean I'm available."

"Are you involved with someone?" He stepped onto the bottom step, bringing their bodies within touching distance again. Even though the night was cooling rapidly, his heat curled out from his body and wrapped itself around her.

"I'm not a cheater," she said in her best holier-than-thou voice.

His wolfish grin hit her below the belt. His gaze roamed over her possessively. She almost stumbled trying to get up another step.

"Just because your girlfriend isn't here doesn't make you available." She held her chin a little higher, proud that she hadn't crumpled under the power of the attraction between them.

"Jules isn't my girlfriend." He stepped again and they were eye to eye, chest to chest.

"But you said—"

"I said she could tell Peterson, a coworker of ours, that we were dating so that he'd stop asking her out. He won't take no for an answer." He reached out and tucked her hair behind her ear. His hand slipped behind her neck and every nerve in her body tingled in response. "I wouldn't betray her or you in that way, Maggie."

"Oh." Her brain completely shut down on her. The blue of his eyes held her hypnotized, waiting for his next move. Her whole body was a shiver of anticipation.

"Found it!" Amber shouted through the door.

Brady touched his forehead to hers. "To be continued."

Brady sat at the table as Amber leafed through the pages of a scrapbook. Maggie had followed him in and disappeared.

"I wasn't allowed to have a dog, but Nana let me put the stickers on this page, anyway." Amber pointed at the little stickers of dogs surrounding a picture of Amber and Mrs. Brown.

"We have a dog out at the farm. His name is Barnabus." Brady tried to not get distracted wondering where Maggie was and if she'd felt the same powerful draw that he had.

"I've never been on a farm. Is it like the zoo?" Amber turned the page. "See, we went to the zoo. It took a really long time to get there."

"Never been on a farm?" Brady needed to stay focused on Amber.

Amber tucked her dark hair behind her ear. A motion he'd seen Maggie do at least a dozen times. "Billy has a farm, but I'm not friends with him."

"We'll have to fix that." Brady pointed to a picture of Maggie with a monkey. "Did you take this?"

"Yeah, Mommy said it was silly, but I liked the picture." She closed the scrapbook and met his eyes. "Would you take me to your farm?"

"It's not my farm," he said automatically. "My brother runs it, but I grew up there. I'd love to show you around."

"This weekend?" Amber gave him a pleading smile and put her hands together. "Do you have horses?"

"Maybe. We don't have horses."

Amber gazed intently at his eyes. "You have the same color of eyes that I do."

Brady held his breath. Would she make the connection?

"Time for bed, baby," Maggie called from the other room.

"Will I see you tomorrow? Please, please, please, say yes."

"I'll try. I have some work to get done, but I'll be over after. Especially if your mother is cooking." He tweaked her nose with his finger.

Amber giggled and gave him a hug around his shoulders from behind him before running upstairs.

He took in a breath. This was familiar, yet foreign to him. Nights at the Ward farm had always been slow and easy, but nothing about his life since Tawnee Valley had been slow or easy. It was hard to remember how it felt to relax.

"You'll be by tomorrow?" Maggie swept past him to the kitchen sink and started filling it with water.

"Planning on it." He scrubbed his face, suddenly tired. "Can I help?"

"Sure." Her voice was tight.

He took the drying towel and waited while she washed a few dishes. How many nights had he spent with his mother, helping with the dishes? The silence between Maggie and him was comfortable and distracting at the same time. How could he recapture that moment on the porch steps? And if he did, would he have the energy to follow through?

They finished the dinner dishes. She scrubbed the counters while he dried the last dish.

She took the towel from him and hung it before turning out the kitchen light. "You'll think about what I said? About telling Amber?"

"Yes." Brady followed her through the dining room to the

front door where she held it open. Apparently, she didn't want to pick up where they'd left off on the porch steps. Maybe she was as exhausted as he felt.

"She needs to know." Maggie finally met his gaze.

What he wouldn't give to wipe away the weariness from her. To ease her burden.

"I'll tell her. I promise."

"More promises." She half smiled.

"Promises I intend to keep." Brady stepped close, but she retreated when he lifted his hand toward her.

"I don't think that is a good idea." Her face was stern, but there was a breathless quality to her voice that encouraged him.

"Not tonight," Brady said.

"Not ever." Maggie leaned against the wall. "I'm tired, Brady. I can't play this cat-and-mouse game as well as you can. I'm attracted to you."

He didn't move, sensing the "but" behind her words. "I'm attracted to you, too."

"I can't be what makes you go away." Her face flushed and her bottom lip trembled.

"I don't understand…" Why would she worry about that?

"My dad left when I was six." Her face went blank as if she felt nothing, but he could feel the pain underscoring every word. "I thought Mom had driven him away and I hated her for a while. Then I thought it was my fault and I hated myself for it."

"I wouldn't do that to Amber." He started to reach out but she flinched away. "Or you."

"You don't know that. I don't know that." She straightened. "We are much better off as friends. That way this doesn't get confused into something it's not. It never was."

Her smile had a touch of sadness to it. He wanted to reassure her, but he didn't know how much of himself he could give…to Amber or to her. When things had gotten rough in the past, he'd run. How could he guarantee he wouldn't do the same now?

Maybe this was for the best. He nodded. "It never was."

Her smile vanished though she tried to hold on to it. "I'll see you tomorrow."

"Tomorrow." Brady stepped out of the house and the weight of the world crashed down on his shoulders. He had people relying on him in New York and people relying on him in Tawnee Valley. Part of him wanted to run away, hide in his work. But as he settled into his rented car, he glanced up as the porch light turned off. Maggie stood silhouetted in the doorway.

No, this time he'd be the brave one. This time he'd build a relationship with his daughter and make sure that it didn't fall apart when something major happened. He'd be her rock, the way Maggie's father should have been for her. He wouldn't run.

The week turned out to be more hectic than Brady had estimated. Contractors had change orders. Reports had to be in on time. Jules was barely staying afloat.

It was Wednesday and he'd sworn to Maggie and Amber that he'd be by today, but someone above must have a sense of humor, because everything was falling apart at work.

The sun beat on his head as he tried to shield the screen of his laptop. He had his earpiece firmly in and was listening in on a conference Peterson had called.

"We need to increase the budget by at least five hundred thousand dollars to make sure the project doesn't have overages," Peterson said.

"The budget is fine as is and with all the current work orders inputted, we should have a small bit of excess left over in case of another change," Jules said. "An increase is un-called for. What we have is sufficient."

Brady glanced up at the sound of a truck coming down the old country road. The only place on the farm that received decent reception was at the top of the driveway near the mailbox. Cars rarely came this way, but a lot of farm equipment went past. Of course, if the driver caught a glimpse of Brady, they would stop and chat for at least ten minutes.

The mail truck came around the corner and stopped at the box.

"Brady, didn't your mother ever teach you to wear a hat?" Betsy Griffin tipped her postal cap at him. "You'll get those good looks burnt right off ya."

Brady muted the conference. "If mine gets messed up at least there are two more just like me."

Betsy chuckled and tucked a strand of gray hair up into her cap.

"You tell that brother of yours that his mutt has been up to no good. There are about five puppies on my farm that look an awful lot like that shaggy dog of his."

"I'll let him know."

"You take care now." Betsy tipped her cap and drove off.

Brady and Sam had managed to maintain a good distance from each other. Sam was always out of the house by the time Brady got going in the morning. He couldn't afford to get into it with Sam if he wanted to stay.

He glanced at his screen and unmuted his phone.

"Brady?" Jules's voice sounded concerned.

"I'm here."

"Did we get cut off?"

"No. Someone stopped by. Meeting over?" Brady eyed the time. If he was going to see Amber tonight, he'd need to wrap up quickly.

"Yes."

"What did I miss?"

Jules filled him in on the proposed changes and how she'd fought to keep the budget the same. Peterson had backed down at the end. Brady could almost hear the triumph in her voice.

"If you need anything, text me nine-one-one and I'll call you." Brady closed his laptop and put it in the bag. "Anything at all."

"Spend time with your daughter. I'll see you when you get back to New York." Jules hung up.

Brady stretched as he stood and looked over the old farmhouse and the land surrounding it. The brothers had spent many days working the fields and helping their father make the most out of the land they had. Generations of Wards had worked these fields before them. Now it all fell to Sam.

The house needed a coat of paint, but the barn looked in good repair. Instead of being held together by whatever scraps their father could find, it looked as though Sam had gone through and made the barn a solid structure.

Unlike Sam, who seemed to thrive on the farm, Brady had never belonged here. Even when he had been at the top of his game in high school, he'd felt as if something was missing. He collected the mail and headed down the drive.

Being in England hadn't helped. He hadn't found anywhere that made him feel whole. Like a puzzle with a piece missing, he kept trying to fill it with work and accomplishments, but it didn't seem to help. Each step forward made him want to reach for the next level.

The screen door screeched as he opened it. Inside the house it was cool with the windows open and the lights out. He flung the mail on the kitchen table and started to set his bag on the chair when he caught sight of an envelope with red on it.

FINAL NOTICE. Brady snatched the bill and sank into the kitchen chair.

"Sam?" he yelled.

No one answered. Sam must be down in the field or in the barn. Brady tore open the envelope and stared at the balance. He shifted through the other mail and found a few more overdue bills.

He stormed out the back door and crossed to the barn. Soundgarden's "Fell on Black Days" blasted from the garage in the back. The garage smelled of oil and gasoline, bringing forward the memory of his father, leaning over their old truck's engine while Brady, barely Amber's age, sat on the toolbox ready to hand him a tool, loving every moment of his father's attention.

"What is this?" Brady demanded as he hit the off button on the dirt-coated boom box.

Sam rolled out from under the tractor on the creeper their father had always used. His face was smeared with grease and sweat. He glanced at the notices in Brady's hands. "None of your business."

He rolled back under the tractor.

"I sent money. How did you get behind?" Brady moved around the tractor, trying to see Sam's face.

Sam stayed under the tractor and swiped at his face with an old rag that was too dirty to do any good. His blue coveralls had rips in one knee and were badly in need of a wash. He dropped the wrench and grabbed a screwdriver.

"Dammit, Sam. This is something you need to pay attention to. You can't ignore these and hope they'll go away." The balance on the bill in Brady's hand was a couple of thousand alone. But combined with the others and the ones he didn't know about, it could be a hefty sum. "They could force you to file bankruptcy."

"I'll take care of it," Sam grumbled.

"If you need money, I can help—"

"Money?" Sam rolled out from under the tractor and sat

with his arms resting on his knees. The expression on Sam's face said Brady was being ignorant. "And that will solve everything?"

"In this case…" Brady looked pointedly at the bill. "Yes."

"Do you remember how to work?" Sam pushed to his feet and dropped the screwdriver into a metal tool chest with a loud clang before slamming the drawer shut.

"I work every day—"

"Behind that little computer of yours. Pushing buttons." Sam made little typing motions in the air before he jerked open another drawer and pulled out a socket wrench.

"And I make money doing it. I use my brains and not my brute strength. I create jobs for people." Brady met Sam's gaze. He wasn't going to give in on this. What he did was important. It took a lot of effort to coordinate the projects to make sure everything went smoothly and according to plan.

"And I don't use my brain?" Sam tapped the socket wrench against his hand, lightly.

"It's different and it doesn't change the fact that you are swimming in a sea of debt that this farm can't sustain."

"How would you know?" Sam dropped down on the rolling cart, planting his feet firmly on the concrete floor. "What do you know about farming?"

Brady opened his mouth and closed it. He'd been away for eight years. Though he'd helped Mom balance the bank accounts and been the one to figure out their father's will and hers, he knew nothing about what the finances were now.

"It took Dad, you, me and Luke to keep this farm running on a regular basis during the summer. If the farm had a good year with sufficient rain for the crops and the coyotes didn't get too much of the livestock, we made ends meet." Sam pointed the socket wrench at Brady. "The money you sent helped pay for part of this barn."

"I sent a hell of a lot more money than—"

"And you had a child that needed taking care of."

"If I'd known about my child, I would have taken care of her."

"I didn't need the money." Sam acted as if Brady hadn't said anything. "We were doing fine. Luke was home for the summers for a few years. But then he got busy with med school. I had to pay for someone to come and work *our* farm." Sam cracked his neck. "I fell behind a little. Sue me."

Sam disappeared under the tractor. Brady wasn't ready to push the fact that Sam had kept Amber a secret. Losing the farm was too important. It would have destroyed his parents.

Brady couldn't erase time and return to Tawnee Valley eight years ago and hang around to help out. He couldn't erase what had happened to Maggie, Sam or Amber. All he could do was offer the future.

"Let me look over your books," Brady said.

"What? So you can tell me what I'm doing wrong?" The sound of metal hitting metal emanated through the garage.

"What do you think I've been doing the past eight years?"

"Besides getting soft?"

"Working on budgets and figuring out how to minimize spending and maximize profits." Brady started to lean against the workbench, but when a daddy longlegs shuffled past, he decided against it. "If you won't take my money, at least let me figure out a payment plan, so you can find your way out of this hole without losing the farm."

"I won't lose the farm." Not even a hint of fear in Saint Sam's voice, but there was an underlying tightness. "You weren't the only one with plans. I was at college when Mom got sick, but I gave that up for her, you and Luke. And when Mom died and left Luke to me, I made you go to college, follow your dreams. Figuring you'd find your way home eventually. Guess I was wrong about that."

"I never meant to dump that on you," Brady bit out. He'd

struggled with the guilt, but he'd known he had to go his own way.

"This farm has been in our family for over a century. I won't lose it now." Sam banged something with the wrench. The sound of metal against metal reverberated in the space.

"Just let me look it over." Brady felt as though he was ten trying to convince twelve-year-old Sam to let him have a turn with the basketball.

Sam rolled out and wiped his hands on the dirty rag. "Only if you get off your damn high horse and make yourself useful around here."

"Do you have any idea how much work I have to do?" Brady could feel his face getting redder by the second. Between Maggie's demands and Sam's, he wouldn't be able to get any work done on the Detrex project.

"I'm sure there's someone as fancy as you working up there in New York, getting things done just fine without you." Sam stood and took the bill from Brady's hands. He glanced over it with his usual stoic face.

Fighting with Sam was as fruitless as fighting with Maggie. He'd done them both a disservice and owed them a little of his time in payment. He had left his brother when he needed him most. Sam *had* raised Luke, no matter how much Brady tried to justify that he'd been away at school. He could have gone to a college closer, so he could help whenever needed. But he'd let his pain control him, and New York hadn't been far enough away. He'd had to detach himself so much that he hadn't bothered to keep in touch with anyone from Tawnee Valley except for Luke. Even then, Luke had been the one contacting him, not the other way around.

Maybe he could make up for the time that he'd lost by helping out. He glanced at his watch and wondered what Maggie was doing.

Brady sighed. "Just tell me what needs to be done."

Chapter Eleven

"A no-show, huh?" Penny snatched a carrot from the plate Maggie was setting on the table.

"He said Sam needed his help." Maggie avoided meeting Penny's gaze, afraid she'd catch on to the disappointment Maggie had felt when Brady called an hour ago.

"Want me to beat him up for you?" Penny straddled a chair and held her fists like a boxer. "I could hit him right where it counts."

"That won't be necessary." When Penny sagged in defeat, Maggie added, "Yet."

"What's for dinner?" Amber came in and sat next to Penny.

"Chicken." Maggie hurried to the kitchen. What she wanted to do was go outside and have a good scream, but she needed to keep it together until Penny went home and Amber went to bed. She hoped this didn't become a habit with Brady.

"Is Brady coming over?" Amber called to her.

Maggie took in a deep breath and forced a smile before returning to the dining room with the platter of chicken. "No, honey, he has work to do."

"Can't he do it over here?" Just a hint of a whine had entered Amber's voice.

"Nope."

"What am I, chopped liver?" Penny tickled Amber's side until Amber giggled and batted her hand away.

Amber leaned in close to Penny's ear and said in a loud whisper, "I think Mommy likes Brady."

Penny raised an eyebrow at Maggie, but turned and whispered, "I think Brady likes your Mommy, too."

Amber nodded and giggled.

Maggie could feel the heat rising in her cheeks. "I do not like Brady."

"They looked like they were going to kiss on the porch," Amber told Penny.

Maggie groaned and refused to look at Penny. "Eat your dinner."

She passed around the food until everyone had a full plate. Penny kept trying to catch her eye, which Maggie avoided at all costs. She didn't want to go into details with Penny until Maggie knew how she felt about Brady.

Amber chatted away about school. Maggie forced herself to participate in the conversation. Ever since last night, though, only one thing had occupied her mind—that kiss. It had been one thing to kiss him in New York. Different place, right mood, old lover, that type of thing. But here? On her front porch?

She'd been on edge since she got home from work, waiting. Waiting for Brady to come over and finish what he'd started. Even though she'd told him it would be better if they didn't. Even though she could almost feel every touch, the slide of his skin against hers, his mouth against hers and traveling lower. God, how she'd wanted him and what she wouldn't give to feel that way. Complete abandon.

Which would be a mistake. Huge mistake.

"Earth to Maggie." Penny waved her hand in front of Maggie's face.

Maggie snapped to attention. "What?"

"Amber asked you a question." Penny gave her an expectant look.

"I'm sorry, baby." Maggie shook off the lingering images from her past. "What was your question?"

"Why don't you ask Brady out on a date? Penny would watch me, wouldn't you?" Amber's blue eyes were huge and innocent and hopeful.

Maggie snapped her gaze to Penny to see if she had put Amber up to this, but Penny held up her hands as if to say, "Don't look at me." She sighed and turned to Amber.

"It isn't that easy." Maggie tried to think of excuses and reasons and anything but Brady's hand on the back of her neck. An involuntary shudder raced along her spine.

"Why not?"

"Yeah, Maggie, why not?" Penny leaned her elbows on the table and added her questioning look to Amber's.

"Because…" Oh, hell, what was she supposed to say? That she didn't like him? Then the question would be why he was hanging around. Until Brady was ready to come forward to Amber about being her father, her hands were tied.

"Go on." Penny was enjoying this way too much.

If things were different, she might have jumped at the chance to ask Brady out. "He lives in New York and we live in Tawnee Valley. It would never work out. Besides, we're just friends."

She took her dishes to the kitchen. Logically, that was true. Brady didn't have a burning desire to move back to Tawnee

Valley anytime soon. In fact, it seemed he couldn't wait to get away from it.

She turned to find both Amber and Penny looking at her from the doorway.

"What now?" she said.

"I like Brady," Amber said. Plain and simple as if that were the cure-all to the world.

Sensing a trap, Maggie hesitated before saying, "I like him, too."

Penny covered her mouth to hide her chuckle. Maggie glared at her, but she waited patiently for Amber to get out what she wanted to say.

"You should date." Amber disappeared into the dining room. The clatter of dishes being stacked filled the room.

"Did you put her up to this?" Maggie whispered and pointed toward the dining room.

"No, but the look on your face is priceless." Penny's grin infuriated Maggie more.

Amber reappeared with the dishes and took them to the sink. "Are you waiting for my father to come back?"

Maggie's mouth dropped open and she honestly couldn't think of a single thing to say. Even if Amber knew Brady was her father, she would probably be wondering the same thing. Maggie hadn't dated because the available men in Tawnee Valley greatly dwindled after high school age. And the ones that were available weren't what she wanted.

Penny gave her a phony serious look. "Yeah, Maggie. What are you waiting for?"

Maggie narrowed her eyes at Penny before squatting in front of Amber. "What's bringing all of this up now?"

Amber scrunched her face as if she were trying to keep the truth from coming out, before bursting out with, "Jessica said that her mom thinks you should get back with Brady."

Maggie closed her eyes. Damned if she does, damned if

she doesn't. What was she going to say to that? That she and Brady had never really been together? Then when Amber found out about Brady being her father, Maggie would have to explain that sometimes people don't have to love each other to have a child.

"Do you love Brady, Mommy?"

That one struck her right in the heart.

"You know what, runt?" Penny said and held out her hand to Amber. "Maybe we should lay off Mommy for a little while. Let's go find that book we were reading the other night."

Maggie mouthed "Thank you" to Penny as Penny led Amber out of the kitchen. Already almost on the floor, she dropped on the old linoleum and sagged against the dark oak cabinets.

Did she love Brady? In high school, she believed she was in love with him, but how could you love someone who barely acknowledged your existence? Okay, she had loved him in that first-crush, puppy-love kind of way, completely unrequited.

But now...he'd changed so much that he didn't seem like the same guy. She saw hints of the guy she'd crushed on in high school, but that wasn't the only thing that drew her. When they'd walked the streets in New York surrounded by people, she'd been the only one that had mattered to him. Or when he maneuvered them though the airport, always careful to make sure she didn't fall behind or get lost. Or when he touched her face to wipe away the tear when she'd confessed about her own father.

To say that she had a crush on Brady was putting it mildly. The way he was with Amber when he was in the moment and focused was amazing. He'd even caved to her request about work. Even if he missed coming over, he'd respected her wishes.

"You okay?" Penny stepped into the kitchen and slid down the cabinets to sit next to Maggie.

"I don't know."

"You know I love to tease you, right?" Penny bumped her shoulder against Maggie's.

"Yeah." Maggie leaned her head against the cabinet and rolled it until she faced Penny. "What am I going to do?"

"First, you are going to thank me for distracting your daughter."

"Thank you." Maggie reached out and took Penny's hand. "Really. Thank you for being here for me. You don't know how much I rely on you."

"What are best friends for?" Penny shrugged but squeezed Maggie's hand. "As for Brady…"

"Yeah. Brady." Maggie thudded her head against the cabinets.

"You've got a great daughter, Maggie. And maybe Brady won't be that bad of a dad for her, but you have to look at the big picture."

"What's the big picture?" Maggie desperately wanted to know.

Penny clasped her hands around Maggie's. "Amber is putting this together faster than either of you expected. Brady needs to come clean and you need to figure out what type of relationship you are going to have with each other and with Amber."

"I already told him that I didn't want to get involved with him because of Amber."

"Why not?"

Maggie struggled to find words, but finally pulled it together. "Because—"

"Brady isn't your dad. He's not going to leave Amber. At his worst, Brady's a workaholic. He earns good money and has kept fit unlike most of the men around here. You could do a lot worse than Brady Ward."

"But—"

"Don't give me the whole New York-versus-here thing. What are you really worried about?"

Maggie took a deep, shaky breath. "That the only reason he wants me is because he loves Amber."

Brady pocketed his phone as he got out of the car. He'd made sure to set the ringer to vibrate in case Jules needed to reach him. All day they'd worked with a contractor who was refusing to listen to anyone but Brady, which was frustrating for both Jules and him. Something he hoped Peterson didn't get wind about.

When Brady hadn't been on the phone or the computer, Sam had kept him busy working the farm.

He wasn't about to let another day go by where he didn't see Amber, though. A sharp high-pitched bark met him as he opened the rear car door.

"Are you ready?" Brady said to the puppy in the cardboard box.

The puppy wagged his tail and barked in response. Brady hooked on the leash to the new collar he'd bought and set the puppy on the ground. Barnabus, Sam's dog, was a pretty big dog and this "puppy" was going to be large like his daddy. He was already the size of a small dog.

Maybe Brady should have checked with Maggie before bringing the gift, but he remembered Amber saying that she'd always wanted one. When Sam had begrudgingly brought home a couple of the pups to pawn off to other people, he'd happily given one to Brady.

The puppy took off toward the house with Brady in tow. Brady knocked on the side of the screen door.

"Just a second." Maggie. The sound of her voice rushed through him.

He tried to stop the direction his thoughts were headed, but when Maggie appeared at the door with her hair wet in a pair of cut-offs and a green T-shirt that made the green in her hazel eyes stand out, his brain stopped altogether.

"Hey, Brady, Amber's bus gets here in about ten minutes." She met his eyes and smiled.

The puppy whined and her smile faded as her eyes dropped to see the white fuzz ball. "You brought a dog?"

"He's a puppy." Brady's brain was occupied with mentally peeling off every layer of her clothing and imagining what they could do in ten minutes.

"*That* is a puppy?"

His gaze lingered a moment longer at her breasts before finally arriving at her not-pleased-at-all face. His brain shifted into gear. Definitely should have checked. "Yeah. Sam's dog got out in the spring and this little guy is the end result."

"There is nothing little about that puppy." Her eyes rounded in horror. "Please don't tell me you brought that for Amber."

"Why? She was saying how much she wanted a dog the other day and how she couldn't have one…" Realization settled in his stomach like a lump of Sam's burned eggs. "And you were the one who didn't want a dog, right?"

"Do you know how much work a dog is? Let alone a puppy?"

He hated hearing the disappointment in her voice. Hated it even more because he was the one she was disappointed with. "I can say he's come for a visit?"

She narrowed her eyes and crossed her arms. "You know the minute she sees that fur ball she's going to love it."

"I guess he doesn't have that effect on you?" Brady said curtly.

"Who do you think gets stuck with the feeding and cleaning and taking him out at three in the morning in the snow? Not to mention housetraining."

"Like I said—"

"You got me a dog!" Amber's squeal of delight was met by little excited puppy barks.

Maggie gave him the see-I-told-you look. But Amber's eyes glowed with happiness as she shrugged off her backpack and knelt before the puppy. When the puppy proceeded to bathe her face with his tongue, her giggles made Brady feel as if he'd brought her the moon and not a mutt.

"You are such a licker. I'll name you Flicker," Amber proclaimed. "Licker would be weird."

Brady cleared his throat to get Amber's attention. "I brought him for a visit."

Her fingers tightened into the puppy's fur and her face fell with disappointment. His heart tightened. He almost said she could keep the dog, but Maggie had already made it clear she didn't want it.

"But I'll see if Sam wants to keep him out at the farm, so you can visit Flicker." Brady knew Sam hadn't been pleased with the idea of more dogs, but in the grand scheme of things, Sam owed Brady more than Brady owed Sam. At least, Brady wanted to think that, but looking at the girl nuzzling this fur ball, he wondered what Sam had given up to take care of Mom, Luke and him.

"Do you have homework?" Maggie opened the screen door. Flicker immediately burst into the house, causing Maggie to scowl at Brady.

"I'll get him." Brady brushed past her. His side pressed against hers for the briefest moment, but it sent electricity coursing through his veins.

Amber was hot on his heels. He managed to grab the leash before Flicker got to the trash can.

"Can we take him for a walk?" Amber looked to her

mother for approval. "I've always wanted to do that. Can we? Please?"

"The dog can stay for dinner, but he has to go home with Brady." Maggie crossed her arms over her chest and met Brady's gaze. "You are responsible for any damage that dog does."

Obviously, Brady wasn't the only one Amber could wrap around her finger. "That's fine."

"The walk, Mom?" Amber struck a similar pose to her mother.

"Go ahead, but then it's straight to homework. And Brady has to go with you."

Amber raced to the front door. The puppy followed on her heels, jumping on her when she stopped.

Maggie grabbed his arm as he passed. When he stopped, she pulled her hand away as if he were burning her. Maybe he had because his skin felt singed from her touch.

"He's too big for her to handle," she said.

"We'll be fine, Maggie." He resisted the urge to kiss her scowl away and pulled on Flicker's leash.

The screen door slammed behind them as Flicker and Amber raced down the stairs. The puppy kept trying to grab the end of Amber's shirt, but she kept it away from him with a little shriek of joy.

Brady jerked on the leash and the puppy came rushing to him. "Maybe if we walk together, Flicker will learn his manners."

"Okay." Amber fell into step with Brady. The warmth of the day had settled with a gentle breeze. The puppy darted from tree to tree and jerked slightly on Brady's hold.

"Are you dating anyone?" Amber walked beside him.

"No."

"Have you had many girlfriends?"

Brady wasn't used to anyone being so direct with him, but

he found Amber refreshing. He already had one lie he had to come clean on. He figured the least he could do was honestly answer her questions. "A few."

"Did you have any girlfriends in London?" Amber watched the puppy as he burrowed underneath some leaves.

"I had a few dates, but no one I'd call a girlfriend." Brady pulled on the leash as Flicker tried to veer off into someone's yard.

"Why not? Don't you like girls?" Amber stopped and cocked her head to the side.

Brady stopped his mouth from gaping. "I do but I didn't have time because of work."

Amber nodded as if she understood completely. He couldn't help but wonder if she did. He had no idea what a seven-year-old thought about or even knew. Apparently, more than he thought.

"Is New York big?" Amber asked.

"Millions of people live there." Brady felt his phone vibrate in his pocket, notifying him of a text.

"How did Mom find you in all those people?"

Brady looped the leash around his wrist and grabbed his phone. Now that they'd settled into a slower pace, Flicker walked beautifully as if he'd been raised on a leash. "The same way you find anyone. She had an address and a phone number."

He flipped on the screen and saw the text from Jules. Nine-one-one. Crap.

"Amber?" Brady stopped. Flicker came bounding back to see what the holdup was.

"Yes?" She had squatted next to Flicker and petted him to keep him calm.

"Do you think you could take the leash for a few minutes? I need to make a quick phone call."

"You want me to walk Flicker?" Amber held out her hands and bounced slightly in place.

Brady glanced at the dog who had decided to chew on his own leg. Flicker hadn't tugged on the leash recently and seemed fairly calm. Amber could handle the puppy. He handed the leash to her. "Wrap it around your wrist and be careful not to let go, otherwise, we'll have to chase Flicker."

"I promise." Amber wrapped the leash around her wrist. "Come on, Flicker."

They all started forward again as Brady called Jules. "Hey, Jules, I can't talk long. What's going on?"

"The contractor wants to charge us double for the most recent change order. I tried to reason with him, but he says that you and he had a deal." Jules sounded exhausted.

Brady stopped, but Amber kept going. "Jules, tell him that you are in charge and you know every deal that I've made. If he's not going to work with you, we'll have to find someone else."

"Flicker, no!"

Brady's heart stopped as he looked up. Amber was tangled in Flicker's leash. Before Brady could even move, Flicker jerked on the leash, and Amber crashed to the sidewalk, landing in a heap. Flicker bounded to Amber's side as Brady rushed to her.

Amber's cries filled the air and made Brady's heart ache, even as his pulse raced. Flicker whimpered and started licking the back of Amber's head.

"Are you okay?" Brady knelt on the ground and pulled the leash away from Amber's legs. He shoved Flicker's nose away from Amber's face as he helped her into a sitting position.

Her dirt-smudged face didn't seem to have any cuts on it. Her tears tore at something deep inside him. He should have caught her. That's what daddies did.

chance to make sure nothing was broken, but being hysterical wouldn't help anyone.

She reached into the medicine cabinet and got out the cleanser and antibacterial cream along with the Band-Aids. The bathroom was small on a normal day but with Brady holding Amber and a rambunctious puppy bounding all around, her nerves were on end.

"Put her down on the toilet."

"She's going to be fine. I had all sorts of cuts and scrapes growing up." Brady sounded as if he was trying to reassure himself more than anyone else.

Maggie handed him paper towels. "Wet these. We need to clean the wound to see what type of damage has been done."

"Of course." Taking the paper towels, he went to the sink. He seemed startled to find the phone in his hand. Setting it on the edge of the sink, he turned on the water.

Maggie squatted before Amber. Amber's tears had started to dry, but she sniffled slightly. The puppy sat in the corner near the tub and started whining.

"What hurts?"

"My hands and my knee." Amber glanced over at Brady before returning her gaze to Maggie. "It's not Flicker's fault, Mommy. I was messing around."

Right. Maggie pressed her lips together. "Why don't we get you cleaned up?"

She had a feeling the fault lay with that phone, but she wouldn't know until she had a chance to talk to Brady. Brady came over with the wet towels and she moved out of the way.

He knelt beside Amber and gently stroked the wet paper towel over her knee. Amber winced, biting her lip.

"When I was six, I was helping Dad out in the barn." Brady moved to one of her hands. "There was an old stool out there that I liked to stand on."

As Maggie stood, she took Brady's phone. He was so engrossed in helping Amber that he didn't notice. On the screen, it showed he was still connected with Jules. She cut off the call and slipped the phone in her pocket.

"Dad needed this special wrench from above his workbench." Brady wiped delicately with the paper towel.

As he cleaned off the blood, Maggie could see that the fall had taken off some skin. Amber leaned forward to watch Brady. Her hair fell forward along her cheekbone. She seemed so fragile right now, even though Maggie had patched up worse in the past.

"I climbed on this stool and onto the workbench to get this special wrench." Brady continued his story.

Just as enthralled with his story as Amber, Maggie handed him some cotton soaked with the cleanser.

"When I went to get off the workbench, one of the stool's legs broke and I hit my head on the edge of the old, greasy workbench." Brady held out his hand for the antibacterial and Band-Aids.

"Did it hurt?" Amber asked.

"Bunches." Brady quickly applied the bandages. "I had to go to the hospital and get stitches and shots and everything. I still have a scar."

He touched a spot above his eyebrow and even Maggie leaned forward to see.

"You had to get shots?" Amber's voice was a combination of horror and admiration as she examined the scar. She reached out and traced the small, white line.

Brady nodded. "But you won't need shots. All done. A little battered and bruised but no worse for wear."

He held out a tissue. Amber blew her nose.

"Will you help me with my homework?" Amber gave him her best I'm-hurt smile. "And maybe we can finish our walk with Flicker?"

She avoided looking at Maggie.

"If your mom says it's okay." He looked at Maggie then.

Maggie got caught in his blue eyes. Creases of worry had formed on his forehead and around his eyes. He did care about Amber, even if work had distracted him.

"Sure, that sounds good." Maggie watched both of their faces light up and felt warm and cold at the same time. Amber and Brady loved each other already. She could almost believe that he would always be there for Amber. That they would have each other for the rest of their lives. That Brady wouldn't get tired of being a dad and walk away.

He wasn't like her dad. She had to get that in her mind. But he did live in New York and would eventually leave both of them behind. She could only hope he would be good about staying in touch with Amber after he left.

As she watched them settle at the dining room table with the dog at their feet, chewing on a freshly unwrapped raw-hide bone, Maggie couldn't help feeling as though she was on the outside looking in.

"I'm going to go finish dinner." She excused herself, but she could hear the two of them talking in the dining room. It felt right, as if this was how things were meant to be. That they could be a family. Which was ridiculous. Just because he seemed to care for Amber, didn't mean that he wanted to be anything more with her. And even if he did, it wasn't possible with his job and her life here. He would never leave New York.

It all came down to work with him. Brady had obviously taken a work call. During which, Amber must have fallen. Amber's laughter pulled her attention back to the moment. Maggie could hear the low rumble of Brady's voice, but not what he was saying. Amber hadn't said anything about Brady's involvement. Was she protecting him?

They had a little over a week left before Brady returned to New York. When he did, their life would go on as it had before, except Amber would know her father was out there.

What if Brady wanted Amber to go to New York with him? For a few weeks in the summer? Was Maggie ready for that?

She didn't want him to walk out of their lives, but what would his involvement in their lives entail? Would Brady pop in and out of their lives whenever it was convenient for him? Would he be here for Christmas and Thanksgiving and Easter? Birthdays?

"I'm really sorry, Maggie."

She set down the cutting knife and turned to face him. He had stopped in the doorway and leaned his shoulder against the jamb.

"What happened?" She didn't raise her voice. It even came out without sounding accusatory. For emphasis, Maggie crossed her arms and gave him the look she gave Amber to make her confess the bad deed she'd just committed.

"She got tangled in the leash." He almost seemed boyish, looking at her with his head dipped, avoiding saying what would get him in the most trouble. Hoping she'd take whatever explanation he gave. He even dared to give her that sheepish smile that had turned her into mush in high school. Too bad for him it wasn't high school anymore.

"And?" Maggie tried not to tap her foot.

He sighed. "I let Amber hold the leash."

"By herself?"

"Flicker was doing great." The tips of Brady's ears burned red, and she guessed there was more to the story.

"You let her handle an animal that weighs as much as she does?" Maggie couldn't keep her hands from flying as she spoke. "Did you think about what would happen if the dog ran out in the street?"

"But he didn't." Brady's face lost its placating look as he went on the defense.

"And where were you?" She stepped closer and poked him

in the chest. "Where was the great Brady Ward to the rescue? If your hands were free, you could have easily caught her before she hit the ground."

"On an important phone call." He straightened from his leaning position. In high school she would have backed down immediately, but now she didn't feel an ounce of intimidation.

"More important than watching Amber?" The fear when they'd come in had merged with her anger at Brady for bringing the dog in the first place until all she could see was red. "You can't apologize and think that makes it okay. We talked about this. No work when you are with Amber. What part of that didn't you understand?"

"The part where I have to sacrifice everything because of something my brother did." Brady's eyes flashed. She should have retreated, but she couldn't. "Work isn't just money to me. It's my life. It's all I have."

"Not anymore." She poked him in the chest with each syllable for emphasis.

"Do you think I don't know that? That I sleep well at night? That I don't think of a million ways to make this work out best for everyone? News flash. I'm not Superman."

"And who asked you to be? I didn't go to New York to drag your ass back here. I thought you needed to know. You were the one who volunteered to come. You insisted you needed to know her."

He captured her hand against his chest before she could poke him again. "You were the one who insisted now or never. Were you hoping I'd say never?"

She sputtered, "No, of course not."

"You didn't feel at all threatened by the fact that Amber is as much mine as she is yours?" The words were softly spoken but hit her hard in the gut.

His hand held her close to him. The air around them was

thick with tension. What was she supposed to say? Yes, she'd gotten used to having Amber all to herself. Would she deny her daughter her father just to keep things the way they were, which was way more comfortable than how she felt right now with Brady so close?

She should back down, but this was too important. "So why don't you go in there and tell her? Fess up. Stop being such a coward."

"And how do you propose I do that? Just come out and say it? Or should I be like you and wait until she's comfortable before striking?" he said.

"I didn't know you didn't know. Sam—"

"Sending a letter wasn't the only way to reach me and you know it." Brady's blue eyes burned. His breath was hot on her face. "You could have tried other ways."

She pressed her lips together and tilted her chin. Refusing to let him inside her head. To make her doubt her decisions all those years ago. Those questions she'd had when Sam had dropped off the money with no note from Brady. As she examined it over the years, she would wonder, but the older Amber got, the harder it was to admit maybe she'd made a mistake in trusting Sam.

"Admit it, Maggie. You were afraid I'd want something to do with Amber. That I would want to be her father."

Somewhere deep inside she found the strength to step away from Brady. She wasn't backing down, just getting breathing room.

"Why would I be afraid of that?"

He narrowed his eyes. "It doesn't matter. I'm Amber's father and that isn't going to change."

"You're my dad?" Amber's voice sent chills through Maggie's body.

They both turned in time to see the hurt in Amber's eyes before she spun around and ran out the front door.

* * *

Brady cursed. This wasn't the way he had wanted Amber to find out.

Maggie was already at the front door, ready to go after her. Brady reached her in three strides.

"I'll go," he said.

"You don't even know where to look."

Flicker bounced between the two of them obviously excited to be going back outside. Brady grabbed his leash.

"Fine. We'll go together. Where would she go?" Brady opened the door and let Maggie go first.

"I saw her go right before she disappeared behind the bushes. There's the park, the school playground, Amber's friend Mary's house, Penny's. There are a million places she could have gone to." Frustration tinged her voice.

He linked his fingers with hers. "We'll find her."

Her chest rose and fell as she took a deep breath. Her fingers remained entwined with his.

Before they left, the phone rang. Amber had shown up at Penny's. Brady's heart started again, grateful for once that Tawnee Valley was a small town. Maggie squeezed his hand.

When they arrived, Penny simply held open the door. "She's in the living room."

As Penny took the leash from Brady's hand and led Flicker away, Brady followed Maggie into the living room. The yellow walls peeked out in the spaces between the framed pictures on the wall. There were some from high school, some from when Amber was a baby and even some from now. On the blue sofa, Amber sat with a mug of milk and a plate with a few cookies.

"Amber Marie, you can't run out the door like that." Maggie looked as though she was going to scold her more, but Brady tugged her hand. She turned to look at him. In her hazel eyes, the relief over finding Amber only barely covered the fear that had been there before.

"I've got this one." Brady squeezed her hand one more time before letting go. He sat in the floral chair facing the couch.

Amber hadn't made eye contact with either of them. She continued to dunk and eat her cookies as if they weren't there.

Brady struggled to find the words that would put this to right. "We didn't mean for you to find out like that."

Maggie moved behind his chair. Her presence offered him the comfort and support to continue.

How could he make this right?

"I should have let your mom tell you right away, but I was afraid." Brady waited for some indication that she was even listening.

She set the cookie on her plate and lifted her blue eyes. "What were you afraid of?"

"Everything." Brady took a deep breath.

"That's silly." Amber grabbed a napkin and wiped the chocolate from her lips. "How can you be afraid of everything? Are you afraid of cookies?"

"I wish this were simple, but I didn't know about you until your mom came to New York. And then all I wanted to do was meet you, but I thought you wouldn't like me." Brady scrubbed his face with his hand.

"Why wouldn't I like you?"

When she put it so simply, Brady was stumped. "I don't know."

"You're my dad?" Amber was keeping her face blank.

Maggie slid her hand over his shoulder. He was amazed that the touch of her hand could make him feel more in control.

"Yes." Brady waited as Amber thought about it.

"You and Mom were married?"

"No." Brady shifted on the seat. This wasn't headed in a

pleasant direction, but being honest had always served him well in the past. He just wasn't sure that Amber was old enough to understand what had happened between Maggie and Brady when they were young.

Amber sat back in the couch and pulled her feet under her. "But you guys dated? I thought you said you hadn't dated Brady, Mom?"

Maggie's fingers curled into his shoulder. "We knew each other in high school. We were friends."

Friends? They'd barely spoken in high school. They'd had one passionate night. Amber had been the result of that. He needed to get Amber off this path.

"I'm sorry I didn't tell you right away. I should have." Brady leaned forward. Maggie's hand slipped from his shoulder. He met Amber's intense gaze. "Do you forgive me?"

Amber looked from Maggie to Brady and back again. Her nose wrinkled. "Are you going back to New York?"

"In a week." Brady could feel the clamp on his stomach as he waited for her to come to her decision.

"Are you coming back?"

He could almost see the wheels turning in her head. "If you want me to."

She scooted to the edge of her seat. "Am I going to go to New York?"

"I'd love to have you come stay with me." Brady could feel the clamp loosen.

"Can Mom come, too?" Amber spared a glance at her mother.

"We haven't worked out all those details yet," Maggie interrupted.

No, they hadn't. It was probably time they started to think about the future, but not tonight.

"Can I keep Flicker?" Amber had a devious glint in her eyes.

"Is that the only way you'll forgive me?" Brady bit back his smile. Negotiations were supposed to be serious.

"You know the rules, Amber Marie."

Brady wasn't used to Maggie's "mother" voice. It was amazing how much she'd changed in the years since he'd known her.

Amber crumpled her forehead and pouted. "No pets as long as my room looks like a tornado hit it. And I learn some responsi-bil-ity."

"I'm sorry about keeping this from you." Brady was eager to hear her words of forgiveness.

"Do I still call you Brady? Or should I call you Dad or Daddy?" Amber cocked an eyebrow, mimicking her mother perfectly.

"You can call me anything you want." Brady's heart stuttered and filled his chest.

"Dad." Amber tested out the word. "Daddy. Brady."

Flicker barked somewhere in the background.

Amber stood and rounded the coffee table until she stood in front of Brady. They were eye to eye. Brady held his breath. His emotions too overwhelming to pick apart.

"I forgive you and like you just fine, Daddy." Amber's arms closed around Brady's neck.

Brady returned Amber's hug, feeling like the luckiest man alive.

Chapter Thirteen

Brady walked out into the night after helping put Amber to bed. His feet felt glued with each step. Thankfully, Penny had decided to keep Flicker.

What Brady needed was some time alone to think about what being someone's daddy really meant. Did that mean seeing her for two weeks in the summer? Or trying to figure out how to watch a child during an entire semester of schooling in New York? Or spending the holidays in Tawnee Valley with Amber?

And Maggie.

He slid into his rental car and glanced at the two-story Victorian house. How many times had he driven down this street when he was young and never thought anything of this house? Now it housed one of the most important people in Brady's life. His daughter.

His career had always come first, but he could make room in his life for Amber.

Work… He checked his pockets for his phone, but came

up empty-handed. He'd been on it with Jules when Amber got hurt. Damn, he'd forgotten about Jules on the phone.

But what did he do with his phone? He must have left it inside somewhere. He pushed open the door and trudged back to the front door of Maggie's house. Knocking softly so he wouldn't wake Amber, he peeked in the window and saw Maggie crossing the kitchen. She probably couldn't even hear him knocking.

He checked the door and found it unlocked.

"Maggie?" he said softly as he walked in.

It had taken both of them to get Amber to bed. Only Brady promising that he was leaving right away and coming back tomorrow had finally convinced her to go to sleep. He didn't want to risk waking her. Besides, Maggie had seemed as worn-out as he felt.

He crossed the threshold into the kitchen and found Maggie sitting at the table with her head in her hands. He froze at the sight of her.

Her hair fell like silk around her face, softening her and making her seem ageless. Her eyes were closed and her fingers were massaging her temples in slow, steady circles. His fingers flexed and his heart sped. The heaviness lifted slightly.

She'd given him a daughter. A beautiful, intelligent daughter that she'd had to raise on her own because of Sam. He should have been here the entire time. Amber shouldn't have had to learn about him like this, to wonder all this time if her father loved her.

"Maggie?" he said softly.

The chair scraped against the linoleum as she scrambled to face whoever was in the room. Her wide eyes connected with his and realizing it was him, she relaxed.

"Brady? I thought you'd left." She grabbed a towel from the sink. Always busy cleaning something.

"I did, but I think I left my phone. I wanted to let you know before I started searching."

She'd dropped her gaze from his almost immediately. She glanced at him quickly before turning away. Maybe she was still angry about what had happened with Amber.

"I meant what I said earlier." He stepped into the room and walked over to where she stood wiping the counter in a circular motion. He settled his hand on hers. She jerked her hand away, dropping the towel.

"I know you're angry with me, but I don't know what I'm doing anymore." He draped the towel over the bar and finally met her gaze. Instead of anger in her hazel eyes, he saw vulnerability and wariness. It made him stop in his tracks. Did she fear him?

She cleared her throat. Her eyes hid her feelings from him once again. "It's late, Brady."

"You know I'd never do anything intentional to hurt Amber?"

"Of course." But there was a hint of skepticism behind her agreement. She moved to the other side of the kitchen and grabbed the broom.

He closed in on her one step at a time. "There isn't anything I wouldn't do to keep her from feeling the pain you felt as a child, Maggie."

Her lips set firmly together and her chin got that stubborn tilt. It made him want to kiss her until she softened beneath his touch. He stood there, debating whether to close the distance between them or retreat. The emotional roller coaster of the past few hours had him warring with himself. She'd clearly stated that she wanted to keep things as friends between them. But when she was this close, his fingers itched to bury themselves in her hair. His gut tightened and his pulse pounded every time she was in the room.

The few tastes he'd had of her hadn't been enough. He

wanted to feel the curves of her body and explore all those hidden spots that would make her sigh with pleasure. He wanted to nibble along her jawline until the hardness left her face and she sighed his name.

He closed the distance between them. No longer thinking of the consequences. His thumb traced her jawline and her lips parted. Their eyes were locked, but neither of them said a word. All he had to do was lean down and kiss her. He knew she felt it, too.

The noise of the vibration of his phone filtered through the haze his thoughts had left him in. Maggie jumped as if something had bitten her. The broom clattered to the floor. Her head bumped against his chin and he instinctively moved back.

The buzzing continued. Brady looked around the kitchen trying to pinpoint the source until his gaze returned to Maggie's red cheeks and downturned face.

"Is that your phone?" Brady stood within touching distance of her and much as he wanted to touch her, he felt as if he was missing something important.

She shook her head, but finally lifted her eyes to meet his and that stubborn jaw was set again. Her blush deepened, but she didn't drop her gaze.

"Is that *my* phone?" Brady asked.

Maggie drew in a breath. "Yes."

He waited, expecting her to do something. Either return it or explain herself. But she just stood there, defiant and beautiful.

"May I have it?"

"I'll give it back if you tell me you can separate your work life and your home life."

"I don't have a home life." Brady ran his hand over his hair.

"You do now." She shoved away from the wall and brushed past him.

His gaze caught the lump of his phone in her back pocket, but that wasn't what caused his heart to send blood rushing through his body. Her jeans hugged her hips and accented her bottom nicely. He had every intention of getting his hands on those hips again.

She spun around and he barely had the sense to pull his gaze to her eyes. She narrowed her eyes on him. "You have Amber. What's it going to take before you realize that work is only a distraction to what life is really about? Does Amber have to get hit by a car because of your inattention? What if she comes to stay with you in New York? Who's going to watch her while you work? What's the point of her even going if all you are going to do is work? One weekend morning isn't going to be sufficient time to spend with her."

"Fine. I'll leave work at work."

Maggie pulled the phone out of her back pocket and held it out to him. "How can I be sure of that? You already broke that promise to me once."

"I'll leave it at Sam's tomorrow." He closed his hand over the phone, but didn't let go of her hand. "You can't tell me you haven't made any mistakes, Maggie."

"Of course I've made mistakes." Maggie threw her free hand in the air. "But I've learned from them."

She stared pointedly at her hand engulfed by his.

"I see." He released her hand and shoved the phone in his pocket. "I was a mistake."

Maggie pressed her lips together as if holding back something. He'd disappointed everyone this week. Amber, most of all.

"I'll be here tomorrow." He held her gaze and stepped closer. "You promised to let me make some mistakes. Well, this is one of them. I'm not perfect. I never claimed to be, no matter what this town tried to turn me into."

She didn't say anything, but she didn't withdraw, either.

The temptation was there. The longing to kiss her, to be with her. Was it totally physical or was there something more going on between them? Shaking those thoughts away, he brushed her cheek with his thumb. "I'll be here. I promise."

Chapter Fourteen

"**D**o you have the latest BlackBerry?" Brady looked over the small cellular phone offerings at the Electronics Hut in Owen. So much for getting his phone from Maggie last night. This morning it had slipped out of his jacket and a cow had crushed it to pieces with her hoof.

"We can order anything you need." The white-haired man behind the counter looked as if he had been at the invention of the phone.

"I was hoping to get something now." Brady glanced over the selection. He was hoping to download his information from the network, which would be easier with another Black-Berry.

"I got in a few new models…" The salesman seemed to drift off for a moment as if lost in a thought, or maybe he fell asleep.

Brady waited for a moment before saying, "Would you please check if you have a BlackBerry?"

"All right. Don't get your panties in a twist." The man

stood as if every joint fought against him. "I'll bring out what we have."

He moved slowly toward the stockroom, leaving Brady alone in the front of the store. He sighed and scanned the small store. Electronics of all sorts filled the shelves. What didn't fit on a shelf was shoved on the floor along the aisle.

The bell over the door jingled as the door slammed behind him.

"Where's Harry?"

Brady turned and saw a brown-haired man, about his age, struggling with a box of parts. He hurried forward as the box began to slip and caught the opposite end.

"Thanks."

Brady helped carry it to the counter. "What is all this?"

"Parts from a failed attempt at an electronics repair shop." They dropped it on the counter. The guy seemed familiar but Brady hadn't placed him. He held out his hand. "Josh Michaels. You're one of Luke's brothers. Brady, right?"

Brady shook Josh's hand, trying to place him. "In town for a few days. You graduated with Luke?"

"Yeah." Josh glanced around the shop, probably looking for Harry.

"The salesman is in the back. He should be out any minute." Brady hoped, at least. He needed to get back out to the farm and then Maggie's.

"White hair, looks like Rip Van Winkle?" Josh asked.

Brady nodded.

"That's Harry. You could be here for an hour before he finds anything in that storeroom." Josh settled against the counter. "How long has it been since you've been back?"

"Years." Brady picked up one of the phones and messed with the settings a little. "A lot has changed."

"The biggest blow was the Phantom Plant closing. Lot of good people had to move to find a job." Josh pointed toward his box. "The rest of us are just trying to make ends meet. Unfortunately, most people prefer to buy new than repair these days."

"I'm surprised they shut the plant." Brady hadn't followed the local news. With shrinking margins in most industries, downsizing seemed to be the only option.

"Businesses fell like dominoes in Owen after that. Money grew tighter until no one was spending anything and no one was hiring anyone." Josh nodded toward the back room. "Even old Harry threatened to close the shop. But I convinced him to carry cell phones. That seems to have brought in some traffic."

Brady turned over the cell phone in his hand. "Smart idea."

"One of my better." Josh smiled, obviously pleased with himself, but his smile fell. "Wish I could turn the whole town around. Get these people back on their feet and give them a reason to be proud again."

"It appears I have some time." Brady nodded his head toward the back room where they could hear Harry moving things around. As far as Brady knew, the old man might have forgotten he was out here. "Want to talk about some of your ideas?"

A few hours later, Brady's mind was churning as he headed toward Maggie's. Harry had called in a favor and should have a new phone for Brady by the morning. But what had him excited were the prospects for Tawnee Valley and the neighboring town, Owen. Josh had a lot of ideas. While some weren't great, some could work. If Josh could find a backer.

Brady had a lot of experience working on new projects and knew what it took to get them off the ground. He was already envisioning the layers of work that would be required to get Kyle to give the approval to go ahead with this project. Brady could help breathe life into this town and make his company a lot of money in the process.

There was almost an extra skip to his step as he walked to Maggie's front door. He felt invincible as if he could handle anything else that life intended to throw at him. What he wanted to do was sweep Maggie into his arms and forget to breathe for a while.

He pressed the doorbell and tried to squelch the half smile from his face. No one answered the door. He checked his watch. The bus should be arriving any minute. It wasn't like Maggie to be late, at least not in his experience.

He rang the doorbell again and waited. His elation from his good business sense was slowly fading to apprehension. What if something had happened to Maggie? What if something had happened to Amber? He didn't even have a spare key to get in to make sure everything was all right.

Leaning over the railing, he tried to peer into the window. Finally, he left the front and walked around back. Maggie's car was in the driveway. He could feel every muscle tensing in his arms and neck.

Whenever things seemed good in his life, something always happened. It was no one's fault, just bad timing. His mother's funeral had been two days before he was supposed to start college. His father had died the day before he turned sixteen. He got Maggie pregnant before he left for England and he didn't return until now to find out about Amber. Nothing good happened to him without a touch of tragedy.

He'd lost so much. He couldn't lose this, too. Not before he could figure out what it would mean to him. He pounded on the back door. They had to be okay.

"I'm up. I'm up."

He heard her over the pounding of his heart and tried to take a deep breath. The door swung open. Maggie stood in a pair of yellow pajama pants and a cat T-shirt with a robe hanging off her shoulders. Her hair was wild as if she'd been running her fingers through it and had attempted to pull it into a ponytail holder. Purple smudges highlighted under her eyes.

"Hey, Brady." No emotion entered her voice, but she looked like she hadn't slept in days or at least last night. Her eyes briefly glanced at him before her hand dropped off the door. She turned and shuffled toward the cabinets.

"Is everything okay?" Brady hesitated as he walked into the house and closed the door behind him. "Are you okay?"

"I'm just great." She emphasized the words with a huge yawn. She held a coffee cup. "Sleep is for wusses."

"Where's Amber?" He felt as if he'd walked into an alternate universe.

"She's in watching TV."

"Didn't she go to school?" Brady knew today wasn't a day off, which meant one of two things. His heart stopped inside his chest. "Is she sick?"

"It's a twenty-four-hour thing." Maggie waved her hand as if waving away his concern would be that easy. "We only have—" she squinted at her watch and sighed "—five more hours to go."

"Mommy!" Amber's voice was rough and had an edge of panic to it.

Maggie snapped to attention and changed before his eyes. The sleep was gone as she raced into the living room. He followed, trying to make sense of all of this in his mind. He'd left them last night and everything had been fine.

"It's okay, baby. Let's get you to the bathroom." As she passed him on the way, she seemed to realize he was there. "You should go home, Brady. You don't want to get sick."

Amber tried to smile at him but her face was pale and sweaty. They went into the bathroom and Maggie closed the door.

Brady stood undecided. Should he go? Maggie seemed to think so, but from the looks of it both she and Amber were on their last legs. He shrugged out of his jacket and draped it over the dining room chair.

Returning to the kitchen, he made short work of the few dishes in the sink and started some water to boil. The bathroom door opened and Maggie's murmured words caught his ear. He could almost imagine her rubbing Amber's back and saying those things only a mother could say when you were sick.

At seventeen, he'd done the same for his mother, trying to make her as comfortable as possible. But this was different. Amber was young and this wasn't cancer. Kids got sick all the time. His grip tightened on the plate in his hands.

She'd be all right.

"You're still here." Maggie sank into the chair at the table and laid her head on her arms.

"Yeah, I'm still here." He finished drying the plate and set it in the cabinet. "Where's Amber?"

"Sleeping on the couch." Maggie couldn't stifle the yawn that made the words come out nearly unintelligible. "You should really…"

Brady sat at the table next to her. "It's okay. I'm here. What do you need?"

Her eyes were shut but a partial smile lit her face. "Sleep."

He stood and lifted her out of her chair. Her eyelids popped wide-open for a second before lowering again. She put her arms around his neck as he carried her in his arms up the stairs.

She snuggled closer as he passed by the open door to Amber's room. Purple walls, a single bed with a purple-flowered cover on it, a shelf full of kids' books. Taped to the walls were art projects progressing from thick lines of paint in no particular pattern to recognizable representations of owls, monkeys, houses.

Hundreds of questions fell over each other to get his attention. Things he'd never thought of before. What was Amber's first word? When did she walk for the first time? Who had been there to catch her when she fell trying? What did she want to be when she grew up? How much time had Sam spent with her? Getting to know his niece? Who was going to hold her when someone broke her heart for the first time? Who was going to check out her dates to make sure they were good enough for her? Where would he be when her next firsts happened?

"You can put me down."

Brady gentled his hold on Maggie but didn't release her. Her hazel eyes were half-open. Who would be there for Maggie? "You're exhausted."

"Am not." Yawns bracketed her words.

One of the other doors had to be hers. He carried her to the next door and pushed it open. A light floral scent wafted over him. His fingers clenched into her. When he was sixty, he'd remember this scent, Maggie's scent. It tickled his nose and played with his senses, making him wish that Maggie weren't so tired and their child wasn't sick on the couch downstairs.

Draped in a multicolored quilt, a queen-size bed dominated the small, light blue room. The room was immaculate. Full of color. Almost picture-perfect. Just like Maggie.

Lowering her to the bed, he sat on the edge. Her eyes had drifted shut as she snuggled into the bed instead of against him. Coldness seeped into him where her warmth had been.

"Sleep, Maggie." He stroked a strand of hair out of her face. "Let me take on the responsibility for a while."

She mumbled in her sleep. He dropped a kiss on her temple before standing and heading downstairs.

Amber lay on the couch with a worn-out stuffed pig in her arms. She gazed at him with her wide, blue eyes. "Is Mommy okay?"

"Just tired." He moved to the end of the couch where her feet were and looked at her expectantly.

She pulled her feet in, leaving enough room for him. "At least I wasn't at school when I puked."

As he settled, she stretched out, her feet in his lap. "No one had to dodge your splattering?"

A small smile appeared. "You want to watch a movie with me?"

"Sure." For the moment, Brady was content to be with Amber and to let Maggie catch up on her sleep. Work pressed slightly at his mind, but he squashed it. Amber needed him to be here. Much as he hated to admit, the company would be fine without him even for a few hours or a few days.

Chapter Fifteen

Maggie stretched in bed. But when she opened her eyes, she could only make out the shadows of her bedposts and dresser. Bolting upright, she rushed out of her room and into Amber's. Her bed was empty. Her alarm clock read ten o'clock.

Downstairs. Amber must be downstairs. Maggie rushed down the stairs, not entirely sure she actually stepped on every tread. She barely noticed the dishes drying in the rack as she passed by the kitchen and stopped in the living room doorway.

The TV was barely loud enough to hear it, but that's not what caught her attention. Propped up by pillows, Brady was sprawled on her couch asleep. Amber was fast asleep tucked on the couch beside him with her head resting over his heart. A small wet spot had formed on Brady's black shirt under her slack mouth.

Maggie leaned against the doorjamb as her heart settled to a normal pace again. She glanced at the TV, which had returned to the main menu of the DVD that it was playing. *Rapunzel,* one of Amber's favorites.

No cell phone or laptop in sight. Had the New York Brady honestly watched a kid's movie without his precious phone to connect him to his office? Had he really carried Maggie upstairs and put her to bed? Warmth spread to her face. Had he seen her without makeup and her hair looking like a whacked-out version of Medusa?

Had she dreamed the gentle kiss to her temple? Lord knows, she'd had plenty of dreams about Brady, but none of those stopped at her temple.

A rustling brought her out of her head. She held her breath as Amber shifted slightly. Brady's snores died for a second. They both settled into sleep. Quietly, Maggie grabbed her camera and took a picture.

She slipped out of the room and headed into the kitchen to grab a bite to eat before she returned to bed.

"Brady says we can go to the park and maybe stop by Penny's to visit Flicker." Amber bounced in her seat at the table.

"Eat your pancakes." Maggie avoided looking at Brady as she put a plate of pancakes in front of him. He'd told them the story of his phone and the cow while she'd gotten the batter ready. Amber's appetite was back now that she was feeling better.

"How are you doing?" The words sounded almost tender. Holy crap, was that concern in Brady's eyes?

She stumbled slightly on her way to the stove. "I'm fine."

"If you need some more sleep, Amber and I can go to the park on our own. But we'd love it if you joined us."

She could hear the smile in his words even though she didn't dare look at him. How the man could sleep on a couch and wake up looking devilishly handsome was beyond her. She'd felt like night of the living dead last night. At least this morning, she'd had a chance to shower, put on some makeup and brush her hair before facing him.

His black hair was tousled. His clothes wrinkled and his shirt stained over his heart from Amber's drool. And all Maggie wanted to do was sit in his lap and feed him pancakes.

"I think they're done." Brady's voice shook her out of her fantasy.

She flushed as she plated the dark pancakes onto her plate. Thankfully, syrup fixed everything. She'd choke them down if she had to. She took her seat at the table across from Brady with Amber in between them.

"What do you think, Mommy?" Amber said around a bite of pancake.

Maggie was too distracted to chastise her about talking with her mouth full. "About what?"

"Coming with us, silly."

"Yeah, Maggie. Come with us."

Two sets of blue eyes were fixed on her. Amber's were wide and pleading; Brady's had crinkles in the corners as if he knew exactly what she had been thinking about and found it amusing. Give him a chance, he'd asked, and she'd agreed to it.

"Should I bring a picnic basket?" Maggie focused on Amber. It was a whole lot less confusing. Amber's eyes, while similar to Brady's, were still the eyes of her daughter. Looking at Brady stirred something within her and if he kept this new act up, she'd be in some deep doo-doo by the end of the day.

"I love picnics," Amber exclaimed.

"Me, too," Brady said, and without meaning to, Maggie looked at him. His face showed his pleasure. Yup, deep doo-doo.

Four hours later, Maggie found a shaded spot under an old oak tree to put out the blanket for their picnic while Brady pushed Amber on the swings. Amber had been swinging by herself for the past two years, but Brady didn't know that. Maggie shook her head as she set down the basket and drew out the blanket.

The air had a hint of nip to it, but it was pretty warm for a fall day. While there were plenty of leaves on the ground, the trees had held on to most of them. In a few weeks the trees would be bare. A good day to come to the park.

"Let me help you with that."

Maggie turned at Brady's voice. She glanced beyond him at Amber happily swinging away. "Did she have you fooled for even a moment?"

His carefree smile tugged at her heart. "Not a chance. Which is why I only pushed her a little, so she'd be done with me quickly."

He reached for an end of the blanket. She quickly passed it before he was able to touch her. She was having enough trouble breathing when he was around. If he touched her, she was fairly sure she'd forget how to breathe at all. And he being the Boy Scout he'd always been would be forced to give her mouth-to-mouth resuscitation. Her heart skipped a beat.

They backed away from each other to spread out the blanket. The whole morning he'd been thoughtful and attentive. A girl could get used to this if she weren't careful. Maggie tried to keep New York Brady in her mind, but even when he was angry at her over something, he turned her on and challenged her. The way he was acting today stirred the memories of the Brady she'd had a crush on since middle school.

Her heart still raced when he was near. The same way as it had back then. Even her skin prickled, waiting for an accidental brush or the touch of his hand. She wasn't a teenager anymore. This was ridiculous. The man turns on a little charm and suddenly she feels like putty? Just waiting for him to mold her.

She snapped the blanket to straighten it and lowered it to the ground. It wasn't as if she was innocent, or that he was all that great of a catch. She sat on the edge of the blanket.

"How's work dealing with you gone?" Maggie asked as she turned to dig out the picnic gear.

"Getting by." Brady's voice was near.

Looking over her shoulder, she saw that he'd stretched out on the blanket. All six-feet-something of him displayed like temptation itself. She needed to find something to remind herself that this Brady wasn't the real Brady. Fast-paced, self-centered, know-it-all was Brady now.

"I saw that you were talking to Jules when Amber got hurt..." *Take the bait. C'mon, you know you want to talk about work.*

"Yeah, one of the contractors was being a dick. Something about only wanting to deal with me." He didn't twitch a muscle.

"Aren't you worried she wasn't able to fix it?" Maggie set the plates next to the bowls of food she'd pulled out.

"Jules is a pretty competent woman. I'm sure she was able to handle herself." Brady finally rolled onto his side and looked at her. "Why are you suddenly worried about my work?"

She could feel the heat in her cheeks but kept getting things out and ready for lunch. "You've been without a phone for nearly two days and you haven't burst into flames yet."

He chuckled and the sound flowed through her. "Like I said, they are competent."

"And what brought you to that conclusion?" She lifted her gaze to his and wished she hadn't. His eyes were soft in the shade of the tree. A pretty deep shade of blue that should seem wrong on a man like Brady, instead sent a pulse of heat through her.

"I'd rather be here with Amber." He glanced toward the

swings. The chains creaked as Amber went back and forth. When he returned his gaze to hers, she inhaled. "And you."

Every unfulfilled wish came rushing back to her. How Brady would come sweeping into their lives at any moment and make things better. How her mother would have been cured and alive today. How Brady would love her.

But this wasn't wish time. She needed to remind herself of that and make him show her the truth. She dropped her attention to the food. "I bet you can't wait to go back to New York and your life."

"New York is good." There was hesitancy in his voice as though he was waiting for her to spring a trap.

"And your friends."

"Sure." Brady sat up and his attention on her made her wish for things that weren't real.

"And your girlfriends."

Only the sound of the creaking swing chains and rustle of leaves filled the void after her statement. Her breath caught in her throat, but she forced herself to continue with getting their lunch ready while waiting for his reply.

"Wow, that's one big land mine you placed right there."

"Excuse me?" She finally lifted her eyes.

There was a hint of anger in his eyes and God help her, if she didn't relax a little bit, even as her breathing hitched. Charming Brady might be difficult to manage, but she was used to angry Brady.

"I already told you that Jules and I aren't dating," Brady said carefully, probably negotiating the supposed *land mine* she'd put out.

"I know." She turned to watch Amber happily swinging. Hopefully, now he would tell her that there was someone in New York. That this was all fake and he was going to leave them.

"I don't have a girlfriend, nor would I want one in New

York. I have enough women in my life currently." He moved. She didn't see him move, but her body was in tune with what his did. His warmth drew closer to her. In the coolness of the shade, she longed to relax into him.

"I'm sure women are ready to toss themselves at you when you return." She managed to keep her spine straight and her tone even.

"What about you, Maggie?" His breath tickled the hair at the nape of her neck. Why had she put it up this morning?

"What about me?" Surely he didn't think she would fall at his feet. Because even if she believed he cared about Amber enough to stick around or even if he didn't care, at least felt a sense of obligation to Amber, Maggie wasn't about to fall into bed with him just because. She respected herself too much to sleep with someone without love. Didn't she? Okay, in New York, she'd gotten a little carried away, but lust was still lust. And it was intoxicating and tempting and arousing.

"Anyone in these parts float your boat?" His countrified accent caught her off guard.

"Float my boat?" Forgetting for the moment that he'd moved close, she turned to him. A breath separated them. A single inhalation would bring her flush against him. His eyes danced with a teasing, seductive light.

"Isn't that what the kids are calling it these days?" He gave her a half smile. Apparently, she hadn't been as off-putting as she'd tried to be.

It would be so easy to kiss him, but she wasn't about to let him win this match. "You must be the talk of the town with your pretty words."

"I get by." His head tipped oh so slightly to the left. An invitation if she'd ever seen one. His eyes said, "kiss me, I dare you." A challenge that she wouldn't accept if she had half a brain.

"I choose to keep it in my pants, as they say." She gave

him a tight smirk but didn't pull away like she should. It was like waving your hand over a flame. The closer you got to the wick the more danger there was of burning yourself, the higher the rush.

He glanced down. "That's a shame."

When he didn't look up right away, she followed his gaze. Her top gaped slightly from her turned position on the blanket, giving Brady a nice view of her cleavage and hints of the red bra she'd put on this morning.

He returned to look at Maggie. All the teasing was gone and his eyes were like the tropical ocean, warm and inviting. "Maggie, I—"

"Daddy, look how high I can swing."

For a breath he stayed where he was. She swore she saw something in his eyes that she'd never seen before. Something she wasn't sure she was ready to understand. The next breath he stood and walked over to Amber, shouting encouragement. She stared at him trying to decipher everything that had been said, and that look.

He had been nothing but sweet and charming this morning until she'd tried to pick a fight. He'd even turned that around on her. Every time they got close, it seemed as if the fire between them had only been smoldering and waiting for him to come closer so she could burst into flames. She had hoped that familiarity would dampen their lust. The day-to-day grind usually had that effect on relationships. Instead, the tension wound tighter and tighter. He didn't seem any less interested than he had in New York. In fact, he seemed more interested.

He glanced at her and caught her gaze. What had he been about to tell her? His lips curved into a smile. Her breathing hiccupped. Maggie swallowed. This day needed to end, because she was getting closer and closer to throwing herself at him.

"Time for lunch," she yelled.

Brady helped Amber slow the swing. Their laughter combined to make a perfect melody of sound. He wasn't here for Maggie. He was here for Amber. To get to know her, not Maggie. The tension eased out of her body. This was what she wanted for Amber. A father who loved her.

Chapter Sixteen

Maggie stood in the kitchen, staring out the window. Amber had insisted that Brady be the one to tuck her in tonight. Which probably meant conning him into reading her multiple books before bed.

Their picnic had gone off without a hitch. In the afternoon they'd spent a little time at Penny's with Flicker and then went grocery shopping, of all things. Maggie had been amazed by what Brady remembered from his days of working on the farm. He'd kept them both entertained with little stories about him and his brothers.

Amber had definitely fallen in love with her father, and Maggie couldn't blame her. Brady had proven today that he was still that boy she'd had a crush on in school. But he'd also shown her that the grown-up Brady was even better with more substance and a way of viewing the world that had to do with life and experience that neither of them had had eight years ago. Crushing on teenage Brady had been easy, but grown-up Brady made her feel unsettled.

"Deep thoughts?"

She spun around. Even knowing he couldn't read her mind, she felt vulnerable. As if she were latching onto an idea of what it would be like to do something insane like fall in love. With Brady.

"Did Amber go to sleep okay?" She had to find something to busy herself with. The dishes were done and put away. Everything was clean. Unless she wanted to pull out the oven cleaner and a scrubbing pad, there wasn't anything left.

"After five books." His smile was tender, as if he would read Amber a hundred books if she asked him to. "She was practically asleep when she asked for the fifth one. I made sure to read very slowly."

"Great." Oh crap, now what?

He looked as if he had absolutely nowhere to be. It was only eight-thirty. Maybe she should pretend to be tired and ask him to leave. She could watch some TV or work a little or...

"Do you want a drink?" Maggie blurted out. She had to say something, and everything else sounded rude after the day they'd spent together and especially last night with Amber. Besides, he just stood there watching her with a look that made her stomach flutter.

"Sure." His gaze never strayed from her as she went to the fridge.

She opened it and pushed things aside to see what she had. "I have some milk and juice boxes and water and a couple of cans of Diet Coke hidden near the back. Sorry, I don't normally have adult company besides Penny. So no real reason to drink."

But damn, could she use a drink about now.

"Water's fine." His baritone voice made her knees tremble.

She straightened and closed the fridge. With a forced smile, she walked over to the sink and flipped on the faucet to cool the water. "Water it is, then."

Her hands shook when she reached for the glasses. His hand curved around hers as his warmth engulfed her back. It would be so easy to go wherever this led them.

"Let me help you with that," Brady whispered next to her ear.

Shivers coursed along her spine, pooling into an empty pulsing between her legs. It was only lust. His other arm crossed her waist and pulled her tight against him. His hardness settled against her backside, leaving no doubt where his thoughts were.

Their hands closed over the glass, and he moved it to the stream of water. While the glass filled, his lips caressed the back of her neck. She forgot to think, to breathe as she succumbed to the desire that hummed to life whenever he was near.

He took the glass from her hand and set it on the counter before shutting off the faucet. Turning in his arms, Maggie met his gaze. His pupils were dilated. His breath shaky.

"No more games, Maggie." His fingers tipped up her chin as his mouth descended. There was no denying the chemistry between them.

His lips parted on hers, and she gave herself up to the feel of his mouth. The slide of his tongue against hers. The passion she'd been denying all week rose to the surface all at once. The kiss turned desperately passionate. She didn't want to think anymore, only touch him and let him touch her.

She pulled his T-shirt loose from his pants. Her greedy fingers found their way under to memorize the ripples of flesh beneath. As long as she kissed him, she wouldn't have to think, only feel.

Brady's hands had found their own way under her top, curving around her back before lifting her onto the counter. Not for one second did he release her mouth, and she didn't give him the chance.

It's as if they both knew if they paused for one moment, reality would come crashing in. His fingertips traced a path of fire beneath her shirt, making her skin tremble, anticipating his touch. She wanted to live in this moment. To ignore the warning bells going off in her head.

His lips trailed down her chin and his teeth grazed her throbbing pulse in her neck. The upper cabinets bumped against her head. No thinking. Thinking wasn't allowed.

But the kitchen? Not the best place in a house with kids.

"We…" she said.

His tongue found a spot on her neck that was as close to divinity as she had ever come. Even her toes curled in response to the flood of longing. Okay, just a second more and she'd stop.

The button of her jeans opened. Then she felt the tug of the zipper.

"Brady?" She tried again to be responsible, but his name came out as a soft moan.

His lips curved into a smile against her neck. He knew she was weak. Captured by his spell. Unable to untangle her thoughts long enough to think about Amber walking in on them.

That did it. She shoved against his chest and was surprised it actually moved him. His eyes were almost black and had that dazed look that she knew was reflected in hers. Their chests moved in time as they drew in much-needed air.

"We can't do this here," she finally managed to say.

"Maggie, you're killing me." His head dropped to her shoulder. His dark hair tickled her skin, keeping the fire on high.

"Brady, look at me." It was about time he actually heard her.

He raised his head and met her eyes before his gaze dropped

to her lips. She felt a corresponding tug deep inside. There was no way she was turning him out tonight.

"Not *here*." She reached out and tipped his chin until he met her eyes again. "Not in the kitchen. Amber might wake up."

His eyes glowed like a child's at Christmas. "Well, why didn't you say so?"

He swung her into his arms before she could make any comment and strode across the kitchen and up the stairs. She patted his arm until he lowered her softly to the floor in the hallway. Grabbing his hand and hoping for the best, she led him past Amber's door and into her room.

He towered over her and walked her backward until the bed hit her knees. She grabbed his shirt as she lowered herself to the bed. He followed willingly. His lips met hers and banished the other thoughts that had bubbled forth.

"Condom?" she mumbled against his lips.

He pulled out his wallet and withdrew a condom, placing it on the nightstand along with his wallet.

"The door?" She had to cover all the bases while she was still coherent enough.

"Shut and locked." He nibbled her bottom lip before kissing her senseless.

The sense of urgency took over again as she pulled his shirt over his head. She could ignore the little warning bell going off in the back of her mind. Especially when his mouth was doing divine things to her neck. It didn't matter that they hadn't discussed where they were going from here.

It hadn't mattered before, why should it matter now? Her shirt followed his to the floor. His warm skin rubbed against hers, and breathing became optional. She fell against the bed as his lips worked magic along her collarbone. Her stomach clenched as he worked his way closer and closer to her breasts, which were confined by her bra.

Why shouldn't she be allowed this? So what if he'd be gone in a week? Shouldn't she enjoy what she could, like Penny always said?

His hands slipped beneath her and released the catch on her bra. With it out of the way, his mouth covered her nipple and she got her wish. Nothing but sensation flowed through her brain. He branded her with his mouth as his hands worked on her pants.

Want and need replaced everything. As his hands continued to explore her body, she nearly came off the bed when he switched breasts.

A small knock broke through the chaos of sensations. It was probably the house settling. Brady's finger teased her panty line.

Another knock followed by a small "Mommy?" had Maggie slamming her hand over Brady's and shoving him to the side. She took three deep breaths before grabbing a shirt and throwing it over her head.

"Just a minute." Suddenly, she was engulfed in Brady's rich scent. She had grabbed his shirt, still warm from his body. She held her finger to her lips when she looked at Brady.

He nodded.

Opening the door a crack, she saw Amber's face covered in tears. Forgetting everything, Maggie dropped to her knees and held out her arms. Amber flew into them, wrapping her arms tight around Maggie's neck.

"I...had a bad...dream," Amber said through her sniffles. Her arms stayed tight around Maggie and her head lay on Maggie's shoulder.

Maggie rubbed her back. Perhaps this was the universe saying *don't sleep with Brady Ward*. "It's okay. Why don't we go to your room and get you into bed?"

Amber's head shook violently on Maggie's shoulder. "I want to sleep with you, Mommy. In your bed."

Danger. Maggie tried to glance at Brady, but her head wouldn't turn far enough. Maybe he'd hidden in the closet. He could sneak out after Amber fell asleep.

"Can I call Daddy?"

No matter how many times Amber called him that, it shocked Maggie. She didn't know quite how to answer. After all, Brady was right there. No need for a phone call.

She wanted to laugh hysterically but instead her mouth opened and closed while she tried to think of some reason Amber couldn't call Brady besides the fact that he was in Maggie's bedroom.

"No need to call me. I'm here." Brady opened the door all the way and knelt beside Maggie. She cringed. What would Amber think?

Amber immediately released Maggie and flung herself at Brady. A stab of jealousy hit Maggie hard. She'd always been the one to comfort Amber. The one Amber clung to when she needed a good cry. The one Amber relied on to keep her safe.

And now Brady was hogging her glory. Not that she wanted Amber to have bad dreams. She just wanted to be the one her daughter wanted to comfort her.

"What happened to your shirt?" Amber asked. She snuggled up to Brady the same way she always snuggled with Maggie.

"Your mom was cold." Brady glanced Maggie's way. How could she begrudge him this when he looked so damned happy?

"That was nice of you." Amber pulled away and smooshed Brady's face between her hands, forcing him to look at her. "Would you stay and sleep with Mommy and me?"

"Of course." Brady didn't hesitate for a moment.

What the hell was going on in her life? First she about had sex with Brady and now she was about to climb in bed with him and their daughter? This was too weird.

Amber grabbed both their hands and led them to the bed. She climbed in and under the covers. "Mommy on this side and Daddy over here."

Not an ounce of the heat from before was in the look Brady gave her. It was questioning and tender. Almost as if he was giving her a choice. Oh, sure, Amber would blame her for driving Brady away.

Maggie shrugged and grabbed a pair of pajama bottoms from her dresser. After pulling them on, she climbed into bed with Amber.

"I don't even get my shirt back?" Brady smiled.

"I'm still cold." Maggie snuggled deeper under the covers. That, and it smelled like him. "If you aren't going to be comfortable, you could always go home."

"Wouldn't dream of it." He sat on the edge of the bed and took off his socks, but kept his jeans on. He lay on top of the covers, put his arms under his head and crossed his ankles.

"I'm glad you're my daddy," Amber whispered.

"Me, too," Brady whispered back.

Maggie reached over and shut off the lamp. As she lay wide-awake in the darkened room listening to the rustles and breathing of Amber and Brady, all the thoughts she'd put to the side while Brady had been kissing her rushed forward. But one question spoke louder than any of the others.

What if Brady wanted to be with Maggie because of Amber? All his charm and kisses were only to stay close to his daughter?

She felt a brush of his fingertips on her shoulder and tried to relax so he thought she'd fallen asleep. He wouldn't even be in her life now if it weren't for Amber.

Well, his charm and kisses wouldn't work on Maggie. She didn't need a man in her life and definitely not Brady Ward. She wanted a man who was in love with her for who she was. Besides, it wasn't as if she were already half in love with the guy.

His hand slipped away and immediately she missed his touch. Oh, for Pete's sake, she was better than this. Falling in love with the father of her child. Ha! Impossible because he lived in New York and she lived here. He was high class and champagne dreams. She was barbecue and beer.

Even if the chemistry was explosive, that kind of thing never lasted. Before long he'd resent her for holding him back. Especially since he didn't love her. Her heart throbbed and a warm well of tears choked the back of her throat.

He would never love her. Could she ever know if he really loved her? He would convince himself that it was the right thing to do. To love the mother of his child.

She drew in a shaky breath to keep from crying because she knew without a doubt that if she hadn't loved him before, she definitely loved Brady Ward now. And she couldn't do a damned thing about it.

Chapter Seventeen

Last night, this wasn't the way Brady had planned to wake up with Maggie. He stared across the bed and the tangle of dark hair at Maggie sleeping on the other side of Amber.

Her light honey hair spread over the pillow. The constant tension in her face had gone soft in sleep. He'd hoped they could ease some of the tension between them last night. The sexual tension had been building since New York and the only way to discharge it was to have sex. It was only natural.

It didn't help that she constantly battled him at every turn. Challenged him about his way of life. Stole his phone. Made him someone's daddy.

Instead of finally succumbing to the spark that hadn't died since they were younger, they'd ended up with Amber taking the middle of Maggie's queen-size bed. He'd never been kicked so much in his life, and he couldn't help but smile because of it.

The morning sun drifted in between the curtains and fell across Maggie's and Amber's faces. Amber had wanted her daddy to comfort her last night. Her heart had beat like a scared rabbit's against his. He'd forgotten to ask what her nightmare had been about. Wasn't even sure if he should ask.

Now she slept as beautifully as her mom. Even though Amber had his coloring, she had her mother's features. His heart was going to burst out of his chest. It almost felt as if they were a family.

What would it be like to have them with him? The thought startled him, but it had been in his mind all day yesterday. He had to return to New York and work. That's where his life was. But why couldn't he take them with him? Both of them.

Not just a week or two in the summer or a weekend a month, but forever. Maggie's nose crinkled in her sleep. Amber threw her arm across Maggie. Surely Maggie would see that they were better as a family. With Maggie there, he'd know someone was taking care of Amber while he worked.

It's not as if there was anything holding them to Tawnee Valley. Maybe the house, but Maggie's mom was gone. His brother lived there, but Sam wasn't exactly their favorite person.

Maggie stretched. Slowly her eyes opened and focused on him.

"Morning," he whispered.

She gave him a sleepy smile and stretched again. His shirt tightened against her body, giving him an image to dream about. If she noticed his interest, she didn't give it away as she rolled out of bed, careful not to disturb Amber.

Before he had a chance to say anything more, she was out the door.

"Do you like my mommy?"

Brady looked into Amber's wide-awake face. "Yeah, I like your mommy."

"Then why did you leave her?" Such a simple question but he didn't have a good answer to it.

His mouth opened as he thought of saying one thing, but then he closed it. He'd left because he needed to put his past behind him. He'd left to forget about a little town called Tawnee Valley where his parents had raised him and where they had died, leaving him and his brothers alone. He hadn't planned on leaving Maggie because she hadn't been part of the picture.

"I don't suppose you'd take an 'it's complicated, you'll understand when you're older'?" Brady tried.

From the look in Amber's eyes, she wasn't buying it. "Jessica says that when a man and woman don't like each other anymore, they move away from each other. But since you and Mommy like each other, why don't you live together?"

"Because Brady lives all the way in New York and our life is here."

Saved by Maggie's voice, Brady lifted his gaze as Maggie walked through the door in a different shirt. She tossed his T-shirt at him as she sat on the edge of the bed next to Amber.

Amber's face bunched up as she tried to work out her next question. Before she could ask anything more, Brady stood.

"I should go back to the farm." He tugged his shirt on over his head. Maggie's scent mingled with his.

"Sounds like a plan." Maggie didn't look as if she was going to offer to walk him to the door or anything.

"Can I come, too?" Amber bounced on the bed before turning her pleading eyes to Maggie. "Can I, Mommy? Please? I promise to behave. I can be ready. Please?"

"I don't mind," Brady said. "As long as you two don't have anything planned."

"No, we don't." Her smile seemed forced. "Go on, Amber. Get dressed so the two of you can go."

Amber hopped off the bed and rushed from the room. Doors opened and closed and drawers slammed before the sound of running water filled the silence between him and

Maggie. Picking at the blue shirt she wore, Maggie sat on the edge of the bed with her bare feet on the runner board. She didn't seem to be in any hurry to move or to talk.

"We should talk." Brady didn't know what else to say, but they really did need to talk about many things. He needed to sort through what he wanted on his own before he gave her his plan.

"About what?" She tried to give him a blank look, but he wasn't buying it. They hadn't discussed what type of arrangement they were going to have after this week or the fact that every time he was alone with her he wanted to touch her and kiss her.

"About a lot of things. Have dinner with me tonight?"

"We have dinner every night." Maggie pulled a length of her hair through her fingers. "When you aren't too busy working."

"Not here. Not with Amber. Out."

That finally got her attention. Her hands dropped to the bed as she looked at him. "Where?"

"Well…" Brady hadn't thought that far ahead. They needed neutral territory to talk things through, for him to have a chance to propose the arrangement and for them to discuss how to implement it. "How about we go to the restaurant in Owen on Main Street?"

No one ever called the place by its current name. Through the years it had been through so many owners and name changes that it had become that place in Owen on Main Street. It was practically the only sit-down restaurant for miles besides the small café in Tawnee Valley.

The only other restaurants were at least an hour's drive away. Brady could think of better things to do with their time than driving to get to a good dining place.

Maggie kept smoothing that one strand of hair. For a moment he thought she wasn't going to answer him at all. It wasn't that far-fetched that he would want to take her out to talk. Especially after last night.

"Okay." Maggie didn't lift her gaze from staring at the ends of her hair.

That was it? Too easy, but he could use a little easy right now. "Great, I'll pick you up at six."

"Who will watch Amber?" Suddenly, her attention was fixed on him. The sunlight glinted off the green in her eyes.

"Oh…" Who would watch Amber? He'd never thought about that. Never had to think about it before.

The water stopped. He only had a few minutes before Amber returned.

"What about Penny?" Brady didn't know Penny all that well. Only what Luke had told him once after a few beers in London. But she didn't seem like that bad of a person. Maggie trusted her. Amber liked her.

"Penny can't on Sunday nights." Maggie padded over to her dresser.

"I'll take care of it." Brady had to find someone. If all else failed, there was one person that owed him about eight years' worth of babysitting.

After a quick stop in Owen to pick up his new phone, Brady and Amber drove the country roads to get to the farm. Brady wished he could watch her face as she took in the countryside, but he kept his eyes on the road.

As he pulled in the driveway, Barnabus started barking and pretty soon the puppy joined Barnabus and started howling.

"Is that Flicker's brother or sister?" Amber leaned her forehead against the passenger-side window to see the balls of fur pacing the car as Brady took it easy over the gravel.

"Sister, I think." Brady parked the car near the old windmill.

"Is it okay to get out?" Amber's voice was timid, but trembled with excitement.

"They won't hurt you." Brady smiled reassuringly. "Just walk as if you have every right to be here and if they get in your way, give them a gentle push and say 'get down' firmly."

She nodded solemnly and opened the door. Immediately, two noses came through the opening and pushed into her lap. Her giggles filled the car as Brady leaned across her to shove the dogs back.

"You don't happen to have a pork chop in your pocket, do you?" Brady said. The dogs were wiggling and pushing regardless of Brady trying to shove them away.

"No." Amber laughed as the puppy licked her face.

A high-pitched whistle made both dogs retreat. Brady watched as they ran across the courtyard toward the barn and Sam.

"That was funny." Amber shoved out of the car and followed the dogs.

Brady hurried after her.

"Hi, Mr. Ward." Amber stooped to pet the puppy, who sat close to Barnabus and wiggled. Sam had trained the puppy quickly.

"Mr. Ward?" Brady gave Sam a questioning look as he caught up with Amber.

"He brings the baby animals to the petting zoo at the end of the school year," Amber explained, not paying any attention to the two men. Her focus was intent on the puppy. Barnabus whined and nudged her with his nose. She giggled and started to pet both dogs at the same time.

The color rose on Sam's neck. "Mrs. Potter asked me if I wouldn't mind. It's before planting season."

"Amber?" Brady tried to pry her attention away from the dogs. Finally, she looked at him expectantly. "Sam is my brother. He's your uncle Sam."

That finally got her attention. She stood and stared at Sam. "I've never had an uncle before."

"You have two. Your uncle Luke is away at college." Brady held his breath as Sam and Amber regarded each other. It was as if they were sizing up the competition. Each taking the other's measure. If she were a grown-up, it would have been intense. But since she had to tilt her neck so far to look at him, it ruined the effect.

"Sarah Beth says her uncle takes her to Dairy Queen on Sundays." Amber crossed her arms over her chest.

"We put little girls to work out here." Sam matched her pose and didn't seem as if he would budge an inch.

"If I work, do I get Dairy Queen?" She raised her eyebrow.

"If you do your job and don't complain, I can see what we can do." Sam couldn't possibly mean for Amber to do chores. The type of chores they used to do as boys were too much for a little girl.

"She's only—" Brady protested.

"I don't do windows," Amber said with all the calm of a seasoned negotiator. Brady had seen corporate negotiators with less talent.

"Neither do I. Do we have a deal?" Sam held out his hand. She took it and shook it once. "A deal."

"Sam, you can't use my kid as child labor." Brady couldn't help but feel betrayed. He'd brought Amber out here to play not to be put to work.

"A promise is a promise, Daddy." Amber smiled at Brady before turning to Sam. "What do you want me to do?"

"This is insane." Brady threw up his hands.

"The baby lambs need to be fed. First, we need to go warm the milk and bottle it." Sam started toward the house and Amber followed. "Then we go out to the barn and feed them. Think you can handle that?"

"Yup."

Brady stood in the driveway with the two dogs. He couldn't help but wonder what had just happened. Since when did

Sam hang out with kids? And how did he manage to make Amber feel needed by giving her something she would have done, anyway?

"You let Amber go with Brady out to the farm?" Penny pushed the bowl of chips closer to Maggie. "You need these more than I do."

"I can't keep spending time with him. I almost had sex with him last night." Maggie slouched on the couch. The TV buzzed with a repeat of a show about house hunting in the background. Neither of them were watching it, but it seemed natural to have it on.

"Whoa, back up the bus, lady." Penny sat up on her knees from her curled position in the corner. "What do you mean *almost?*"

"Amber had a nightmare and then we all ended up sleeping in my bed. It was so freaking domestic, it was scary." There had been part of her that had been grateful that she hadn't been the only one carrying the burden of Amber's fears.

"Okay, we'll deal with that in a minute." Penny hit the off button on the remote. "Let's talk sex."

"It was nothing." Why she'd felt the need to confess, especially to Penny, she'd never know.

"That bad, huh?" Penny patted Maggie's knee sympathetically.

"No." Maggie couldn't seem to stop herself. Maybe Penny could sort out this mess. "It would be easy just to have sex. The tension is there. All. The. Time. I know now that he won't leave Amber because of my stupidity, but I think I want it to be more than it was before."

"You mean more than just sex?" Penny relaxed against the corner. Her forehead crinkled as she tapped a finger to her lips thoughtfully. If she'd come to a conclusion, she kept it to herself.

"Yes, more than sex. More than hey, you're my baby's daddy, why don't we knock boots." Maggie pulled the elastic from her hair and straightened her ponytail before slipping the elastic back on it.

"That's a good one. Knocking boots." Penny raised her eyebrow and quirked her lips into a smile.

"I'm afraid." Maggie put the bowl on the coffee table and stood. All this energy pulsed through her.

"You're always afraid."

"What?" Maggie hadn't expected Penny to say that.

"Think of everything you've been through." Penny ticked each thing off on her fingers like a grocery list. "Your father left, your mother's cancer, your unexpected pregnancy. We both know that it was awfully suspicious when Sam dropped off the money the first time. But the fact is, you were afraid of Brady then and you are afraid of Brady now. Because you love him."

Maggie's heart felt as if it was going to crumble into bits in her chest. "It doesn't matter."

"Why doesn't it matter, Maggie?" Penny finally stood. "Because the Brown women never get what they want? Because your mother couldn't make your deadbeat father stay? Because you're afraid to love anyone who isn't obligated to love you back?"

A touch of anger scorched the pity party happening in her body. "I love *you*. And you aren't obligated to love me."

"But I've always been there." Penny flipped her red hair. "And you have no reason to believe I'm going anywhere. But Brady is only obligated to Amber."

Tears welled in Maggie's eyes. "But what if he feels obligated to me because of her? What if everything he thinks he feels for me is only because of her? He doesn't love me. I would know it."

Penny grabbed a tissue box from the coffee table and held

it out to Maggie. "How would you know? You are so blind you couldn't even tell you've been holding out for Brady for the past eight years."

"That's not true—"

"Really?" Penny narrowed her eyes. "Not one date—a date, Maggie—has been good enough for you since you found out you were pregnant. You hid behind your mom's illness and then your daughter. It's time to stop hiding, Maggie."

Maggie breathed in deep. Everything Penny said touched at the heart of the matter.

"What happens if you put yourself out there?" Penny grabbed Maggie's hand. "What happens if you sleep with Brady and he doesn't want you anymore? It'd be freaking awkward for a while, but you'd get over it and so would he. But what if he wants you?"

That feeling of drowning came upon her quickly. She'd felt it before when she'd found out about her mother's cancer. Overwhelmed, confused, but she'd found clarity in one moment. One moment that had cost her. A night with Brady Ward. It had been impulsive and she'd paid for it. She would never regret her daughter. Amber was her life.

"I keep asking the same question, but you never give me the right answer." Penny sat on the couch and grabbed the bowl of chips before resuming her position in the corner.

"What's the answer, then?" Maggie wanted this to be over.

"The worst thing that could happen is that you could never try to be with the man you've loved since high school. That you let him go because you are too scared to find out that he might love you, too."

Chapter Eighteen

"You left her with Sam?" The accusatory tone in Maggie's voice couldn't distract Brady from a dressed-up Maggie. Her red dress wasn't particularly fancy, but it hugged her in just the right places, making his thoughts less than pure.

"Sam promised her Dairy Queen, a movie and chores in the morning. Besides, Sam owes me a lot more than one night." Brady offered her his arm. "Are you ready to go?"

She hesitated for a moment, almost as if she wanted to bolt up the stairs and hide in her bedroom. Instead, she gave herself a slight shake, which made her dress dance around her knees. "I'm ready."

He led her to his rental car and opened her door. All afternoon he'd worked on the logistics of how to get her to New York. He'd even put together a presentation. More for himself than her. It was the way he worked through things. It was comfortable.

He climbed in and started the car, turning the music to a soft volume. Now that he was with her, all the preparation flew out the window with one look at that dress. The soft floral scent that emanated from her didn't help the tightness in his pants. He'd be lucky if he could get through dinner—let alone the important conversation they needed to have—before he kissed her.

They had fifteen minutes to drive to the restaurant, an hour to eat, then the drive back before he could kiss her. When he kissed her tonight, unless she objected, he had no intentions of stopping.

"Did Amber enjoy the farm?" The thought of his daughter cooled him.

"She fed the lambs, and Sam let her try milking a cow." Brady pulled away from the curb as he told Maggie all about the "pet" cow that Amber spent the better part of an hour trying to milk. By the time they reached the restaurant, he was completely in control.

The hostess sat them in a booth toward the back. Very few people were in the restaurant.

"I think last time I was in here it was a barbecue joint," Maggie said from behind her menu.

"Looks like they decided fried chicken might work better."

"Until next week." Her smiling eyes peeked over the menu.

He couldn't resist returning the smile. The waitress came over and took their order. When she left, she removed the menu Maggie had been hiding behind.

Maggie smiled at him and it seemed as though she wasn't hiding anything like she normally did. Her makeup was subtle, but her hazel eyes seemed even more intense than normal, and a slight blush touched her cheeks. Almost the same flush she had after they kissed.

"You wanted to talk?" Maggie closed her hands on top of the table.

"We need to figure out where we are headed and what situation would be best for Amber." This was what Brady was good at, presenting a solid plan to corporate for a new venture. He never felt nervous about it anymore, but now his stomach twisted slightly.

"We're both adults, Brady. I think we can come up with some arrangement that makes sense." Maggie leaned forward. "I'm glad you want to spend time with her."

"I hope I'll always be part of her life."

"Of course. We could probably come out to see you for a few weeks in the summer. Maybe you could come here for holidays. Since Sam is here. We usually have holidays with Penny."

"I was hoping for more than that." Brady interrupted her flow, which seemed to throw her off balance for a moment.

"More?" Maggie sat against the booth back and grabbed the locket around her neck. "You mean like a month in the summer?"

"No, Maggie, I mean—"

"Here we go." The waitress put down the plates, oblivious to the fact that she'd interrupted them. "Can I get you anything else?"

"Not for me," Maggie said.

"Thank you." Brady waited until the waitress was gone.

Maggie picked at her food. Tears hovered in her eyes when she lifted her gaze. "I can't let you have her for half the year. It's not going to happen. She's my life. I know that's not fair to you, but I can't."

He reached across and grabbed her hand. "I'm not asking you to, Maggie. I would never take Amber away from you."

Her chest rose and fell as she searched his eyes. She drew in a deep breath and nodded. "I'm sorry. I assumed that's what you were building up to."

"You have every reason to want Amber with you. I can't imagine missing one more day of her life." Brady took a bite of his chicken, trying to figure out the easiest way to propose his suggestion. She wasn't a CEO. She was a woman who had an emotional attachment to what he wanted. If he had some way to convince her that if they went through with his plan everything would be fine, he would tell her. But it might fall flat. He didn't think it would, but there was a small chance it could.

She watched him warily as she nudged her mashed potatoes around her plate.

"Remember at Luke's party, I couldn't find a way to tell Sam that I wanted to take the internship in London?"

Confusion lit her face. "Haven't we been through this—"

"Bear with me." He smiled to reassure her. "You approached me when everyone else at the party ignored me."

"Nobody was ignoring you."

"Okay, avoided me." He winked at her to try to put her at ease, but his heart warmed from her rising to his defense. "I wasn't exactly good company that night, but you sat and listened. I'd barely acknowledged your presence in high school, but you listened to me. Instead of telling me my dreams were ridiculous, you encouraged me to follow them."

"Everyone knew you were going places, Brady. You didn't need me to tell you that." Maggie tucked a lock of hair behind her ear.

"But I did that night." Brady took in a deep breath. "I needed someone to tell me it was okay. That running away from my brothers didn't make me a bad person. Not that I asked you that, but you made me feel like I was making the right decision. Even if it was for the wrong reasons."

"What is wrong about wanting to go to college?" Maggie had stopped the pretense of eating and intently listened to him.

"It wasn't just the opportunity that I wanted." He swallowed. "Only Sam knew the truth of it."

Her brow furrowed, but she reached out a hand to him.

He accepted her offer and tangled his fingers in hers. She gave him strength. She deserved the truth. "I was running away, Maggie. I couldn't stay in Tawnee Valley after my parents were gone. Everywhere I went they were there, but they weren't anymore. The constant reminder was driving me nuts. I was weak. I couldn't have Sam and Luke relying on me."

"They did okay." Maggie squeezed his hand.

"Luke had a rough time of it and Sam was too controlling for his own good. But none of that matters now." Brady shook off the past. "I wanted you to know that I've run in the past, but that I don't plan to this time."

"What are you saying, Brady?"

"Come to New York with me. You and Amber. We'll find a good school for her."

She started to pull her hand away.

"We don't have to sleep together. I can find a bigger place, if you want. But I can't deny that I want to be with you. To see where this thing between us can go. Aren't you the least bit curious?" Brady could almost see the shutters shut over her eyes as she closed him out.

"Curious?" Maggie finally pulled her hand back. Touching him did funny things to her brain. Made her hear things that surely Brady hadn't said.

"Amber would be better off with two parents who loved her, right?" Brady's blue eyes turned calculating.

"I'm not denying that Amber needs both of us. But New York is far away…" Would it be so bad to go with him? To stop hiding like Penny thought she was doing?

"We'd be there together. I can help both of you through the transition." Brady reached across the table but she pulled her hands into her lap.

Something was wrong with what he was saying. If he touched her, she wouldn't be able to figure out what it was.

Everything he said was what she wanted to hear. Almost everything.

"What happens when we don't want to be together?" Maggie folded her arms across her chest. "What if all we have is a shared past, a child and lust? What if that isn't enough?"

What if she wanted love?

"It's a start, isn't it?" Brady straightened. "We don't have to decide anything tonight. You can take a few days to think it through. I want you and Amber with me, Maggie."

"We're supposed to leave Tawnee Valley and everything we've ever known to run off to New York and start over?" Maggie couldn't wrap her head around it. "Where would I work? What if things didn't work out? I couldn't support Amber and me in New York."

"Think it over. Please, Maggie. The one regret I have is not knowing what you were going through." Brady held up his hand to get the waitress's attention. "Let's go somewhere and talk. Not here, okay?"

She nodded. He hadn't offered her love. Not even marriage. Even though she had pushed it aside for years, she wanted the whole package. A man who loved her. A marriage that would last until they were old and gray.

He wasn't offering that. He was offering her a maybe. Maybe this could grow into something, but what if it didn't? What if he never loved her the way she loved him?

Before she knew it, they were in his car parked outside her house. Neither of them made a move to leave the car. His fingers curled around the steering wheel.

"Would you tell me what happened during those years?" Brady didn't look at her but stared ahead with his head resting against the car seat.

She undid her belt and shifted in the bucket seat until she was comfortable. "Do you want the long story or the short?"

"Whatever you are willing to tell me." Brady dropped

his hands into his lap and turned his head to her. "You're an amazing mother. Any fool could see that. But I know that wasn't your only struggle. I want to know you, Maggie. Not the brave facade you put on for the rest of the world, but you."

She breathed in deep. How much should she tell him? What did he really want to know? "I found out about my mother's cancer a month before graduation. I think I was still in shock by graduation. I canceled my college plans including the scholarship I'd worked hard to get. My friends were leaving, and all I could do was hope that treatment worked for my mom. While they were going off to begin their lives, I was staying behind to save hers."

"We don't always get a choice." Brady held out his hand and she took it. "Knowing someone might die is difficult."

"At the party, I wanted something I could have control over. I wanted to find out if the guy I had a crush on for as long as I could remember might possibly want me, too." She smiled softly in the dark, remembering the fanciful, romantic thoughts she'd felt that night.

"And then you found me?"

She squeezed his hand. "I went searching for you. All I could think was how this might be the last time I did something for me. Something entirely selfish. Something I'd wanted for so long."

His thumb stroked over the back of her hand. In the weak streetlights, she caught his gaze.

"You were leaving. I knew it was a one-time thing. I wasn't trying to trap or trick you."

"I know." Brady's low baritone sent shivers down her spine.

"I found out I was pregnant when I was as sick as my mother after her therapy. I didn't know what to do. I didn't want you to think I did it on purpose. I didn't want you to think I needed you. So I wrote a damned letter." She laughed self-deprecatingly. "A letter I hoped you never received. But when Sam brought me money, I didn't question anything."

His fingers tightened on hers, but he stayed quiet.

"We needed the money. I wanted to believe you were that type of guy. The guy who thought throwing money at a problem made it go away. Because it would be easier to lose you if I never had you. I knew what Mom had gone through with my dad and I was scared." She used her other hand to wipe away a tear that slipped out.

"Amber was born. Mom went into remission. Things were good for a while. When Mom got sick again, we had a rough year and then it was over. She was gone."

"And you were alone again." He reached out and brushed another tear from her cheek. His hand cupped her cheek, making her feel cherished.

"Amber and I carried on. The end." If only it had been that easy. If only it hadn't been a constant struggle for her.

"You're a wonderful person, Maggie." His soft words startled her.

She searched his eyes for the hidden meaning behind his words. "I kept you from your daughter for eight years and you think I'm wonderful?"

"You were protecting yourself and Amber." Brady touched his forehead to hers. "We all run away sometimes. In our own ways."

He was right. She hadn't run away physically but she had emotionally. Too afraid that the voices telling her he would hate her would be true. Too afraid that he didn't want Amber.

Now he wanted them both to go to New York with him. She'd never considered that he'd want them as a package deal. She'd never considered that he would want them at all.

Could he learn to love her? She pressed her lips to his. The brief touch sent warmth throughout her body. She loved him. Maybe not when she'd been eighteen, but the man he was now, the one she'd gotten to know over the past week. In all her life, she'd never loved anyone the way she loved Brady. He made her think. He made her laugh. He made her sigh with pleasure. He made her feel as if everything would be okay as long as he was in her life.

"Let's go inside," she whispered. The decision for New York could wait until morning. Denying that she wanted him was only driving them in circles.

"Are you sure?" His thumb caressed her cheek. His blue eyes searched hers.

"Aren't you?" She leaned into his hand. They both needed to heal and they needed the other to help. Even if it was only one more night, she wanted this.

Chapter Nineteen

Maggie held Brady's hand as they made their way upstairs to her bedroom. No disruptions tonight. No mindless passion.

Tonight Maggie would give Brady her heart the only way she knew how.

He turned her until they were face-to-face. "I've always wanted you, Maggie."

Want. Lust. Desire was easy. Just standing next to him had her pulse racing, her nerve endings waiting for his touch, her breathing choppy. His thumb traced a path of fire over her bottom lip.

She met his eyes and began unbuttoning his shirt. No rushing. No hurry. Every moment would be savored and remembered. His blue eyes glittered in the dim light of her room. His hands smoothed over her shoulders. He paused at her zipper and lowered it until his hands reached the base of her spine.

Helping him shrug out of his shirt, she never broke eye contact. It kept her centered, reminded her that this was for her heart. To be with Brady and see if she could stand loving him, when he didn't love her in return.

He drew her closer and lowered his lips to her forehead. Light kisses trailed over her face, closing her eyes and making her body pulse with need. When his lips finally took hers, she drew in his breath as her own.

The urgency of last night was forgotten as he sipped slowly on her lower lip. As he rediscovered her mouth, his fingers slipped through her dress's open back and touched the trembling flesh beneath.

She didn't want to hurry, but her body was beyond ready to move to the next step. Her fingers threaded through his hair as she deepened the kiss. He followed her lead and slipped the dress from her shoulders. She kicked off her heels without relinquishing his mouth.

This time wasn't about hiding behind passion. Or even about succumbing to a chemistry neither of them could deny. This time she wanted the way her lover touched her, the way he kissed her as if it were the last time they would be together or the first, to touch her soul.

The rest of their clothes followed the dress and shoes. Each piece brought a new sensation until nothing but air separated their bodies. Her breasts pressed against his lightly haired chest. Her stomach shivered inside as it pressed against his heat.

And yet his hands remained low on her hips. He wanted her to lead this dance. She broke off the kiss and gasped in air, causing her body to fit tighter to his.

He groaned as he kissed the side of her neck. "You are so beautiful," he muttered against her skin. His fingers flexed into her hips, pulling her tight against him.

Fire and heat coursed through her veins, pooling between her legs. She pulled away from him slightly and caressed the stubble growing on his cheek. The words *I love you* hovered on her lips, longing to be released. To share with him the joy and fear, but she couldn't.

"I've waited a long time for this." She pulled the covers back on the bed and held her arms out to him. "Do you remember what you said to me that night?"

Closing the distance between them, he wrapped his arms around her. Her ear rested against his beating heart. She wondered if hers pounded like his.

"I said that I wished I hadn't wasted my time." He kissed the top of her head. "That I'd really seen you when we were in school."

He tipped her chin up and lowered his lips until his barely touched hers. "That we had more time."

"We have time now." Maggie met his gaze, hoping he could see how much she wanted him to love her. Knowing it left her vulnerable but not caring.

"We have the rest of our lives." His words sent a shock wave through her being as his lips claimed hers. They moved together on the bed, connected lips to lips until they lay beside each other.

She forgot to breathe as his hand wandered over her breast, encircling her nipple until it hardened. When his hand left her, his mouth claimed her other breast. His fingers drew circles down her belly until he cupped her in the palm of his hand.

The need to touch him, to give him the pleasure he was giving her, filled her. Her fingers traced over his tightened abs and caressed his hip bone. His moan made her smile, but then he changed positions, taking her other breast into his mouth. Her breath hitched. His fingers moved over her until she could think of nothing but the next touch, the next sensation. The heat built until she feared she'd burst into flames if something didn't change soon. If he didn't let her find the release that had been building for the past week.

Her fingers closed over him and he stilled. His harsh breath bathed her breast in warmth. She explored him with the lightest touch. His tongue flicked out at her nipple. His hand resumed the slow tortuous pace until her hips rose to meet him.

It was right there, so close she could almost touch it. He moved up her body and took her mouth with his. She clung to him as her body burst with sensation and pleasure.

Her breath caught as he caressed her breast. The fire started to rise within her again. He shifted on the bed until they were chest to chest, stomach to stomach, thigh to thigh.

He made short work of a condom. When he lifted his head, his eyes were liquid pools in the darkness. She could feel her heart quietly singing as his thumb stroked her cheek.

He entered her slowly, making their bodies one. Never once taking his gaze from hers. She needed to see his eyes, to see if there was even a little hope that he could love her. A little hope that she could cling to as her heart broke.

As he moved within her, the flames built until thought became impossible. His lips found hers in the storm and they clung to each other, reaching for something just out of their reach. In this moment, they made sense. They fit each other perfectly. Matched each other unlike anything else she'd ever felt. As they climbed closer, he held her tighter, and her heart wished it was because he was afraid to let her go.

Sparks burst behind Maggie's eyes as a new rush of sensation flowed through her and she felt him join her as they were engulfed.

Brady woke slowly, a little disorientated in Maggie's bedroom. Maggie's warmth covered his side, and her hair tickled his nose. They must have fallen asleep at the foot of the bed. Covers were thrown over them and spilled onto the floor.

He hugged Maggie to him. For once, his heart felt settled. This felt right, having Maggie with him. Last night had been amazing. There hadn't been the normal awkwardness of sleeping with someone for the first time. Granted it wasn't their first time, but it had been eight years.

In a week, he could have Maggie and Amber in his apartment in New York. He'd written an email to his assistant yesterday to start a folder on Josh's ideas for Tawnee Valley, including the files he'd started the other day. He'd also requested that the refrigerator in his apartment be stocked. He'd sent her a couple of pictures for the guest bedroom to be transformed into a little girl's room for Amber. Fresh flowers were to be in every room when they arrived.

Two weeks ago when he'd been preparing for the Detrex presentation with Jules for corporate, he would have laughed if someone told him he'd have a family in a week. It surprised him that he hadn't even thought about the project in the past few days. So consumed with Maggie and Amber that it hadn't been as important as it always had been. They could be a family. Brady hadn't had any part of a family since he was eighteen. He'd been driven to fill that emptiness with his career. Now he had Amber and Maggie.

He wanted to shout from the rooftops, proclaim to the world his happiness. Instead, he stared at the woman in his arms. Who knew Sam would be right years ago? Maggie was a keeper. Brady had been stupid to let her out of his life before. He wouldn't make the same mistake twice.

Maggie stretched and looked at him with sleepy eyes. "Morning."

Yup, this was how he wanted to wake up every day. "Morning."

She glanced around, noticing their feet near the pillows. She shrugged and put her head on his chest.

"Want to go over to The Rooster to get breakfast before going to pick up Amber?" He tucked his hands beneath his head.

She propped her chin on her hands to look at him. "You're lucky today wasn't a school day."

"I'm one of the luckiest men alive. Come on, we can't spend all day in bed."

If she had protested even a little, he would have stayed in bed with her all day. Instead, she sighed before getting up. The sunlight lit her skin in a golden haze. He sucked in a low whistle before she put on her robe and slipped out of the room.

A half hour later they sat in the only café in Tawnee Valley, where they served cholesterol with an extra helping of cholesterol and a side of burned caffeine. A few older farmers sat at the counter nursing their coffees. Brady was getting better at recognizing people. Bob Spanner had sold Dad a few head of cattle. Russ Andrews helped Sam with the crops in the west field. Guy Wilson's property abutted the Ward farm on the north side. Brady had run into probably half the town in his week here. Nothing changed in Tawnee Valley. It was comforting and exasperating.

He needed to put a spare set of clothes at Maggie's. Maybe he should bring his whole bag and spend the rest of this little vacation from reality with her.

He gave Maggie a smile that made her blush. Nothing could touch him this morning. Not even the email from Jules saying the project was going poorly in New York. He hadn't even felt compelled to answer right away. It could wait until this afternoon.

"Morning, Maggie and Brady." Their waitress was Rachel Thompson, who used to babysit Brady and Luke. "What can I get for you?"

"Two specials." Maggie handed the menu back. "Over easy with bacon."

"All righty. I'll have those up for you in two shakes." Rachel winked at Brady before sauntering off toward the kitchen.

"About New York…" Maggie didn't meet his eyes.

"Like I said, up to you if we sleep in the same room or not. You don't like the apartment? We can get a different one.

There's a few schools we'll need to contact to see if we can get Amber in on such short notice. I can have my assistant put together everything we need."

"Hey, Maggie." Brady recognized Josh's voice behind him. "We don't see you here often."

Brady stood and held out his hand to Josh. "Josh. Been meaning to call you."

Josh took Brady's hand, but stopped shaking it. His gaze darted to Maggie, then back to Brady. His light mood darkened. "*You're* the deadbeat?"

"Josh. This isn't the time." Maggie's tone was level and meant to cool things down.

"*Deadbeat?*" Brady repeated. He released Josh's hand. For some reason the connections weren't coming together for him. He and Josh had had a great conversation the other day. He'd even seemed pleased to see him for a minute. What was different now?

Maggie's eyes were huge, but she had that under-control look she had when taking care of a problem. Was there something going on between her and Josh?

"I always figured it was Luke." Josh glared over Brady's shoulder, obviously speaking to Maggie and not Brady.

Brady didn't like his tone. The other diners had stopped talking to see what was happening. What was Josh accusing Luke of?

"Not here, Josh," Maggie said through her teeth.

"Why the hell not, Maggie?" Redness seeped into Josh's face. "Oh, I even thought it was Sam for a while. But Brady?"

"It's none of your business, Josh." Maggie stood and moved to Brady's side.

"I'm missing something here," Brady said. Maggie's angry eyes locked with Josh's. He was keenly aware of the other diners and unlike in New York when they had been curious strangers, these people knew him, knew his parents, knew his brothers. "What do my brothers have to do with Maggie?"

Ignoring Brady, Maggie and Josh continued to have their silent battle, but it didn't seem to be getting them anywhere. The only thing he and his brothers had in common was looks. Like a spark igniting tinder, Brady's brain made the connection. This had to be about Amber.

"Why don't we calm down, have a seat and discuss this like rational people?" Brady gestured toward their booth. This wasn't an issue for the other diners.

"Seriously, Maggie?" Josh finally gave Maggie a disappointed look before turning his anger on Brady. "Do you know what kind of hell you put her through?"

"Josh, no." Maggie stepped forward, but Josh held out his hand.

"Do you?" Josh asked again.

"I have some idea." Brady straightened, ready for whatever came next. He'd already made amends with Maggie over the past. "I didn't know about Amber."

"Didn't know?" Josh turned to the people at the counter. "He didn't know, and that makes it okay."

"Josh Michaels, you cool it right now." Rachel came from inside the kitchen to stand next to Maggie.

"How can you all just sit there and watch? Eight years this woman went through hell. We were all here. We all saw. Grace Brown had been a loving, thoughtful woman. She'd loved that little girl with all her heart." He spun to Brady and shoved Brady's shoulders, but Brady absorbed the impact.

"All it would have taken was one phone call. One visit. And you would have known, but you were too busy in London to think about the girl you impregnated. And how devastated she was when her mother died."

"Maggie says it's none of your business." Had Brady been

so self-centered? So focused on forgetting that he hadn't had the decency to at least check on the people he'd left behind?

"I would have married her, if she would have had me," Josh spat out. "Because that's the right thing to do."

Maggie gasped.

What could Brady say? He hadn't been aware? All he could do was stand here and take it. Josh wasn't going to be done until he'd had his say. The tips of Brady's ears burned as every eye in the diner turned on him. What did they expect of him? What they always expected from him?

To be the better man. To be their champion. But in this case, he wasn't.

"I wouldn't have sent her 'hush' money." Josh looked down his nose at Brady.

The diner went silent as if everyone held their breath to see what Brady would say.

"Brady?" Maggie touched his arm. "Let's go."

"That's right, Maggie." Josh stepped away with his arms wide, inviting Brady to hit him. "Protect the man who did you wrong."

"Please, Brady," Maggie said.

Brady had never been the type to fight. He'd always solved his battles through negotiation. Luke had been the passionate one who had been in more fights than Sam and Brady combined. But in this case, Brady had no standing. He deserved whatever this man flung at him.

Brady took his gaze from Josh and searched Maggie's eyes. What had he done? What had he forced her to live through alone?

"Let's just go." Maggie tugged on his arm. "I'm sorry, Rachel."

"Men." Rachel seemed to think that was the most reasonable explanation.

Brady let Maggie lead him out. The stares of the people

who had once deemed him the golden boy of Tawnee Valley burned through him. He wasn't even worth their regard now. He'd used Maggie for one night of passion a long time ago and had never once thought about the possible consequences. He'd barely thought of her at all throughout the years.

When they were seated in the car, he said, "I'm sorry, Maggie."

It would never make things right. It wouldn't change the past eight years. But he had to try. He had to fix this.

"It's not all your fault." Maggie didn't meet his gaze.

"I never even checked to make sure you were okay. For all I knew you could have been killed driving home from our house at four in the morning." Those looks. Brady would never get them out of his head. Disappointment, disapproval.

"I could have tried harder to reach you. I knew you and Sam didn't get along." Maggie's voice was soft. When he turned to her, she was gazing out the window away from the diner.

She could have married Josh. Amber would have had a dad and maybe even some brothers and sisters. But she hadn't. She'd chosen to stand on her own.

"I admire you." The words came out softly, almost unintentionally.

Finally, her hazel eyes met his. Her smile was wistful as she took his hand. "Let's go get Amber, okay?"

It didn't matter what the town thought of him and Maggie. It mattered that she was with him now.

Chapter Twenty

The drive to the farm didn't dispel Brady's sour thoughts. With every mile, one fact burned in his mind. If Sam hadn't been such a control freak, Brady would have known about Amber from the beginning. Whether he would have returned or not would have been on Brady. He could have been the *deadbeat,* but they would never know.

When he parked near the house, the anger Brady had been repressing for years churned within his gut. Maggie had been silent the whole car ride.

"Why don't you go in and get Amber. I need to talk to Sam." Brady didn't wait for Maggie's reply before heading to the barn where music played.

He pushed open the barn door and stopped. Amber was in the process of painting a wooden chair while Sam tinkered with his tractor.

"Morning, Daddy." She smiled at him from her task.

"Morning. Why don't you run in and get cleaned up?" Brady waited while she rushed to the house.

Sam wiped his hands on a greasy rag. "That kid can sure pack away the food. I think she ate more than me."

The whole world was off-kilter this morning. First the diner and now Sam acting as if Amber had always been a part of their family. "Don't act like you like having my kid around."

"Why not? She's a good kid." Sam looked over the tools on the workbench.

"If you thought she was such a good kid, why wait eight years to tell me about her? All you had to do was tell Luke, if you were worried about being the first to cave."

"Is that what you think happened?" Sam was a little too cool for Brady's taste.

"Just another way for you to control everything on this farm." Brady paced the barn door opening. "You interfered with my life. With Maggie's and Amber's lives. Why don't you tell me what happened?"

Sam set down the tools as if he didn't trust having them in his hand before he faced Brady. "I was protecting you."

"By keeping Amber a secret? How the hell was that protecting me?" Brady could feel the burn on the back of his neck as anger pulsed through him.

"What would you have done if you'd known?"

"I sure as hell wouldn't have expected Maggie to take care of everything. I would have done something." Brady felt flustered. He had no idea what he would have done.

"For God's sake, Brady, Mom raised you better than that."

"Where do you get off—"

"Do you think my life has been all that great? Do you think I wouldn't have given anything to be able to get away for at least a while?"

Brady hadn't given it much thought. It had always been Sam who would take over the farm.

"I did everything in my power to make sure you and Luke were able to live the lives you wanted. Did I make some crappy decisions along the way? Hell, yeah. What do you want? I was only twenty years old with the responsibility of two younger brothers and a farm to deal with. I was happy Luke graduated at all."

"You didn't have to—"

"Didn't I? Think, Brady. Who did Mom turn to when Dad died? She asked me to stay and I did. I don't regret the decision, but sometimes I hate it. I hate the farm and I hate our parents for leaving me with everything."

"I tried to help."

"Your ambition has always outstripped this town. Did I want to see you get stuck here in a marriage you felt obligated to offer? Watch you turn bitter and disillusioned about life?"

"It was my life. My choice. You could have trusted me to make the right one." Brady's chest hurt as if Sam had punched him. "And even if I had been impulsive at twenty, why wait eight years before letting anyone know?"

Sam's lips tightened and his brow furrowed. He turned to the tractor without another sound.

His silence was the only proof Brady needed. As much as Sam had claimed he needed Brady, he hadn't wanted him around.

"Dammit, Sam. Not this time. You don't get to turn your back on me and act like a freaking martyr. If you aren't going to say anything, you might as well listen."

Brady took a deep breath to clear his mind. "Eight years. You could have told me anytime in eight years. You could have waited until I was older and time had healed whatever wounds I had, but you didn't. You owe an explanation to me."

"A month ago, I had to get a chest X-ray for insurance. My heart is enlarged, but since I don't have any other symptoms, I'm monitoring my blood pressure and going to the cardiologist in a month."

It felt as if the floor fell out beneath Brady's feet. "You're sick? Have you told Luke?"

"What? So he can stare at me like you are?" Sam moved around to the other side of the tractor, obscuring his face from Brady's view. "I'm fine. I feel fine. I thought you should know about your daughter since you came back to the States. In case something happened to me." Sam the martyr. Brady hated this side of Sam.

"We can't fix the past, Sam. What's done is done. I'm sorry I wasn't around to help more. I'm sorry that I left you to raise Luke on your own. I'm sorry you had to take on everything. I'm sorry about your heart."

"That's an awful lot of sorry," Sam grumbled.

Brady sighed. Sam wouldn't even lift his gaze.

"I know you won't say you're sorry for what you've done." Brady let the anger slip away. "But I forgive you."

"I painted a whole chair by myself," Amber proclaimed in the car.

Brady had been stiff and silent since the conversation with Josh at the diner. Maggie wondered if she should talk about New York. Last night had been wonderful, but it wouldn't work long-term. If she kept sleeping with him, she would fall deeper in love with him.

"Sam wouldn't let the dogs sleep with me last night, even after I threatened to sleep outside." Amber gave her prettiest fake pout.

"Dog kisses, yuck." Maggie made a face for Amber.

"When I'm older, I want to have ten dogs."

The car slowed to a stop at her house. Maggie dared a glance at Brady's profile. He seemed to be processing something.

"Here's my key. Amber, go inside and get ready for lunch."

Amber wrapped her arms around Brady's shoulders from behind. "Are you staying for lunch, Daddy?"

"Maybe, but I might have to go." He touched her arm with his hand. "We'll do something fun this week together. I promise."

"'Kay." Amber bounced out of the car. Within seconds, she disappeared into the house.

"You know what I can't get out of my mind?" Brady stared straight forward through the windshield and into the distance.

"No, I don't." But she wanted to know.

"How much better my life would have been if you and Amber had been in it all along."

Not exactly what she thought he would say. She couldn't keep it inside anymore. "We can't move to New York."

That got his attention. She wanted to clap her hands over her mouth and take it back.

"It's scary, Maggie, but we can make this work."

She took a deep breath. "I'm sure your life is great in New York. You don't know how flattered I am that you want me and Amber to be part of that, but..." She wished she hadn't put that disappointment in his eyes.

"We can take it slow. It doesn't have to happen right away." He traced the line of her cheekbone with the back of his fingers. "Think about it?"

"It's not going to happen, Brady," Maggie said firmly. "Our lives are here. New York isn't the best thing for Amber and me. I know how attached you've become to Amber. We'll visit and our door is open anytime you want to come down."

"Marry me."

"What?" She leaned against the car door.

"We have a wonderful daughter. We're obviously compatible in bed. It would guarantee that I wouldn't just leave you in New York alone. If that's what it takes to have you with me, that's what I'm willing to do."

Her heart stopped pounding for a moment. Had he just rationalized a marriage proposal? When she'd found out she was pregnant, she'd hoped for this. For him to offer to take care of her forever, but when he didn't show up, she'd had to become stronger and start taking care of everything herself. No one was going to sweep in and do everything for her.

"If you'd known about Amber, you would have proposed to me because it was the so-called right thing to do. But you didn't love me then, any more than you love me now. I would have said yes because I was scared out of my mind to be alone."

"It doesn't have to be about love. It makes sense for us to be together for Amber."

"Don't you see, Brady? I'm not scared anymore." She rolled her shoulders back and opened the door. "I've raised Amber on my own. I don't want 'good enough.'"

He opened his mouth.

Maggie smiled even as her eyes filled with tears. "I love you, Brady Ward. But I don't think you could ever love me the way I deserve to be loved."

Before he could change her mind, she slipped from the car and hurried into the house.

"Peterson has a meeting with Kyle on Wednesday. He wants to put an ax in our project."

Brady looked up at the sky, wondering why he'd suddenly become some butt of a cosmic joke. Everything seemed to be going wrong. The report on his computer screen claimed the project was aiming to go over budget in thirty days. That couldn't be correct. Brady had been diligent in making sure the budget was spot-on.

"Have you talked with Kyle?" Brady rubbed his hand over his hair and looked out over the farm from the top of the hill.

"I'm going to go in tomorrow morning, but your files have

disappeared from the server." Jules sounded as upset as he felt. "This project is going to die before it got started."

Which wouldn't look good for either of them since a significant amount of money had been spent up front. Brady had lost his brother and possibly Maggie and Amber. He couldn't lose his job, as well. What more could he do here? At least if he went to New York, he could fix the project. After all, it seemed as if work was the only thing he was good at.

"Schedule with Kyle for tomorrow morning. I'll call my assistant and book on the next plane out."

"Brady, you don't have to do that. Email me the files. I'll try to reconstruct what you did. You have your family to worry about."

Sam walked from the house to the barn. A small figure on the gravel drive below. Sam had almost sacrificed the farm to keep giving money to Maggie for Amber from what Brady sent home. Sam had given up his dreams so Brady and Luke could have a chance at theirs. He'd gone about it the wrong way, but he'd been as young and impulsive as they had been.

For once, Brady wanted to make Sam proud, to honor that sacrifice. This was what Brady was good at.

"I'll see you tomorrow morning, Jules." Brady hung up the phone. He double-checked to make sure the files weren't on the company server before logging out. A quick phone call and he was on the next flight headed to New York. He would save this project and he'd go on with life as it always had been. Maybe Maggie would come to her senses after a while.

But first, he had to say goodbye.

After several moments of searching through the winding rooms of the barn, he found Sam in the back garage. A stripped-down version of a '69 GTO sat on wheel ramps.

"Is this your old car from high school?" Brady strode forward to touch the silver hood. "I remember when you and Dad worked on it that summer."

"I remember you kept trying to help and how I wished you would just go away," Sam said from under the car.

"I felt the same way." Brady smiled at the memory. Each of them vied for their dad's attention but Sam had always won.

"I tried to go away."

"I'd almost forgotten about when you went to college." Brady leaned against the workbench in a space that looked a little less dirty. "You went to Iowa State. Mom and Dad were so proud. You'd only been there a week when Dad had his heart attack."

Sam rolled out from under the car and sat on the creeper. "I got home in time to say goodbye. Dad told me that you were all my responsibility now."

"You never told me that." Brady lifted a hammer that had been around the farm longer than he had.

"You didn't need to know." Sam rested his arms on his knees.

Brady let his gaze roam over the old car that he used to want so badly. He'd begged Sam to let him ride in it. Eventually, Sam had caved and took him around the back roads. It had been like flying. "I have to go back to New York. A situation has come up at work."

"You don't owe me any explanation." Sam's voice was gruff.

"Actually, I owe you an apology. I ran out on you and Luke, and when you didn't try to reach out, I thought you were telling me to stay away. I didn't mean for things to end up like this. I should have been here with you."

Sam stood. "I wished I could trade places with you. That you would be the one stuck on the farm with no escape, while I was the one living the good life somewhere far away.

"There's no need to apologize, Brady. I wanted you here, but I wanted you to have a better life outside of Tawnee Valley. To make something out of yourself and make our parents proud."

"They'd be proud of you, Sam." Brady took in a deep breath inhaling the smell of old oil and grease and that slight hint of dirt. Things that would always make him think of his dad and Sam. "Why didn't you tell me about all this?"

"Because you were angry and hurt when you left. Because I was angry and hurt that you were leaving. I didn't know how to make it okay after everything that had been said. You were better off without me."

"I've never been better off without you, Sam. If anything, I should have let you know that. I want to work on this. I want to be part of this family again. I want what Mom would have wanted, us three brothers together." He held out his hand to Sam. "Do you think that's possible?"

"I hope so." Sam took his hand and jerked him into a quick one-armed hug.

"I'll try to come back soon." This time Brady meant it. He would schedule it months in advance if he had to, but he would make sure that he had time to visit Tawnee Valley. He had one last stop before leaving town. One last chance to convince Maggie to come with him.

Chapter Twenty-One

Brady knocked on Maggie's door. He wanted to talk to Maggie alone.

The door opened and there she was. His mood lightened at the sight of her.

"Amber's not due home for another thirty minutes from Penny's." Maggie had that stubborn tilt to her jaw, but now it made him want to smile. "If you are here for the internet—"

He stepped closer and kissed her. Her hands went to his shoulders as if she was going to push him away, but instead he felt her fingers grip tight to his shirt. He could spend days kissing Maggie and never get his fill. Thirty minutes suddenly didn't seem like enough time.

Gently he guided her into the house with his body, because he was damned if he was going to stop kissing her if this was all he was going to get for a while. He closed the door with a kick. Like a starved man presented with food, he couldn't help himself when it came to Maggie. She filled a need he hadn't realized he had.

Her tongue lightly stroked his. Heat surged in his system. No other woman had this effect on him. Scary as it was, he didn't want to leave her behind. If that took marrying her, he would do it. Whatever she needed to feel comfortable.

He lifted his lips from hers and touched her forehead with his. Their heavy breaths mingled in the small entryway. She clung to his shirt. He held her like a desperate man, hoping to never let go.

"Reconsider, Maggie." He wanted to beg, to grovel, to worship her until she couldn't think straight.

Her hazel eyes met his. The green sparkled in the light while the brown around her pupils pulled him into their depths. A touch of wistfulness filled her eyes. Her smile tugged at the little piece of hope he had left.

"You are persistent."

"When I want something? Yes." He didn't step back. Wanted her to remember what it felt like to be with him. She said she loved him, but he was reluctant to use that as a bargaining chip.

"Why don't we go inside and talk this through? We should be able to find a manageable solution." Maggie pressed lightly against his shoulders.

He released her for the moment. *"Manageable solution?"*

She shrugged and took a seat at the dining room table, patting the chair next to her.

Time was against him in this negotiation. Maybe he should pull out all his big cards right away. He took the seat.

"I know you want us to move with you to New York." She held up her hand to stop him from talking. "This town is the only home Amber and I have ever known. You aren't asking us to move across the town but to another dimension."

He raised his eyebrow. *"Dimension?"*

"I've been there. I've seen all those people so driven to get to the next spot that they are as likely to mow you down as go around you. That style might suit you, Brady. But it's not who Amber and I are." She folded her hands together on the table. "It's not who I want Amber to become."

"You would get used to it. We would be together. Isn't that what family is about?" A low blow, but time was running short.

"Family is about finding what is best for everyone," Maggie said softly.

"My being employed—isn't that what's best?" Brady stood. Energy bounced through his body, making it impossible to sit still. He paced the carpeted floor. "What I do for a living isn't something I can do anywhere. I have to be in New York to be effective at my job. We don't have to live in Manhattan. We could move to a suburb."

"It's not just the city. You are asking us to give up what we have here. You aren't the only one who works. The furniture store lets me work flexible hours with Amber's schedule. I have friends who love me. A community that looks out for us. You can't offer that to us." Maggie remained surprisingly calm.

Didn't she realize what this meant? Didn't she realize his plans now included her? What would make her change her mind? "Isn't that what family is for? Isn't that what love is about?"

Her expression clouded over as she stood. "You have no right to tell me about love."

"Show me. Teach me what I need to know." Brady didn't want to leave like this. He wanted her to come with him.

She shook her head and backed away. "I can't."

"Why not?"

"Because it isn't something you learn." She hugged herself and leaned against the wall. "I wish I could help you, but you have to find it on your own."

Brady moved in front of her and caressed her cheek. "Maggie, I have to leave. Today. I don't want to go until I have your promise that you will consider the possibility of moving. Of making our family whole."

"More promises?" Her eyes filled with tears. "What about your promise of time?"

"It's unavoidable. My career is hanging on this project. I have to fix it." Brady dropped his hand. A few days away from work and the whole project depended on one meeting. He couldn't lose everything. He had to keep his career.

"Your career." Her voice was flat, emotionless. But her eyes were a deeper shade of green than he'd ever seen them.

"What's that supposed to mean?" he said.

She shook her head. That hated pity came into her eyes. "When you figure it out, let me know."

The door opened behind them.

"Daddy!" Amber tackle-hugged him from behind. "I'm glad you're here."

Maggie slipped away from him, but he couldn't wash her image from his mind. Why couldn't she understand?

Amber let go and rummaged through her backpack. He had to resolve this thing with Maggie. Amber deserved to have a family.

"How was school?" he asked. Maggie had disappeared, maybe to give him time to say goodbye to Amber or maybe to clear the tears. Eventually, she'd give in and come to him. He needed to give her more time to adjust to the idea.

"It was awesome." Amber held out a piece of red paper. "We are having an art show this Thursday. Can we make this our special outing?"

Her eyes sparkled with hope and love. He loved Amber. It was natural. But he couldn't reconcile what he felt for Maggie. Right now, the fact that he had to cancel Amber and his outing ripped his heart in two.

"I'm sorry, Amber." He wished he didn't have to ever say those words to her again. "I have to go to New York today."

Her smile turned into a frown. "But you'll be back."

Needing to be eye to eye, he got on one knee in front of her. "It's not that simple. I need to go back to work, but as soon as I get time off, I'll be back."

She sniffled and her lower lip trembled. He felt like the world's biggest jerk.

"It's okay, Daddy." She put her arms around his neck. "I'll miss you."

That made him feel even lower, but he wrapped his arms around her tight. "I'll miss you, too."

She pulled away and smooshed his face in her hands. She placed a single kiss on his forehead. When she pulled away, he smiled at her.

"What was that for?"

"Nana says that when you love someone and they are going to leave you, you should kiss their forehead to seal you into their memory. Nana always kissed me right here before I went to sleep." She pointed to a spot on her forehead.

"Your nana was a wise woman. I bet you miss her."

Amber nodded. "But she's right up here whenever I miss her too much."

"Would it be okay if I kissed your forehead, too? That way you don't forget about your daddy?" Tears welled in the back of Brady's throat as she nodded yes and leaned her forehead forward.

He kissed her lightly next to the spot her nana always kissed her. "I'll get back as soon as I can. I promise."

"I'll wait for you." Amber grabbed her bag and ran into the kitchen.

Brady stood slowly. This house was home to two people he cared so much about. If only he could box it up and take it with him. Including the wobbly kitchen chair and the recliner it took a good shove to recline in. It was as unique as Maggie and Amber.

A movement by the kitchen doorway pulled his attention. Maggie stood there. Her blond hair in a ponytail. Her hazel eyes watchful. Her lips slightly curved in a sad smile.

He wanted to stay, but he had to go. Within two strides, he had her in his arms. Maybe he couldn't convince her to go with him this time, but he'd keep trying. He kissed her lightly on her mouth before touching his lips to her forehead.

"Don't forget me, Maggie."

Back in New York that night, Brady stood alone in his apartment. Since he was early, no flowers warmed every room. However, the guest bedroom had begun its transformation. A soft lavender covered the walls and the old furniture was gone. Painter drop cloths were placed on the floor to protect the wood.

It remained an empty shell. Brady sighed and went to his bedroom to unpack. Maggie's red silk scarf called to him. He dropped to the bed and pulled the silk into his hands. Though it seemed like the only living thing in the apartment, it wasn't truly alive. That spark had come from Maggie.

His phone rang, breaking the silence.

"I'll get the files from my backup drive," Brady told Jules.

"I could have handled the meeting on my own."

Maybe she could, maybe she couldn't, but the fact of the matter was Brady had returned for just this purpose. To save his career and the job that consumed all his time.

"What time?"

"Nine." Jules paused. "Are you okay, Brady?"

His sanitized white room stared back at him. The emptiness of his apartment mocked him. No Maggie. No Amber. Just him.

"Yeah. I'll be fine. See you then." He disconnected the

call. When he went to work in the morning, he'd fall into his routine and have barely any time to think about what he'd left behind in Tawnee Valley.

He downloaded the files from his home server for the meeting tomorrow. Reviewed his notes and what Jules had emailed him. Everything was ready for tomorrow's meeting.

His apartment was empty. His life was empty. As he looked around, he wished he were in Tawnee Valley. Even the prospect of fighting for his project didn't thrill him. He couldn't imagine being here without Maggie and Amber. In a little over a week, they'd come to mean everything to him. But all he had left was his career. Maggie had made it clear that she did not want to move to New York.

Unfortunately, he couldn't get Maggie out of his head as he lay in bed, trying for sleep. He'd offered marriage, but she'd turned him down. Because she loved him. His chest filled with warmth. He hadn't had time to process her words before. Maggie Brown loved him. The sacrifices she made for her mother had been out of love. The sacrifices Sam had made had been out of love. And he'd expected her to follow him, sacrifice the life she'd built for herself and their daughter, because he wanted her with him. While he sacrificed nothing.

Brady pulled the red silk scarf through his fingers. How much more should everyone else sacrifice for him?

By the time exhaustion claimed him, his alarm clock went off. Even as tired as he was, Brady almost wished he had chores to do. Feeding the animals usually helped clear his head.

Instead, he rode the subway to his office and grabbed a coffee from the shop in the lobby. He needed a few days to settle back into his normal routine. Everything would return to normal.

Paperwork had piled up on his desk from last week. When

his meeting alert went off, Brady was feeling mostly human. The coffee and the monotony of paperwork had helped.

Jules came around the corner as he left his office. Her dark green suit was the top-of-the-line businesswear, but it didn't do anything for him. All he could think of were Maggie's bare feet on the runner board of her bed.

"I'm glad I caught up with you before the meeting," Jules said as they walked together toward Kyle's office.

"I've recovered all the files. We should be able to reassure Kyle that the project isn't leaking funds." Brady kept pace, but couldn't help remembering the slower walks with Amber and Maggie. Crisp autumn air and light conversation. Amber's giggles ringing through the streets.

"I had a chance to look through the preliminary numbers for the Tawnee Valley project you sent me," Jules said. "I think you might have something there. With a few tweaks, I bet we can get Kyle on board with the project."

"That sounds good." Brady paused outside Kyle's door. He placed a hand on Jules's sleeve to stop her from going in. "Do you think it's possible to love someone and not know it?"

Her forehead wrinkled as her perfectly arched eyebrows pulled toward each other. "What do you mean?"

"Sorry. Just preoccupied." Brady stepped aside for Jules to lead the way into Kyle's office.

"Have a seat," Kyle said.

The last time Brady had been in here he'd been focused on finding a way to make the project work and finding time to meet his daughter. On the far wall were portraits Brady hadn't noticed before. They showed various poses and ages of Kyle with his wife and their two children. Staged photos meant to show a happy family.

Very few of the family photos in Maggie's house had been staged with studio lighting.

"How did your visit with your family go, Brady?" Kyle regarded him with a piercing gaze.

"It went well. Very well." Except for the part where Maggie didn't want to live with him.

"Good. Jules, you had some problems to discuss." Kyle leaned back in his chair.

"We were able to recover the files for the budget. I think you'll be pleased with the calculations we've done. We're scheduled to come in right on budget with the Detrex project." Jules was all business, from her hair to her outfit to the way she carried herself. She had been everything Brady had thought he wanted.

"Peterson called to try to reschedule his meeting for this morning. Do you know anything about this?" Kyle looked at Brady first, but Brady turned to Jules.

"Given that Mr. Peterson grabbed my ass yesterday and suggested that the project would be back on track if I went out with him, my guess is he wanted to turn himself in on sexual harassment charges." Her cool demeanor didn't change.

"Why didn't you tell me this happened?" Brady could have done something about it.

Jules turned her cool gaze to him. "I don't need a protector, Brady. I can handle myself fine."

She'd said that before, but all of Brady's life he'd been taught to protect women. Now it seemed as if none of the women in his life needed him. Not Jules. Not Maggie.

"Those are some strong accusations. We take sexual harassment seriously in this organization. Would you be willing to report this in an incident report?" Kyle kept his gaze on Jules.

"Of course."

"Do you mind if I call in Mr. Peterson?"

Jules crossed her arms. A smug little smile formed on her lips. "No, sir. I don't mind at all."

Within minutes, Peterson stood in the room as far away from Jules as possible. Both Brady and Kyle stared at the bruise on the man's cheekbone. Brady resisted the urge to smile.

"Suspension without pay pending litigation." Kyle didn't seem unhappy to watch security escort Peterson grumbling from his office. When the door closed, Kyle addressed Jules, "It doesn't have to go that far before we step in, Jules."

She nodded. All this time, Brady had thought he was protecting her, but she could handle it on her own. Just like Maggie. It wouldn't matter if Detrex succeeded because Maggie wouldn't be there. If he wanted his family, maybe it was time to stop asking them to sacrifice for him and instead make some sacrifices of his own.

"I want off the Detrex project."

Surprised, Jules and Kyle faced him.

"Jules doesn't need my help. She can handle the account and take the project where it needs to be."

Jules flushed, but didn't say anything. Kyle nodded his agreement, but Brady wasn't finished yet.

"I want to talk to you about another project, though. If you have time," Brady said.

"My ten o'clock just got escorted from the building. What were you thinking?"

Chapter Twenty-Two

"And Jessica said pineapples come from special pine trees." Amber walked backward to face Maggie. Obviously looking for confirmation.

"I'm pretty sure this time Jessica is wrong." Maggie made a circle motion with her finger to get Amber to face front and watch where she was going.

"Daddy called yesterday."

Maggie stumbled but caught herself. "Did he?"

"Yup."

It had been almost a week since he'd left. The only other time he'd called she'd been outside. Amber had been hanging up the phone as Maggie walked in. Maybe it was better this way. Cut off all contact with him.

"He misses us." Amber spun in a circle. They were walking home from her Girl Scout meeting.

"Does he?" Maggie highly doubted that. He was probably too wrapped in whatever his next project was to even make time to think about them.

"Yeah, and he hopes to see us real soon." Amber took off running for the house.

Maggie hoped that Brady meant it. Not for her sake but for Amber's. Amber would get her hopes up and when Brady failed to meet her expectations, it would be Maggie's responsibility to soothe the hurt. Maggie's own father had contacted her two times after he left. Both times he'd promised to stop by next time he was in town. She'd sat outside and waited until she fell asleep on the porch swing.

Amber shouldn't have to go through that.

Penny had convinced Sam to watch Amber Friday night. Penny was determined to take Maggie out drinking and to find someone to take the edge off, as Penny put it.

A small part of Maggie held out hope that Brady would come to his senses, but even if he did, she wasn't sure she could trust it. What would he be willing to say to be able to have Amber in New York? After all, he'd already proposed marriage.

"Mommy, hurry." Amber's voice sounded far away.

Maggie searched the sidewalk, but she was only a few houses away from their house. Amber must have run ahead and let herself in.

As Maggie reached their sidewalk, she happened to look on the porch. Sitting on the top step holding a bouquet of fresh-picked wildflowers was Brady Ward. She stopped as her breath caught and her heart skipped a beat.

In jeans and a gray T-shirt, he sat on her porch, looking at her. Her mind couldn't process anything.

When he walked her way, she noticed movement in the screen door behind him. Penny and Amber smiled before they ducked away.

"I picked these for you." Brady held out the bouquet. A jumbled mess of goldenrod, black-eyed Susans and a blue flower she couldn't remember the name of. They were the most beautiful flowers she'd ever received. She took the bouquet warily. If he started in on New York again... She had to stay strong.

"I realized something while I was away."

She wasn't sure she was strong enough to meet his gaze. This was the man she loved, but it didn't take a degree to realize he wasn't going to love her in return.

"What did you realize?" Maggie took a deep breath filled with the scent of wildflowers.

"I've been searching for something my whole life. In high school, I thought if I was number one all the time that I would feel like part of this town. When I went to England, I thought if I rose to the top of the corporate ladder, I would feel like part of the company. When I moved to New York, I thought maybe this time it would be different."

When he didn't continue, she finally lifted her gaze to his. Her heart beat out of control. This was the one man who could get under her skin and stay there even though he was hundreds of miles away. How many times could she tell him no? How many times would her heart break over Brady Ward?

"When you came to me in New York, I thought maybe this was it. All I had to do was be an awesome dad and I would fill this hole in me." He reached out and brushed a strand of hair from her face.

"Did it?" Maggie was terrified to hear his answer but if she was ever going to be free to find love, she had to.

"Maggie, I didn't need to leave this town to find what I needed most in life. I got a little screwed up along the way, but when you walked back into my life, you gave me clarity again. You gave me a daughter. You gave me your love. Without wanting anything in return."

She held her breath. But she did want something in return. She wanted his love more than she wanted her next breath.

"I suck at this without PowerPoint." He smiled as he closed the distance between them, without touching her.

"I can't." Tears welled in her eyes. "I can't move to New York. If I thought it was the best thing for Amber, I would do it in a heartbeat, but I would die every day, knowing you don't love me."

His thumb caught her tear. "See, I'm making a mess of this. Amber told me the other day about how much fun she had with her friends. How they'd spent the afternoon picking flowers. I can't imagine taking that away from her. Or from you."

Maggie drew in a breath of air, aware of the press of her chest against his. "Then why are you here?"

He took her hands. "Because this is where I belong, Maggie. You are where I belong. All this time I thought I needed to be number one, but the only one I need to be number one for is you, Maggie Brown."

"What?" Tears raced down her cheeks, even as her heart lifted in her chest.

"I thought that by you moving to New York I would have everything, but I would have fallen into the same patterns. Work too much and not stop to really listen to you and Amber. My whole world there centered on work and getting to the next level."

"What are you trying to say?"

"You sacrificed your college for your mother and Amber. Sam took care of Luke and almost sacrificed the farm to help you out. I've done nothing to prove to you that I love you and want to be with you." He took her hands in his.

Her heart raced. "How do you know you love me and not just the idea of a family?"

He smiled and pressed a quick kiss to her lips. "I've been a fool. Afraid to love, afraid to have a family need me. You are the one who soothed me when things felt out of control.

You are the one who gave me strength when I needed it. Before Amber was even in the picture, I needed you. Even before I knew the real Maggie Brown. Something about you has always drawn me.

"I love you with all my heart. I want us to be a family. I don't need New York as long as I have you and Amber. I want to show you how much I love you for the rest of my life. Right here in Tawnee Valley. My company is starting a new project and I've asked to take lead. We're building a factory here. If I have to stay at Sam's and come to your house every day to ask you if you'll marry me, I will."

Tears welled in her eyes and choked her throat. Never in her life had she imagined he would love her.

"I hope those are tears of happiness. I love you, Maggie Brown. I want to marry you. If I have to beg, I will." He started to drop to his knee, but she caught his elbow.

She drew in a deep breath and blinked rapidly to help the tears go away. "All I ever wanted was your love. If I thought you loved me, I would have moved to New York in a heartbeat."

"Now you don't have to." He kissed her. "Say you'll marry me, Maggie. That we'll live here in Tawnee Valley and grow old together."

Looking into his beautiful blue eyes, Maggie knew she was lost and found at the same time. "Yes, I'll marry you."

Her heart felt as if it was going to burst from happiness as he gathered her in his arms.

* * * * *

Mark's dilemma was as strong as ever.

There was something about Emily's spark, her spirit, that made him feel more alive than he had in months. But he couldn't ignore the other part, either—the part that wanted to protect his son's heart by keeping her at arm's length.

"Don't get close, don't get hurt," he mumbled under his breath.

It was a good motto. One that would keep him from ever seeing the kind of heart-wrenching hurt he'd been unable to erase from Seth's eyes during Sally's illness.

Emily.

Once again, the woman who'd captivated his son over a sand castle and a pepperoni pizza flashed before his eyes.

Emily was struggling on the first rung of a ladder he knew all too well. He saw it in her face when he talked to her about the foundation. He heard it in her voice when she brushed off his concern about the pain in her leg. And he sensed it in the unbendable determination that made her refuse help for even the simplest of things.

She needed a hand.

STORYBOOK DAD

BY
LAURA BRADFORD

MILLS & BOON

First published in Great Britain 2013
by Mills & Boon, an imprint of Harlequin (UK) Limited,
Eton House, 18-24 Paradise Road, Richmond, Surrey TW9 1SR

© Laura Bradford 2012

ISBN: 978 0 263 90636 3
ebook ISBN: 978 1 472 01228 9

23-0613

Harlequin (UK) policy is to use papers that are natural, renewable and recyclable products and made from wood grown in sustainable forests. The logging and manufacturing processes conform to the legal environmental regulations of the country of origin.

Printed and bound in Spain
by Blackprint CPI, Barcelona

Since the age of ten, **Laura Bradford** hasn't wanted to do anything other than write—news articles, feature stories, business copy and whatever else she could come up with to pay the bills. But they were always diversions from the one thing she wanted to write most—fiction.

Today, with an Agatha Award nomination under her belt, Laura is thrilled to have crossed into the romance genre with her all-time favorite series.

When she's not writing, Laura enjoys reading, hiking, traveling and all things chocolate. She lives in New York with her two daughters. To contact her, visit her website, www.laurabradford.com.

For Jenny,

You were, without a doubt, Mommy's biggest hero
during a very difficult time.
You are an amazingly special little girl
and I'm blessed to be able to call you my daughter.

Chapter One

Emily Todd stared down at the sparkly silver castle and the blue-eyed prince standing in front of its door, a familiar lump rising in her throat. Oh, what she wouldn't give to rewind time back to when planning life's path had been as easy as reaching for the next crayon in a brand-new sixty-four-count pack.

Back then, with the help of Giddy-Up Brown, she'd been able to ride the perfect horse through a canopy of Burnt Autumn leaves. A mixture of River Brown and Nautical Gray had captured the hue of an angry river with the indisputable eye of a future rafter, while Foliage Green had breathed life into the woods she'd navigated with a slightly oversized compass. And Rocky Ledge? The curious mixture of brown, blue and gray? That had made the mountain she'd squeezed onto its own piece of eighteen-by-twenty-four-inch manila paper seem both majestic and ominous at the same time.

It was hard not to look at the framed pictures on the wall behind her desk and not be impressed by the colors her pint-sized self had selected when mapping out her life in crayon. Though why she hadn't grown bored with the whole notion of drawing her dreams after the fourth picture was anyone's guess—even if Milk Chocolate Brown hair and Ocean Wave Blue eyes were still her ideal for the prince who'd never materialized.

Shaking her head, Emily slipped the decades-old castle drawing back into the folder and pushed it across the desk at her best friend. "Look, I know what you're trying to do here, Kate, but this doesn't mean anything to me anymore. It's a drawing. A silly, stupid drawing. I mean, really, what guy carries a woman across a threshold these days unless she's an invalid and can't make it through the door herself?"

She considered her own words, compared them to the nightmare that had driven her out of bed before dawn, the same one that had robbed her of sleep many times over the past few weeks. "Hmm. Now that I think about it, I should have spent my Saturday afternoons running a fortune-telling operation instead of all those lemonade stands we used to have as kids, huh? I think I actually had a visionary gift."

Ignoring the blatant sarcasm in Emily's voice, Kate Jennings pointed at the series of framed pictures behind Emily's head. "You framed *those* drawings, didn't you? So what's the difference?"

She glanced over her shoulder, mentally comparing herself to the girl in each of the four drawings. Her hair, while still the same natural blond it had always been, was now fashioned in a pixie cut in lieu of the long locks she'd preferred as a child. Her big brown eyes hadn't changed at all, really, only they didn't sparkle quite as much. And the faint smattering of freckles noticeably absent in the drawings was right where it had always been, sprinkled across the bridge of her nose like fairy dust. "I can think of one huge difference, Kate. The dreams depicted in the frames? Those actually came true. That one—" she pointed at the folder "—didn't."

Kate pushed the folder back toward Emily. "So what? You drew them all at the same time."

She felt the tension building in her shoulders and worked to keep it from her voice. "Do you think a doctor would frame a term paper she'd failed, and hang it in her office beside her medical school diploma? Do you think an architect would want to showcase her first ever set of plans—the ones where she forgot to add the foundation that would have actually kept the structure *standing?*" At Kate's scowl, Emily continued. "I think it's cool that you found these pictures after all this time, Kate, I really do. It's why I framed the four I did. But you can't expect me to be too eager to glorify an unrealized dream alongside ones that actually came true, can you?"

Without waiting for a response, Emily pushed back her desk chair and stood. "I've got to get back to work. I have an orienteering class starting in five minutes." She strode across the office, stopping at the door. "But I'll see you and Doug on Friday night at the barbecue, right?"

"Definitely." Kate grabbed the folder and her purse and met Emily at the door. "It's not supposed to be too hot that day, so you should be——"

"I'll be fine no matter what the temperature is," she snapped. Then, realizing how she sounded, she softened her tone. "This diagnosis is not going to beat me, Kate. You of all people should know that. I've done everything I said I was going to do and then some."

"If that were true, this picture——" Kate waved the folder in the air "——would be in a frame like all the others."

"Would you give it a rest, please? I'm not going to hang my failures on the wall. Seems kind of morbid to me."

"I get that," Kate said, tucking the folder under her arm. "But the horseback riding, the kayaking—all of it—came true because you set your mind to it and you made it happen. I mean, c'mon, Emily, how many people do we know from our childhood who have started their own company? How many people do we know that have taken said company and made it the talk of, not only this town, but every other town in a hundred-mile radius? None that I can think of. And why is that? Because you made up your mind about what you wanted in life a very long time ago. So why should finding Mr. Wonderful be any different now?"

"Because *I'm* different now," she whispered.

Kate reached out and brushed a wisp of hair from her friend's face. "Did you ever consider the possibility that all this other stuff came true first because you were *able* to do it at that time?"

Emily closed her eyes, the familiar pull of fear that had accompanied the doctor's diagnosis threatening to envelop her all over again.

No. She refused to go there again. Not now, anyway. Not when she had a class to teach.

Opening her eyes, she gave Kate a hug and then shoved her through the door, her voice settling somewhere between frustration and determination. "I was and *am* able to do it, Kate. Nothing is going to change that. You just wait and see."

"But if you'd just slow down long enough to meet someone, you might—"

"Please. I've got to go. I'll see you Friday evening."

Without waiting for a response, Emily made her way toward the classroom at the end of the hall. Her friend was wrong. Scenes in the pictures on the wall had come true because they were up to *Emily*. The Prince Charming picture she'd sent back home with Kate was nothing but a childhood fantasy born at a time when she'd been blissfully naive about words like *disability* and *burden*.

She was wiser now.

Squaring her shoulders, she yanked open the door and walked into the room to find five pairs of eyes greeting her arrival with the same determination that had driven her throughout her life. It was a determination she admired and understood. "Welcome to Bucket List 101. My name is Emily Todd, and I'm here to help you realize your dream of learning how to orienteer your way through the woods with nothing more than a compass and some coordinates. As you probably know from the course description that lured you here, we'll spend our first hour in the classroom learning about the compass and how to use it, along with our maps. Then we'll head out into the woods for some fun."

The left side of the conference table held a trio of retired men who were hanging on every word she spoke. To the right sat the mother-daughter team who'd called the day before looking for some memorable bonding time. "It looks like we've got a good group here," Emily said.

"I hope my presence won't change that."

Spinning around, Emily took in the sight of the man standing in the doorway, registration papers in hand, and froze, her heart thudding in her chest.

"My name's Mark Reynolds. Your assistant at the front desk said I could still get in your class if I hurried."

She knew she should say something. But for a moment she was at a complete loss for words.

Mark Reynolds was like no man she'd ever laid eyes on—at least not outside the confines of her imagination. Even then, the flesh-and-blood version was much taller than she'd always envisioned. Either way though, his hair was the epitome of Milk Chocolate Brown and his eyes a perfect match for Ocean Wave Blue....

But it was his arms—the kind capable of sweeping a woman off her feet and carrying her across the threshold of a make-believe castle—that yanked Emily back to a reality that no longer had room for such silly dreams.

Mark looked down at his registration papers and then back at Emily. "So...am I too late?"

Slowly she expelled the breath she hadn't realized she'd been holding. "It's never too late, Mr. Reynolds. Not for *learning,* anyway."

HE HUNG BACK as they neared the parking lot, his thoughts as much on Emily Todd as anything he'd learned that morning. During the first hour of class, before they'd ventured outside, they'd sat around a table, and Emily had taught them how to use a compass to find a set of coordinates. He'd tried to listen politely to the questions his classmates asked, and had worked hard to focus on the answers, but in the end, all he knew for sure was the fact that his teacher was gorgeous.

Emily Todd was straight out of the pages of one of his son's favorite fairy tales, right down to the wispy blond hair, slightly upturned nose and big brown doe eyes. But unlike those winged characters that flew around in the dark, sprinkling pixie dust in the air, this woman's feet were firmly on the ground, and she carried herself with a confidence that was anything but childlike.

He admired the determination that had driven her to start a company like Bucket List 101. It took guts and— judging by the list of outdoor activities the company offered—she had to be in great physical shape. Her toned legs and taut body attested to that.

"Did you enjoy yourself, Mr. Reynolds?"

Mark shifted his attention from Emily to her teenage assistant. "I had a great time, Trish. Spending the last two hours in the woods was really cool."

"It's one of my favorite classes, too." Trish swept her clipboard toward Emily, who was disappearing into the woods with a drawstring bag. "Every time I think Emily has come up with the coolest class ever, she trumps it with another one the next time around. Come January, she'll be offering this same class, but on skis."

"Skis?"

"Sounds awesome, doesn't it?" Without waiting for his answer, Trish headed across the parking lot, glancing back over her shoulder in his direction. "If you're interested, I'll be in the office tomorrow morning. We can get you signed up before the fall and winter program guide even goes out in the mail."

"Thanks, Trish. Sounds like fun." And it did.

Especially since it meant spending more time with Emily Todd...

"Don't you think you should give that back to Emily before you get in your car and drive home?"

Mark pulled his gaze from Emily's receding back and fixed it instead on one of the retired guys, who'd kept the class in stitches with his nonstop jokes throughout the three-hour course. "Huh?"

The man pointed at Mark's left hand. "You still have your compass. You were supposed to set it on the porch railing when we came out of the woods."

"Whoops. You're right. I'd guess I better catch up with Trish and turn this in before Emily thinks I made off with her equipment."

"If I were you, young man, I'd bypass Trish and take it straight to Emily. Gives you an excuse to look at her for another few minutes."

Raking his hand through his hair, Mark released an audible breath. "No, man, it's not like that. Really. I've got a kid at home and I'm not in any place to be—"

"She's a cute little thing. Spunky, too." The man took a few steps and then paused. "And she don't have no wedding ring on her finger, either."

Mark looked down at the hand that gripped the compass, a familiar lump building in his throat at the sight of the half-inch band of skin that no longer stood out the way it once had when his ring was off. What on earth was he doing? He'd taken this class as a release, not to pick up chicks. It was way too soon. Seth needed his complete focus. *He* needed his complete focus....

Mark started back across the grass and along the path where Emily had just disappeared. Step by step, he ventured farther into the woods, and found the excitement he'd felt during the hands-on portion of the class resurfacing in spades.

It was as if the sunlight that randomly poked through the heavy leaves, warming him from the outside in, had somehow managed to rekindle a part of his spirit that had disappeared along with any respect he'd once had for himself prior to Sally's death.

Mark climbed onto a stump and looked from side to side, his heart rate picking up at the sight of Emily heading back toward him, the bag she'd been carrying into the woods now looped over her shoulder, a pad of paper and a pencil in her hand. "Emily? I saw you head back here. Everything okay?"

She stopped midstep and gave him a funny look. "Just jotting down a few new coordinates for next time. Did you forget something, Mr. Reynolds?"

"No, I…" He glanced down, saw the compass he held in a death grip. "Actually, yeah. I forgot to turn in my compass. By the time I realized it, Trish had already collected them and I didn't want to just leave it sitting around."

The smile he'd found so engaging all afternoon returned. "Kind of got used to holding it, huh? Well, don't worry about it. I've found myself driving home with a compass still in my hand after one of these kinds of outings, so you're in good company. Means it started to feel natural."

He tucked the compass into his pants pocket and swept his gaze across the woods, nodding. "I can't believe how good it felt to be out here…playing."

Her laughter echoed around them. "Welcome to my job. Where I get to play—and help others play—all day long."

"Sounds like heaven to me."

"Really? Because the last time *I* checked these woods were in the middle of Winoka, Wisconsin," she joked, before beckoning him to follow as she wound her way back through the trees. "If you don't mind me asking, what made you decide to take this class, Mr. Reynolds?"

He considered the best way to respond. If he shared too much, the lift in his heart from stepping out of his reality would be gone. If he didn't give her any kind of answer, he'd come across as rude. He opted for the safest reply he could find. "First of all, it's Mark. Mr. Reynolds makes me feel as if you're talking to someone much older than I want to be. And as to why I came today, I guess you could say I'm looking for something that'll help me unwind."

"Sounds like a good reason."

They emerged from the woods side by side, then cut across the clearing toward the old converted barn that served as the offices for Bucket List 101. When they reached the front door, Mark tried to think of something else to say, something to allow him even a few more minutes in her orbit, but he came up empty.

"Well, thanks for today. It was really great."

"I'm glad you enjoyed it, Mr. Reynolds."

"Mark," he reminded her gently. At her nod, he turned and headed toward his car, the sound of the door opening and shutting behind him making it both easier and harder to breathe. Never in his recent and not-so-recent memory could he recall a woman who affected him quite the way Emily did.

Except, of course, for Sally. And even then, it was for very different reasons....

When he got to his car he reached into his pocket for his keys and froze.

"Oh, no..." He wrapped his fingers around the circular object and pulled it out, denial quickly morphing into self-recrimination. "What an idiot I am!"

Shaking his head, he retraced his steps to the barn and went inside, his feet guided down the hall by the sound of music and a pinpoint of light streaming through the crack under a door.

He knocked and heard Emily say, "Come in."

Pushing the door open, Mark peeked inside, to find her hunched at a desk, poring over some sort of outdoor catalog. "I'm sorry to bother you, but I forgot to actually *give* you my compass after tracking you down in the woods. I'm a head case, I know."

Her laugh echoed off the walls and brought his body to attention. "Considering the fact that you showed it to me twenty minutes ago and I didn't take it, I think it's safe to say your state of mind isn't the only one in question at the moment. But no worries. I happen to believe momentary insanity is par for the course after running through the woods for two hours the way we did. It rattles brains, I think."

He took a few steps into her office and leaned against the wall, her sincerity and her genuineness speaking to him on some unexpected level. "Do you ever get tired, running around like that?"

The sparkle in her eyes dimmed. "No, never."

"Wow." Despite his best intentions, he found himself glancing around the room, looking for any excuse to stretch out their time together. It was as if by being there, talking to her, he could almost forget the unforgettable. He pointed at the illustrations on the wall behind her desk. "Looks like you've got a budding artist on your hands."

The sparkle returned. "Nope. Just a dreamer who happens to have a very sentimental friend."

"You lost me."

She grinned. "I drew those when I was ten. Kate, my sentimental friend, just uncovered them in her hope chest a few weeks ago, and felt the need to share them."

He took a step toward the pictures. "And this is you in all of these?"

"Minus the freckles, of course. I hated my freckles when I was ten."

"You shouldn't have." He pointed at the first drawing. "Trail riding?"

"That'll start back up in the spring."

Stepping to the right, he considered the second. "Nice rapids in this one."

Her laugh sent a skitter of awareness down his spine. "If I took my customers white-water rafting without helmets today, I'd lose my license."

"Artistic liberties, that's all." He matched her laugh and took in the third picture. "Something tells me I didn't look quite as confident in the woods just now with *my* compass."

"You did great." Emily swiveled her chair a hair-breadth to study him. "Everyone did."

Aware of her gaze, he pointed to the final picture. "I've always wanted to rock climb."

"Then why haven't you?"

He stared at the drawing, his lips forming the words he'd only recently come to acknowledge. "Procrastination, I guess. I figured there'd always be time. "

"And now?"

"I know better." He cleared his throat of its sudden gruffness and gestured toward the line of framed pictures. "Looks to me like the dreamer who drew these hit a grand slam."

Her silence made him turn just in time to see her open her eyes and force another smile to her lips. "Considering my sentimental friend uncovered a fifth, which I opted not to hang, I'll settle for a home run."

"Oh? What happened to *that* dream?"

She waved his question aside. "To borrow your words, Mr. Reynolds—I mean *Mark*—now I know better."

Momentarily unsure of what to say, he shoved his hands into his pockets and reclaimed his spot against the wall opposite her desk. "Well, four out of five is nothing to sneeze at. Hell, when I was ten, all I thought about was being a firefighter and trying to kiss the red-head who sat behind me in math."

"And how'd you do?"

"One for two."

She laughed. "You're a firefighter, then?"

"No. An accountant."

"So the redhead inspired your academic path?"

"She inspired me to quit putting off until tomorrow."

"Oh?" Emily's eyebrows rose. "Does she need a job? We could use a spokesperson."

"No. No, she doesn't need a job." With his good mood rapidly spiraling, Mark tipped his head forward and pushed himself from the wall. "I'd better get out of here. Lunch-making duties await." He took two steps toward the door and stopped, a flash of color out of the corner of his eye hijacking his attention to the floor. "Oh…hey, you dropped something."

Squatting down, he retrieved a tattered pamphlet from the carpet beside the trash can and turned it over in his hands, the headline, Multiple Sclerosis, catching him by surprise. "You know someone with MS?"

When she didn't answer, he reached into his back pocket and pulled out a business card. "I volunteer with an organization called Folks Helping Folks. We help people with disabilities by building wheelchair ramps, installing handrails in bathrooms, funding specially equipped automobiles, and that sort of thing. You know, whatever can make their day-to-day life a little easier."

Placing the card on top of the pamphlet, he held them out to Emily. When she didn't respond, he held them out farther. Again, she didn't take them, her hands remaining on top of her desk as if glued to its surface. And in that instant he understood why she sat there and said nothing, why she looked at the pamphlet and business card as if they were poison capable of seeping through her skin and into her soul.

He understood because he'd been where she was. He'd loved someone who was sick, too. He knew the fear. He knew the sense of denial that came on the heels of such a bitter experience. And he knew the gut-wrenching pain that came with pulling back.

Leaning across her desk, he set the paperwork in front of her, his heart aching for this beautiful woman who'd allowed him to shed his well-worn cloak of regret and live in the moment for three glorious hours. "I understand where you're at, Emily. I really do. But please, take this anyway. Pass it on to whoever it is you know that's sick. By denying what's going on, all you're doing is hurting yourself and your loved one. Trust me on this."

Then, without realizing what he was doing, he gave her shoulder a gentle squeeze, the warmth of her skin beneath his hand lingering in his thoughts long after Bucket List 101 had faded from his rearview mirror.

Chapter Two

Tossing her paddle to the shore, Emily maneuvered her way out of the kayak and tugged it onto the sand, the satisfying soreness in her upper arms a welcome relief. No matter how hard she'd tried to bury herself in work the rest of the day, the images spawned by Mark's words had risen to the surface again and again, gnawing at her convictions like a beaver hell-bent on toppling a tree. She'd resisted, of course, but the doubts had claimed a foothold, reappearing throughout the remainder of her workday.

When she'd been teaching her introduction to rock climbing course, she tried to imagine dangling over the side of a cliff in a wheelchair.

When she'd taken a call inquiring about an upcoming white-water rafting trip, she envisioned herself piercing the raft with the end of a cane.

And when she'd locked up her office for the evening and actually considered the notion of wallowing in pity from the confines of her bed, she knew she had to do something. Fast.

Now, two hours later, she felt like herself again. Ready to conquer anything and everything that crossed her path.

Raising her arms in the air, she stretched, the faintest hint of a smile tugging at her lips as she spotted the pint-size towhead feverishly digging in the sand some thirty feet from where she stood. Curious, she closed the gap between them to take a closer look at what the child was doing.

"That's a really nifty castle you're building," she said.

The little boy's hand stilled long enough for him to look up and smile, the deep, penetrating blue of his eyes bringing a momentary hitch to her breath. "Thanks, lady."

She forced her attention back to the castle. "I like all those turrets you built onto the corners."

His cheeks lifted farther as he dropped his shovel in favor of directing Emily's attention toward the tower on the back left corner of his creation. "See that one? That's the princess's room. She's real nice. And this one here—" he shifted his finger to the right "—that's where my room would be if I lived there, too."

Dropping onto the sand beside the boy, Emily retrieved a stick from the ground and secured a nearby leaf to the top. When she was done, she spun it between her fingers while he eyed her across the top of his sand pail. "When I was little, I used to dream about living in a castle, too," she told him. "Only instead of a princess, mine had a handsome prince who would sweep me off my feet every morning and carry me around the castle all day long."

At the child's giggle, she, too, cracked a smile. "That sounds funny," he said.

"Now it does, but when I was young, I thought it sounded romantic." Shaking her head free of the images that threatened to ruin the innocence of the moment, she poked her makeshift flag into the sand by her feet and scrunched up her face. "But don't worry, I don't intend to be carried around by anyone. Ever."

The little boy rocked back on his heels, then jutted his chin in the direction of her stick creation. "That sure would look nice on my castle, don't you think?"

She plucked it from the sand and handed it to him, the answering sparkle in his eyes warming her from head to toe. "But just because my dream was silly doesn't mean you can't share a castle with your princess one day. In fact, I hope you do. Dreams that come true are mighty special."

When he'd positioned the flag just the way he wanted it, the child nodded. "I found an old tree house in the woods behind Gam's house. I like to climb up the ladder all by myself and dream with my eyes open. That way they don't get scary like the ones in my bed."

She studied him for a moment, guessing him to be about four. Maybe just turned five. Either way, he was too young to be alone on the beach....

"What do you dream about in your tree house?" she asked, before squinting down the shoreline.

"Smiles. Lots and lots of smiles."

Startled, she brought her full attention back to the little boy. "Smiles?"

He nodded. "Happy ones. Like the ones me and Daddy used to smile before my mom got sick and went up to heaven."

Emily cast about for something to say, but he didn't give her much of a chance.

"I want us to make great big smiles like that again one day."

"That sounds like a special thing to dream about," she whispered.

"It is." Jumping to his feet, the child surveyed his castle, deeming it a success with a clap of his small hands. "Wow! This is my very bestest castle ever!"

She swung her focus out toward the water and noted the absence of any swimmers or fellow boaters in their immediate vicinity. "You seem awfully little to be out here by yourself."

"I'm not by myself. I'm with my dad." Shooting a pudgy index finger over Emily's shoulder, he pointed toward a man fishing from a line of rocks that led into the lake some twenty or so yards away. "See? He's right there. Fishing."

Shielding the last of the sun's rays from her eyes, she strained to make out the outline standing on the rocks—the tall stature, the broad shoulders, the gray T-shirt and black shorts, the brown hair...

No. It couldn't be.

She looked back at the boy. "That man over there is your dad?"

"Yupper doodle." He dropped to a squat and stuck his finger in the sand. Then, slowly but surely, he drew a snake that nearly reached her toes. "My daddy is so smart he taught me how to make my name. See?"

Stepping back, she looked again at the wiggly line and recognized it as an *S*. Three additional letters later, he was done. "Your name is Seth?"

"Yupper doodle." His broad smile reached his bright blue eyes.

His Ocean Wave Blue eyes...

She glanced from Seth to the man and back again, the confirmation she sought virtually certain. But still, she asked, "Do you know your last name, Seth?"

"Of course I do, silly. But I can't write that name yet. It's too big and kinda tricky. Especially the first letter." Seth cupped his left hand to the side of his mouth and tipped his head upward. "Gam says I just need to pretend the circle at the top changed its mind and is runnin' away from the line."

Squatting down beside the boy, she left a space between Seth's efforts and her own, talking him through the letter he'd just described. When she was done, she nudged her chin in its direction. "Is this the letter?"

"Yupper doodle." He leaped to his feet and came to stand on the opposite side of Emily. "*R* for R-R-R-Reynolds!"

MARK CRANKED THE REEL slowly, hoping the slight movement would be enough to capture the attention of even one member of the fish population that inhabited Lake Winoka. If it did, at least he'd have something else to think about besides Emily Todd.

From the moment he'd left Bucket List 101, his thoughts had continuously returned to the attractive woman, earning him more than a few curious looks from Seth throughout the afternoon. Mark understood the fear she felt, sympathized with her need to pretend her loved one wasn't ill. He'd been there and done that throughout the entire year leading up to Sally's death.

It had been a mistake. A mistake he'd undo in a heartbeat if given the chance.

But there would be no more chances. He couldn't rewind time no matter how much he wished he could. Instead, he had to find a way to live with the guilt of choosing his job over his dying wife over and over again. At the time it had made such sense. Work was how he coped. The more he worked, the less time he had to think, and to feel.

But it had been wrong. For Sally. For Seth. And for him.

No. Mark wasn't going to let Emily make the same mistakes. Somehow, some way, he was going to help her realize that by facing her loved one's illness head-on, she'd be saving herself the added torture of guilt at the end.

Determined to help, he reeled in the rest of his line and made his way across the rocks. Once he had Seth settled in bed for the night, he could go about putting together a packet of information for Emily. Maybe with more information, she wouldn't feel the need for denial.

And maybe, just maybe, helping Emily would enable him to shed some of his own insomnia-inducing guilt.

He stepped off the last rock and onto the sand and looked toward the castle he'd left Seth to finish while he fished. But instead of finding his son elbow-deep in sand, he spotted him standing beside a kayak and a petite blonde woman.

Mark quickened his pace, only to slow it again as the identity of the women became clear.

"Emily? Is that you?"

"Hi, Mark," she answered.

Eagerly, he jogged forward, fishing pole in hand. "Can I help you get in your kayak?"

A look of something resembling irritation flashed across her face. "If I can lift a kayak on and off my car, and carry it from the parking lot to the lake all by myself, I'm quite certain I can get into the water, too."

He drew back at the animosity in her voice. "Oh, okay. No sweat. We'll leave you to it, then." Cupping his son's shoulder, he tried to steer him in the direction of the parking lot, but Seth wiggled free and ran back toward Emily.

"Take me with you. Pretty, pretty please? I've never, ever, *ever* been in a boat like that before."

"Seth!" Mark stepped forward, waving his fishing pole. "You can't just invite yourself in someone's boat like that, little man. It's rude."

The boy's shoulders slumped. "I'm sorry," he murmured. "I didn't mean to be rude, Daddy. I really didn't."

Emily dropped to her knees in front of Seth, her black-and-gold bikini top and black spandex shorts evoking a rapid swallow or two on Mark's part. "Maybe your dad can take you out for a few minutes and let you see what a kayak is all about." Peeling her attention from his son long enough to make eye contact with Mark, Emily gestured toward the kayak with her chin. "I've already been out once this evening. Why don't you take him out for a little while?"

"I can't take your boat," Mark protested.

"Sure you can. Have you ever been in a kayak before?" she asked.

He willed himself to focus on her face, to refrain from looking back at her sweet curves, but it was hard. "Kayaks, no. Canoes, yes."

"Then a crash course is in order. Though, since I wasn't expecting this, I don't have a life jacket that'll fit Seth."

"That's okay." Seth raced toward a bag several feet from his castle and tore through its contents, returning with a pair of inflatable armbands. "See? I've got my Floaties!"

Emily made a face. "Not exactly the same thing, I'm afraid. But if you don't go out too far, they'll be okay this one time." Turning to Mark, she said, "And you? What kind of a swimmer are you?"

"Solid."

She considered his response, then gestured toward the boat. "When you sit in a kayak, you need to keep your legs together and your knees slightly bent. Keep your weight over the center line. Remember that and you won't flip."

She retrieved the paddle from the sand. "Now, for locomotion, you grip this with both hands, see?" Placing her hands slightly wider than shoulder width apart, she demonstrated the correct way to hold it and move it. "The blade of the paddle can also be used as a rudder, for steering, if there's somewhere in particular you're trying to go or trying to avoid."

Ten minutes later, Mark knew enough about the boat and the paddle that he was out in the lake with Seth as Emily watched from the shore. "Wow, Daddy! The next time I play castle with my blocks at Gam's house, I'm gonna give my prince and princess a boat just like this."

"You don't think they'd prefer a sailboat or maybe a regular rowboat?" he teased. "Kayaks are kind of narrow and might not fit your princess's dress too well."

"The princess will be fine. She has short dresses, too, you know."

"Oh, I didn't know that." Mark paddled about, glancing back at Emily more than he probably should.

"I like my new friend, Daddy. She's really nice. And she likes castles, too!"

He forced his focus back on his son, noting how the late-afternoon sun was haloing his head. "Oh? You made a new friend at preschool? What's her name?"

"Not at school. Here." The motion of Seth's body as he tried to turn and point toward the shore made the kayak rock. "Whoa! Did you feel that, Daddy?" he asked, wide-eyed.

"I did. And it's because you're moving around. Remember what Emily said about staying in the center?" Mark tilted his chin toward the shore, but knew it was futile, considering Seth was facing forward, his back to him. "So you were talking about Emily just now when you said you made a new friend?"

"She made a flag for my castle!"

Mark had to grin at the enthusiasm in his son's voice. "Wow, you're right. She *is* really nice, huh?"

Seth's head bobbed up and down. "How did you know her name, Daddy?"

Because once she told me, I couldn't get it out of my head....

Surprised by the thought, he willed himself to find a more appropriate answer, one that wouldn't get the kayak rocking again. "Remember how I went and played that big-boy game in the woods today? Well, Emily was the teacher."

What Seth said in response, Mark didn't catch, as the mere mention of the beauty on the beach had him glancing over his shoulder once again. She was sitting on the sand, watching their progress. When she spotted him looking, she flashed a thumbs-up.

"Daddy, Daddy, look! Look at that fish!"

At the sudden jerking movement, Mark swung his head back around, but it was too late. Before he was able to reprimand the boy for leaning too far to one side, they were in the water.

Emily jumped up and dived into the lake with record speed. "Are—are you okay?" she called as she stroked toward them.

"Yeah, we're good," Mark assured her, gripping Seth with one hand and the overturned kayak with the other. A moment later he had his son settled safely on his back. "And, oh…remember that tip about staying in the center of the boat? That was a good one," he sputtered through gulps of lake water. "M-maybe you could add a class on kayaking to your company's lineup."

Her laugh cut through the sound of his splashing and warmed him in ways he didn't expect in the chilly water. "I offer kayaking classes all the time, Mark."

Hooking a thumb over his shoulder, he gestured toward his son, who was pretending Mark was a white horse if the words making their way into his left ear were any indication. "We might want to put Seth in the front row of that particular class. So he'd be sure to catch all the helpful little tips you might decide to share."

"I'll keep that in mind," she joked as she stopped momentarily to tread water and take a breath. "How are you holding up?"

"We're fine. My ego, though, hasn't fared quite as well."

"Your secret is safe with me." Nibbling back the full effect of a smile she couldn't hide, Emily swam between Mark and the kayak, her bikini top clinging to her rounded breasts as she flipped the boat right side up. Then, with lithe grace, she hoisted herself into it before he could register much of anything besides how alluring her legs looked as they broke the surface of the water. "Now hand Seth up to me and we've got this."

Chapter Three

Emily could feel the weight of Mark's stare as she secured the kayak to the roof of her Jeep, his still-labored breath matching her own. She'd felt it as she'd paddled through the water with Seth safely seated between her legs. She'd felt it as Mark had pulled them onto the beach and plucked his son from the boat for a firm yet loving lecture. She'd felt it as they'd stood dripping on the sand, trying to catch their breath. And she'd felt it as she led the way to the car after he insisted on carrying the kayak.

In fact, the only time she wasn't aware of him watching was when she was stealing glances in his direction. But she couldn't help it. Mark Reynolds was easy on the eyes.

"Thanks for making that unexpected swim to help us out. It was above and beyond," he finally said as she hooked the last clip into place. "One minute he was pointing at a fish and the next...well, you know what happened."

She couldn't help it; she laughed. It was either that

or get caught enjoying his dripping, shirtless chest even more than she already was. "Kayaks tend to flip a little easier than canoes. It's why people who are skittish around water tend to shy away from them in favor of a bit more stability."

"Yeah, I get that now." He bent to Seth's level, buying her time to catch her breath. "How about you, little man? You doing okay?"

The boy jumped from foot to foot, the adventure of the past twenty plus minutes further fueling his natural energy. "I had my Floaties on, remember, Daddy?"

She felt Mark's appreciative glance. "And we have Emily to thank for that, don't we?" he continued, his attention trained once again on his son's face. "Did you learn something from that adventure?"

"The lake isn't as warm as the bathtub."

"And…"

Seth's brows furrowed in contemplation. "You should always wear your Floaties?"

"And…"

"Emily is a really good swimmer, just like you, Daddy!"

She tried to cover her ensuing laugh, but Mark's exasperated eye roll made it next to impossible.

"Yes, Emily is a good swimmer. But didn't you also learn that it's better to look at fish from the beach?"

"But I got to get wet!" Seth exclaimed gleefully. "And so did you, Daddy."

A playful smile stretched across Mark's mouth.

"Yeah, but so did Emily. And she'd still be dry if we hadn't commandeered her boat."

"Pizza might make her feel better."

She looked questioningly at Mark as the four-year-old rattled on. "Daddy said we'd go to Sam's for pizza when my castle was all done," he said. "You can come, too, if you want."

"I—I think I better head home, sweetheart." Squatting down in front of him, she pushed a strand of wet hair from his forehead, then tapped the tip of his nose with her finger. "It was very nice to meet you, Seth. You are truly the best sand castle maker I've ever met."

"Please, Emily? The pizza is really yummy. It was my mom's favorite."

Emily tipped her head to afford herself a better view of Mark, noting the hint of sadness in his face at the mention of his late wife. So much about his taking her class made sense now. The drive to check things off one's bucket list always intensified after losing a friend or family member to an early death. It was as if the loss served as a wake-up call about the uncertainty and lack of promises in life. She saw it all the time.

Still, such a loss was hard to rationalize when it came to someone as young as Seth. "That sounds like some extra special pizza if it was your mom's favorite," she finally said.

"It is! Especially the pepperoni kind." Leaning forward, Seth brought his mouth to Emily's ear as if sharing a secret, the excitement in his voice negating any attempt at whispering. "Sometimes, if I smile really big at the waitress lady, she makes the pizza look like a great big smiley face...with funny hair at the top! So please? Won't you come, too? Pretty, pretty please?"

Gesturing at her damp bikini top and drenched shorts, she scrunched up her nose. "I don't think the folks at Sam's Pizza would be too happy to see me in wet clothes."

A snort of disagreement from the boy's father brought a warm flush to her cheeks.

"I'm wet, too. So's my daddy," Seth argued.

"And Sam's has outdoor tables," Mark added.

Slowly she looked from one to the other and back again, the pull for a moment of normalcy making her relent in the end. "Okay. I'm in. It sounds like fun."

Twenty minutes later, any residual worry over wet clothes and disapproving pizza eaters was gone, in its place the kind of happy-go-lucky fun she'd been craving for months. Any tension that came from being huddled so close to Mark evaporated as Seth kept them entertained with tales from his summer preschool program, most of which came back to a castle in some way.

"The other day? At lunch? I built a great big castle out of everybody's *milk cartons*. And then Liam? He's my bestest friend. He made one out of Pixy Stix during playtime," Seth said. "But then Tyler—he's a meany—he came over and kicked Liam's castle down!"

Seth widened his eyes expectantly at Emily and waited.

"You're supposed to gasp at the things Tyler does," Mark whispered in her ear.

"Oh, sorry," she whispered back, before giving the desired response.

Satisfied, Seth continued. "It's okay. Me and Liam, we cast a spell on Tyler."

She glanced at Mark, then back to Seth. "A spell?"

"Uh-huh. And you know what happened?"

Mark paused from taking a drink and narrowed his eyes on his son. "No-o-o…what happened?"

"He got in trouble with Miss Drake. She said she had eyes in back of her head, which means me and Liam are good at casting spells!"

"Then I guess I'd better watch out," Emily declared. "I don't want any eyes in any funny places."

Seth elevated himself onto his knees. "Oh, I wouldn't cast a spell on a princess. That would be bad."

Mark winked at her over the top of his glass before addressing his son once again. "And Emily is a princess, huh?"

"Yupper doodle."

When the pizza arrived and Seth took a break to eat, Mark took over the conversation, peppering her with questions about Bucket List 101 and the clients she'd encountered since starting the business four years earlier.

"When you drew those pictures I saw on your wall, did you know back then that you wanted to teach people how to do all those things?"

She nibbled at the crust of her first piece and then

tossed it on her plate. "Back then, I just knew *I* wanted to do all those things one day. By the time I was half-way through college, I knew I wanted to do them in conjunction with a business."

"Who's your typical client?"

"I'm not sure I have a typical client. People come for all sorts of reasons. Some want to conquer a fear. Some come simply because they love the outdoors. And some, like yourself, are motivated by a personal goal."

Seth pointed at his dad with his slice of pizza. "My mommy taught my daddy not to wait for tomorrow."

Mark drew back. "Where did you get that, little man?"

Turning the pizza toward his mouth, Seth shrugged. "I heard you saying that this morning when you were standing in front of the mirror, trying to decide if you should play in the woods or not."

Emily watched Mark's eyes close only to reopen mere seconds later. "I was talking to myself."

"Then you should be more quiet, Daddy." The little boy took a bite of pizza and started chewing.

"Apparently you're right." Mark looked at Emily with an impish grin. "Nothing like getting a behind-the-scenes look at my many shortcomings, eh?" Suddenly uncomfortable, he grabbed a slice of pizza for himself and raised it in the air like a champagne glass. "Next topic, please…"

Story by story, they ate their way through the rest of a pizza that was every bit as good as Seth had promised.

But it was the time with Mark and Seth that affected Emily most, temporarily filling a void that had been lurking in her soul for years. It was as if Seth's sweet stories and Mark's genuine interest allowed her to pretend, if only for a little bit, that they were her family, sharing the details of their day over dinner.

"You know how to *rock climb?*" Seth asked around a piece of pizza crust bigger than his face.

"It's not polite to talk with food in your mouth," Mark reminded him.

Seth dropped his crust onto his plate. "Do you, Emily?"

Pulling her paper napkin from her lap, she brushed it across her face, then crumpled it into a ball beside her empty glass. "I do."

"Wow!"

"Emily can do all sorts of things." Mark shifted beside her, the brush of his thigh against hers sending a tingle of awareness through her body. "She can pilot a raft through rapids, she can ride a horse through the woods, she can rappel over the side of a mountain and climb huge rocks."

At the naked awe on Seth's face, she turned a playful scowl on the child's father. "You do realize you just made me out to sound like Superwoman, don't you?"

"Nah. Superwoman is a little taller. And her hair is a lot longer. Besides, you're much, *much* better looking."

Mark's words, coupled with the huskiness of his tone, brought her up short. Unsure of what to say, she was more than a little grateful when Seth leaned across the table. "Could you teach me how to rock climb?"

With a steadying breath, she nodded, acutely aware of Mark's hand beside hers. "After you shared such yummy pizza with me, I'd be happy to teach you how to rock climb. If it's okay with your dad, of course."

"Daddy?" Seth's eyebrows rose upward, making both adults laugh out loud. "Please, please? Can Emily teach me how to rock climb?"

A moment of silence had Seth nearly falling out of his seat in anticipation.

"Hmm. If it's okay with Emily, it's okay with me—under one condition."

Bracing herself for the inevitable clean-your-room or put-away-your-toys bribe, she was more than a little surprised—pleasantly surprised, if she was honest with herself—when he revealed his nonnegotiable terms. "I get to learn, too."

Beaming triumphantly, Seth brought his focus back to Emily. "Daddy has this whole week off and I do, too. So we're free tomorrow."

She bit back the laugh Mark was unsuccessful at hiding.

"Oh we are, are we, son?"

"Yupper doodle!"

"Think ten o'clock would work for you?" she asked, with the most serious face she could muster.

Seth hopped down from his seat and consulted his

father in a series of back and forth whispers before repositioning himself at the table. "Ten o'clock works great!"

When the last of the tables around them had been cleared for the night, Mark reached for the check, plunking down thirty bucks and declaring their dinner a delicious success. "Well, little man, I think it's time we walk Emily to her car and give her a big thank-you for rescuing us from the lake and accepting our invitation to dinner."

The little boy moaned. "Do we have to stop eating?"

"We stopped eating an hour ago, when we finished the pizza." Mark pushed his chair back and reached for his son's hand. "Besides, if we want Emily to teach us how to rock climb in the morning, we really should let her go home and get some sleep."

Sensing the boy's reluctance, she took hold of his other hand and gave it a gentle squeeze. "Rock climbing is serious stuff, Seth. You need to be well rested so you can listen extra carefully when I tell you what you need to do."

"Oh. Okay."

They walked through the pizza parlor and out into the night, the answering silence of the crickets marred only by the sound of Seth's flip-flops slapping the pavement. It was a sweet sound, one she'd never really noticed until that moment.

"I had a really nice time tonight, Seth. Thank you for including me—" A shot of pain zipped up her leg, making her drop his hand and reach for the support of a nearby car.

"Emily? Are you okay?"

She smiled through the pain, praying that would wipe the worry from the boy's face. But it didn't work.

In an instant, Mark was at her side, his strong arm slipping around her shoulders and drawing her close. "Hey...talk to me."

As the untimely pain released its grip, she did her best to shrug away the incident. "I'm okay. I just had a quick pain is all."

"Do you get those often?"

Wiggling out from beneath his arm, she did her best to sound nonchalant as she made her way across the parking lot. "Yeah. Well, sometimes, I guess. It's no big deal."

Mark jogged to keep up, her pace quickening as she neared her Jeep. "No big deal? Are you kidding me?" He pointed at the nearest lamppost while studying her face. "Even in this lighting I could see your color drain away."

She shrugged. "It happens from time to time. And it always stops."

"If that happens again, maybe you should call your doctor. You know, to get it checked out or something."

And just like that, the magical spell that had transformed the evening was gone, wiped away by the reality of her life. Turning her back, Emily reached into her purse and pulled out her car keys, her response barely audible to her own ears. "I can't do that."

He took hold of her shoulders and spun her around, raising her chin with his hand. "Why not?"

"Because I can't call him every single time I get a pain. I can't call him every time my arm goes numb. I can't call him every time a bout of fatigue decides to rear its ugly head and confine me to bed for three days. I have a *disease,* Mark. It's life."

MARK TIGHTENED HIS GRIP on the steering wheel and resisted the urge to close his eyes. When he'd picked the multiple sclerosis pamphlet off the floor of Emily's office that morning, it had never dawned on him that it was she who had MS. She was too beautiful, too energetic, too much of a go-getter to have such a debilitating disease.

Yet now that he knew, so many things made sense. The angst she'd exhibited over accepting his business card wasn't denial over a loved one's condition. Her refusal to let him help her with the kayak wasn't some over-the-top display of feminism. And her insistence at racing Seth from the car to the restaurant, even though Mark had pointed to their unexpected dunk in the lake as a reason to take it slowly wasn't about some bottomless well of energy.

No, Emily Todd was angry, and she was determined to show anyone within a stone's throw that she had things under control.

He understood that stage. He'd been there once, too.

"Daddy?"

The sound of his son's tiny voice from the backseat derailed Mark's thoughts and forced him to focus on the moment. "What is it, little man?"

"Is Emily gonna die like Mommy did?"

The question was like a punch to his gut, grabbing hold of the arm's-length thoughts and bringing them much too close for comfort. Sneaking a peek at his son's worried face peering at him through the rearview mirror, Mark did his best to change the subject.

"You know what? I think it's time we dust off your bike and start working on getting rid of those training wheels sometime soon. What do you say?"

He released a sigh of relief when the little boy nodded and turned his gaze toward the passing scenery, leaving Mark to his own thoughts once again.

It was still so hard to believe. How could someone who looked like Emily be sick?

The same way Sally was...

Just the thought of his late wife brought a lump to his throat. Sally had been so healthy one minute and so sick the next, her all too quick downward spiral made even quicker by the way he'd handled everything. Burying his head in work might have made much of what was happening seem more distant, but it had also robbed him of the little time they had left.

Instead, it was Seth who had been by her side day in and day out, watching his mother slip away until she was gone for good. The memory made Mark sick. What kind of father placed a burden like that on a little boy?

A coward, that's who...

Somehow, some way, Mark was going to make things right. He had to. He owed that much to the boy. And to Sally.

But try as he did to engage Seth in conversation for the remainder of the ride home, the worry he'd seen in his son's eyes in the rearview mirror was still there when they returned home. It was there when they'd shared a bowl of ice cream at the kitchen counter. And it was still there when he kissed Seth's forehead and tucked him under the sheets for the night.

Mark had seen that worry in his son's eyes for far too long. He'd watched it eat away at the pure joy that had been Seth's existence prior to Sally's cancer diagnosis. And he'd sat by, virtually paralyzed by his own fear, while that worry had morphed into a steely determination to be what Mark himself seemed incapable of being.

But no more.

Seth had suffered enough for one lifetime.

It didn't matter how hot Emily Todd was. It didn't matter that her enthusiasm and boundless energy breathed life into Mark's stagnant world.

All that mattered was Seth.

All that mattered was keeping his son from ever reliving the kind of grief that had consumed his young life to this point.

Pulling Seth's bedroom door shut behind him, Mark wandered across the hall and into his own room, where the picture of Sally with Seth on his third birthday brought a familiar mist to his eyes.

With fingers that knew the way, he lifted the frame from his nightstand and slowly traced the contours of his wife's face. "His heart is safe with me, Sally," he whispered. "You have my word on that."

Chapter Four

Emily pressed the intercom button on the side of her phone, working to make her voice sound casual and upbeat. "Trish? Any sign of Mr. Reynolds and his son yet?"

"Still nothing, boss."

"Oh. Okay. Thanks." She pulled her finger back, only to shove it forward once again. "Um, Trish?"

"Yeah, boss."

"My next class is at noon, right?" She glanced at the clock on the wall and noted the rapidly approaching hour.

"Noon it is."

Her shoulders sank along with the tone of her voice. "Okay. Thanks."

With her connection to her assistant broken, Emily pushed back her chair and stood, the enthusiasm that had marked the start of her day giving way to a serious case of unease.

Granted, she didn't know Mark Reynolds all that well. How could she when they'd met just a measly twenty-six hours earlier? But no matter how hard she tried to pin his failure to show up for their first rock-climbing adventure on something as trivial as forgetfulness, she couldn't.

Especially when it had meant so much to his son.

"Seth," she whispered. That was it. Something must have come up with the little boy to cancel their outing and prevent Mark from calling to let her know. It was the only explanation that made any sense.

Perhaps the child was in bed with the flu, or a tummy ache from eating too much pizza the night before. Maybe he'd fallen on the way out to the car that morning and broken his arm, or something crazy like that. Or maybe he'd had a rough night without his mom, and Mark felt it was more important for the little guy to get some rest.

Emily knew it was silly to be so worried about a child she'd just met, but she couldn't help herself. There was something special about Seth, something innocent and pure that spoke to her heart as nothing else had in years.

The fact that he'd been through so much in such a short period of time only served to bolster her gut feeling that Mark wouldn't deny Seth an opportunity to make a new memory unless something fairly serious had intervened.

Her worry at an all-time high, Emily sank back into her desk chair and opened the top drawer. There, where she'd left it, was the card she couldn't get out of her hands fast enough the day before.

Mark Reynolds
Field Worker
Folks Helping Folks Foundation
555-555-5555

Inhaling deeply, she reached for the phone and punched in the number, the final digit quickly followed by a ring that led straight to a nondescript voice mail. When the recording completed its request for her name, number and reason for calling, she obliged, her voice a poor disguise for the worry she wasn't terribly adept at hiding.

"Um…hi. Uh, it's Emily. Emily Todd. From yesterday? At Bucket List 101…and, um, the pizza place?" Realizing she sounded like an idiot, she got to the point, the disappointment she felt over having to wait for a response undeniable. "I got your number from your business card. Could you please give me a call when you get this? Thanks."

She reeled off her phone number, returned the handset to its cradle and then dropped her head into her hands. She'd done everything she could, short of driving back and forth across town trying to guess where Mark and Seth Reynolds lived. All she could do now was wait.

And pray that the images continuing to loop through her thoughts were the by-product of an overactive imagination rather than a spot-on radar that made absolutely no sense where a virtual stranger and his son were concerned.

MARK CROUCHED DOWN beside Laurie's desk and placed a gentle yet firm hand on his son's shoulder. "Now remember what I told you, little man. Miss Laurie has work to do. So it's super important that you sit in this nice seat right here and keep yourself busy, okay?"

Seth nodded.

"And as for me? I'll be in that conference room right there—" he pointed toward the open door just beyond the secretary's desk "—if you have an emergency. But since I just took you to the bathroom, and I'll only be in my meeting for about a half hour, you should be good on that front, right?"

"I'll be good," Seth whispered. "I promise."

Mark reached for the backpack he'd placed beside the chair and unzipped the center compartment to reveal a plethora of activities designed to make the wait as easy on his son—and Laurie—as possible. "I packed your favorite picture books, along with a *Mr. Spaceman* coloring book I managed to score while you were napping at Gam's this afternoon."

At Seth's silence, he reached inside and extracted the new book, flipping it open to reveal page after page of all things space related. "Isn't this the coolest coloring book ever?"

A search of his son's face failed to net the enthusiasm Mark was hoping to see. Disappointed, he tried a different tactic. "If you get hungry, there's an extra yummy cherry lollipop in the front pocket of your backpack that's got your name all over it. Sound good?"

Seth's automatic nod stopped midway as his un-usually dull eyes locked on Mark's. "Daddy? I really would've been a good listener for Emily."

Mark raked a hand down his face before clasping his son's shoulder. "My decision against taking you rock climbing this morning wasn't about listening, little man. It was about keeping you *safe*."

It was a decision he still felt was right even now, some seven hours later. Any residual angst over the whole thing had more to do with his failure to call and cancel their private lesson than anything else.

"Mark? They're ready to start."

He glanced over his shoulder at the woman in her sixties situated behind the gray metal desk. "Thanks, Laurie." Then, turning back to his son, he offered what he hoped was a reassuring smile. "Maybe we can get some ice cream when this is over. How's that sound?"

Seth shrugged. "We have to eat dinner first, Daddy."

Mark didn't know if he should laugh or cry at the sol-emn response more befitting an adult than a four-and-a-half-year-old boy. It made sense, considering everything Seth had been through the past year, but it made Mark all the more protective of his son's childhood.

"Maybe we can make an exception this one time." He brushed a kiss across Seth's head and then stood, his trip to the conference room requiring little more than a stride or two. When he reached the door, he took one last peek at his son, who was still standing in the mid-dle of the foundation's reception area.

"We'll be fine," Laurie assured him. "Now go. The sooner you get in, the sooner you'll be out."

"Thanks, Laurie."

"My pleasure." She swiveled her chair to her computer screen, only to turn back just before he disappeared completely. "Oh, and Mark? A call from a potential client came in for you today. I gave the details to Stan."

"I'll make sure to ask him about it after the meeting." He stepped inside the room and took the empty chair indicated by Stan Wiley, board president of the Folks Helping Folks Foundation. An all-around good guy, Stan made volunteering with the organization a pleasant experience. Stan had gotten involved with the foundation for reasons not dissimilar from Mark's. Regret was a powerful motivator.

"I certainly appreciate everyone coming in on such short notice for a meeting that wasn't on your agenda," Stan began. "But as I told each of you on the phone, it really couldn't be avoided. Not if we want the foundation to be the recipient of a quarter of a million dollars."

A collective gasp rose up around the table.

Stan laughed. "See? I told you this was a meeting worth having."

"Wow. Seriously?"

"That's incredible."

Mark listened to the sentiments of his fellow volunteers, nodding along with each before adding his own.

"That sure is going to open up a lot of possibilities for our clients."

"That's exactly right. And it's why we needed to have this brief meeting. Now that the offer is there, we have to put our heads together and make sure we don't let the money slip out of our grasp." Stan plucked a pile of manila folders from the table in front of him and sent half down each side of the conference table. "That quarter of a million dollars will be the foundation's, provided we meet one very specific and necessary condition stipulated by Jake Longfeld."

Taking the top folder, Mark passed the remaining pile to his left. "Longfeld? As in Longfeld Motors?"

"One and the same," Stan confirmed. "He's been watching the work we've been doing the past few years, and felt it was time to throw one of his always-generous donations in our direction. And we're grateful, of course. But there is this condition we need to find a way to meet."

"Condition?" a woman on the other side of the table repeated.

"That's right." Stan waved his hand. "As you probably know, Jake Longfeld walks with a cane. The reason dates back to an injury he sustained in the armed services some thirty years ago. He's gotten through life just fine in spite of his challenges, but he's wise enough to know that's not the case for everyone with a physical disability, particularly when that disability comes as a result of the kinds of diseases our foundation deals with on a regular basis.

"Which leads me to why we're all here. If you'll open your folders, you'll find a copy of the letter Mr. Long-feld wrote to our foundation, detailing his wishes for his very generous donation. About halfway down the page, you'll see that he wants this money to help two groups near and dear to his heart—those with disabili-ties, and small business owners."

Mark skimmed the letter from top to bottom, nod-ding as he did. "So the entire donation doesn't have to go to a small business owner with a disabling disease, just a portion?"

"Exactly," Stan said. "We satisfy that stipulation and we'll be able to help a lot of people."

"Do we have any clients that fit that bill?" a field worker asked.

The president's gaze settled on Mark. "Perhaps." Leaning forward, he flipped through his folder until he came to a pink slip of paper, which he handed to Mark. "A call came in to the foundation for you today, Mark. From a woman named Emily Todd. Ms. Todd owns a small business on the outskirts of Winoka called Bucket List 101. I'm taking it she has physical limita-tions, if she reached out to us here?"

An image of the petite, pixieish blonde flashed in front of his eyes—the curve of her hips, the sinewy tease of her legs, the tantalizing rise of her breasts, the unforgettable twinkle of her large doelike eyes, the heartfelt smiles she solicited from Seth....

"Mark?"

The sound of his name snapped him back to the present—that and the fact that all eyes in the room were suddenly trained on him. "Uh..."

"Does this woman have physical limitations?" Stan pressed.

He forced himself to address the question, to abandon the image that had him loosening his collar and wishing for a cool glass of water. "At the moment, none that I can see. But with the nature of her disease, that will change."

"Then perhaps we've just met our stipulation."

Stan's words took root. "Wait. Wait. Em—I mean, Miss Todd—isn't a client of ours yet. She, um, well, let's just say she's still in quite a bit of denial about her situation."

"Then I'm counting on you to help her through that stage and onto our client roll." Stan closed his folder and rose to his feet, a triumphant smile making its way across his well-tanned face. "You do that and we can start divvying up the rest of the donation in a way that will enable us to do the most good."

"But I can't force her to seek help," Mark protested.

"She called us, didn't she?" Stan quipped, before adjourning the meeting until the following week. "That fact suggests that our Miss Todd is starting to move toward acceptance at a faster rate than you may have realized."

HE LEANED HIS HEAD against the back of the couch and released a long sigh, his dilemma over what to do as worrisome as ever. Sure, there was a part of him that wanted nothing more than an excuse to drive out to Bucket List 101 again and see Emily. There was something about her spark, her spirit, that made him feel more alive than he had in months. But he couldn't ignore the other part, either—the part that wanted to protect his son's heart by keeping her at arm's length.

"Don't get close, don't get hurt," he mumbled under his breath.

It was a good motto. One that would keep him from ever seeing the kind of heart-wrenching ache he'd been unable to erase from Seth's eyes during Sally's illness.

His mind made up, Mark reached for his cell phone and the foundation's volunteer list. Bob McKeon was aces. Clients seemed to really love his gentle, straightforward approach. And with any luck, Emily would feel the same way.

Emily.

Once again, the woman who'd captivated his son over a sand castle and a pepperoni pizza flashed before his eyes, causing him to pause, his finger on the keypad of his phone.

Emily was struggling on the first rung of a ladder he knew all too well. He'd seen it in her face when he talked to her about the foundation. He'd heard it in her voice when she'd brushed off his concern about the pain in her leg. And he'd sensed it in the unwavering determination that made her refuse help for even the simplest of things.

She needed a hand.

The kind of hand Seth had given Sally when Mark had been stuck on the same rung as Emily, ignoring reality because he'd thought it would be easier somehow.

But it wasn't.

In fact, in many ways, lingering on that rung had made everything more painful in the end.

The whole reason he'd gotten involved with the foundation was to make up for his selfish behavior during Sally's illness. To push Emily off on Bob when she needed a friendly face and an encouraging word would dishonor the vow he'd made to himself over his wife's grave.

No. Mark wasn't turning his back on people during difficult times. At least, he'd never intended to be that way.

Closing the phone, he tossed it onto the coffee table, the determination he'd once prided himself on prior to Sally's illness and death returning for the first time in entirely too long.

He would talk to Emily. *He* would help her reach the next rung of the ladder, by convincing her to accept assistance from the foundation. And he would do that for her just as he would for any other potential client.

Because that's what she was, what she *needed* to be.

For Seth's own good.

Chapter Five

Emily was just wrapping up a class on outdoor survival when Mark walked in, his tall, well-built form commanding attention and drawing the heads of all three female students in his direction. A quick search of his face and stance turned up nothing to indicate there was trouble at home. But still, not to call? Something had to have come up.

In a flash, Mark was at her side, his hand on her arm, his husky voice in her ear. "Are you okay?"

Feeling the questioning eyes of her students, she yanked free of his grip, dropping her voice to a whisper. "What the hell do you think you're doing?"

He stepped back as if he'd been slapped. "You were in pain again. I saw it in your eyes just now."

"Pain? I wasn't in any..." Her words trailed off as she put two and two together, then turned to address the three women and four men who had just taken the first of four classes designed to teach them how to survive in the wild. "I want to thank all of you for such a fun and energetic class today. Hopefully I answered all of your great questions and that you're looking forward to next week's class as much as I am."

A muted chorus of agreement rang out as all seven made their way toward the door, several of them stopping to glance back first at Mark and then Emily, the unease on their faces igniting her fury all over again.

When they were safely out of the room and down the hall, she turned back to him. "How dare you make my students doubt my ability to run this class!"

"Doubt your ability? Where on earth did you get—wait. Wait just a minute. I didn't do that," he protested. "I just wanted to make sure you were okay."

"By making a production in front of them? About pain I wasn't having? Oh, okay." She heard the sarcasm in her voice and forced her mouth closed over the rest of her rant.

He stared at her and then broke left and began pacing around the classroom. "But I saw the flash of pain in your eyes when I walked into the room."

She rested her hands on her hips. "That wasn't pain. It was *worry*."

He stopped midstep and met her eyes. "Okay. And I get that. It's why I'm here, actually." He lifted his left hand to brandish some colorful brochures featuring the same logo as the business card he'd given her two days earlier. "We got your call at the foundation and we're so glad that you're reconsidering the idea of accepting help from us. These pamphlets will give you an idea of the kinds of things we can do to help—"

"You're here because of the message I left on your voice mail?"

"Yes."

She brought her hands to her cheeks and worked to steady her breathing, the meaning behind Mark's statement becoming crystal clear. "I didn't call because I want some sort of help from your foundation," she snapped.

His eyebrows rose. "Then why did you call?"

"Why did I call?" she echoed in a tone that was bordering on shrill. "Hmm, I don't know. Maybe I was *worried*?"

"About what?" he asked.

"Not what, *who*." She kept her focus firmly on his face as she filled in the blanks he was so obviously missing. "As in worried about Seth. And you."

"You were worried about Seth and me? But why?"

She considered turning her back on him and simply walking away, but opted instead to have her say. "Maybe because I saw the way his face lit up when we agreed on a time for our first rock-climbing adventure, which should have had the two of you walking through that door yesterday morning." Sure enough, the color drained from his face as she continued, his genuine cluelessness over his faux pas making her even angrier. "I know what kind of dad you are. I'd be an idiot not to see that. So I think it's fairly understandable why I'd chalk up your no-show to something being wrong, instead of just you blowing off a promise you made to your kid."

Taking two steps backward, he sank into a chair and raked a hand across his face. "And so you called the foundation to see if we were okay?"

"It was the only number I had."

He closed his eyes momentarily, only to open them again with obvious hesitation. "Oh, man. I'm sorry, Emily. I didn't realize…"

Feeling her anger edge toward an unexplained sadness, she waved his words aside. "Look, just tell me he's okay. Beyond that, I don't need or want to hear anything else."

Mark's eyes stopped just shy of meeting hers. "He's fine. We just, um, had other things to do."

"Other things to do," she repeated, as if hearing the words out of her own mouth would somehow take the sting out of them. It didn't.

And it was her own fault. So they'd talked on a beach—big deal. So they'd laughed together for hours over pizza—big deal. So Seth had seemed to respond to her as strongly as she did to him—big deal. It had been one evening—one measly two or three hours.

The fact that she'd given the encounter a second thought, let alone allowed it to excite her while simultaneously meaning so little to the man sitting in front of her, was embarrassing.

She turned toward the door. "Well, I'm sorry you drove all the way out here just to inform me you had better things to do yesterday than show up for a class *you* scheduled. Take care of yourself, and say hi to Seth for me."

"Emily, wait. It's not what you think."

She stopped. "And you know what I'm thinking now, too?"

"Yeah. That I'm an insensitive jerk."

She opened her mouth, only to shut it without uttering a word. Really, why argue the truth?

"But it's not like that. Not in the way that you think, anyway." The legs of Mark's chair scraped against the linoleum floor as he rose to his feet and closed the gap between them. "I decided to refrain from coming here with Seth yesterday because of him. Or, rather, *for* him, actually."

"I don't understand." She dropped her hands to her hips again. "Your son was beside himself with excitement at the pizza place just thinking about learning how to climb. How could your decision not to show up be for him?"

Mark shifted foot from foot to foot, clearly uncomfortable with their discussion. "I—I can't allow him to hurt like he has this past year. Not knowingly, anyway. To do so would make me a pretty crappy dad."

"Teaching him how to rock climb would make you a crappy dad?" she asked in confusion, just as some semblance of a reason hit home. "Is this about safety? Because if it is, you have to believe I know what I'm doing.

Teaching these kinds of skills is my job, Mark. It's how I make my living. He would have been perfectly safe."

An awkward and all-too-telling pause caught her by surprise.

"Wait a minute. Please don't tell me you doubt my ability because I have MS?"

For a moment, she didn't think he was going to answer, but in the end he did, his words suddenly making it difficult for her to breathe. "It's not your ability in light of the MS that I'm worried about, Emily."

"Then what?" she whispered.

"It's the threat your condition wields over my son's heart."

"Your son's heart? What on earth are you talking about?"

She watched as Mark walked aimlessly around the room, clenching and unclenching his hands. When he finally turned to face her, the pain in his eyes was like a lightning bolt to her chest, swift and unmistakable. "Most three-year-olds spend their days playing. Girls with their dolls, and boys with their cars and trucks. When they grow tired of that, they retire to a couch to watch their favorite show on TV, snacking on a hot-from-the-oven chocolate chip cookie with a tall glass of cold milk and a straw. It's the way it's supposed to be, you know?"

Without waiting for a response she was at a loss to provide, he continued, his words, his tone, taking on the emotion evident on his face. "Seth didn't have that. Not beyond his first three years, anyway. No, *Seth's* play-time was spent in medical offices and hospital rooms. And instead of watching cartoon characters chasing each other all over the television screen, he watched his mom grow sicker and sicker, and sicker until she slipped from his life completely."

Swallowing over the lump that grew in her throat, Emily took a step forward. "Oh, Mark, I'm so sorry. I didn't realize just how awful it was for the two of—"

He held up his hands, cutting her off. "I can't take that experience away from him. I can't go back and air-brush out all his pain and anguish, regardless of how much I wish I could. But what I *can* do is protect the rest of his childhood. Keep him from having to go through something like that ever again."

Suddenly the reason the pair had failed to show the day before was as plain as the nose on her face. And she didn't like it one bit.

"Wait, please. Are you telling me you didn't want to bring him here to *rock climb* with me because you're afraid I'm going to die on him like his mother did?"

Mark's glance at the floor was all the answer she needed.

"First of all, a quick fact check. I have multiple scle-rosis. And while MS can be a debilitating disease, the likelihood that it's going to kill me is slim to none. Will it shorten my life? Maybe, but only by about five per-cent. *Five percent*. The chance I'll die being run over by a bus in downtown Winoka is probably higher than that."

Slowly he lifted his head. "But—"

"And second, Seth barely knows me. I mean, c'mon, you really think a few hours at a pizza parlor and a few more spent learning to climb rocks would leave him so enamored with me that he'd be seriously impacted by some unexpected decline in my health? Because I certainly don't—"

"Didn't you see how taken he was with you at the pizza place? How he hung on every word out of your mouth? How he tried to endear you to him with the best knock-knock jokes making the rounds of his summer preschool program? Didn't you see how he looked at you with such awe and genuine happiness? Because *I* did, and it took my breath away."

At her quiet gasp, Mark continued, his voice growing raspier by the second. "But that wasn't all. I also felt his fear when he asked about your illness on the way home that night. It was...*crushing*."

She blinked at the tears that threatened to cut paths down her cheeks. "He was afraid? Of me?"

"He was afraid *for* you. And trust me when I say that kind of fear is worse, far worse." Mark tipped his head back and looked up at the ceiling, the nature of the conversation, coupled with the countless memories it surely dragged to the surface, sapping him of physical energy. "I don't care how perfect that smile of his was the other night when he looked at you. It's not worth watching him hurt the way he did with his mom. Not for me, anyway."

IT WAS QUICK. Fleeting, even. But he'd seen it as surely as if a chorus of angels had underscored its presence.

Emily was taken by Seth, too.

The knowledge made Mark pause and search for a softer, easier way to get his feelings across. But before he could utter another word, the moment was gone.

"So why show up now if you didn't have the guts to call and tell me all of this yesterday morning? Surely you could have popped your precious pamphlets in the mail and saved yourself the trip."

He looked down at the brochures he'd forgotten he had, and held them out to her once again. "Because I—I wanted to talk to you. To see if I could convince you to let the Folks Helping Folks Foundation help you through this difficult time."

"There is no difficult time," she said through clenched teeth before sweeping her hands toward her body. "Look at me. Do you really think I'm having a difficult time?"

"Maybe not now, but down the road—maybe. Probably. But that's why I'm here. That's why I'm trying to tell you about the foundation. We can equip your house and your office with the things you might need later, like a wheelchair ramp or a special tub for your bathroom that will protect you from slipping." Realizing she wasn't going to take the brochures, he dropped them onto the nearest desk. "In fact, the foundation stands to get a very large donation if we can find a local business owner who can benefit from our work. And since this—" he spread his arms and gestured around the room "—is your business, we thought maybe—"

Her eyes narrowed. "Oh. I get it now."

He rushed to soothe away any misunderstanding. "Wait. It's not like that. You know I wanted to help you the other day, long before I knew a thing about this donation."

"Right. Only now it's even more important to pressure me into something I don't want because my…my *disease* helps you and your precious foundation put a checkmark in some stupid little box." She pivoted and paced across the room, stopping when she reached the far wall. "I'm fine, Mark. Just fine. Find someone else to help you tick off your boxes."

"But you have a debilitating disease. You said so yourself."

For the briefest of moments he actually thought she was going to come back and smack him. Instead, she raised her hand and beckoned to him.

Scooping up the brochures, he followed her from the classroom and down the same corridor as two days earlier. When he reached her office, he stepped inside.

She grabbed an overstuffed album from a nearby shelf and slammed it onto her desk. With a flick of her wrist, she snapped back the cover to reveal page upon page of news clippings and pictures highlighting her many outdoor skills. "Can you climb a tree that looks like that?" she asked, pointing at a photo of her near the top of a blue spruce. "And how about this?" She turned to the next page. "Can you scale the side of a mountain, Mark?"

There was lots more of the same—Emily paddling through stage four rapids. Dangling from the edge of a cliff. Jumping over a series of fallen trees, bareback on a horse. Scuba diving and waving at an underwater camera. And all the while, no matter what she was doing, she was looking incredible.

He swallowed once, twice. "No. I'm afraid I can't."

She pushed the album shut and turned to face him, her lips lusciously plump as they parted to dress him down once again. "I may have MS, Mark," she hissed. "But MS doesn't have me."

Reaching out, he cupped his free hand around the back of her head and pulled her close, the intoxicating feel of her soft hair giving way to the reality that was her mouth—warm, enticing and oh so exciting.

When her lips parted to allow access to his probing tongue, he pulled her still closer, their bodies melding against one another effortlessly until the ring of her phone snapped them both back to reality.

She stepped away, her eyes glazed, her voice breathless. "I have to get that. Trish is out today." Without waiting for a response, she grabbed the receiver. "Bucket List 101. This is Emily."

Mark took the reprieve offered by the call to get his

body under control, the intensity of their kiss making his thoughts run in a direction not conducive to their present setting. Never mind the fact that he barely knew her....

"Oh, hi, Kate. Yeah, yeah, I'm fine. Really. I don't know why you think my voice sounds funny. I was just a little busy, that's all."

He tried to give her privacy, to refrain from eavesdropping on the one-sided conversation, but it was hard. Especially when he'd always been sort of good at lip reading, and he couldn't seem to keep his gaze off her kiss-swollen lips....

"Yes, yes, I'm still coming." She glanced in his direction, focusing on his face for mere seconds before taking in the clock over his head. "No, I didn't realize how late it was getting. I'll be there in fifteen minutes. Uh-huh. Yeah. Okay. I'll see you then."

Slowly, she lowered the phone to its base, her cheeks crimson. "That was my friend Kate. The one who found all of—" she turned and pointed at the framed childhood drawings that had captivated him the day they met "—*those*. Anyway, I was due at her house for a barbecue thirty minutes ago and, well, I'm late."

"Can I come?" he asked, before realizing what he was saying. But instead of retracting the bold question, he let it stand, buoyed by the memory of her lips on his.

"Don't you have to get home to Seth?" she asked.

"Seth is spending the evening with my mother. He

won't be home until late tomorrow, probably after dinner."

Emily opened her mouth to speak, but closed it again when he reached for her hand, his voice husky with the kind of emotion he knew he'd have to dissect later—when he was alone.

"Please, Emily? I'd like to go with you."

Chapter Six

The second they looped around the side of the house and into Kate's line of vision, Emily knew she'd made a mistake.

To bring a guy who looked like Mark to a barbecue with a heavy concentration of couples versus singles was bound to raise a few eyebrows under any circumstances. Add the fact that it was Kate—a woman who bemoaned Emily's single status on a regular basis—who was throwing the barbecue and, well, she was doomed.

"Emily! You're here!" Her friend disengaged herself from a small group of people Emily recognized from the Memorial Day barbecue Kate and her husband had thrown six weeks earlier, and met them just inside the hedge that bordered the east side of the couple's property. Extending her hand, Kate widened her eyes at Emily and then beamed up at Mark. "Hi, I'm Kate. Emily and I have known each other since our finger painting days."

His laugh was strong and sure. "And I'm Mark.

Emily and I have known each other since she stuck a compass in my hand and tried to lead me astray in the woods three days ago."

"I didn't lead you astray," she protested. "I gave you the same coordinates as everyone else. You just seemed to be a little distracted in the beginning, that's all."

He swept his hand in her direction, making her keenly aware of the white skirt and powder-blue tank top she'd donned that morning, knowing her day would be spent in a classroom rather than in the woods or on the lake. "Who knew I had to focus on the compass?" he quipped to Kate with a wink for good measure.

Emily felt her mouth gape, and worked to compose herself even as her friend's eyes crackled with the kind of excitement that left her own stomach in knots.

Great.

"Come. Come. You have to meet my husband, Joe." Looping her arm through Mark's, Kate fairly dragged him across the French patio and over to the pickup game of basketball taking place on the other side of the yard between Joe and an eight-year-old guest. "Joe and I met in high school. He was distracted by me when we crossed paths at the diner."

Hoping the lump in the pit of her stomach was a by-product of hunger rather than her shortsighted concession in bringing Mark to the barbecue, Emily headed over to the food table, her history with Kate filling in the rest of the story Mark was no doubt hearing. It was one she knew well, considering that she had been sitting at the same table in the now infamous local hangout when Joe had walked in with four of his buddies from the basketball team that fateful day. The second Kate and Joe had spotted one another across the restaurant, their romantic fate had been sealed.

But it hadn't worked that way for Emily. Ever.

Sure, she'd dated her fair share of guys throughout high school, college and beyond, but none of them had ever quite reached the bar she'd set for someone who would be her life's mate. No, that person had to be smart, funny, motivated, creative and outdoorsy. He had to enjoy conversation and silence. And he had to look at her as if she was someone special.

Like Mark had just now when he was telling Kate about the orienteering class....

Emily stilled her hand over the bowl of pretzels and shook her head. Oh, no. She would not allow Kate's you-need-to-find-your-soul-mate-and-you-need-to-find-him-now mantra start playing in her head.

Four out of five goals was good enough. Especially in light of her illness.

"Em, he's gorgeous. Gor-geous. I am so, so, *so* happy for you."

She swatted away her gushing friend with a handful of pretzels before popping one in her mouth and removing herself from the earshot of a few other guests.

"What?" Kate persisted, staying on her heels. "Am I wrong? Is Mark not gorgeous?"

Lifting her hand to block the sun, Emily scanned the

backyard until her friend's outstretched finger pointed the way to the basketball court and the game that had grown to include five men and the eight-year-old. Even from where she was standing she couldn't help but enjoy the view.

Mark Reynolds was truly a fine-looking man. His hair, which had caught her attention from the start with its rich brown color, was the kind a woman could get her fingers lost in. His smile, whether flashed in her direction over a piece of pizza, or accompanying some good-natured trash talk, as was the case at that moment, was of the knee-weakening variety if she'd ever seen one. And his chiseled jawline...

She closed her eyes, popped a second and third pretzel into her mouth, and then opened her eyes again, this time honing in on her closest friend. "Yes, he's attractive—I'd have to be an idiot not to see that. But I'm not interested."

Kate's left eyebrow rose. "Not interested? Are you nuts?"

"He's just someone I know. Barely." At Kate's foot tapping, she continued. "He stopped by the office today to drop off some, um, paperwork I didn't need, and I felt sorry for him. So I invited him along. No big deal. Really."

The right eyebrow rose alongside the left. "And dinner at Sam's Pizza, what was that?"

Emily pulled her focus back from the basketball court where it had strayed once again, seemingly independent of her brain and the conversation she was trying to have and discard. "He told you about Sam's?"

Kate grinned so widely that Emily actually found herself glancing at the patio for evidence of any canary feathers her friend may have swallowed. "He did."

Emily folded her hands across her chest. "And did he happen to tell you the only reason I went at all is because his son was so insistent and I didn't have the heart to say no?"

"His son?" Kate sputtered. "He has a son?"

"Seth is four and a half. And if you saw him, and he'd asked *you* to come along for pizza, you'd have gone, too. Trust me."

Turning her head, Kate looked back at the court. "So he's divorced, then?"

"No, he's a widower. His wife died sometime in the last six months or so."

"He sure seems happy to be here with you."

She had to laugh at that. "You mean playing basketball with your husband, right?"

"Have you not seen how many shots he's missed since we've been standing here?"

"So maybe he's not a basketball guy, Kate. Believe it or not, those do exist. Difficult to fathom, I know. But still…"

Her friend made a face. "I know that. But I also know he *is* a basketball guy, based on what he told Joe when I introduced them."

"Maybe he lied," she quipped, shrugging.

"Or maybe he's spending more time looking over at you rather than focusing on the game."

"Kate. Please." She heard the exasperated tone in her voice, saw the heads of several people turn toward them as a result. Gritting her teeth, Emily tried her best to get a handle on her increasing agitation before every eye in the place was trained in her direction. "We're just *friends*. That's it."

Without waiting for the retort she was quite sure would come, she headed back to the food table and a recently added plate of brownies. She was about to reach for one when Mark appeared at her side, breathing heavily.

"The…game just…ended so Joe could start on the burgers and dogs. So what do you say we…we check out that horseshoe pit…over there—" he gestured toward the back edge of the property "—while he cooks? That way…maybe I can…catch my breath a little."

For a moment, she considered declining. To accept would mean giving Kate another reason to keep needling her. But in the end, Emily agreed. After all, with any luck, Joe would need Kate's help at the grill and her friend would finally turn her attention to something else.

One could hope, anyway.

"I'm in," Emily said, grabbing one last handful of pretzels from the bowl at the end of the table. "Anything to get out from under this scrutiny for a little while."

"Scrutiny?" Mark echoed. "What kind of scrutiny?"

Oops. She hadn't meant to share that thought aloud. She simply shrugged. "Never mind. Let's go."

HE TRIED TO FOCUS on the game, he really did. But it was hard. Damn hard.

Emily was the kind of girl who would make cars swerve off roads when she went jogging down a busy street. She just was. But what took his own first swerve all the way into a tree with no hope of recovering was the fact that her beauty was only part of the story. She was also smart and engaging, with a completely unpretentious and slightly self-deprecating manner where her looks and her body were concerned.

Her physical prowess, however, was a different matter. That, she took pride in. Not a boastful kind, but rather a self-satisfied one. As if she'd worked hard to learn certain skills and didn't feel the need to hide her ability in those areas from anyone.

"It's your toss, Mark."

In fact, she was so skilled at so many things, he found himself wanting to start stretching his own limits a little. See what he could do, too...

"Earth to Mark... Come in, Mark."

The repeated sound of his name brought him back to the moment. "I'm sorry?"

Emily pointed to the horseshoe in his hand. "It's your toss."

"Oh, yeah." He pulled his arm back and then swung it forward, his horseshoe sailing through the air and landing a full twelve inches from its target. "Wow. That was lame." Her laugh tingled down his spine and brought an answering smile to his own face. "You think that's funny, eh?"

She held up her hands and gave them a little shake. "I shouldn't be laughing. Don't mind me."

"Like it's easy to ignore the woman who's beating your pants off at horseshoes." Before she could respond, he moved on, tackling a subject he'd been wondering about since they'd arrived. "So tell me...why aren't you married or coupled off, like most of your friend's guests seem to be?"

Emily launched her last horseshoe at the target, the sound of metal on metal bringing another smile to the lips he couldn't seem to forget kissing. "Well, that's a bit of a loaded question, don't you think?"

"Sorry. I didn't mean to come across as nosy. I guess I just can't fathom why you haven't been snatched up by at least a dozen different guys by now."

Shrugging, she wandered over to a pair of Adirondack chairs nestled beneath a large oak tree and claimed one as her own. "It's okay. I don't really mind. I guess I'm just on edge about that particular topic, thanks to Kate."

He took the other chair. "She's a little pushy where your love life is concerned, huh?"

For a moment, he was afraid he'd offended Emily again, but when she finally answered, her words painted a very different picture. "Kate is one of those people who has a life plan. One that's actually written out on a piece of paper. All the goals she wants to hit are spelled out right there, in order, with bullets. Last I checked, she was on number six, I think."

"Number six?"

Emily nodded, her gaze fixed on the trunk of the oak tree. "The sixth bullet point. Which, between you and me, means she's trying to have a baby. It could be a girl or a boy this first time around. But whatever it is will necessitate a specific gender where bullet point number seven is concerned. Because she's supposed to have one of each, you know, according to her life plan."

"A life plan? Really?"

"Uh-huh. And Kate believes the things on her list are the same ones everyone else is supposed to want. You know…get married, work for a few years, develop a few hobbies, have a child, and so on and so on. It's why she's having a little difficulty accepting the fact that my life has taken a very different path. And while sometimes I think she gets it—at least in a grudging way—there are other times where I actually feel as if I've disappointed her."

"By not getting married?" he asked. "Come on, I can't believe that's true. Besides, there's still plenty of time for you to hit a few bullet points of your own. Lots of women these days wait to get married into their early thirties and beyond. Sally and I just did it a little early. More like Kate and Joe." He silently cursed the way his tone softened at the mention of his late wife, afraid that

Emily would jump on the same apology bandwagon his friends rode and pull him from the place he was at that moment....

With Emily.

"I guess that's it. But as I try to tell her all the time, sometimes plans change. And that doesn't always have to be a bad thing, right?"

Silence enveloped them as they slipped into their own thoughts—his about the events he hadn't anticipated when he'd met and married Sally, and hers about things he could only guess at.

"Come and get it before it's gone!" Joe bellowed from the grill. "Got plenty of burgers and hot dogs for everyone. But if you snooze, be prepared to lose, folks."

Despite the answering rumble of his stomach, Mark found himself wishing for another moment or two alone with Emily. There was something about her quiet confidence that made him feel alive—a feeling that had been sporadic at best since Sally's diagnosis, illness and subsequent funeral. Maybe part of it was simply having the chance to talk about something other than his wife's death and how Seth was coping—subjects few of his friends seemed capable of deviating from these days. More than that, though, was the growing attraction Mark felt for the woman seated by his side. Stealing a glance in her direction, he searched for a way to put a smile back on her face. "Hey, what do you say we grab something to eat and have a rematch? And this time I'll actually *try*."

Her eyes crackled to life. "Are you implying I only beat you because you weren't trying?"

"I'm not implying that, I'm saying that," he teased.

"Oh, okay. But just so you know, you might want to go easy on the trash talk, mister. Because if you don't, you may find yourself eating way more than one of Joe's famous burgers by the time we're done."

"You think so?"

"I know so," she quipped.

Sure enough, two hamburgers, one corn on the cob, a hearty helping of potato salad and three losses later, he collapsed onto the same Adirondack chair he'd sat on earlier. Only this time, instead of stealing glances at Emily and hesitating over which way the conversation should go, he was interacting with her as if they'd known each other for years. She laughed at his corny jokes, teased him about his less-than-stellar horseshoe skills and smiled at him as if she was every bit as aware of the sparks flying between them as he was. And it felt good. Undeniably good.

All too soon, however, dusk gave way to darkness and Mark found himself reluctantly conceding that it was time to call it a night. His hand found the small of her back as they made their way around the side of the house and headed toward her car. "Emily, I had a really great time tonight. I can't tell you the last time I did something like this. Except, of course, the other night."

Her feet slowed as they approached the Jeep. "You were at a barbecue the other night?"

"No, I was at Sam's. With you." A nearby streetlamp cast an alluring glow across her face, and he swallowed.

"Then I don't get it. Did something like what?"

He looked to the sky, taking in the crystal-clear view of the stars above. It had been so long since he'd allowed himself simply to breathe, without traveling down the familiar road of should-haves and could-haves where the past eighteen months were concerned. When he was ready, he allowed himself to look at her again, noting the way her skirt clung to her ass in a sweet yet flirty kind of way, and how the tops of her breasts peeked out along the upper edge of her halter top.

"Like have fun. Like laugh. Like...*live*."

Reaching out, he traced the side of her face with his fingertips, drawing her in for a kiss that had his heart accelerating in a way no pickup game of basketball ever could.

Chapter Seven

If it weren't for an approaching car, Emily could have stayed in Mark's arms all night, tasting his lips, marveling at the sensation of their mingling tongues and feeling the heat of his growing excitement against her body. She disengaged herself far slower than circumstances called for, resulting in some rubbernecking from the teenage occupants inside.

She stepped back, swiping at her lips in an unexpected burst of shyness that brought a crinkling to the skin around Mark's eyes. "I—I...wow. I don't know what to say," she confessed, once the car had passed.

"Say you don't want to call it quits for the night yet. Say we can hang out a little longer. Say I don't have to stop kissing you for at least another couple of hours."

Lifting her wrist into the glow of the streetlamp, she took note of the time, her heart sinking at the late hour. "But it's already eleven o'clock and—"

"It's a Friday, remember?"

She paused. Mark was right. There was no pressing need to get home, other than to take her medication.

And that could wait another couple of hours if necessary. In fact, the notion of not allowing her condition to impact her evening in any way was very appealing.

"So what do you suggest?" she finally asked, the resulting smile on his face warming her from head to toe.

"I don't know. But I'll think of something."

She savored the feel of his hands on her hips as he leaned against the car and pulled her close, the look in his eyes as he stroked her cheek threatening to render her speechless if she didn't think fast. "What about a little preview of what you missed the other morning?"

"What I missed?" he asked absentmindedly, as his hand moved to her hair and then her neck.

"The back entrance to my office opens to a room two stories tall. The climbing walls I have in there aren't quite the same as scaling the side of a mountain, but they're perfect for someone wanting to learn. If you're interested, that is."

"Are you serious?"

"Sure. It'll be fun." She disengaged herself from his arms and pointed her key at the car, the quick chirp-chirp of the locks accompanied by a flash of the headlights. "I've got a pair of shorts and a T-shirt I can change into at my office. Then we're good to go."

He stopped en route to the passenger side and made a T with his hands. "Whoa. But I like the outfit you're wearing now."

"I can't rock climb in a skirt, Mark."

"Darn."

She laughed. "I can put it back on when we're done. Though why it'll matter at midnight or later is beyond me."

"Because you look spectacular, that's why."

She slid behind the steering wheel and put the key in the ignition, the purr of the engine, coupled with the intensity in Mark's eyes, making her more than a little nervous. She'd gone rock climbing hundreds of times. She'd taught men of all shapes and sizes how to do the same on the very wall they'd be scaling in under twenty minutes. Yet in that moment, she would have second-guessed her ability to teach someone their ABC's, let alone how to climb a two-story wall, with her heart thudding in her chest the way it was.

And she knew why.

For as much as she bemoaned Kate's life plan, Emily wasn't much different herself. She might not have made an actual bullet-point list designed to take her from college to her death bed, with a nod to every major milestone in between, but she *did* like to be prepared.

It was why, she always suspected, she liked the kind of activities she'd built her life around. To kayak, she needed to be prepared—with a paddle and a life jacket. To take a survival trip through the woods, she needed to be prepared—with things like flint and a knife. To rock climb, she needed to be prepared—with rope, a harness and connectors. To scuba dive, she needed to be prepared—with a diving helmet and suit, weights, a regulator and a tank.

And when the doctor had walked into her hospital room six months earlier and uttered the words *multiple sclerosis,* she'd begun the mental preparation necessary to abandon all hope for her fifth and final childhood dream—of becoming a wife and mother. She'd prepared herself for living alone. For finding things that would fulfill a life shared by no one.

But Mark Reynolds, and the way he looked at her as if she was someone special, was throwing a monkey wrench in those plans.

"You do know that, right?"

She peered at him across the center console and shook her head. "I'm sorry, Mark. I think I may have missed what you just said."

"Is something wrong?" he asked.

"No. But I zoned out there for a minute." She slid the gearshift to Drive and pulled the car from the curb, the motion a welcome reprieve from the thoughts she was having at that moment. "So what is it I'm supposed to know?"

"That you look spectacular."

And just like that, the thoughts were back. Mark Reynolds hit every single one of the must-haves she'd set for a mate. He was smart, funny, motivated, out-doorsy—all of it. He was, essentially, a no-brainer, as Kate was fond of saying about all sorts of things in life. But the problem wasn't him. Or even the notion of him. It was Emily.

Sure, she wanted to believe there was hope that

someone would love her despite her condition. But the recurring nightmare she had three or four times a week said otherwise. It didn't matter how supportive her face-less prince tried to be, because the part that woke her in a cold sweat was having her prince slowly giving up his own wants and needs to be her caretaker.

"I'm guessing by your silence that you don't know that. So let me be the one to tell you that you do. And as I always tell Seth, I'm a pretty smart guy when it comes to the easy stuff in life."

She had to laugh. "Isn't *everyone* smart when it comes to the easy stuff?"

"You don't get out much, do you?" Mark quipped. "Then again, who am I to make a statement like that? I *never* get out."

His comment hit her like a slap to the side of the head. Tonight wasn't about looking inward. It was about having fun.

Mark needed that.

And so, too, did she.

Pulling her office keys from her purse, she climbed out of the Jeep and gestured for Mark to follow. "C'mon, let's go."

When they reached the main door of the barn, she unlocked it and stepped inside, the motion-sensor light she'd mounted in the hallway switching on instanta-neously. "Why don't you head downstairs, and I'll join you as soon as I get changed."

"Don't take too long, okay?"

"I won't." And she didn't. Less than five minutes later she was standing with him at the base of the climbing wall, with a harness for each of them. Dropping one to the ground, she helped Mark into his and connected it to his rope. "Take your time. This wall here—" she touched the one directly in front of them "—is the beginner wall. Your hand- and footholds are closer together on it. Once you've mastered this section, you can move on to the intermediate wall, where the hand- and footholds are farther apart and the climb is a bit more challenging."

"What about that wall?" Mark asked, pointing to the far side of the room.

"That's the expert wall. We'll save that for another day."

Mark snorted. "Or maybe another year."

She secured herself into her own harness and hooked herself in as Mark's belay. "No, another *day*. You'll get this, if you try. The folks who don't are the ones who let fear slow them down. Then the doubts take over and knock them the rest of the way out. I see it all the time. But if you think about it, climbing a wall or scaling the side of a mountain is really no different than wanting to write a novel or become a world champion chess player. You just have to check your hang-ups at the door and do what needs to be done to make it happen.

"As for what you need to do here, keep your body close to the wall. People tend to think their knees should be pointed inward, but if you turn them out a little bit, you'll be much more successful."

When she was done sharing a few more true tips, she motioned toward the wall. "Now it's time for you to give it a go. I'll be your belay a few times, then I'll hook you up to one of the electronic ones."

HOLD BY HOLD, Mark moved higher, Emily's advice about turning his knees outward helping immeasurably. His first trip up the wall was about trial and error, his second time solely about improvement. But by the third trip, he'd discovered that the best way to move was to do it in two parts—first his limbs, then his weight. Employing that technique again and again ensured this was his most skillful effort yet.

He glanced down over his shoulder as he hit the bell at the top of the wall, Emily's enthusiastic praise bringing an even bigger smile to his face. "Think I'm ready to move on to the next wall?" he called down.

"Absolutely. But you need to know that the chance of falling increases as the holds decrease in number." When he reached the bottom, she unhooked him from the rope and led him over to the intermediate wall, where she proceeded to hook him in once again. "Now, if you feel yourself start to slip, you need to push away from the wall right away. If you keep your feet out in front of you as the rope comes tight, you can brace yourself and keep from hitting the wall as you swing inward. Okay?"

"Feet out, push away...got it." He moved toward the wall, only to stop as he reached the base. "Is this your favorite?"

She shook her head and pointed to the wall behind them. "I like the expert wall best."

Now that he knew a bit more about the sport, he took a closer look, finding the distance between each hold far more impressive than he'd first realized. "Actually, I was asking more about rock climbing as opposed to the other sports you do. Is it your favorite?"

Her eyes widened with an excitement he envied, and he found himself hanging on her every word, her enthusiasm for exploration and life in general transforming her already beautiful face into something truly captivating.

"Wow. That's a tough one to answer. I like climbing because of the challenge. Being out on a real mountain, it's almost like a puzzle. You have to figure out the best hold to get you to the next level." She wandered across the room and took a seat on the bottom step of a narrow riser. "Rafting is exhilarating. One minute everything is calm and peaceful and you're paddling along a river, and then all hell breaks loose and you're forced to think and act fast. I love that part."

He unhooked his rope and sat down, too. "What about horseback riding?"

"That's one of those things I enjoy doing when I need time to think. I guess I find the cadence of the horse like a lullaby of sorts."

"What about when you're jumping over a fallen tree or a rock? Doesn't that kind of mess with the lullaby?"

She leaned against the upper step and closed her eyes. "Mess with? No, not really. Alter? Yeah, a little. You know how sometimes an exhausting activity can clear your mind of things that seemed such a big deal before you started? Well, working a horse hard does that for me. And the slow, wandering part gives me a chance to catch my breath and come up with a solution."

Mark's laugh brought her focus back on him. "So what you're telling me is that I need to learn how to ride a horse, huh?" Before she could respond, he moved the topic into a broader arena, desperate to keep the evening light and fun. "You ever think about changing the name of your company to Outdoor Therapy?"

"Sometimes the stuff on a person's bucket list is put there for therapeutic reasons." She swung her body to face him, hugging her knees to her chest. "But most of the time, learning how to ride a horse in adulthood, or rafting your way down a picturesque river, is about a dream. Sometimes it's a carryover from childhood— maybe from a television show or a book with a character who rafted or climbed or snorkeled. In those cases it's something my client has always wanted to do, and they're determined to do it before age makes it too difficult. But sometimes it's part of a broader dream that starts in a person's thirties or forties. Maybe they've always played life safe, or maybe they've been so busy caring for an elderly parent or a sickly kid that they need a diversion. Or maybe they're so intent on accomplishing some sort of personal feat that they show up at my door saying, '*I don't care what we do just so long as I can say I did something.*'"

"That happens?"

"All the time."

Mark considered her words and compared them to his own reasons for having enrolled in her orienteering class. His reasons, his motivations, put him in the latter group. "I guess I'm kinda like those folks. At least on some level."

"How so?" she asked.

"I think I needed to prove something to myself. Prove that I can change, can get myself out of a rut if I just make myself do it."

"And?"

"I did that," he replied. "Only now I want to see what other kinds of things I can do."

She released her legs and jumped to her feet, a sly smile tugging at her lips as she reached for his hand. "Okay, so let's see how you do with the intermediate wall."

He allowed her to guide him back there, only to wave off her attempts to hook him back up to the rope.

"Oh, come on, Mark, you can do this."

"And I'll give it a whirl in a few minutes. But first I want to see *you* climb."

"Why?"

He looked from the expert wall to the beginner's

and back again, finding the difference between the two substantial. "Because I want to see that someone can actually climb that thing."

Two minutes later, he was mentally patting himself on the back as he watched her climb the wall with the help of an electronic belay, the harness emphasizing her ass in a way that made him wish he was climbing right behind her, his body melding against hers as they moved from hold to hold.

Unfortunately, he wasn't in Emily's league, as evidenced by his repeated slips off the harder, more complex wall. But it didn't matter. He was having a blast nonetheless.

Here, the stress of day-to-day life was noticeably absent.

Here, he could laugh without guilt and live, rather than remember.

So he threw himself into the process of climbing, discovering what techniques worked for him. But even when he miscalculated, even when he out-and-out failed, it was still fun. Energizing, even.

Eventually, though, his arms and legs began to protest the workout, forcing him to unhook himself from the rope. "Emily? This was awesome! I don't know why I waited so long to try this kind of stuff. It's… *motivating*."

She came down from yet another successful climb on the expert wall, and met him in the center of the room, her hand reaching for the straps of her harness, only to be shooed away by his.

"Please. Allow me." Snaking his arms around her midsection, Mark slowly unhooked them, the feel of her lower back beneath his fingertips making his shorts tighten in response. Carefully he set her harness on the floor, then pulled her close once again, the ache to kiss her stronger than ever before. But this time, instead of kissing her mouth, he drew his lips across her eyes, her cheeks, her chin, eventually sinking still lower, to the base of her neck.

When she laced her fingers in his hair, he moaned, her taste, her touch like some sort of magnetic pull he was powerless to fight. Seconds turned to minutes as his lips left her neck and traveled back up to her mouth, the warmth and yearning he found there making him moan again.

"Mark," she whispered against his mouth. "It's almost one in the morning."

"And your point?" he countered as his tongue slipped past her protests.

Bracing her hands against his chest, she stepped back. "Most people are heading to bed by now."

"Most people aren't standing in a room alone with *you*, Emily Todd." Her laugh caught him by surprise. "You think I'm kidding?"

When she didn't respond, he continued. "I can't tell you the last time I laughed as much as I have tonight. Or the last time I didn't want to escape into bed just to get the day over with. But tonight, with you, it's been different. Which means I now have a much better understanding of how much it stinks for Seth when I make him clean up his toys before he's ready to stop playing."

SHE MET HIM in the parking lot in the same outfit she'd worn when they arrived, the hint of appreciation on Mark's face worth the time it had taken to stop in her office and change again. "Everything's locked up, so we're good to go," she announced.

At the feel of his hand on hers, Emily looked up and smiled. "This was fun, Mark. It really was."

"Uh-oh."

She drew back. "Excuse me?"

"I said 'uh-oh.'"

"I got that. But why?"

"I was bracing myself for the big black moment."

She wiggled her hands free of his and rested them on her hips. "What are you talking about?"

"The black moment. You know, like that instant when you reach into your wallet to pay the toll and realize you're flat broke. Or when you've been craving some peace and quiet, only to get home and find that your water valve broke and your basement is flooded. Or better yet, that moment when you're standing at the baggage claim in your oldest pair of ripped blue jeans and you realize your suitcase is lost, and the meeting with your boss's boss regarding your long-awaited promotion is less than an hour away."

"Ooh-kay. So what black moment are you bracing for right now?"

He lifted his hand to her shoulder and then circled it around her neck, drawing her to him with a gentle force that nearly took her breath away. Slowly, deliberately, he brought his lips down on hers for what had to be the sweetest, most passionate kiss she'd ever had— the kind she wasn't likely to forget in this lifetime or the next. When he was done, he hooked his index finger beneath her chin and lifted her face just enough to leave a long, lingering kiss at her hairline, making her shiver in response.

"I'm bracing myself for the moment you say good-bye."

Chapter Eight

Emily tried to make her laugh sound carefree, but it was obvious even to her that she'd failed miserably. She was falling for this man. To pretend otherwise required a kind of theatrical prowess she simply didn't possess.

"I don't want this to be a black moment," she finally whispered.

"Then say you'll follow me back to my house and come inside for a little while. Say you're not ready for our time together to end yet, either."

Startled, she glanced at the ground momentarily while she searched for something to say. All she came up with, though, was an echo of his words. "Your house?"

The lone light in the parking lot caught the concern on his face as he rushed to offer an explanation she wasn't entirely sure her body wanted to hear. "Oh. No. Not like that. It's just that I've really enjoyed hanging with you tonight, and I'm not too eager for reality to take over, you know?"

Problem was, she did know. She, too, found herself

in a world of married friends who were suddenly much harder to nail down for a movie or a coffee or even a walk in the park. She wasn't thrilled with the change, but she was used to it. Mark, however, probably wasn't. After all, his status as a single father was still fairly new.

"I could start a fire in the pit outside and we could sit on the patio and talk. Or if you'd rather, we could see if there are any good movies on cable. Whatever you want."

It took everything she could muster not to ask if he could kiss her again the way he had outside Kate's house, or even the way he had just now, on her forehead. Never in her history of kissing had such encounters zipped along virtually every nerve fiber in her body, waking up senses that had obviously been in a deep slumber for most, if not all, of her life.

Instead, she nodded, the answering smile on Mark's face one she wished she could bottle.

Reaching into her purse, she felt around for her keys and then headed to the driver's side of her car, the prospect of spending a few more hours with Mark intriguing. Once she was settled in her vehicle and he in his, he gave her the high sign from his window and motioned for her to follow him to the home he shared with his son.

When they arrived, she slid the Jeep into Park and looked to her right, absorbing the small white bungalow situated peacefully between two large oak trees. The front porch, while not terribly deep, welcomed with its whimsical summer flag and cozy wicker swing suspended on thick chains. The pathway that led to the steps boasted an assortment of black-eyed Susans, bee balms and even a few holdout blue flags.

His tap against her window prompted her to roll it down. "I see you garden?"

"Sally gardened. I'm just doing my best to keep everything—" his voice dipped ever so slightly "—*alive*. You know, so things look the same for Seth. He needs that sense of continuity and stability right now." Gesturing toward the walkway, Mark met her gaze through the open window. "Well? Shall we?"

"Um, sure." Squaring her shoulders, she stepped from the car and allowed him to place a guiding hand at her back.

Slowly, they made their way up the sidewalk and onto the porch, the answering silence of the crickets sending an unexpected shiver down her spine.

"Are you cold?" he asked, draping an arm over her shoulders.

"I think the more accurate word would be *nervous*." The second the comment was out of her mouth, she regretted it.

"Hey." He turned to face her, the concern in his eyes impossible to miss. "There's no need to be nervous. This is just another setting for an evening that's been mighty special so far. That's it, okay?"

Two seconds later, as she stood in his front hallway, she knew Mark was right. The barbecue had given them a chance to size each other up. The time spent climbing had been about having fun and not worrying about Kate's prying eyes. And being here in Mark's house was just another opportunity to enjoy each other's company before their day-to-day lives took over.

Glancing about, she couldn't help but notice the homey touches that magnified the welcoming feel of the porch. Knickknacks and memorabilia dotted the shelves of a corner hutch off to her left, while a smattering of pictures lined the wall on her right, creating a sense of warmth and familiarity.

Emily approached the first picture, the image of a newborn Seth drawing her. "His hair back then was the same color as yours."

Mark's breath was warm on her neck as he, too, moved in closer. "It was. But it didn't stay that way for long. When he wasn't much more than five or six months old, the hair on the sides of his head started to disappear. Funny thing is, we never saw any clumps in his crib or on the floor. It just kind of disintegrated, replaced with the blond hair he has now."

"Your wife was blonde, I take it," Emily mused before stepping to the right to take in the next picture, of a slightly older Seth with a smile so big it transformed his penetrating blue eyes into a virtual carbon copy of Mark's. "Wow. He was every bit as adorable here as he is now."

And just like that, the same sparkle she saw inside the frame ignited in the eyes of the man who shadowed her footsteps. "He *is* a cutie, isn't he?"

"The cutest," she echoed. "But even more than that, he's sweet and kind and quite the little conversationalist. I've found myself actually missing him since the other night at Sam's."

Mark drew back. "You mean that was real the other night?"

"*Real?*" she parroted.

"Yeah. I mean, I kind of assumed you were just being nice and, you know, humoring him because he's four and still hurting over his mom."

She pulled her focus from the photograph and fixed it on the larger, dark-haired man beside her. "*You* don't humor him, do you?"

"No. But he's mine. It's only natural for me to think he's brilliant and funny and the best kid in the world."

Sinking against the wall, Emily did her best to explain the lift the little boy had given her by simply being himself. "Well, he's *not* mine. And as you know, I'd never laid eyes on him before that night. But it took all of about five minutes—which, for the record, happened sans you—for me to find him engaging, thoughtful and very sweet. It's like—" she looked past Mark as she searched for the right words among an unexpected minefield of emotion "—being around him erased reality for a little while and actually enabled me to step back into the part of the picture I *didn't* draw when I was ten, yet always knew was there."

"Wait." Mark held up his hand. "You mean the pictures in your office? I thought you drew them all. They certainly looked like they'd been drawn by the same—"

"There was one more. One you didn't see because I opted not to frame it, much to Kate's chagrin, I might add. But I'm talking about one I *thought* about drawing but didn't." Suddenly aware of how idiotic she must sound, Emily straightened and made her way to the next photo, farther down the hallway. It was of Seth at about two, his face not much different than it was now. "While I can't be sure how I would have drawn a little boy at that time, my dream son would have been everything I saw in Seth the other night. The same joy, the same curiosity, the same beautiful heart. And he would have been a spectacular big brother to the little girl I would have drawn in his arms."

"You were quite the little artist back then, weren't you?"

"No, I was quite the *dreamer*."

"So you want kids? One boy, one girl?" Mark reached around her to straighten the frame, which had slipped off center by a fraction.

"I did. But I'm older now. Wiser, too." Feeling her mood begin to slip, she cast about for something to get things back on track. "Seth is just one of those kids who stick in your head and your heart long after they've run off, you know?"

At the feel of Mark's breath on her neck again, she turned to find his mouth settling on hers with an urgency that both stunned and excited her. Rising on tiptoe, she slipped her arms around his back and reveled in the feel of his strong, healthy body.

She gasped ever so slightly when he ran his fingers through her hair, pulling her head back so his lips could explore her chin, her jaw, the base of her throat. Her body responded with an undeniable warmth that left her heart pounding mere seconds before his hands started untying her halter top.

His gaze followed the straps as they cascaded down the front of her body to reveal even more of her breasts than her attire had already provided. Her breath hitched when his tongue slid over his lip in response.

"Emily?" he asked hungrily, before meeting her eyes and seeking permission to continue.

With a gentle yet deliberate finger, Mark lowered the fabric enough to reveal the lacy, strapless bra she'd bought during an extra girlie moment, his moan of desire instantly wiping away any regret she'd had over the price tag.

Slowly, deliberately, he moved his lips over the tops of her breasts, while his hands slipped behind her back and unfastened her bra. As the last hook was freed, the flimsy material fell away revealing the effects of his nearness. She cried out as his urgent mouth settled on her hardened nipples, teasing, caressing....

Suddenly he pulled back, desire blazing in his eyes. "Emily, I want you."

She answered by slipping her halter top the rest of the way off, her efforts rewarded by the appreciation in his eyes and the unmistakable bulge in his pants. Reaching around her waist, he undid the lone button on her waistband and watched her skirt fall into a puddle at her feet, revealing her white lacy thong.

"Oh my God, you are sexy as hell, Emily," he murmured against her ear. Grasping her hand, he led her through a small but tasteful family room and into a second, darker hallway beyond.

When they stepped inside his bedroom, he pulled her close, his fingers slipping around her waist, only to travel to her ass and tug her against his still-clad body, evoking a moan of her own.

He wanted *her*.

Emily.

MS and all...

RELEASING HIS HOLD on her, Mark stepped back long enough to take stock of the woman standing in the middle of his bedroom, his erection straining against the fabric of his shorts in response. Never in his wildest fantasies had he ever come across a female quite like Emily Todd.

Her eyes, her hair, her face spoke to his protective side, the innocence he found in her gripping his heart and threatening to never let it go. And her breasts spoke to him in a different way—tantalizing and teasing him with rock-hard nipples that confirmed his desire was reciprocated.

With determination befitting a Jedi warrior, he

forced his eyes from her breasts and allowed them to travel south, down her flat and sexy abdomen to the alluring scrap of fabric that separated him from a heat he craved as he'd never craved before. He sank to his knees and guided her panties down her legs with his mouth, letting the garment drop to her ankles so he could taste her sweetness.

Her answering moan of pleasure was followed by the feel of her fingers as they buried themselves in his hair. He wanted this woman. Wanted her now.

Rising to his feet, he steered her hands to the waistband of his shorts, watching her face as she released his erection with a tug. When she was done, he pulled her to him, the heat of their skin mingling as he laid her on the bed and lowered himself to her, their bodies joining effortlessly.

She felt so good and so right as he moved inside her—slowly and gently at first, then with gathering strength and desire. With thrust after thrust he claimed her, the intensity of his efforts making her cry out for more—a request he was all too happy to oblige, until neither one of them could resist any longer, their release coming so strong and so decisively it left his body craving an encore before the spinning in his head had even stopped.

Chapter Nine

It was a full ten minutes or so before Mark opened his eyes, the fleeting confusion in his face at her empty spot in the bed giving way to a smile that warmed her the moment he spotted her standing in the bedroom doorway, wrapped in a bath towel, watching him.

The thin cotton sheet slipped from his chest as he rose on his elbow to give her a more thorough and appreciative once-over. "How long have you been standing there?"

She held her hand to the opening of her towel and picked her way across the clothes-littered floor, her other hand clutching the skirt and halter top she'd rescued from the hallway. "Not long. I—I took a shower in your guest bathroom. I hope that was okay. I got up about an hour ago and did some exercises that made me a little sweaty."

She could feel his gaze as she bent to retrieve her panties. "Exercises?"

"Uh-huh. Sit-ups, push-ups, that sort of thing."

"Naked?"

The huskiness of his voice warmed her face, rendering her unable to answer with anything more than a nod.

"Wow." He dropped onto his back and laced his fingers behind his head, a mischievous smile playing across his lips. "I'm getting worked up just thinking about that."

She glanced at the part of his body still covered by the sheet, the sudden elevation of the fabric just below his waist confirming his words. She swallowed.

Mark patted her side of the mattress. "Get back in here. I miss you."

"But my hair's all wet," she protested.

"Get back in here."

She set her recovered clothing on his dresser and made her way around the edge of the bed. "If you're sure."

He rose on his elbow a second time, the sheet slipping farther down his well-toned body. "Oh, I'm sure. Trust me. But lose the towel, okay?"

She paused, a sudden burst of self-consciousness making her apprehensive about granting his wish.

"Oh, no, don't go getting all shy on me now. Your body is exquisite."

Slowly, she peeled away the soft blue towel and slipped into bed beside him, where he coaxed her onto her side and pulled her back against his chest. She snuggled there, keenly aware of his still-hard length pressed to the base of her back. "It might not always be that way, you know," she murmured in a voice that was suddenly sleepy.

He kissed the top of her wet head a few times. "What?"

"My body. It could change in lots of ways."

The pressure of his lips ceased temporarily. "You've got a long way to go until you're old enough to worry about body changes. And even then, I suspect those worries will pass you by, with good reason."

She rolled over and planted a kiss on the tip of his chin. At his happy moan, she kissed him one more time and then looked up at the ceiling. "I'm not talking about age-related changes, silly. I'm talking about disease-related changes."

At his silence, she continued, transported back to countless nights and mornings over the past few months when this exact topic had played its way through her thoughts. With no one next to her to hear her fears.

"There are the obvious ones, of course, that most people think of when they hear the words multiple sclerosis. You know, wheelchairs, walkers, a funny lilt to your walk, that sort of thing. Then there's the chance that I could wake up one day and be temporarily blind, or unable to feel my legs or my arms or even both."

On a roll, she kept talking, the need to say everything out loud far stronger than she'd realized. "Sure, I know the meds I'm taking three times a week are designed to help stave off the disease as long as possible, and I'm grateful for them. But even those bring their fair share of issues. When I have to take a shot, I try to do it just before bed so I can sleep off the flulike effects. And if I don't get enough sleep on those nights, I pay for it with aches and pains in the morning. If I fail to take it before bedtime, as was the case last night, then I have to take it in the morning and basically deal with feeling lousy all day."

She drew a deep breath, letting it out slowly. "And then there's the bruising and stuff at the shot site." Shifting ever so slightly, she guided his gaze to the back of her arm, her abdomen, her hip and upper thigh, tapping a small red spot some eight inches above her knee. "You might not be able to see the marks a whole lot right now, unless I just took one, like I did before my shower. But over time, after months and years of injecting myself in the same places again and again? Well, they'll be impossible to miss regardless of how toned I might—"

A quick, yet persistent buzz cut her off midsentence.

Mark rolled to his left and reached toward the nightstand, retrieving his cell phone from beside the lamp. He looked at the display screen and sat up, flipping the phone open. "Good morning, little man. How'd you sleep?"

For the briefest of moments, Mark's lack of response to what Emily had shared stung ever so slightly. She'd kept everything to herself for so long it had felt good to know someone else was listening. To go from that to a phone call without so much as a squeeze or nod of acknowledgment was disconcerting.

Then again, he hadn't asked for the phone call to come at that exact moment, and it was Seth, after all. The same little boy who'd managed to grab hold of her heart with barely more than a smile. Yes, Seth Reynolds was a sweet boy, of that she was sure. She'd seen it in his devotion to his sand castle and the careful thought he'd given to the life he'd have inside its walls if he were truly a prince. She'd seen it in the way he'd listened so intently to his father's inquiries about her job and her clients while they ate, interjecting a few well-thought-out questions of his own on occasion. She'd seen it in the way he'd hopped down from his chair to retrieve a slip of paper a passing patron had dropped on the ground. She'd seen it in the way he'd shared tales about summer camp and his favorite times with Mark. And she'd seen it in his eyes when she'd first told Mark about her diagnosis.

Kids like Seth didn't become that way all by themselves. They were shown how by someone who was like that, too.

Stealing a glance in Mark's direction, she felt a warmth spread throughout her body that had absolutely nothing to do with physical desire and everything to do with genuine affection and admiration.

Maybe she really could frame that final drawing one day....

Maybe there really was a prince who could love his princess no matter what....

Content for the first time in a very long time, she

rolled onto her side and drifted off to sleep, the sound of Mark's voice as he spoke to his son the best lullaby and postinjection anti-ache ointment she could ever imagine.

"So TELL ME WHAT YOU DID with Gam last night. Did you get pizza?"

"Yupper doodle! And ice cream, too."

Mark closed his eyes at the happiness in his son's sweet voice, allowing it to soak into every pore of his being, and feeling his shoulders and neck muscles relax as it did. He was grateful for the result, but perplexed by the need.

He'd had an amazing time with Emily last night. She'd been both fun and funny at the barbecue, patient and encouraging on the climbing walls, and beyond his wildest expectations in his bed. They'd made love several times throughout the night, her enthusiasm and passion elevating the encounter into the best-ever category. And even when he'd awakened to find her watching him, he'd been happy. Truly happy.

Yet here he was, sitting inches from her sheet-covered body, and feeling the tension roll in all over again. It was subtle in nature, residing primarily in his upper body and temples, but it was present, nonetheless.

"And you wanna know what else we did, Daddy?"

Why on earth was he tense? It made no sense at all.

"Daddy?"

Mark shifted his focus from Emily to the dresser on the opposite wall. There, beside the pile of clothes she had placed on top, was the picture of Seth and Sally that greeted him each morning. It had been taken on their last outing together before the cancer had confined his wife to bed. Their smiles, so like one another's, still brought one to Mark's lips, too. Yet today, unlike all the other times he'd looked at that same picture and experienced the same reaction, the joy was fleeting.

Because there, on his son's face, was something he'd overlooked each of the other thousand or so times he'd stared at that photo.

Seth's mouth might have been smiling—a by-product, no doubt, of having spent a special day with his beloved mom—but his eyes weren't. In them there was sadness—the kind of sadness only those who'd witnessed the suffering of a loved one could ever truly understand.

Mark swiped at the tears he felt forming, and willed himself to concentrate.

"Daddy? Are you still there?"

He tightened his jaw in determination. "I'm here, Seth."

Focus...

"Gam and me had *two* whole bowls of ice cream!"

There were so many things Mark wished he could go back and change from the moment Sally had received her diagnosis. Things about himself and the way he'd handled the situation that still haunted him six months after her passing. But of all the mistakes he'd made, all the regrets that had him pacing his bedroom at all hours of the night, the one he shed the most tears over was the one that concerned his son.

Or, rather, the way he'd let his son down during the most difficult time of the little boy's life.

"Did you hear me, Daddy?"

Focus, damn it...

"I'm sorry, little man. Can you say it again?"

"Gam and me had *two whole* bowls of ice cream! With whipped cream *and* candy pieces on top!"

"You mean one for her and one for you?" he asked.

"No! Two for each of us! And you know what else? Gam's new frigerfrator came and it was in a great big box!"

Mark resisted the urge to correct his son's pronunciation of refrigerator and addressed his enthusiasm, instead. "Sounds to me like you're more excited about the box than you are about her refrigerator."

"It's really, really big, Daddy. Bigger than me, and even bigger than *Gam* if she could stand up."

Closing his eyes, he imagined the smile that accompanied his son's words. He'd taken Seth's smiles for granted once. Now he knew better. "Wow. That must be a really big box."

"It is! And you know what? Gam said we can get out my crayons and turn it into a castle that I can actually go inside!"

Before Mark could weigh in, Seth chattered on. "And then guess what, Daddy? Guess what she told me?"

"What?"

"She said we can keep it in the playroom for as long as I want!"

He made a mental note to have some flowers on hand when his mother dropped Seth off that evening. Maybe even a box of candy, too.

"I love you, Seth," he whispered. "You know that, right?"

"Yupper doodle! And I love you, too, Daddy. Bunches and bunches and *bunches!*"

Long after his son had hung up, Mark held the phone to his ear, his focus trained on the photograph of Seth and Sally and the haunted look he was slowly but surely trying to eradicate from his son's deep blue eyes.

A warm hand on his bare back made him jump, and he snapped the phone closed.

"Everything okay with Seth?" Emily asked in a voice thick with sleep.

"Yeah." He propped his pillow against the headboard and reclined against it with a quiet sigh.

Emily rolled onto her side and smiled up at him. "So did he have some more pepperoni pizza?"

"Uh—what?"

Her smile faltered a smidge as he turned his head and met her gaze. "Seth. Did he have pizza last night?"

"I think so. I don't really remember."

Glancing back at the picture of Sally and Seth, he sighed again, this time more loudly and with a hint of impatience that made Emily sit up, his sheets drawn around her chest.

"Is there a problem with Seth?"

He looked from the image of Sally to the one of Seth in her arms, the hurt and loss of innocence in his son's eyes clawing at Mark's insides in a way he simply couldn't ignore.

And in that instant, he knew what had been nagging at his subconscious.

The tension he'd been feeling when Seth's call came in wasn't a coincidence. It was a warning bell. One he needed to heed before it was too late. He owed him that much.

Emily's hand closed on his and squeezed. "Mark? Is there a problem with Seth?"

"No." He cast about for the best way to remove the Band-Aid her presence had placed across his heart, and finally settled on the tried-and-true yank method that got it all over in one shot. "There's a problem with *us,* Emily."

"Us?" she echoed, all sleepiness slipping from her voice in favor of confusion. "I don't understand. What's wrong?"

He bit back the urge to halt the conversation and pull her into his arms before he ruined everything, because he had to say it. "I can't do this."

"Do what?"

He forced himself to meet her eyes. "This. You know, with us." He moved his hand back and forth between them. "Seth deserves…*better.*"

A wave of self-loathing washed over him as his

words hit their mark, but it was short-lived. His responsibility, his duty, was to Seth. It had to be.

"Better?" she echoed in confusion. "Mark, I don't understand what you're saying. Please tell me what's going on. Everything was fine five minutes ago."

"No. It wasn't."

"Yes, it was. And you know that as well as I do."

He had to make her understand. "I have to make a better choice for Seth. It's my job."

"A better choice?" she whispered through suddenly clenched teeth. "Wait a minute. I get this now. This isn't about finding someone better. It's about finding someone healthy, isn't it? Someone who doesn't have to take shots, or have bruises all over her body? Someone who won't slow you down or embarrass you because she slurs her speech in front of your friends."

When he didn't respond, she scooted to the edge of the bed and traded the sheet for the towel she'd shed on the floor. With three easy strides, she crossed the room and pulled the pile of clothes off his dresser.

He fought back tears as he watched her march toward the door, the sight of her retreating back making it hard to breathe. But he had to let her go. He really had no choice. His life choices weren't about him. Not anymore.

Yet as she reached the doorway, he couldn't help but call her back one more time. For one more glimpse at the ray of sunshine that had graced his life and his bed for one amazing evening he knew he'd never forget.

"Emily?"

Without turning to look at him, she paused there.

"Please know that the Folks Helping Folks Foundation is here to help you in whatever way you need as this disease progresses. It's what we do, and we're really very good at it. And the Longfeld donation I told you about yesterday? That could really help you in ways you may not even be able to realize yet." He could hear his voice growing hoarser with each passing word, the overwhelming sadness at losing this woman making it difficult to speak. "So, please, give it some thought. If you decide to come on board and let us help, I'll assign Bob to your case—he's the best. He'd take good care of anyone, but if I give him a heads-up that I know you, he'll take even better care of you. I promise."

Slowly she turned, her clothes clutched against her body with trembling hands. "Let me make this crystal clear to you, Mark. I don't want or need Bob's help and I most certainly don't want or need yours, either. I am fine, and I will continue to be fine. On my own. The way it's supposed to be."

He opened his mouth to protest, but shut it as she continued, her voice, her demeanor, taking on an icy quality.

"And just in case it's unclear, being on my own is the way I *want* it to be."

Chapter Ten

Emily pulled into the parking lot beside Perk It Up and cut the engine, the only tangible remnant of her morning a dull ache above her eyes that more than served her right. She'd been a fool giving Mark a second thought, and an even bigger one for giving him a chance at her heart.

But it wouldn't happen again, that was for sure.

Leaning forward, she peered into the rearview mirror for any sign of the tears that had birthed the headache, aware of the trouble she'd be in if Kate suspected she'd been crying. Then again, she could always pin her red-rimmed eyes on the aches and pains that had racked her body all morning long.

A rap on her driver's side window made her jump.

"Would you stop checking yourself out in that mirror and get moving, already? I'm in desperate need of my jumbo size mocha latte. *Now.*"

With a quick swipe of her hand through her hair, Emily grabbed her purse from the passenger seat, mustered the best smile she could and met Kate on the walkway that led to their favorite coffee shop. "Long morning?" she joked as they headed inside for their weekly get-together that had been a tradition since they graduated from college.

"Long night, long morning, take your pick. It's all kind of blending together at this point." Kate swept her hand toward the seating area. "Why don't you get us a table and I'll get our drinks. That way there won't be an issue finding a table. You want your usual?"

Emily considered saying no and asking for a simple glass of water, but knew it was best just to nod. Any deviation from normal where Kate was concerned was too risky. Especially today, when Emily was one funny look away from screaming at the top of her lungs until the men in white suits arrived to cart her off to some padded room somewhere.

No, her best chance of getting through the next hour was to act as normal as possible and keep control of the conversation, steering it toward innocuous subjects like work, Kate's favorite reality show, Joe and the status of Kate's baby-making quest.

Selecting a table beside the large plate-glass window, Emily peered out at the comings and goings of downtown Winoka. Everywhere she looked there were couples—teenage couples, young married couples, elderly couples, and everything in between. It was as if the only way people got from point A to point B in this town was by holding hands and stopping every few feet to make googly eyes at one another.

It was maddening, really. A little nauseating, even.

"You do realize I've been climbing the walls ever since you left the barbecue last night, don't you? I think I checked my cell phone close to a hundred times before Joe finally hid it in his den somewhere." Kate paused beside Emily's chair and studied the bold black initials snaking their way down the seam of both foam cups. "Okay, here you go, this one is yours."

Claiming the empty lattice-back stool across from her, Kate perched on the edge and widened her eyes, waiting. "Well? What do you have to say?"

Emily looked from her to her coffee cup and back again. "Oh, yeah. Sorry." With an appropriately timed cringe, she remembered her manners. "Thanks for the coffee, Kate. I'll pick them up next week, okay?"

Her friend shook her head and laughed. "Nice try."

Slowly she lifted her cup to her mouth and took a sip, Kate's gaze never leaving her face. "What? What am I failing to say?"

A squeal from her friend took her and the rest of the patrons in the coffee house by surprise. "I want to hear everything. And by everything, I mean *everything*. Don't leave anything out. Not one single, solitary thing."

"That last sentence was rather redundant, don't you think?" Emily set her cup back on the table and wrapped her hands around it. "But really, Kate, I have no idea what you're talking about."

Pushing her own cup to the side, She leaned in. "You know, I told Joe you were going to do this. In fact, I think I nailed your line almost verbatim." A pause for reflection gave way to a slow, yet self-satisfied nod. "Actually, you know what? There's no *almost* about it. I got every last word with the exact same inflection and everything. Wow. I've really got you down, don't I?"

"Kate. Would you knock it off, please? I have absolutely no earthly idea what you're babbling—"

And then she knew.

There would be no time-killing conversation about her upcoming fall classes, no stories starring Joe as the perfect husband, no idle chitchat about the latest fashion trends being worn about town that day. And there would be no graphic details about Kate's ovulation cycle or the number of times the happy couple did it during the primo thirty-six hour target that month.

No, the conversation had already been picked out for them hours earlier, when she'd made the mistake of bringing a male guest to Kate and Joe's barbecue....

"You do realize I could sit here and give you all sorts of grief over you having gone out to dinner with this guy and his son *days ago* and never saying a word, but I won't. I could also give you all sorts of grief over your failure to call and fill me in on everything when you got home last night, but I won't. Part of being a good friend is patience and understanding, right? Which, technically, I gave you by not bugging you for details until now." Kate grabbed her cup and took a big sip, fanning her mouth as she did. "Ow. Hot."

"There's nothing to tell, Kate."

"You have pizza with a super hot guy, bring him along to my barbecue and then forget to call me with all the deets afterward, and you expect me to believe there's nothing to tell? Are you nuts?"

Pushing away the image of Mark's bare chest as it rose and fell above her body countless times throughout the night, Emily addressed her friend's inquiry as quickly and succinctly as possible. "Look, I saw him and his son at the beach when I was kayaking. I let him take Seth out in the kayak for a few minutes, and they tipped over. Seth was fine because he had on Floaties, but I swam in and got him nonetheless. To thank me, they took me out for pizza. No big deal."

"Most no-big-deals don't look at a woman the way yours looked at you last night," Kate said.

Emily lifted her cup, only to set it back down as her hands began to tremble ever so slightly. "I don't know what you're talking about. Mark wasn't looking at me in any special way last night."

"Oh, no? Then I guess every single one of my friends who commented to me about the two of you last night was imagining the same thing I was?"

"And what was that?" she asked, exasperated.

"That your no-big-deal is more than a little hot for you."

Hot for her.

She couldn't help it—she laughed. It was either that or cry. And she knew if she opted for the latter, she wouldn't be able to stop anytime soon. "I think you *and* your friends all need your eyes checked."

Kate took another sip. "It sounds to me like you're the one who needs your eyes checked. I mean, c'mon, Em. That guy couldn't keep his eyes off you. And when you talked…either to him or with one of us? He *listened*. And I mean, really listened. As if the words coming out of your mouth were the most fascinating things he'd ever heard." Kate eyed her across the lid of her cup. "Are you really going to sit there and tell me you weren't aware of that?"

Emily pulled her hands from around her own drink and dropped them into her lap. She'd revisited Kate's barbecue innumerable times that morning, reliving many of the things her friend was spouting. Of course she'd seen the looks Mark had sent in her direction. Of course she'd been aware of the way he listened when she spoke. And yes, she remembered every single minute of their time together. But none of that erased the cold hard facts.

Kate released a long, dreamy sigh through pursed lips. "I mean, Emily…really. Mark turned heads last night. Happily married heads, I might add. And it wasn't just because he's good-looking. A lot of it was because of how attentive he was to you." A quick laugh gave way to a faraway look. "He was gentle and kind and funny, and so helpful with everything where you were concerned."

Emily glanced up. "Helpful?"

"He carried your plate out to the Adirondack chairs, didn't he? He opened the door for you every time you went in the house, and picked up your horseshoes after every round you played."

Before she could fully process everything Kate was saying, her friend continued on in a voice that had suddenly grown more hushed. "He really seemed to care about you, Em. Like he'd do just about anything you needed him to do, if you'd only *let* him."

Instantly, she remembered being in his arms, the sensation of his hands on her face so strong in her mind that she could actually feel them.

"I mean, you're so wrapped up in this stupid nightmare you keep having about being a burden that you're missing the possibility of what could very well be right in front of your face. In an extremely attractive package, I might add."

"Stupid nightmare?" Emily echoed.

"Yes. A stupid nightmare. I mean, come on, Em. Don't you realize how silly it is to let some recurring dream keep you from the one thing you've wanted since we were little?"

"I wanted lots of things when we were little," she reminded Kate before slipping off her stool and tossing her nearly full cup into a nearby trash can. "And I'm living them right now."

"Not all of them."

"I'm living the ones I have control over."

Kate grabbed Emily's hands and held them tight.

"No man who has a clue what you're worth would ever shy away from you because of the MS. It just wouldn't happen."

She clenched her teeth and muttered, "Oh? You don't think so?"

"Of course I don't. Joe doesn't, either. You just need to let the right guy see the true you—without that silly nightmare clouding the picture. The rest will fall into place. We're sure of it."

Emily weighed her response as she gathered her purse in her hands and hooked it over her shoulder, her desire to hide her hurt superceded by a need to make things clear. "Then perhaps it's not your eyesight that needs to be checked, but rather, your intuition. And if you have Joe's checked, too, maybe you can get a discount. You know, a check-one-check-the-second-for-free kind of thing."

It was Kate's turn to protest. "Why are you being so negative? This isn't like you."

Closing her eyes, she counted to ten, praying for patience and something resembling civility.

"Are you going to let your diagnosis make you shut down Bucket List 101?" Kate challenged.

Emily opened her eyes as she hit five. "Of course not. You know better than that."

"Then why would you let it keep you from finding someone special? That makes absolutely no sense to me, Em!"

"Then let me spell it out for you, Kate. Living my dream with Bucket List 101 affects me and me only."

"That's not true. What about Trish?"

Emily rolled her eyes. "Trish is nineteen. She'll be married in a few years. And once she and Tommy have kids, she won't be working anymore. But if I build a life with another person, this illness will affect him at some point, too. *That* isn't fair."

"And you think a guy like Mark couldn't handle your MS?"

"I don't *think,* Kate. I *know.*" She saw the way her friend jumped back at the anger in her voice, but she couldn't help it. She'd had enough. Her head had come out of the clouds the second the neurologist had walked into her hospital room and uttered her diagnosis six months earlier. It was time for Kate's head to come out of the clouds now, too. "So Mr. No-Big-Deal can find someone else to open doors for, and carry plates for, and pretend to listen to as if she's the only woman on the face of the earth."

Emily's breath hitched as the tears she'd vowed she wouldn't cry in front of her friend began to form in the corners of her eyes. "I just hope, for her sake, she has a super strong immune system, capable of withstanding the common cold and flu. Because if she doesn't, she'll surely be getting the Mark Reynolds seal of disapproval where it comes to him and his son."

Kate's gasp netted more than a few curious looks in their direction. "Emily! You can't truly believe that."

"Oh, no? Hmm. Do you know why I didn't call you last night when I got home from your barbecue?"

"No…"

"Well, here are some deets for you, Kate. I didn't phone because I didn't go home after the barbecue."

Emily lowered her voice, abruptly aware of the hush at several neighboring tables. "I took Mark to the office and taught him how to climb. We laughed, we joked, we had a great time. And then, when we were done climbing, I went home with him…and we slept together. When we woke up, I shared a few of my realities with him, only to have him essentially toss me out of his bed *and* his life. So don't you dare sit there and tell me I can't believe what I just said, because I can and I do."

Stopping for a much-needed breath, she steadied her voice and her emotions until she could finally escape to the privacy of her car. "But no worries, Kate, I'm fine. I'd much rather live my life in a way that fits *me*. Besides, for what it's worth, the days of wanting that fairy tale prince—from that silly picture I drew at your kitchen table a lifetime ago—to sweep me off my feet are long gone. And you know what? I'm okay with that. A-okay, as a matter of fact."

A flash of pain skittered across Kate's face. "But—"

"Because when it comes right down to it, I'd much rather walk on my own two feet than count on anyone else, anyway. It's the surest way I know to get where I'm going, don't you think?"

Chapter Eleven

Mark made his way through the house, turning on lights and fluffing throw pillows as he went, his ear turned toward the driveway for the sound of his mother's car. For far too long, he'd sat in the gathering dusk replaying his time with Emily—remembering every smile and every laugh they'd shared.

Desperate for something to deaden the ache in his chest, he strode into the kitchen and over to the refrigerator, liberating a rare can of beer from the top shelf and popping the tab. Try as he might, he couldn't get the image of her beautifully toned and naked body out of his thoughts.

One-night stands had never been his thing, even during his pre-Sally days. And last night, when he'd made love to Emily, that hadn't changed. What, exactly, he'd thought they had or could have, he wasn't sure, but he knew he'd wanted to see her again.

Yet all that had changed the moment he'd heard Seth's voice juxtaposed against the last photograph he'd taken of Sally and Seth together.

It didn't matter what he thought of Emily. It didn't matter how alive she made him feel or how perfect it felt to be inside her. He wasn't a single man. He was a single father. There was a big difference between the two.

"Daddy?"

He placed his beer can on top of the refrigerator and met his son in the hallway, squatting down and holding out his arms. "Little man! You sure are a good tiptoer. I didn't even hear you come in."

Seth stopped just shy of Mark's arms. "I didn't use my tippy toes, Daddy. I even banged the door, but you were making that silly face."

Dropping his arms, he studied his son closely. "Silly face? What silly face?"

"This one." Seth leaned against the wall, opened his mouth a little and stared off into space, before breaking the pose with a giggle. "See?"

Mark had to laugh. "Oh, sorry. Daddies get distracted, I guess." Then, opening his arms once again, he greeted his son in the way he'd intended before letting his thoughts stray to a topic best left in the shadows. "Do you have any idea how glad I am to see you, little man?"

It was true. Seth was the glue that kept his life together, the reason he got up every morning and came home from work every evening. Without him, Mark would be lost, his life empty of any real purpose.

Seth squeezed him with all his might, a curious

aroma of Play-Doh and chocolate chip cookies clinging to his hair. "Gam wants you to wave before she leaves."

Lifting his son into his arms, Mark made his way to the front door and blew his mom a kiss before locking up for the evening. "So did you make your castle with Gam out of that great big box you told me about when you called?"

Seth nodded. "I did! And it is so-o-o neat, Daddy. Gam said I could show it to you next week when I'm back in camp and you have to pick me up at her house after work."

"I can't wait to see it." He carried his son into the living room and set him down on the couch, claiming the cushion to Seth's left. "Maybe, if I can find another box, we can add on an addition. Like a throne room or something."

His son's eyes brightened with genuine excitement. "I bet my princess would like a special room for all her fancy dresses."

"Your princess, eh? Is she pretty?" Mark teased, ruffling Seth's hair with his fingers.

"Yupper doodle. The prettiest."

He considered the little boy's words with all the seriousness he could muster, and consciously relaxed his shoulders. "That's quite a claim, little man. Tell me about her."

Tucking his legs beneath him, Seth took a deep breath, releasing it along with a lengthy description. "She's got great big brown eyes that twinkle with so much pixie dust that some of it falls over the top of her nose and across her happy cheeks. She's got short yellow hair that curls right here—" he pointed at the sides of his face "—and a really big smile all the time."

"Wow. She *does* sound pretty. Special, too. Just like you." Mark pulled the little boy's head onto his lap. "I missed you last night and this morning. I didn't have anyone to make my special pancakes for."

Seth giggled. "You could make me some tomorrow morning."

"Yes, I can."

"So what did *you* do, Daddy?"

"I ate cereal."

Seth's giggle grew louder. "No, silly. What did you do last night while I was at Gam's?"

Mark forced a smile and did his best to keep his voice light. "I played some horseshoes."

"Is that a game?"

"Yes, it is." He tapped Seth's nose with his finger and animated his voice. "You use real horseshoes, just like the kind real horses wear on their feet."

"Where'd you play with those kinda shoes, Daddy?"

"At a barbecue I went to."

"Whose barbecue?"

"No one you've ever met."

Seth sat up, eyes wide. "You went to a stranger's house, Daddy? You know you're not s'posed to do that. It could be dangerous."

He tried not to laugh at his son's solemn expression.

"Well, they weren't strangers, exactly. The people having the barbecue are friends of the person I went with."

"Who'd you go with?"

He exhaled into the palm of his hand, his discomfort over the shift in topic increasing exponentially. "I went with Emily."

"Emily!" Seth parroted, just before a smile spread his lips wide. "Oh, wow, I like Emily. Bunches and bunches!"

Clapping his hands together, Mark seized on the only sure-fire conversation changer he could find. "You know what I found in the cabinet earlier today?"

Seth shook his head.

"Butterscotch sauce and a bag of mini chocolate chips. And I figured, if you're up for it, maybe we could make our own ice cream sundaes right here at home," he said in his best conspiratorial voice. "So what do you say, little man? Does that sound like a yummy plan for after dinner?"

"I already had dinner. At Gam's. She made me eat all my broccoli." Seth looked toward the door and lowered his voice to a near whisper. "It wasn't very good."

"But it's good for you." Mark scooted to the edge of the couch and glanced back at him. "Come on. Let's have a treat."

"Did you find whipped cream, too? 'Cause sundaes are s'posed to have whipped cream, Daddy."

Grateful for his son's one-track mind where ice cream was concerned, Mark rose to his feet and motioned for him to follow. "As a matter of fact, I did. A great big tub of it."

When they reached the kitchen, Seth climbed onto his stool at the counter and Mark grabbed a pair of bowls from the cabinet, along with two spoons from the utensil drawer. Then, with as much pomp and circumstance as he could muster, he set about getting everything they would need for their sundae bar, including the jar of sprinkles Seth spied while Mark was extracting the chocolate chips from the pantry.

"Do you think Emily likes ice cream, Daddy?"

He paused with his hand on the freezer door, his back to his son. "I can't answer that, Seth." Reaching inside, he pulled out two cartons and held them up. "So what'll it be? Vanilla or chocolate? Or—" he winked "—a little bit of *both?*"

"I betcha she likes vanilla best, just like me," Seth declared.

Mark's shoulders drooped. So much for changing the subject.

He carried the cartons to the counter and set them beside the bowls. "Maybe. I don't know." Then, with the help of the old spoon-under-warm-water trick he'd learned from Sally, he scooped two small mounds for Seth and two for himself. "Mmm. Finding that butterscotch sauce today was a pretty nice surprise, wasn't it?"

Seth propped one elbow on the counter and reached

for the sauce with his other hand. "Can I put it on all by myself, Daddy? Please?"

If it'll make you forget about Emily...

Aloud, he said, "If you're really, really careful, sure. But let's try to make that bottle last for a while, okay? That way we can have sundaes again another day."

"Okay! Maybe Emily can have some then, too, right?" Seth pulled the lid off the butterscotch sauce and carefully tilted it in the air above his bowl. Slowly, carefully, he poured some across the top of his ice cream, and then did the same to Mark's. When he was done, he turned the container upright and smiled. "See? I saved plenty for Emily."

Not wanting to stomp all over his son's mood, Mark made a show of adding a dollop of whipped cream to both bowls and then allowing Seth to decorate them with a few tiny handfuls of chocolate chips and a quick shake of the sprinkle jar. Once the last chip was placed on each sundae, Mark declared their concoctions ready to eat.

"Now, what do you say we try and see which one of us can eat all our ice cream from start to finish without making a peep? Whoever wins gets to pick which story we read before bed."

"Can I say it's yummy if it's yummy?" Seth asked.

"No, sirree. No yummies, no lip smacking of any kind, and—" he sat on the stool next to Seth and touched his finger to the little boy's nose "—most especially, no burping."

A fit of giggles gave way to the quietest ice cream eating Mark could ever remember, and he was glad. Whatever it took to keep Seth from talking about Emily. Mark's feelings for her were still way too close to the surface.

All day long he'd revisited moments from the barbecue, his favorites revolving around the game of horseshoes he'd failed at again and again. She'd been so good-natured and easygoing that she'd coaxed the same qualities out of him despite his lack of prowess or points. And when they'd gone climbing inside her office building, she'd made him feel as if there wasn't anything he couldn't do.

But it was the part that came later—in his bed—that he'd found himself lingering on. Every touch, every sound, every move was replayed in his thoughts until he'd had to force himself to focus on something else.

Now that Seth's chattering had ceased, though, Mark found himself pressing the play button in his mind once again. And sure enough, an image of Emily looking up at him as he made love to her flashed before his eyes, making him drop his spoon into his bowl with a metallic crash.

"Daddy, you made a noise!" Seth accused. "A great big loud one!"

Shaking away the memory, he turned to the towhead sitting beside him. "So I did."

"I won! I won!" Seth jumped off his stool and headed

down the hallway to his bedroom. "And I know exactly the story I want to read. It's my very, very favorite!"

Thirty minutes later, once Seth had had a bath and brushed his teeth, Mark settled atop his son's covers with the selected book—a story about a young prince and princess and their fairy-tale castle in an enchanted forest. Mark tried hard to make the story come alive by calling on his best repertoire of voices for all the main characters. The effort delighted his son.

When they reached the end, Mark closed the book and laid it on the night table. "I think that's my favorite story, too."

"Daddy?"

He looked down at his son and smiled. "Yes, little man?"

Seth let out a big yawn. "When can we see Emily again?"

Closing his eyes, Mark searched for yet another way to change the subject—something he could say to end their evening on a happy note instead of one tinged with guilt and the kind of highlight reel that was sure to haunt him as he slept. Yet all he could come up with was a truth Seth needed to hear, if for no other reason than Mark's own sanity. "Son, I'm afraid we won't be seeing Emily anymore."

Seth's eyes widened with questions Mark was simply too tired and too strung out to answer. Instead, he swung his legs over the edge of the bed and made his way to the door, stepping out into the hallway and flipping off the overhead light as he did. "Good night, little man. Sweet dreams. I'll see you in the morning."

SETH STARED UP AT THE sliver of light the moon cast on his ceiling, and wiped the wetness from his cheeks. The lump in his throat kept getting bigger and bigger no matter how hard he tried to swallow it away.

He was trying to be brave, like a big boy, but it was hard. God kept taking all the happy, smiley princesses for himself.

Like Mommy.

And now Emily, too.

Rolling onto his side, Seth pulled his stuffed giraffe, Geronimo, against his damp cheek and stared out the window into the night, the sadness on his daddy's face when he'd told him about Emily making the tears come faster.

He remembered Emily saying she was sick, but he hadn't known she was going to leave so fast. And once again, just like with Mommy, he hadn't gotten to say goodbye.

Daddy had. Daddy got to hold Mommy's hand when she went to be with God. But *he* was too little. He'd had to stay with Gam.

Daddy got to go to a barbecue with Emily and see her smiles one last time. But *he* didn't. He was having two whole bowls of ice cream with Gam.

Why didn't anyone ever let him say goodbye? Didn't his goodbyes matter, too?

Sitting up, he looked into the giraffe's black shiny eyes. "I want to say goodbye, too, Geronimo. Don't you think Emily wished I could say goodbye just like Daddy got to?"

He nodded the animal's long neck in agreement.

"Yeah. Me, too, Geronimo."

His mind made up, Seth slipped from his bed and tiptoed over to the closet for his quietest pair of sneakers and his favorite backpack. Then, being extra quiet, he put his softest baby blanket and his special picture of Mommy inside the main pocket and zipped it up tight, his uneaten Pop-Tart from yesterday still packed safely in a side compartment.

Careful not to make any noise, he made his way across his room to his bedroom door, which Daddy always left partway open. With a quick left and a right, Seth headed over to the sliding glass door in the living room and stopped. Then, peeking over his shoulder toward his daddy's room, he pushed the little silver lever into the unlock position. When he was sure Daddy hadn't heard the click, he stepped outside and slid the door shut.

"C'mon, Geronimo," he whispered as he crept around the house and onto the street, his feet taking him in the same direction Daddy's car always went. "It's our turn to say goodbye."

Chapter Twelve

Emily propped her elbows on her desk and stuck her fingers in her ears in a futile effort to drown out the steady *whump whump* of the helicopter flying back and forth over Bucket List 101.

She tried to concentrate on the course description she was composing for the upcoming fall calendar, but the incessant noise made writing difficult at best. No matter how many times she consulted the list of skills her students would learn during the four-day extreme camping expedition, she forgot them the second she began typing, her thoughts, derailed by the persistent feeling that something wasn't right…

She knew it was silly, paranoid even. It was a helicopter, that was all. Its very nature was to push down air, thus putting pressure on a person's eardrums. Pulling her fingers from her ears, Emily rose from her chair and made her way to the window, the maddening *whump whump* of yet another pass overriding her need for fresh air.

"Hey there, boss." Trish breezed into the room, her

slim legs making short work of crossing to the desk. "I compiled a list of twenty former clients who expressed an interest in a survival-style camping trip when they filled out their comment cards at the end of class. Gives us a nice solid base to start with, don't you think?"

Emily turned away from the window. "That sounds like a great idea. Nice work, Trish."

She rounded her desk and dropped back into her chair, repositioning her hands atop the keyboard. "Now, if Mr. Helicopter Instructor would just take his student a few miles east, I might actually get the darn course description written and ready for you to paste into the fall program guide."

Trish strode over to the window and peered out. "That's not a flying lesson, boss. It's a search team."

"Search team?"

"Uh-huh. According to my mom, they're looking for some little kid who was missing from his bed this morning."

Emily's stomach tightened with fear at the mere notion of what that would be like for a parent. "Boy or girl?"

"A little boy."

"How old?" she asked.

"I think my mom said he's four, maybe five, but I'm not exactly sure. I *do* know he's not school-aged yet."

Jumping up, Emily joined Trish at the window. "Call the local police station. See if they'll fax you some information on this little boy. If they can do that, tell them

I'm willing to call in some of our more seasoned hikers and see if we can get together a search team to go out into the woods on foot."

Ten minutes later, Trish was back, fax in one hand, pink sticky note in the other. "Got the info you requested, boss. A picture, too."

"Tell me."

Consulting the note, Trish began filling in the blanks. "Okay, the kid's name is Seth Reynolds and—"

Emily's gasp echoed against the walls, only to be drowned out by an eighth helicopter pass and Trish's voice relating, "He's four and—"

"A half," Emily cried. "Four and a half. Oh my God, Trish, I know him."

Her assistant's eyes widened. "You do?"

She reached out, grabbed the fax from her hand and stared down at the face of the little boy who'd smiled so sweetly at her across the dinner table at Sam's. "This is Mark's son."

"Mark?"

"Yes. You remember Mark."

Trish looked questioningly at her. "I do?"

"He's the guy who came to my orienteering class late the other day! The one who…" She let the words trail off. There wasn't any other meaningful correlation to be made for Trish or anyone else. Not now. Not ever.

Looking back down at the paper in her hand, Emily read the word for word quote Mark had given the police department's dispatcher: "My son isn't the type to wander off, but he's been through a lot lately, losing his mom and all. I mean, I thought he was doing okay—as okay as he can be, anyway, but maybe I was wrong. Maybe I missed something. But he's a sweet little guy who loves his toys and dreaming about fairy tales and castles."

"Dreaming about fairy tales," she whispered. Suddenly she was back on the beach at Lake Winoka. Seth's sand castle was to her left, while Seth himself played in the sand, wide-eyed and happy. In her hand was the flag she'd crafted out of a stick and a leaf. She was glued to the spot by Seth's tales of royalty and secret hideaways....

"Secret hideaways," she whispered, before grabbing Trish by the arm. "Oh my gosh, Trish, that's it! *That's it!*" She released her assistant's arm, only to grab for her purse and keys. "I've gotta go. Cancel my class for this morning and the one this afternoon, too. Tell people we'll reschedule for next week—same day, same time. If they can't make it, give them a refund."

DESPITE THE TEARS that had clouded her vision on the drive home from Mark's twenty-four hours earlier, Emily was able to find her way through downtown Winoka and out the other side with little to no effort, her hands instinctively turning the wheel down one side street after another until she was back on Crystal View Drive. Any hesitation she entertained as to which house was the right one was quickly wiped away by the smattering of police cars parked outside the fourth bungalow on the left.

She pulled alongside the curb behind the last of four Winoka police cruisers and cut the engine, her heart thudding in her chest. All the way there she'd second-guessed her decision to come, her worry over getting Mark's hopes up unnecessarily almost making her turn around. But every time she slowed the car to do just that, Seth's voice had gotten louder in her head.

If she was wrong, she was wrong. But if she was right, and she did nothing...

Dropping her keys into her purse, she stepped from the car and crossed the street to Mark's house, a huddle of police officers quickly disbanding as she approached. "Can I help you, miss?" one asked her, not unkindly.

"I'm a friend of Mark's. I'd like to see him if it's okay."

The officer hesitated a split second before waving her through. "Yeah, okay. But he's in bad shape right now. Might be helpful if you can get the poor guy to eat something. He's gonna need his strength if this drags on."

She nodded and continued up the driveway, her feet guiding her to a door she'd vowed she would never step foot in again. But this was different. Her being here had nothing to do with her and nothing to do with Mark.

This visit was about Seth and only Seth.

When she reached the front porch she knocked,

only to be instructed to enter by the same police officer who'd given her permission to pass.

Was she crazy for being here? For pretending she actually knew Seth in a way that made her privy to his thoughts?

Maybe.

But it was worth the shot. *Seth* was worth the shot, she reminded herself.

This time, when she entered Mark's home, she didn't linger in the hallway looking at pictures. She knew they were there, knew Seth's eyes were on her as she nodded toward the officer standing there and turned her focus to the living room and the man with the chocolate-brown hair who sat slumped in a chair, staring at the carpet beneath his feet.

She hesitated, for a moment, his private pain slowly thawing the anger she held for him. She couldn't imagine what he was going through—the raw fear he must feel, wondering if he'd ever seen his precious little boy again.

But before she could muster the courage to speak, before she could settle on just the right sentiment to offer, a board creaked under her feet. At the sound, Mark's head snapped up and his eyes widened. "Emily?" he choked out. "What are you doing here?"

Pushing aside all residual anger for the man, she crossed the room and stood awkwardly beside his chair. "I heard about Seth."

Mark's head pitched forward once again, his shoulders caving inward. "He was in his bed when I went to sleep last night. I kissed his head and tucked him in bed with Geronimo. And then…this morning…he was *gone*. They both were."

Gathering her courage along with her breath, Emily put words to the scenario that had played itself out in her thoughts again and again throughout the drive. "Did you check his tree house?"

Mark's head moved from side to side. "Seth doesn't have a tree house."

"Yes, he does," she said. "He told me all about it at the beach the other day."

In a flash Mark's eyes were on hers, penetrating, questioning. "What are you talking about? What tree house? Seth *doesn't* have a tree house."

Slowly she lowered herself onto the couch across from Mark and reached for his hand, the feel of his skin against hers and the subsequent thumping in her heart something she'd have to chastise herself for later, when she was alone. "The other day, at the beach, before you came over…Seth and I talked about the castle he was making and which room he'd live in if it was real."

Mark's eyes closed and he gave a tired shrug. "Seth is big on fairy tales. Has been ever since he was old enough to sit on Sally's lap at bedtime and follow along with the pictures in a book while she read the story aloud. Something about her voice when she read the princess stories left an impression on him. By the time he was two, those had become his favorite, and that hasn't changed."

Emily shook his hand ever so gently until his focus was on her once again. "Please, Mark. I need to tell you this. After he showed me his room in the castle, I told him that I used to dream about living in a castle when I was little, too."

"Emily, I don't see why any of this matters. My son is *missing!* Don't you get that?" Pulling his hand from hers, he raked it through his hair. "He could be wandering around lost, or be with someone who intends to do him harm."

She continued on, undaunted. "I told him that just because my dream didn't come true, there was no reason to think his couldn't...because dreams are good and special, and no one can ever take them away from us unless we give up on them ourselves."

Sensing Mark's growing frustration, she plowed on, desperate for him to see the tree house tidbit the way she did—as a viable place for finding Seth. "That's when he told me about his tree house. He said he found it in the woods."

Mark straightened in his chair. "Woods? What woods?"

"I'm not sure, exactly. I think he called it Gem's Woods or something like that," she recalled, unsure of whether she was saying the right name. "I suppose it could be a place in his imagination, but he talked about it like it was real. Like it's a place he's gone before."

"Say the name of the woods again," he prompted.

"Gem…Gum…Gam… Something close to—"

He drew back. "Did you say Gam?"

"That's the closest I can remember. I'm sorry.…"

"No. No. Don't be. That's what he calls my mom. It's a carryover from when he had a hard time saying his *r*s when he was first learning how to talk."

"Are there woods behind your mother's house?" Emily asked.

"There are, but her house is easily a mile away from here. He couldn't walk that by himself. He's only four."

She nodded, even as she relayed the rest of the conversation she'd had with Seth. "He told me he liked to climb the ladder and sit there. He said he liked to go there and dream with his eyes open."

"Dream with his eyes open?" Mark repeated in confusion.

"He said that he likes to dream that way best because then they're not as scary as the ones he has at night in his bed."

This time, Mark brought both hands to his face and peered at Emily across the tips of his fingers, clearly trying to absorb everything she was saying. After a few seconds, he jumped to his feet so forcefully his chair tipped over backward. "Oh my God, do you think that's where he went?"

She rose in turn, finding the hope on Mark's face both encouraging and frightening at the same time. "I don't know. I really don't. But if there's even a tiny chance that's where he went, it's worth trying to find it, don't you think?"

"Absolutely!" he shouted as he ran toward the door, with Emily at his heels. "Anything is worth a shot at this point!"

Chapter Thirteen

The police car had barely come to a stop in his mother's driveway before Mark was out of the front seat and opening the back door for Emily. "Come on, let's go! Hurry!"

Together, they took off in a sprint around the neatly kept house where Mark's mother lived, and headed into the woods, their path slowed from time to time by a downed tree and the occasional large rock that posed a tripping hazard to anyone not paying attention. With unspoken agreement, they split off in opposite directions when the trail they were following did the same, one branch leading toward a rushing creek, the other farther into the woods.

Emily turned left and darted around an old rusty fence that marked some long-ago property line at the base of a steep hill. Without breaking stride, she ran to the very top, her gaze flitting from side to side for any indication of the tree house Seth had spoken about that day at the beach.

He hadn't given her anything to go on, no concrete

description of the path he took to get there that could now serve as a map. What she did know was that the tree house had a long ladder, which meant the structure was elevated a fair distance. From the perspective of a four-year-old, anyway.

Running through the woods was something she was good at. Emily could weave her way around trees and toppled limbs like a football player tasked with the job of getting the ball down the field and into the end zone. But that was when she was looking straight ahead, not up, as was currently the case.

Everything she knew about missing children pointed to the importance of time. The longer a family went without finding their child, the less likely they ever would. So the urgency to locate Seth's tree house and rule it out as a possibility was critical. With that in mind, she lowered her head and began searching for the ladder rather than the tree house itself, enabling her to run faster.

And that's when she saw it—a rotting, weathered affair that looked as if it could barely support the weight of a curious squirrel, let alone a human. But Seth was light and compact.

Without altering her stride, Emily stuck her fingers in her mouth and gave a long, low whistle to alert Mark to her find. The ladder she'd spied grew closer and closer, until she could just make out the bottom of an old tree house that had clearly seen better days. When she reached the actual tree, she said a silent prayer, hoping against hope that her gut was right—that Seth was inside, dreaming, safe and sound and completely oblivious to the massive search now under way in his honor.

With barely a pause to collect her breath, she began climbing, the second board of the makeshift ladder giving way beneath her feet and prompting her to grab hold of the fifth board and pull herself upward. Two more big pulls and she was emerging through the floorboards into a dank and dusty place that smelled vaguely of strawberry Pop-Tart. Squinting into the darkness, she choked back a sob of relief at the sight of the little boy and his stuffed giraffe sleeping peacefully beneath a blue-and-white baby blanket, a framed photograph of Mark's late wife peeking out from under the soft fleece.

Slowly but surely, a parade of tears made its way down Emily's cheeks. "Seth? Seth, wake up, sweetie. It's me, Emily. From the beach and the pizza parlor the other night."

"Emily?" the little boy repeated in a voice heavy with sleep. Slowly, he sat up, furiously rubbing his eyes, then peered at her between the ears of his giraffe. "Emily? Is that really you?"

She heard the crunch of leaves on the ground below as Mark reached the tree, prompting her to move away from the hole in the floor to afford him access to his son. "Yes, Seth, it's really me."

"But how did you come back?" he asked, his eyes round with confusion.

"Come back?" she echoed. "Come back from where?"

"From God's house!"

She moved aside as Mark pulled himself into the tree house and lunged across the floor, drawing his son into the fiercest bear hug she'd ever seen. "Seth… Seth…*Seth!* You scared me half to death! What were you *thinking* by leaving the house like that in the middle of the night?"

The little boy pointed over his father's shoulder. "Daddy, look! It's Emily! She came back from dying!"

She looked from Seth to Mark and back again, the child's bizarre statement throwing her for a loop. "Dying? Seth, I didn't die. I'm right here, perfectly fine as always. See?"

Wiggling out of his dad's arms, Seth turned a questioning eye on Mark. "Daddy, you told me we wouldn't be seeing Emily anymore, remember? You told me that last night, when you were kissing me and Geronimo good-night."

Mark's mouth gaped. "Is that why you ran away, little man? Because you thought I meant that Emily had died?"

Seth nodded solemnly. "I didn't get to say goodbye. So I came here…to say goodbye in my wake-time dreams. Just like I did when Mommy died."

"Oh, little man, come here." As he gathered his son in his arms once again, Mark's shoulders began to shake, an indication of the tears Emily suspected were streaming down his face and onto Seth's head.

Mark was right.

Seth cared about her way too much. Especially for someone so young, who had been through so much already. He'd grieved enough for one lifetime.

Swallowing painfully, she made her way back across the floorboards to the ladder. She'd done what she'd set out to do. She'd found Seth and reunited him with his dad. It was time to go home.

SECONDS TURNED TO MINUTES and minutes to half an hour as Mark sat there in the tree house, holding his son close, grateful for the chance he'd been so sure he'd lost.

When he was convinced the moment was real rather than a cruel dream from which he'd soon waken, he brushed a hand across his eyes and released Seth for a long-overdue once-over. "Do you have any idea how worried I was when I woke up this morning and you weren't in your bed? Or how scared I was that someone had gotten into the house and taken you? Or that I'd never get to hold you in my arms again?"

Seth's cheeks turned crimson and he cast his eyes downward. "I'm sorry, Daddy. I didn't mean to scare you."

"I was afraid you were all alone and waiting for me to find you." He heard the words as they left his mouth, the fear, relief and anger in his tone shaking him to the core once again. Now that Seth was safe, Mark realized just how terrified he'd been while he'd sat waiting for some word. It was a feeling he wouldn't wish on his worst enemy.

Seth raised his stuffed giraffe in the air and waved it around for Mark to see. "I wasn't alone, Daddy. Geronimo was here to keep me safe. Mommy, too."

"M-Mommy?" he sputtered.

"I talk to Mommy here. And she listens to me."

Mark sucked in a breath as he searched for the right words. Clearly, it was time to bring in a professional—someone who was trained to help his son through his grief. Raking his hands through his hair, Mark asked, "What do you say to Mommy when you're here?"

Seth rocked back on his knees, and smiled. "The first time, when I just found my tree house, I got to tell her goodbye. And then I made sure to tell her that I love her very, very, very, very, very much. Because she needed to know that, Daddy. She really did."

"Mommy knew how much you loved her, little man. It's why she smiled like she did all the time." Shifting slightly, Mark reached for Seth once again, this time pulling him onto his lap. "There wasn't a day that went by when Mommy didn't know how much you loved her and how very special she was to you. And you know what? That was the greatest gift you could have ever given her."

"But I wanted to tell her goodbye *before* she went with God. Just like you got to, Daddy. Only you and Gam didn't let me. You said I was too little. But little people can say goodbye just as good as big people. Geronimo thinks so, too."

Mark considered his son's words and compared them

with the decision he'd made as Sally's death neared by hours rather than days. "I'm sorry you didn't get to say goodbye to her, Seth. I really am. It's just that…well, all I can say is that sometimes big people have to make a decision they think is right. And I thought it was more important for you to remember Mommy the way she was the day before she died—when you were able to cuddle up next to her, looking through the pages of your favorite storybook together." He heard his voice give way under the weight of the memory, and he worked to compose himself so he could say what needed to be said. "I didn't want your last memory of Mommy to be one where she could no longer say anything to you. Because that's what it was like for me, and it was really sad."

Seth nestled against Mark's chest, his hand wrapped tightly around Geronimo. "It's okay now, Daddy. I said goodbye to Mommy in my wake-time dreams. And she heard me, because she made a rainbow right out there—" he lifted his giraffe and pointed it toward the square opening that served as the tree house's lone window "—as soon as I told her. It was big and had lots and lots of pretty colors. Even purple!"

Mark wanted to ask about the rainbow, but opted to leave the topic alone. If Seth needed to see a rainbow to make peace with his mom's death, then he needed to see a rainbow. Telling him that such a sighting in thick woods was nearly impossible served no real purpose.

Sometimes being right didn't matter. And this was one of those times.

Instead, he lifted his hand to Seth's head and smoothed back the crop of blond hair that was so like Sally's. "How did you find this tree house? Because I know you couldn't have gotten Gam out here all by yourself."

"I found it the day Mommy died."

"I get that," he said. "But how did you find it?"

Seth shrugged. "I found it all by myself."

He swallowed. "Gam let you go out in the woods by yourself?"

"No. Gam didn't know. She was crying in her room. But I knew why. I knew God had given Mommy her wings so she could fly like the rest of his angels. 'Cept she's extra special because she's a princess angel."

Mark gave the nod he knew Seth needed, but stuck to his line of questioning. "So how did you end up all the way out here? By yourself?"

"Gam fell asleep. She didn't mean to, Daddy, but sometimes crying makes you sleepy. So I asked Geronimo if he wanted to help me find the hospital, and he said he did. But we found this tree house instead. When Mommy made the rainbow, we went back and woke up Gam."

Mark shook his head at his lapse in parenting. His own pain had been so raw when Sally passed that he hadn't thought to go home for Seth until his own tears were in check. "Did you tell Gam about the rainbow?"

Seth grew quiet on his lap.

"Seth?" he repeated. "Did you tell Gam about the rainbow?".

This time, his son shook his head and whispered, "No."

"Why not?" he asked.

"Because the rainbow was *my* goodbye, Daddy."

Seth's goodbye.

A goodbye that could have proved disastrous if Emily hadn't remembered Seth's mention of a tree house.

"Emily," he mumbled under his breath, before glancing toward the ladder for the first time since finding Seth. "Where'd she go?"

"She climbed back down the ladder a long time ago, Daddy. Right after she winked a big wink at me."

"Why didn't you say anything?"

"Because you were crying, Daddy. And Emily put her finger to her mouth, like it was a secret."

"I was crying because I thought I'd lost you." Leaning his head against the wall of the tree house, Mark thought back over everything he'd heard. "And I can't ever lose you, little man. I love you too much for that, okay?"

"Okay, Daddy." Seth gestured around the tree house. "So do you like it?"

He let his eyes follow the path indicated, and nodded. "Did you at least tell Gam about the tree house?"

Again Seth shook his head. "Gam wouldn't like the ladder. She'd tell me I'm too little to climb it. Then all my dream time would be the scary nighttime kind again."

Opting to bypass the notion of nightmares temporarily, Mark asked the one question that still remained. "Seth? If you didn't want to tell Gam or me about the rainbow or this tree house, what made you tell Emily about it that day at the beach?"

"Because she wanted to live in a castle when she was little, just like me, Daddy. And just like Mommy did."

His breath hitched. "Your mommy wanted to live in a castle when she was little?"

"Uh-huh. And she got to!"

Mark smiled despite the tears that pricked his eyes once again. "She did?"

"Yupper doodle. And she lived in it with you and me, Daddy. She told me her castle was our house."

"She did?" he asked, blinking rapidly.

"Uh-huh. Every night when she kissed me and Geronimo good-night!"

It took everything Mark had not to break into wrenching sobs, the sadness he felt nothing short of overwhelming. "I'm sorry, little man. I'm sorry you had to lose Mommy when you're still so little."

With a lopsided shrug, Seth tossed his beloved animal into the air and caught him with a giggle. "That's okay, Daddy. It was better to have a special mommy for a little while than no special mommy at all."

Chapter Fourteen

Emily pulled into the parking lot of Bucket List 101, her thoughts running in a million different directions, yet converging all in one spot. Seth was safe and sound, and that was all that truly mattered.

It was time to put the rest of the story behind her, where it belonged. Her passion was her company. She needed to focus on making it the premier outdoor adventure destination in the region.

No, she didn't have a husband and the prospect of children to look forward to, like Kate. But she had a company that was changing lives. Was one really better or more important than the other?

With a quick shake of her head, Emily grabbed her purse from the passenger seat and her keys from the ignition and headed toward the large white barn she'd converted into her offices, on the western edge of town. Here, she could be herself—adventurous, free-spirited and healthy. At least as far as her clients were concerned.

She pulled the door open and stepped inside to find

the reception desk empty. "Trish? I'm back. You still here?"

The soft squeaking sounds of her assistant's shoes preceded her appearance in the outer office. "My mom just called. She said the good news is all over the television and radio stations."

Emily felt the smile spread across her face. "We found him. Sleeping peacefully inside an old tree house in the woods behind his grandmother's place, completely oblivious to the search taking place all over Winoka."

"Is that why you went tearing out of here this morning?" Trish asked, claiming her spot behind the desk.

"I'm sorry about that, Trish. I really am. But all of a sudden I remembered something Mark's—*Mr. Reynolds's*—son had told me when I saw them at the beach after work the other night. He'd mentioned a tree house he'd found, and that he liked to go there to be by himself."

"Be by himself? Why does a four-year-old need to be by himself?"

Emily placed her purse on the floor, and perched on the edge of the desk. "Well, considering this particular four-year-old lost his mom to cancer six months ago, I imagine he's probably got more reasons than either of us could fathom."

Trish tsked softly. "Wow. That's rough. Thank God you found him, though." Reaching into her top drawer, she pulled out a couple of apples and offered one to Emily.

"Oh, thanks, I missed lunch." She reached for the fruit and took a bite, her mind wandering back through the morning, but stopping short of the many reasons seeing Mark had been so hard.

"Wow. So that guy—the one who was in here for the orienteering class? He lost his wife and then he couldn't find his son? Wow." Trish narrowed her eyes in thought as she crunched her own apple. "I think if I were that kid's dad, I'd be tempted to stick him in a bubble where he couldn't ever get lost, or sick, or whatever."

Pulling the apple from her mouth, Emily tossed the barely eaten fruit into the trash and stood, her appetite suddenly squashed. "No. Mark's preferred bubble isn't one that keeps Seth *in,* it's one that keeps everyone else *out.* Of Seth's life."

She heard the bitterness in her voice, felt the weight of Trish's questioning eyes and literally grasped for the first topic she could find to change the subject. Her hand closed over the first in a long line of pink sticky notes attached to her assistant's desk. "I take it I missed a few calls while I was out? Anything important or truly exciting?"

Trish glanced downward, running her fingernail along the line of messages. "I signed up this person… and this person…and this one, all for next week's Intro to Nature's Workout Room and…oh, yeah, this woman—" she peeled off the fourth note and gave it a quick glance before handing it to Emily "—is from *Winoka Magazine*. She wants to do an article on you."

Taking in the reporter's name and information, Emily nodded. "You mean an article on the company, right?"

"No. On you. She says she'll touch on the company in the story, but this particular piece is on female entrepreneurs and the spark that lit their proverbial match, as she put it."

"My proverbial match, eh? Hmm. Something tells me a little kid with a big imagination and a sixty-four pack of crayons probably isn't the kind of tale she's looking for."

"I'd read it," Trish quipped, moving her finger to the next note and pausing.

"Yeah, I guess I'd read it, too. And I'd probably send a copy to my mom for her scrapbook. So I guess we'd have three readers, if nothing else."

"Boss?"

At the change in Trish's tone of voice, Emily glanced up from the notes in her own hand. "Yes?"

"There was one other call. From a man named Jed Walker."

"And?"

"He started out as a prospective client at first, but then…"

She looked from Trish to the note in question and back again. "But then what? Is there a problem I should know about?"

Her assistant peeled the note from her desk and

crumpled it in her hand, shrugging as she did so. "Nothing we can really do anything about. But I still felt bad."

"Bad about what?"

"Not being able to help this guy. I mean, he knows he can't go wheeling through the woods with a compass or whatever, but it's kind of a shame that he can't take one of your survival seminars simply because he can't get down the stairs and into the classroom, you know?"

Finally, Emily was able to make sense of what she was hearing. "Is this guy disabled or something?"

"He's in a wheelchair. Lives on his own. He's got this dream of learning how to scuba dive one day despite the fact that he's paralyzed, and he was hoping he could sign up for one of your scuba trips to the Caribbean this winter. I told him that wasn't possible, but that we might be able to get some people in here to carry him in and out of the classroom if he wanted to sit in on one of your survival classes, but he said no. Said he gets where he needs to go on his own, without anyone carrying him around like a baby." Trish tossed the paper wad into the trash beside her desk. "The guy was a real firecracker, I tell you. Real determined to live life on his own terms, just like you. When I mentioned the survival class idea, he said it wouldn't do him much good anyway, since most campgrounds have gravel parking lots and are situated much too far from the actual facilities.

"Made me kind of sad when he said that. I guess I'm so used to being able to walk that I never really stopped to notice how life isn't set up for people like Mr. Walker."

Emily peeked into the trash can. "And this guy wants to learn how to scuba dive, when he can't walk?"

Trish nodded. "Said it was his dream long before the car accident that confined him to his wheelchair—"

The ringing of the office phone cut their conversation short, sending Trish into full-blown assistant mode and Emily down the hall toward her office, the image of the wadded-up pink sticky note front and center in her thoughts.

She understood all about determination. It was why she was standing in the middle of a building she'd purchased with the intention of starting her own company. A company that was now thriving, thanks to her own refusal to give up.

She understood the desire to live life on one's own terms. It was why she wouldn't let Kate cajole her into a life she was no longer meant to have.

And she understood the man's refusal to let people carry him around. The mere thought of being in that position one day with her multiple sclerosis was enough to drive her batty.

So how could she continue to tout Bucket List 101 as a way to fulfill lifelong dreams if she wasn't equipped to do that for everyone—especially someone as driven and full of heart as the man whose name was scrawled across a piece of paper now crumpled in Trish's trash can?

Deflated, Emily reached inside her office door and flipped on the overhead light, her gaze going to her desk and the pamphlets Mark had left behind prior to the barbecue and a night she wished she could forget, but knew she never would.

She'd been so angry when he'd brought the literature by, so quick to tell him she didn't need any help from him or his foundation. But now, in light of the man Trish had had to turn away because they were unable to accommodate his challenges, maybe it was time to rethink that notion.

When she was sure her assistant was off the phone, she pressed the intercom button. "Trish?"

"Yeah, boss?"

"We're about helping people realize their dreams, aren't we?"

"That's what the little thingy out here in the waiting room says."

"That's what it says in here on my desk, too." Leaning forward, she poked a finger at the replica of the sign that greeted her customers from atop a table in plain sight of Trish's desk. "Which means we've got a whole bunch of work to do to make that happen."

"Isn't that what we're already doing, with the course descriptions and the classes we keep adding?"

"But we can do better. We can do more. If we don't, we'll need to take down the sign we're both looking at right now." She swiveled her chair to the right and flipped on her computer, ready to begin the initial legwork for something she should have done a long time ago. "Oh, and Trish? When you get a chance, would you bring that message in here?"

A pause gave way to a funny little snort. "Uh, boss? I already gave you all your messages."

"I'm talking about the one in your trash can...the one with Mr. Walker's phone number on it. There are some things I'd like to discuss with him."

MARK PULLED HIS CELL PHONE from the side pocket in his car door and scrolled through his recent calls, finding the number for Bucket List 101 among them. He found it hard to believe it had been only five days since he'd first laid eyes on Emily. So much had happened.

She'd affected him in a way he hadn't seen coming. Sure, he wished things were different, that they could have met twenty years in the future, when he didn't have to worry about Seth quite so much. But they hadn't and he did.

His son had to come first.

Seth.

Leaving him with Gram for a much needed nap had been difficult. But the only reason Mark had been able to tuck Seth in for a nap at all was because of Emily. The least he could do was say thank-you.

Unfortunately, it was all the other things Mark wanted to say and do to her that kept pushing their way into his thoughts and leaving him more than a little unsettled. He wanted to shower her face with kisses of gratitude. He wanted to run his hands down her exquisite body. He wanted to peel off her clothes and make love to her all over again.

But he couldn't.

She was sick. And he was a father.

His mind made up, he pressed the button for Emily's office number and put the Blue Tooth device to his ear, the clamminess of his hand a shameful reminder of why he was suddenly so nervous. If a friend had led on a woman the way he'd led Emily on the other night, Mark would have been disgusted.

And he was. At himself.

Emily deserved an apology as much as she deserved a thank-you, and he would make sure she got both by the time their call was over. As he listened to the phone ring, he prepared himself for what to say and how to say it. But when it became apparent no one was going to pick up, his nerves gave way to disappointment.

What was with him? Why couldn't he just shut this girl out?

A sixth ring yielded to a seventh before the call was finally answered. "Bucket List 101, this is Trish, how can I help you?"

He steered his car around a parked car at the end of his mom's road and stopped, his uncertainty over what to say rivaled only by his uncertainty over where, exactly, he was going in the first place.

"Hello? Is anyone there?"

Say something, idiot...

"Uh…yeah, hi. This is Mark. Mark Reynolds. I took a class on orienteering from your company the other day and I—"

"Mark, hi. Wow. I couldn't believe it when Emily told me the missing boy was yours. I bet you haven't let him out of your sight since she found him in that tree house for you."

He closed his eyes momentarily, the image of his son alive and well in the corner of the dilapidated tree house bringing a tightness to his throat. It was all still so surreal. "You have no idea, Trish. No idea."

She paused, then said, "I bet you want to talk to Emily and say thanks, huh?"

Among other things, he thought. To Trish, he said, "I do. Can you put me through to her?"

"Emily is out of the office at the moment. And since she didn't tell me where she was going, I can't be sure when she'll be back—if she even comes back this afternoon at all. But I can certainly put you through to her voice mail, if you'd like."

It wasn't the way he wanted to do it, but maybe it was for the best. That way he could thank her for finding Seth, apologize for his own shortcomings and then leave her to her life. "Yeah, okay, that'll work."

But the second he heard Emily's voice in his ear, he knew he couldn't leave a message. Calling her wasn't just about saying thanks. Or even apologizing. He wanted to hear her voice—talking specifically to him. He wanted to look into her eyes, wanted to scale a mountain with her by his side, wanted to learn about her past. He wanted to tell her one of Seth's jokes and hear the way she laughed with her whole being. Heck, he just wanted to be close to her again....

No. A voice message was not the way to tell her how he felt, or to explain why he couldn't see her again.

Ending the call, he turned left at the next cross street, his destination suddenly clear.

Chapter Fifteen

Mark paused, his fist inches from the door, and turned toward the telltale sounds of a garden hose being used somewhere off to his left. Sure enough, in a quick peek around the corner of the house, he spied the very woman he was there to see, quietly humming to herself as she watered the same flowers and bushes he'd admired two days earlier. Without a moment's hesitation, he retraced his steps to the sidewalk and then cut across the side lawn.

Kate's cat-green eyes widened in surprise as she released her hand from the hose's trigger. "Mark? What are you doing here?"

"Hi, Kate. I was hoping you'd remember me." He held out his hand in her direction and was aware of the hesitation that accompanied hers in return. "I was wondering if we could talk. About Emily."

"What about her?" Kate squeezed the trigger once again and aimed the water across a row of zinnias.

He followed the stream with his eyes and searched for the best way to explain the jumbled mess in his head and why it had brought him to Kate's door. But before he could start, she'd moved on to the marigolds and her own assessment of him. "You know, I thought you were a nice guy the other night. So did my husband and the rest of our friends. In fact, if you want to know the truth, I kept Joe up for hours that night, going on and on about how perfect you were for Emily."

A flick of Kate's wrist brought the water dangerously close to Mark, yet he resisted the urge to flinch. She was angry, of that there was no doubt.

"But boy, was I wrong," she hissed. "In fact, I'd go so far as to say that it's guys like you who give the entire male gender a bad rap."

"I like her, Kate. I like her a lot." He linked his hands behind his head, only to release them just as quickly. "Do you think I'd be here, subjecting myself to the possible drenching that's mere centimeters—and quite likely *seconds*—away if I didn't?"

The spray of water came even closer. "Candy and flowers, or even—get this—*a date,* are generally the preferred ways to show a woman you like her, Mark. Telling her you're not interested because she has a life-altering condition doesn't really have the same ring, you know?"

He pushed his fingers through his hair and tugged, the frustration coursing through his body almost enough to make him pull it all out by the roots. "And if I handed my four-year-old son a toy truck and told him to take it out onto the middle of Highway W and play with it there, would you think I was a horrible parent?"

Kate turned the hose back on the zinnias, but kept her anger focused squarely on Mark. "Oh, are you one of those analogy guys? The kind who are always looking for some stupid little anecdote to justify their pathetic selfishness?"

His head was beginning to spin. "No. I'm just a dad who loves his son more than himself."

Rolling her eyes, Kate released the trigger. "What on earth are you babbling about?"

With the threat of a drenching removed, he gestured toward the corner of the patio. "Can we sit out back and talk? Please?"

For a moment, he thought she was going to refuse, maybe even turn the hose back on and actually point it at him this time. But in the end she nodded, lowering her arms with reluctance. "You've got five minutes. So you'd better get to the point. If you actually have one, that is."

Oh, he had one all right. Even if he wasn't entirely sure what it was yet.

He followed her through the break in the dwarf bush honeysuckle hedge and onto the patio. Once she'd claimed a spot on a cushioned chaise, he settled on a nearby Adirondack chair. "I don't know how much Emily told you about me, but I have a son, Seth. He's four and a half. In fact, if you watched the news at all today, you probably saw him on television."

"I didn't. I slept in and then I had an appointment."

"Anyway, his mother—my wife—passed away six months ago after a yearlong battle with cancer. It would have been a tough go for any kid to lose his mom, but Seth's anguish was magnified tenfold by my selfishnes."

Looking down at the stone slabs beneath his feet, Mark continued. "You see, I shut down. I couldn't stand watching her deteriorate, knowing there wasn't a thing I could do to stop it. I couldn't fight it away with my fists, I couldn't hug it away with my arms and I couldn't cajole it away with my words. I was utterly helpless and, well, I guess you can say I don't do helpless all that well. Or, as was the case with Sally's illness, at all."

At Kate's silence, he stole a glance in her direction, finding the blatant irritation that had all but seeped from her pores earlier suddenly gone. Temporarily, at least.

Not wanting to miss the opportunity her change in mood offered, he went on. "So while I buried myself in my work during her struggle, my three-and-a-half-year-old son was everything I should have been. He was her arms, he was her ears, he was her comfort and her companion. Which means he *watched* her die, Kate." His voice breaking, Mark dug his elbows into his thighs and cradled his head with his hands. "I failed her. And I failed my son. That's a mistake I'll have to live with for the rest of my life."

The creak of Kate's chaise was followed by a warm and steadying hand on his shoulder. "There isn't a rule book for something like that, Mark. You didn't know."

He snapped his head up, the pain in his voice replaced by the intense anger he felt for himself. "While I think that's a piss-poor excuse for my actions, I could only use it once. If I failed him like that again, I'd be the worst father on the face of the earth."

"Failed him again?" Kate asked, her eyes locked on his. "I don't understand what you mean."

"There was nothing I could do about Sally getting sick. It just happened. I should have been there for her, as a husband is supposed to be, and I should have been there for Seth, too. But I wasn't. And as a result, my innocent little boy saw far more of his mother's suffering than he should have. Losing his mom at that age was horrific enough. Having to experience that and play the part of the adult in the house at the same time? There are no words for that except *inexcusable* and *pathetic*."

At her obvious confusion, he filled in the blanks as succinctly as possible. "I cannot sit back and allow my son to love a woman I already know to be sick. It's like telling him to take that toy truck I mentioned earlier and play with it the middle of a four-lane highway. It would be certain disaster."

Kate's gasp brought him up short. "Wait. You don't think Emily is going to *die,* do you? Because she's not."

For the briefest of seconds he felt a hint of hope, only to have it disappear just as quickly. "Look, I'll be the first to admit I don't know that much about multiple sclerosis, but I know it can be extremely debilitating over time."

"That's true."

"I don't want Seth to have to watch someone he loves suffer ever again."

"And if you get sick, Mark? What then? Are you going to abandon him on the steps of some church, just so he doesn't have to watch you die? Do you really think that would be better?"

He pushed himself from the chair and paced across the patio, the thought of Seth being left orphaned one he hadn't visited before. "That falls into the category of things I can't really control, beyond doing my best to eat right and exercise more. But there's a big difference between something that's out of my control and something in my control."

Kate perched on the edge of the chair Mark had vacated, and exhaled. "Oh. I get it now. If you let Seth get attached to Emily and she suddenly starts going downhill, you've essentially handed his heart over to be broken once again."

Mark stopped midstep, deflated. "Yeah."

"Have you seen Emily? Have you seen the kind of shape she's in?"

In the interest of avoiding saying anything that might get him slapped, he opted to nod rather than put his feelings about Emily's body into words.

"You've got to know she's not going down without a fight." Kate stood and made her way over to him, a genuine smile on her face now. "Couple that with the fact that the medication she just started taking is designed to hold this thing at bay for a long time and, well, I don't think your reason for denying yourself a second chance is all that valid. Especially since it would be a second chance for Seth, too. A second chance to love and to be loved."

A second chance.

Was that what he wanted?

Mark wasn't sure.

And what about Emily? Was she even interested in a relationship? He posed the question to Kate.

"Oh, to hear her talk? No. But like you, Em has let the fear of what-ifs in life keep her from her dreams."

He had to laugh. "Are you kidding me? From what I've seen, Emily is all about chasing down her dreams."

"That's true for all but one of them."

"Huh?"

Wrapping her hand around his, Kate pulled him toward the back door. "Come. I want to show you something."

Five minutes later, standing in her sunny kitchen, he found himself staring down at a child's drawing. The blonde figure depicted on the page seemed vaguely familiar. "Is this one of Emily's?"

"Yep."

He couldn't help but smile as he took in the glittery crown on the subject's head and the huge smile on her face as a brown-haired boy, also wearing a crown, carried her into a castle in his arms. "She dreamed of being a princess?" he finally asked.

"She dreamed of finding her prince." Sweeping her hand toward the drawing, Kate dropped her voice to a near whisper. "It's the one dream that's yet to come true. Though if you ask me, it's closer than she realizes."

He took in the innocence and hope that had belonged to a ten-year-old Emily, and then handed the picture back to Kate. "So what's holding her back from making that dream come true, like all the others?"

Kate looked from Mark to the picture and back again before depositing it in his hands again with purpose. "She's afraid she'll be a burden to her prince because of her diagnosis."

"That's ridiculous," he argued. "You love the person, not the illness."

"You love the person, not the illness," Kate echoed. "Hmm... I couldn't have said that any better if I tried."

AS HEAVY AS HIS HEART had been when he pulled into Kate's driveway, the opposite was true on the way out. Mark really didn't know if it was a second chance he wanted or not. He was okay raising Seth on his own. He was okay filling his days with work, volunteering at the foundation and being a dad to the greatest kid on earth.

But whether it was about second chances or something entirely different, he knew he wanted Emily. He wanted the lift she brought to his heart. He wanted the hope she sprinkled around with the mere flash of her smile. He wanted the contentment he felt with her in his arms. And he wanted the pure joy he saw in Seth's face whenever he was around her.

The ring of his cell phone broke through his thoughts. Seeing the name and number of the foundation's president, Stan Wiley, on his caller ID screen, he answered. "Good afternoon, Stan. What can I do for you?"

"I saw you on the news just now. So glad you found your boy safe and sound."

Mark smiled. "Yeah. You and me both." He pulled to the side of whatever street he'd gotten himself onto. "I'm not even going to ask how I looked. I barely remember talking into the microphone outside my mom's house."

"You looked fine. Rattled, sure. Relieved, absolutely. But no worse for the wear."

"Good." He made a mental note to call his mom the second he and Stan were done talking, to give her a heads-up on his estimated return and to hear Seth's voice. "So what can I do for you?"

"You can pat yourself on the back, Mark, for a job well done."

"I wish I could take credit for finding Seth, but I can't. That was a woman named—"

"No. No. I'm talking about getting us that Longfeld donation. Your hard work is going to end up benefiting a lot of people, Mark. A *lot* of people."

"You mean we got the donation?"

"You bet we did. And it's because of your hard work."

"*My* hard work?" he echoed. "Stan, I'm not sure what you're talking—"

"Of course, there's still work to be done, but that's usually the case with any accomplishment in life."

Mark tried to make sense of the conversation, his confusion growing with each word Stan uttered.

"I need you to take a welcome packet over to our newest client, along with a hearty thank-you from all of us here. So, do you have a pen handy?"

"Uh…yeah, sure. Hang on." Shifting the phone to his left hand, he opened the center armrest and extracted a scrap of paper and a pen from its depths. Then, wedging the phone between his shoulder and his cheek, he propped the paper on his steering wheel and prepared to write. "Okay, shoot."

"Eight-one-six Sunset Street, Winoka."

He repeated it, then capped his pen and popped it back in the armrest compartment. "Got it."

"I know you've been through a lot today, Mark, but as soon as you're able to get this taken care of, the better?"

Oh, how he wanted to say no, to continue on his journey to Bucket List 101 and the conversation he wanted to have with Emily. But tomorrow would be here before he knew it. A new day with the chance for a new start…

"I'll check in on Seth first. If he's still sleeping, I'll deliver."

Chapter Sixteen

Emily crossed the living room and pulled open the front door, her breath hitching at the sight of Mark standing on the porch, an enormous envelope in his hands. And for a moment, as she drank him in, she allowed herself to remember the way his arms had felt as he'd cradled her after they'd made love—the contentment that had been eluding her for months, if not years, finally hers for the taking.

Yet it had all been a farce.

What had meant so much to her had meant nothing to the man standing on her porch now, looking from her to a scrap of paper in his hand and back again, as if he'd been dropped in the middle of a foreign land.

"What do you want, Mark?" she asked.

"I…" He looked down at the paper one more time and then held it up for her to see. "This is 816 Sunset Street, isn't it?"

And then she knew why he was there. He'd been assigned her case. Though, by the look on his face, she guessed he was still in the dark about that.

"Yes, it is." She knew she was being curt, but couldn't help it. He'd hurt her in a way no one ever had before. And while she understood his stance, it didn't negate the way he'd used her before he dropped the proverbial hammer on her heart and her self-respect.

"I don't understand. I'm virtually certain I jotted down the address exactly as Stan told it to me."

"Considering that's the address I gave him, I'd say you did a good job."

The hand that held her address dropped to his side, and he stared at her, confused. "You talked to Stan? At Folks Helping Folks?"

Met with her silence, he stuffed the paper into his pants pocket and shifted from foot to foot. "Why?"

"Because that's who the receptionist put me through to when I called."

"You called the foundation?"

She shrugged. "How else were they supposed to know I need assistance?"

Mark stepped forward, only to stop when she held up her hands. "Why? Did something happen today after you found Seth? Are you feeling bad?"

It took everything in her power not to turn around and slam the door in his face. This man, who knew nothing about her beyond the lapse of judgment that had allowed her to be a one-night stand, was so quick to assume she was weak. Sickly. And it made her angry.

"For the umpteenth time, Mark, I'm fine. I've been

saddled with a scary-sounding condition, but I'm fine! Not that you'll ever get that or, rather, *want* to get that."

For a moment it was as if she'd slapped him. He drew back, blinked, and then simply looked sad.

She couldn't take it anymore. "Look, I called because I realized I could use my condition to help other people."

At his raised eyebrows, she continued. "By making my business more accessible, with the help of the foundation, I'll be able to provide opportunities to clients I couldn't have otherwise. And if I'm going to hang my hat on being the kind of company that helps people check off items on their bucket lists, I can't ignore the fact that individuals with disabilities and conditions have lists, too."

"So you're going ahead with the assistance just to help others?" he inquired.

Emily hesitated briefly. "At this particular moment in time? Yes. But anything can happen, with me just like with this segment of the population I've been over-looking for far too long. I don't need help now, but I may very well in the future."

"Oh, Emily, I know how hard it must have been to make that call." Mark took another step this time trying to draw her in for a hug. But she stepped back out of his reach.

She didn't need his touch. She didn't need him, period.

"I assume that's the paperwork Stan said he'd send over?" She pointed to the envelope under Mark's arm, and then reached for it at his nod. "I'll look it over, sign what needs to be signed and have Trish bring it by the foundation before week's end. Will that work?"

He relinquished his grasp on the packet and nodded. "Uh...yeah. That should be just fine."

"Well, then, we're done here, yes?" Without waiting for a response, she wrapped her fingers around the edge of the door and tried to push it closed. But when it was just shy of the click, Mark pushed it back open.

"Emily, please. We need to talk about it."

"I'm sure the paperwork is self-explanatory. If I hit a snag, I'll call the office."

He moved his hand from the door to her cheek. "No. We need to talk about what happened the other night. With us."

She covered his hand with hers and closed her eyes for a moment, her heart in a losing battle with her head. "There is no *us,* Mark. Now go home. Be with Seth."

"But—"

Fighting back tears, she kept her voice as steady as possible when she said, "I'd ask you to give him a hug for me and tell him once again how glad I am he's safe and sound, but I also know you don't want me tarnishing his world with my sickly presence."

Again, she tried to close the door. And again, Mark stopped it with his hand.

"Please, Emily. I need to talk to you. For me *and* for Seth."

HE SUPPOSED HE SHOULD look around, maybe comment on the framed photographs or various knickknacks he couldn't quite make out from his spot on her living room sofa, but Mark couldn't.

Not yet, anyway.

All that mattered at that exact moment was finding a way to explain himself and his actions in a way that would wipe the hurt from her big brown eyes once and for all.

"I didn't shut down on you yesterday morning because I didn't care, or because I'd gotten what I wanted and I was done with you." He leaned forward and studied her, her defensive posture alerting him to the battle he had ahead. "Please tell me you know that, Emily. Please."

When she didn't respond, he continued, his desire to cross the space between them and pull her into his arms almost more than he could handle.

Take it slowly, buddy...

"You touched something inside me the first moment I laid eyes on you in that orienteering class. It was like someone opened the curtains on my world for the first time in over a year." He saw her swallow, and knew he had her ear, if nothing else. "I guess you could say that part was all physical attraction, and maybe you'd even be right. I mean, look at you! You have the most expressive eyes and breathtaking smile I've ever seen. I'd be a fool if I didn't notice that, Emily. I'd be a fool, too, if I didn't find the way your hair curls around the edges of your face sexy as all get-out. And I'd be a blind fool if I couldn't see how unforgettable your body is."

A hint of red tinged her cheeks and he felt his body react almost instantly. "But it wasn't just a physical reaction. I've seen attractive women before—they're on virtually every corner, if you're of a mind to look. But that initial reaction to you was different, and I'm not sure how, exactly, to explain it beyond that. And then you started talking, and I found myself getting excited about things. *Important* things like life...and living."

"I'm glad my class impacted you like that," she whispered.

He dropped his hands to his thighs and stood up, his attention trained on the woman seated on the other side of the room. "It wasn't the *class* that impacted me like that, Emily. It was you.

"It's one of the reasons I took Seth fishing that night. Because I needed to clear my head. I've only been a widower for six months now, Emily. Six months. What kind of heel can have feelings like that for another woman within six months?"

He was mentally chastising himself for the way his voice was growing raspy when she finally looked up, her eyes fixed on his. "And then there you were...as gorgeous and fun as you'd been in the classroom and in the woods, and you were making my son *smile*."

Running a hand across his mouth, Mark tried to rein in the emotions that threatened to annihilate the courage that had him talking in the first place. "It wasn't an I'll-smile-because-Daddy-just-told-me-a-silly-joke smile or a hooray-we're-having-ice-cream smile, Emily.

It was a real one—the kind I haven't seen on his face in far too long."

"I got as much from Seth as he got from me that night," she finally said. "He made me smile a real smile, too."

"A real smile?" Mark repeated.

She uncrossed her arms and laced her fingers together, twisting them ever so slightly. "Ever since I was diagnosed six months ago, I feel like everyone is always looking at me funny—my mom, Kate, Trish… My clients don't know, of course, but that's a different relationship, anyway. But with Seth, it was like he saw me. The *real* me. The me that even *I* was beginning to doubt was still there."

Mark took a tentative step forward and gestured to the vacant space on the sofa beside Emily. "May I?"

A pause gave way to the faintest of nods.

"It all came crashing down, though, on the way home in the car after pizza. Suddenly that smile on Seth's face was gone, and in its place was worry." Shifting his body, Mark reached for her hand, then stopped, uncertain. "Seth is only four, Emily. *Four.* He's not supposed to worry about anything beyond which kind of milk he wants, chocolate or regular, and which crayon will make his latest castle the most glittery. Yet there he was, sitting in the backseat…worried about you."

"I'm sorry," she murmured.

Pushing aside any residual hesitation, Mark took her hand and squeezed it gently. "No, *I'm* sorry. I'm sorry I didn't call and explain when I decided to bail on the rock climbing because of my own hang-up. But I thought I was doing the right thing. I thought I was protecting my son from another broken heart."

Emily tried to pull her hand away, but Mark held on tight. "That's what I don't get," she stated. "How was rock climbing with me going to break Seth's heart?"

"I saw the worry on his face after spending only two, maybe three hours with you. Can you imagine the concern he'd have for you after really getting to know you?"

At the understanding in her eyes, Mark continued, his voice breaking once again. "I promised Sally I would look after Seth. That I would do everything in my power to keep him happy and safe. And the way I was seeing it at the time, allowing him to get close with someone I knew to be sick would be like purposely ignoring that promise."

"But I'm not going to die from this, Mark. I may not ever show any outward signs that anything's wrong at all."

"I know that now. But even so, there's also a possibility that you could be in a wheelchair in five years. Such a fate for someone as active as you would be awful. Seth is the kind of kid who feels that. Truly feels that."

The slump of her shoulders told Mark she understood.

"But when I saw you again after we didn't show up for the lesson, and we spent all that time together at Kate's, and then later on the climbing walls at your office, it was like I'd forgotten all the reasons I had to stay away from you. And when we made love…in my bed…I was whole again. Until Seth called, anyway. And that's when I remembered that my job, my promise, has me being a father first."

"And so you put up a wall," she mused.

"Yeah, I put up a wall." Taking hold of her other hand, Mark slowly lifted it to his lips and brushed a kiss across her fingertips. "But Seth and Kate made me see that that wall isn't just holding back potential hurt and pain, it's also holding back any chance at true love. For me and for Seth."

Mark watched as Emily closed her eyes and worked to steady her breathing, his own hitching in response when she finally looked at him again through tear-dappled lashes. "True love?" she rasped.

"True love."

Chapter Seventeen

Emily wanted nothing more than to wrap her arms around Mark and shed the happy tears that were making it difficult to see.

This man loved her. Loved her so much that he was willing to take a chance with his heart and that of his son's.

On her.

She'd dreamed of a moment like this for more than half her life. Yet now that it was here, she knew it couldn't be. Not for her, anyway.

To let Mark and his son love her would be unfair.

Slipping her left hand from his, she wiped a finger beneath her eyes, dislodging all tears. "I appreciate what it must have taken for you to come here and say these things to me. And I'm touched. I truly am. But I don't want a relationship, with you or anyone else."

He pulled her hand from her face and held it tightly, scooting closer as he did. "Look, I know I was a jerk, Emily. But I was wrong. I know that."

"Maybe you were, maybe you weren't. But as for you

and me, it's not going to happen." She hated how cruel she sounded, but it needed to be said.

This time, when she pulled her hands away, he let them go, the bewilderment in his face impossible to miss. "Emily. I don't get this. I'm telling you I love you. I want you to be a part of Seth's and my future."

She drew back. "Your future?"

"Of course. What do you think I've been trying to say?"

Silence fell between them as she let his words sink in, their meaning, their sincerity making her wish things were different. That *she* was different. But she wasn't.

She pushed herself off the couch and wandered over to the fireplace, where the countless photographs lined the mantel. There was the picture of her and Kate on a river in Tennessee, the look of horror on her friend's face as they paddled through rapids a stark contrast to the grin on Emily's face. There was the photograph she'd taken while rappelling down a rock wall in Montana. And the gag one Kate had framed of Emily's hair after a week of survival camping in the Colorado Rockies.

Each picture represented a milestone along her path to fulfilling some of her biggest dreams. No, there weren't any wedding poses or cute babies smiling out from any of the frames, but that was okay. In just over thirty years, she'd accomplished more of her dreams than most people did in a lifetime.

"You're in need of a few new pictures, don't you think?"

She spun around to find Mark standing not more than a foot away. "Excuse me?"

"You missed a picture in your office and, because of that, you're missing a few here." He motioned toward the photographs in front of them and smiled. "Fortunately for you, I have one of them with me."

Unsure of what he was talking about, she followed him over to the packet she'd set on the coffee table, and watched as he opened the back flap, withdrawing an all-too-familiar, golden-hued paper.

Emily lifted her hands. "How did you get that?"

Holding the whimsically illustrated page next to his face, he flashed his best knee-weakening smile. "Notice the hair?" He pointed from the prince's head to his own. "Do you see the color?"

"It's Milk Chocolate," she whispered.

"Uh-huh..." He pointed to his own hair once again, before drawing her attention back to the picture. "And the eyes? What were those? Royal something or other?"

She swallowed and shook her head. "Ocean Wave Blue."

"Ocean Wave Blue, eh?" He smirked. "Uh-huh. Got those, too, don't I? And if you use just a little imagination, you'll see that my muscles aren't so far off, either." He hooked an arm upward and flexed his biceps, eliciting a laugh from her.

When her laughter began to fade, he grabbed her

hand once again. "I can be this guy, Emily. I can be your prince. I just happen to have a second, and far cuter, prince in tow. That's the only difference."

Oh, how she wished that were true.

Wriggling her hand free of his, she took the drawing and turned it so he could see the whole picture. "But that's not the only difference, Mark. Not by a long shot."

"Then help me see what I'm missing," he pleaded.

She smacked her free hand against the other figure depicted there. "*She's* different!"

"Not really." He stepped forward and, reaching out, captured a piece of Emily's hair between his fingers. "Same blond locks, just a little shorter." He released it and brushed the back of his hand down the side of her face. "Eyes are just as big and brown as ever. Though you left off one of my favorite parts when you opted not to draw in your freckles."

She closed her eyes against a burning that had nothing to do with happiness and everything to do with the fact that her heart was breaking over the one dream she knew she couldn't have, no matter how desperately she wished otherwise. When she opened them again, she saw the face of a man who'd spent the past thirty minutes being honest about his feelings. The least she could do was do the same.

"I'm not talking about the stuff you can see. I'm talking about the stuff you can't."

"Like what? Because I can't see your spirit in this drawing, but it's plain as the nose on my face. And I can't see inside your heart in this, either, but I saw it when you made Seth feel special on the beach, and at the pizza parlor later that same night. And I *felt* it when we were together at Kate's barbecue, and when we held each other after we'd made love."

"Stop!" she shouted. "I'm not talking about that kind of stuff. I'm talking about being a burden."

He held up his palms. "Whoa, whoa, whoa. A burden? A burden to whom?"

"To you, to Seth, to anyone who signs on to spend their life with me." She allowed herself one more glance at the drawing she'd been so proud of twenty years earlier, and then tossed it into the hearth, to be burned on the first cool night. "I may not die from this disease, but I might very well be in a wheelchair or wasting away on a couch, making you feel as if you can't enjoy your life or Seth's because you're stuck at home taking care of me. And then what kind of life will you have? What kind of life will Seth have?"

"Emily, hold on a minute. Wasn't it you who said you might live out the rest of your days as if nothing was wrong with you?"

"Might is the key word, Mark. *Might.* That's not enough of an assurance for me."

"And if the worst case happens, I'll take care of you. I'll carry you to the car so we can go for a drive. I'll carry you up the side of a mountain so we can have a picnic with a view. I'll carry you to bed so I can make love to you and then hold you all night. And I'll do all of those things because I *want* to."

"Carry me?" she spit. "*Carry* me? Oh, no…" She crossed the living room with quick, even strides and stopped just shy of the front door. "A very wise man recently told me something that will stay with me forever. He said we come into this life alone, and we'll leave it that way, too. So living it that way from point A to point B really isn't such an *awful* thing."

"Awful? Maybe not. But *sad?* You bet it is."

She felt the sting in her eyes and knew it wouldn't be long before tears made it past her lashes. "He's not sad. He's determined. Like me."

"Maybe he is. And if he is, then good for him. But being determined and allowing yourself to love and be loved aren't mutually exclusive things, Emily. Sure, you made all those pictures on your office wall come true on your own. That's awesome. But is there any reason those same dreams couldn't have come true with a supportive partner by your side? I don't think so. And if that supportive partner can step in and make things a little easier along the way, is that so wrong?"

"Maybe I *want* to do it by myself."

"Do you?" Mark pressed. "Do you really? Because I don't think you do—"

She opened the door and stepped to the side to indicate her desire for him to leave. "I won't push this disease off on anyone else. It's mine to live with, not yours."

After several long moments, Mark joined her by

the door, the determination in his eyes taking her breath away. "Love isn't a burden, Emily. It's a journey. Through good times and bad. And I for one would rather have five minutes of wonderful than a lifetime of nothing special."

She brought her hand to her mouth in an effort to stifle the sobs that were building. "I never wanted to be carried through life. I wanted to be the perfect wife, the perfect mother."

"And being in a wheelchair negates that?"

"When your child wants to play with blocks and you have to watch from five feet away, yes. When you want to make your husband his favorite dinner, but can't because the ingredients you need are too high for you to reach from a seated position, yes. When you can't walk your child to the bus stop, hand in hand, on his first day of school, yes."

"Emily, it doesn't have to be like that."

"The fact that it might be is enough for me." She tried to resist when Mark pulled her close, but she couldn't. More than anything she wanted to savor the feel of his arms one more time, to find whatever comfort she could in knowing that her dream could have come true.

All too soon, though, he stepped back, his hand reaching for hers in the process. "Come with me. There's something I want to show you."

HE HELD HER HAND all the way to the front door, a wave of second thoughts accompanying him. While there was a part of him that liked the idea of Seth being present when Mark asked Emily to marry him, there was another part that was just plain scared. Scared she wouldn't see things the way he saw them.

"You can open your eyes now," he prompted. "Just don't look around too much out here, okay?"

"Don't look around too much?"

"Humor me." He wasn't entirely sure she would remember the house, considering the heightened stress level they'd been under when they'd pulled up the driveway the first time. But he didn't want to take any chances. Her focus was needed inside.

"Where are we?" she asked as he gave a quick knock and opened the door for her to enter.

"You'll see." He knew he was being cryptic, but he wanted her to see reality with her own two eyes. With any luck, it would have more impact than any picture he could try to paint with his words.

Step by step, he led her down the main hallway, his slow, careful gait designed to give her time to soak up the various degrees and awards that were displayed on the walls.

"Rose Reynolds?" Emily read as they passed. "Who is that?"

The sound of his son's happy chatter saved Mark from having to verbalize an answer. "Do I hear my little man?" he called.

"I'm in here, Daddy. With Gam."

Emily tugged him to a stop. "You brought me to your

mother's house?" she whispered. "Mark, what on earth are you doing?"

His only response was to guide her the rest of the way down the hall and into the hearth room. When they rounded the corner, he released her hand and stopped beside the card table he'd erected before leaving for Kate's that afternoon. "Mom? I brought someone special I'd like you to meet."

Rose Reynolds craned her neck around in greeting, but it was Seth's voice that dominated the room. "Emily! Emily! You're here!" Jumping down from his chair beside his grandmother, he ran to Emily and wrapped his arms around her legs. "Gam and I are building a castle with my blocks. You wanna see?"

"Uh, sure, sweetheart. I'd love to see it." Without glancing in Mark's direction, Emily followed Seth around the table, stopping beside Mark's mother and extending her hand. "Hi. I'm Emily Todd. I'm a friend of—"

His mom's eyes twinkled in the reflection of the overhead light. "I'm Rose and I know who you are. My grandson has talked nonstop about you since the other night at the beach."

At the first hint of a blush on Emily's face, the woman laughed. "In fact, this room right here—" she pointed toward the elaborate block castle's second story "—is yours."

"Mine?" Emily repeated.

"Yupper doodles," Seth exclaimed. "It's big enough for you *and* Daddy!"

The corner of Rose's mouth twitched just before a sly smile broke out across her gently lined face. "Emily, would you like something to drink? I have wine, lemonade, water, tea...."

At Emily's questioning glance, Mark nodded.

"I'd love a glass of water if it's not too much trouble."

"No trouble at all."

Seth's finger shot up into the air. "I'll be right back, Emily. Don't go anywhere, okay?" Then, in a flash, he was around the table and climbing up onto his grandmother's lap as she wheeled herself from the table and into the kitchen.

Mark watched as his mother transported his son across the kitchen and then went about the task of filling Emily's drink order. After a moment, he looked back at Emily.

"Your mom...she's in a wh-wheelchair," Emily stammered.

"Yup." He pointed toward the card table between them. "Doesn't stop her from building a castle with her grandson, now, does it?"

When Emily said nothing, he nodded toward the kitchen. "And Seth? He's just as happy to ride around the house on his grandmother's lap as he would be to walk by her side. It's his grandma and that's all that matters."

When Emily finally spoke, her voice was quiet and

unsure. "But what about when he gets too big to ride in her lap?"

"He'll push her...just like I did."

Emily's lower lip trembled ever so slightly. "She was in that when you were a kid?"

"She's been in it since *she* was a kid. Mom lost her leg in a fire. She's got an artificial one, but that's mostly for vanity, as she's fond of saying. Which means—" he looked closely at Emily "—she was in it when she married my dad."

Mark watched as Emily peered around the room.

"He's not here anymore, unfortunately."

"Oh? Did he pack up and leave when he realized how much work she was going to be?"

"He died just before Seth was born. Mom cared for him right up until the end."

Emily's face turned crimson. "Mark, I'm sorry. That was out of line."

He shrugged. "I imagine a first glance at the two of them would have had lots of people assuming he cared for her. But by the second glance, anyone with half a brain in their head would realize they were as much a partnership as any other marriage out there. The only difference was the fact that Mom did most everything from a seated position."

"But she has all those awards and degrees," Emily mused.

"You're right, she does." Mark knew it was premature to get his hopes up, but things were looking good.

Emily was getting a taste of a reality she needed to see. "And knowing Mom, she's likely to add a few more to her collection before she gets around to admitting she's old. Heck, she'd probably remarry one day if she could find someone to keep up with her."

Even as he spoke, he could tell Emily wasn't absorbing what he said. Instead, her eyes were focused to the side, as if she was trying to remember something.

"Wait. One of those degrees we passed was for..." Her words trailed off as she headed along the hallway, with Mark on her heels. When she reached the row of framed certificates, she stopped in front of the one that was dead center. Tapping her hand on the glass, she looked from the official document to Mark and back again, the confusion in her face making him chuckle. "This says she's scuba qualified."

"Because she is."

"But how?"

"When she and Dad were in Australia on vacation fifteen years ago, she came across a place that offered scuba classes to people like her."

"But you can't scuba dive in a chair, Mark," Emily protested.

"And she didn't. They removed her artificial leg, attached an extra-big flipper to her good foot and away she went, compliments of—"

"The water's buoyancy," Emily finished. "Wow. I had no idea."

"It's been like that with my mom for as long as I

can remember. Everything she's done in life, every-thing she's ever accomplished, she's done *in spite* of her chair." Seeing in Emily's eyes the emotion he'd hoped to stimulate, he took her hand and led her back to the living room. Then, with determination, he pulled her close, his shoulder quickly growing damp from her quiet tears. "Which is how I've always loved her. And how Seth has always loved her, too. Why I didn't look at things that way from the start is beyond me, but I guess I just needed to step back and take in the big picture. And you do, too."

"I can't make any promises," Emily whispered.

"Neither can I. Not about that kind of stuff, any-way. But there is one promise I know I can make if you'll let me."

"What's that?" She stepped back and peered up at him.

"Seth? Can you come here a second?" Mark called. "I need your help with something."

"Sure, Daddy." The boy rode across the kitchen on his grandmother's lap, then climbed down carefully with the water glass in his hand. "Here you go, Emily. I hope it's really yummy."

Taking his son by the hand, Mark knelt on the floor at Emily's feet and whispered to Seth to do the same. Then, looking up, he met and held her gaze. "I prom-ise, from this day forward, to sweep you off your feet and carry you in my arms only if you ask. With one caveat, of course."

The smile he'd grown to love in such a short period of time slowly made its way across her face in spite of the tears that streamed down her cheeks. "What's that?" she asked quietly.

"That I don't have to ask permission to carry you over the threshold of our home on our wedding night."

Epilogue

Thirteen months later

Trish looked up from her desk the second they walked in, the smile on her face surely a reflection of the one Emily felt spreading across her own.

"Hey, boss. Hey, Seth. Ready for the big day?" Spinning around in her desk chair, Emily's assistant yanked open her top drawer, pulled out a bouquet of lollipops and held it out for Seth to see. "They taste just like vanilla ice cream, only not so cold."

Emily shook her head and laughed, releasing Seth's hand as she did. "Now, wait a minute, Trish. Are you *my* assistant or *Seth's?*"

"I got a cherry one for you, boss."

"Good answer," she joked before reaching for the series of pink sticky notes lined up across the desk. "So everything's all set for noon?"

"Everything is all set. I even gave a call to that reporter from *Winoka Magazine* who did that article on you last spring. Told her what's going on, and she said she'd send a photographer by to snap some pictures of the ribbon cutting for the next issue."

"Outstanding." Emily flipped through the messages that had come into the office while she'd been away for her appointment. When she got to the fourth in the pile, she stole a peek in Trish's direction. "Kate called?"

Pulling an orange lollipop from her mouth, her assistant nodded, her expression giving nothing away where Kate's call was concerned.

"And? What did she say?"

"She's on her way over."

"Did she say why?" Emily prompted.

Trish made a face. "We're talking about Kate, aren't we? Everyone around her is supposed to be an open book. But her? Not unless she's in your face."

"True." Emily smiled at Seth as he hopped across the main office and down the hall, a lollipop held tightly in his hand.

Trish watched him go and then turned back with a questioning look. "Have I missed the memo about our little prince turning into a frog? Because if I did, might I remind you it usually happens the other way around. You know, first the frog, then the prince."

Glancing at the note containing nothing but Kate's name, Emily shrugged. "He's still a prince. He's just a prince who's learning about the letter *B* in his kindergarten class this week. Bunnies start with *B,* so there's going to be a lot of hopping going on."

"Ah-h-h… I see." Trish lowered her voice. "Everything go okay with your neurologist this morning?"

"Nothing I didn't anticipate."

At the sudden shift in her tone, Trish's eyebrow shot upward once again. "You okay?"

"Yeah, I'm okay. Just found myself marveling once again at the psychic ability I appeared to have had when I was ten."

When she didn't elaborate, Trish waved her down the hall. "And apparently you and Kate both excelled in whatever class you guys took on the art of being cryptic."

Emily made a face at her young friend before heading off to her office. She wasn't trying to be cryptic. It just didn't make much sense to talk about something that simply wasn't going to happen. It was like strapping on her climbing gear, only to find herself standing in the middle of a flat desert. There was no point. Not in her eyes, anyway.

Besides, if she shared the reason for her appointment aloud, it would seem as if she wasn't happy with the life she had, and that couldn't be further from the truth. She already had so much more than she'd thought she'd ever have.

"Hiya, Memmy."

She couldn't help but smile at the nickname the little boy had bestowed on her after the wedding, his creative merging of her name with the role she'd be playing in his life resulting in a moniker they both treasured.

"Your *bunny* hop was very good, sweetheart."

Seth beamed around his lollipop. "Really?"

She crossed the room to perch on the edge of her desk. "Actually, I'd say it was *beautiful, brave* and very *believable*."

His closed his lips around the sucker for a quick taste and then popped it out of his mouth. "That's very good, Memmy. Miss Olson would be proud of how well you know your *B*s."

"I'm pretty proud of Memmy, too. But for lots of other reasons, little man."

Hearing her husband's voice coming down the hall, Emily turned toward the door, the sight of her real live prince making all her petty worries disappear. This man, whom she adored with everything she had, had given her back her dream. Life didn't get much better, in her opinion.

He opened his arms wide enough for both of them, his first kiss finding the top of Seth's head and the second one lingering on Emily's lips. "How'd it go today?" he whispered in her ear.

"I asked those last few questions we discussed, and I think it's best if we just stay the course."

When Seth wiggled free and returned to the reading corner Emily had set up for him behind her desk, she allowed Mark to pull her close, the comfort she found in his arms making her decision a little easier.

"You know I'll support whatever you decide."

She gestured over her shoulder at the fifth drawing,

now framed and hung on the wall beside all the others, and lowered her voice to a near whisper. "I drew all of those because they represented my fondest dreams. And one by one, they've all come true. There are no other drawings to be framed, because I already have everything I ever wanted, Mark. To risk jeopardizing my ability to care for Seth just so I can complete a picture I never drew in the first place just isn't worth it to me."

"I love you, Emily."

"I love—"

The buzz of the intercom cut her off midsentence. "Boss? Are you ready?"

She glanced from the clock over the door to Mark and then Seth's face. All her life she'd been a go-getter, determined to make her dreams and the dreams of everyone around her come true. Ninteen months ago, an obstacle had been erected in her quest to reach her greatest dream of all. Thirteen months ago, Mark and Seth had stood beside her as she made the choice to see that obstacle as an opportunity to grow.

Now it was her turn to do the same for a man she'd only met over the phone.

"We're ready." Holding her hands out to her two greatest gifts, Emily made her way back down the hallway with her big prince on one side and her little prince on the other. When she reached the end, she turned right instead of left, bypassing the front door in favor of the new, wider one that had been installed by the Folks Helping Folks Foundation.

Pushing it open, she closed her eyes and lifted her face to the late August sun. "Mmm…"

"Mrs. Reynolds?"

Her lashes parted to reveal the man who, in many ways, was responsible for leading her back to Mark. A man who knew what it was to dream, and embodied the very spirit needed to make those dreams come true. She started to walk down the ramp to shake his hand, but stopped when he shook his head and wheeled himself up to her instead, the smile on his rugged face making her blink back tears.

"Mr. Walker, I am honored to finally meet you. Our time on the phone together so many months ago made such a difference in my life. All I can do now is hope that what we've added here today will make a difference in yours, too."

"It's a start, that's for sure. At least now I can come here and learn about some of the things I put off doing until I wasn't able to do them anymore."

Emily glanced up at Mark, saw him nod, and knew the moment she'd been researching and working toward was finally here. At least the first part, anyway.

Pointing toward the door she'd just come through, she addressed Mr. Walker with what she hoped was a semidecent poker face. "Before we get started with the foundation's ribbon-cutting ceremony, would you mind coming inside with me for a second? I'd like to show you something."

"Sure." Jed rested his hands on the wheels of his

chair and spun them forward, through the door Mark held open. Room by room, Emily guided him through the building, pausing to explain about the various on-site classes they held throughout the year, as well as a few details about the adventures that took them to various locations throughout Winoka and beyond.

When they reached the last classroom before the hallway that led to her office, she stepped inside and took a seat, gesturing for him to follow in his chair. "Mr. Walker, you already know it was that initial phone call you made to Trish last year that set the ball rolling to get our doors widened and that ramp put in place. And for that, we're grateful. You see, I'm a big believer in helping people realize their dreams, and making our building accessible got us a little closer to doing that."

At Jed's nod, she continued, motioning for a teary-eyed Trish in the doorway to join them for the rest of the surprise. "Anyway, I know you'd like to be able to do more than just wheel your way through a door and sit in on a few classes. And you should be able to, as should anyone else who's confined to a wheelchair. So I sent out a call a few months ago to find an adventure instructor who is familiar with physical challenges."

Jed's mouth gaped ever so slightly as he looked from Emily to Trish and back again. "And?"

"When the ribbon-cutting ceremony is done, I'd like to introduce you to Peter Cummings. He's a dynamite kid with some really great ideas and the know-how to implement them."

Her eyes began to burn at Jed's obvious struggle for words. Unable to contain herself anymore, she took both his hands in hers and smiled. "And as for you, Mr. Walker? You're the first name on my list for a scuba trip to Saint John this winter."

"Scuba?" he repeated in a voice thick with emotion.

"That's right. *Scuba*." She looked toward the door once again and cleared her throat. Less than thirty seconds later, she was reengaging eye contact with Jed as Mark piloted Rose into the room. "And my mother-in-law, right here, will be on that trip, too. Seems the first five times she went diving weren't enough."

Jed's hands trembled in Emily's, though his focus was on no one but Rose. "You've done it? You've been under the ocean like that?"

The older woman's smile lit up the room. "You bet I have. And in a few months, you'll be able to say the very same thing."

Grateful and deeply moved, Emily released one of Jed's hands in order to grab one of Rose's. "Jed, you made me realize my vision for Bucket List 101 was lacking in one very important way. The changes you see here today have hopefully altered that. But I've learned something else, too. I've learned that doing things on my own is very different than doing them alone. And while you may have been right on the phone all those months ago when you reminded me that I came into this world alone and will leave it the same way, I have to tell you that all the time in between is so much better when you have someone you love and respect by your side. The key is finding someone who really sees you, regardless of whether you're sitting, standing or somewhere in between."

SHE WAS ROUNDING UP the last of the paper plates when Kate came bursting through the door with her four-month-old daughter, Lizzie, fast asleep in her carrier. "Oh, thank God. I was hoping the two of you would still be here."

Mark popped his head up from the corner where he was dismantling the PA system they'd rented for the ribbon-cutting ceremony, and laughed. "Was that your car that just came screeching into the parking lot a second ago?"

"Nope. That was Miss Trish heading out. Which works perfectly, since I need to talk to the two of you alone." Kate scanned the room and then poked her head into the hall. "Where's Seth?"

"He's in my office drawing a picture." Emily dumped the stack of dirty plates into the trash and made a bee-line for Lizzie. "Am I ever going to get to see her when she's awake?"

"Come by around dinner or anytime during the night and you'll see her wide-eyed and bushy-tailed." At Mark's snicker, Kate rolled her eyes. "You think I'm kidding?"

"No. Actually, I don't. Seth was like that, too, when he was that age."

Emily ran a gentle hand down her goddaughter's leg as Mark and Kate swapped the kind of stories she'd never experienced. Not firsthand, anyway. And knowing what she now knew about the risk to her health if she became pregnant, they weren't the kind of stories she'd ever be able to relate to. But that was okay. She'd come into Seth's life at such an early age that she hadn't missed too much.

"Woo hoo? Earth to Emily! Come in, Emily."

At the sound of her name, she looked up to find both Mark and Kate gazing at her curiously. "I'm sorry, I guess I zoned out there for a minute."

Mark pulled up a chair next to her and draped his arm over her shoulders. "That's okay, Em. You've more than earned yourself a little zone-out."

Kate sat on the table next to Lizzie's carrier and got straight to the point. "So, have you made a decision?"

From anyone else, the question would have been too much. But from Kate, it was okay. Normal, even. Taking a deep breath, Emily willed herself to choose her words wisely.

"Having MS doesn't mean I can't have a child. We can. But in order to try, I'd have to stop my injections. If it worked, and we became pregnant, I'd have to stay off them throughout the duration of the pregnancy. Lots of women with my condition do it all the time. But a large percentage of them experience an acceleration of the disease within six months of giving birth."

Mark whispered a kiss across the side of her head as

she continued. "If we didn't already have Seth, I might be tempted to take the chance. But we do. And I want to be healthy for him and for Mark for as long as possible."

Kate covered her eyes with her palms.

"Kate? Are you okay?" Mark asked.

Slowly, she pulled her hands from her face and nodded. "I'm better than okay. In fact, I think I have some news that'll blow your minds."

"Okay, shoot."

"Joe's cousin called the other day. The two of you met him at one of our barbecues last spring. His eighteen-year-old daughter is pregnant, and she's going to be giving her baby up for adoption as soon as it's born."

"That's too bad," Mark murmured, tightening his hold on Emily.

"Well, it is and it isn't. You see, Reagan doesn't want to be a mom right now. She's one of those kids who has a life plan, and having a baby doesn't figure on the list right now. She wants to go to college and travel before she even considers settling down and starting a family. The father has relinquished his rights already, and Reagan is ready to do the same, provided she can find a loving family for her little girl."

Mark sat up tall. "Little girl?"

Kate grinned. "Yup. You interested?"

Emily turned to Mark, their simultaneous "yes" eliciting a squeal from Kate and summoning Seth from the hallway.

"Seth, is that you?" Mark called, buying Emily time to wipe the tears from her cheeks.

"Yupper doodle. I have a picture for you and Memmy."

"Hi, Seth!" Kate said. "Come and say hi to Lizzie. Daddy and Memmy woke her up."

Seth hopped over to the baby, who rewarded his efforts with a smile. Smiling back at her, he held his picture up in front of his face and then peeked back and forth between Lizzie and his drawing.

"Can I see your picture, Seth?" Kate asked.

"Sure!'

Kate's eyes widened as she took the golden-hued paper from his hands. "Em? Mark? Uh, you might want to check this out."

Together, they stood and came around the table, their son's latest artistic efforts making everyone gasp.

There, on the paper, was Seth's version of Emily and her prince. Only in his drawing, there were two additional faces.

The first, a little boy, looked just like Seth. Right down to the Sunshine Yellow hair and the same eye color as the prince. In his arms was a baby girl with Strawberry Banana hair and Emerald Green eyes....

Emily turned to Mark, unable to form the question he was able to ask.

"What is this, little man?"

"It's the next picture for Memmy's wall."

* * * * *

Have Your Say

You've just finished your book.
So what did you think?

We'd love to hear your thoughts on our
'Have your say' online panel
www.millsandboon.co.uk/haveyoursay

- 🌹 Easy to use
- 🌹 Short questionnaire
- 🌹 Chance to win Mills & Boon® goodies

The World of Mills & Boon®

There's a Mills & Boon® series that's perfect for you. We publish ten series and, with new titles every month, you never have to wait long for your favourite to come along.

Blaze.
Scorching hot, sexy reads
4 new stories every month

By Request
Relive the romance with the best of the best
9 new stories every month

Cherish™
Romance to melt the heart every time
12 new stories every month

Desire™
Passionate and dramatic love stories
8 new stories every month